Advance praise for *The Sy*

"Thank goodness Frannie James was taking notes... *The Sylvan Hotel* is a tapdance down memory lane for those of us who came of age in Seattle in the 1990s. She evokes the disaffected "are we adults yet?" vibe of Gen X, and draws a vivid portrait of the time and place through the eyes of an earnest young woman longing for love and her own fulfilled promise. I saw myself in Joann, and people I used to know in her cohort of hotel staff. What a gift it is, to remember! Well done, Frannie."

~ Alexis M. Smith, author of *Glaciers*

"A vibrant salute to Capitol Hill, hotel workers, and the heady heydays of Seattle."

~ Jim Lynch, author of *The Highest Tide*

"James deftly describes Joann's powerful attraction to [coworker valet] Robert—a "gravitational alchemy" that makes him, like the hotel itself, feel like home. Moreover, the author impressively illuminates one of the central conflicts of early adulthood: the draw of one's cozy youth, set against the exciting promise of full-fledged adulthood."

~ *Kirkus Reviews*

"Frannie James employs Joann's vivid reflections to bring to life not just one person's ambitions and issues, but the entire milieu of a hotel "family" in all its strengths and weaknesses. Her approach cements the notion of microcosms of community and growth, lending to much thought-provoking reading ... It is highly recommended reading for audiences seeking stories of attraction and change."

~ *The Midwest Book Review*

"Thoroughly enjoyable and engaging! A heartfelt story that took me back to the 'in-between' chapter of my own life—an experience many other readers will relate to as well. I was sorry to see my time end with Joann and her crew."

~ Maggie Carr, Co-founder, Elliott Bay Book Company, Seattle

THE SYLVAN HOTEL

a Seattle Story

BY

FRANNIE JAMES

Hinton

The Sylvan Hotel: a Seattle story
© 2025 Frannie James

This publication © 2025 Hinton Publishing. All rights reserved.

Aside from established & agreed-upon commerce platforms, no part of this publication's design may be reproduced or transmitted in any form or by any means, electronic or mechanical, including photocopy, recording, or any information storage and retrieval system now known or to be invented, without permission in writing of the publisher, except by reviewer who wishes to quote brief passages in connection with a review written for publication in print and electronic form.

No AI Training: Without in any way limiting the author's and publisher's exclusive rights under copyright, any use of this publication to "train" generative artificial intelligence (AI) technologies to generate text is expressly prohibited. The author reserves all rights to license uses of this work for generative AI training and development of machine learning language models.

This is a work of fiction. Names, characters, businesses, places, events, locales, and incidents are either the products of the author's imagination or used in a fictitious manner. Any resemblance to actual persons, living or dead, or actual events is purely coincidental.

Cover design & illustrations: Vladimir Verano

Book design: Vladimir Verano

Acknowledgments photo © Frannie James

print: 978-1-60944-165-4

ebook: 978-1-60944-166-1

Published in the United States by
Hinton Publishing
Seattle, WA

marcus@hintonpublishing.com

hintonpublishing.com

Hinton is an imprint of Vertvolta Press

vertvoltapress.com

Please contact the publisher for Library of Congress Catalog Data

For K & G.
LIVE your life.
Feel the joy. Feel the sadness. Feel it all.
Believe in yourself. Trust yourself.
Know that you are beautiful in every way.
Know that you are enough.
Know that love is real.

With love to E.B. and the Sylvans.
With love to the universe.

"In vain, I have struggled ... My feelings will not be repressed."

~ Jane Austen, *Pride and Prejudice*

"When the bird of the heart begins to sing,
too often will reason stop up her ears."

~ Hans Christian Andersen

"I'm youth, I'm joy ..."

~ J. M. Barrie, *Peter Pan*

"Nothing gold can stay."

- Robert Frost, *Nothing Gold Can Stay*

THE SWING SHIFT

Ding!

The boy band was on its way down.
Static. Pop. Hiss …
The walkie-talkies were heating up.
"Security to Manager on Duty: *Nobody* gets on the elevator."

In the lobby, hotel executives excitedly chatted, busily standing by. Rock-star sightings were imminent, and an entourage swarmed. Players jockeyed for position, handlers held court, and roadies were getting their moves on. Baggage was everywhere, and the smell of hard living chased notes of orchids and afternoon tea.

Beep!

In a tiny "PBX" room right behind reception, Joann tussled with a petulant switchboard—but she was glad for the chance to rest her feet and duck for cover. It was raining cats and *crazy*. She answered a call, then listened as Kathryn's voice rose above the din out front.

"Welcome to Seattle, Mr. and Mrs. Stewart, and welcome to the Sylvan!"

"Thank you. These polished walls are divine. What kind of wood—"

Kathryn cheerfully recited the "Honduran Mahogany" explanation.

Meanwhile, Joann faced rougher walls, the whitewash fading with years of wear and tear. Even so, PBX housed a communications epicenter. Here, the goings-on of hospitality grind sparked between busy circuits, coursing alongside other affairs of the day. Traveling like lightning, multitudes of transmissions raced through the recesses, tearing from top to bottom, over and back.

Slouching and swiveling, Joann spun in a wheeled chair between two narrow counters. One held the switchboard panel and a reservations computer. A typewriter rested on the other, next to three walkie-talkie radios. Just inside the doorway, another chair was squeezed into a corner. Regularly dragged across the floor, it had forged a path in thin carpeting through grayish threads.

Beep!

The panel lit up, and Joann worked through a stream of transfers and messages. Then the operator pushed herself toward an innermost wall with a small window—her portal to a circular drive that doubled as the hotel courtyard. Bramble shrouded most of the glass, but flashes soon came into focus. Taxis and rental cars whisked visitors to and fro, while valets appeared and disappeared in a whirl of navy jackets, gray slacks, and black shoes. Iron gating ringed the genteel "circle," and string lights clung to palm trees, where they could twinkle their best come nightfall. At the center, a Mediterranean-style fountain awaited the next wish.

Joann pushed back to the switchboard, but things had fallen into silence again. She tapped a pen and tilted her gaze, eyes climbing the walls. Directly above, bulletin boards were heavy with the business at hand. On one side, checklists loomed, and layers of old calendar pages battled freshly pinned forecasts. On the other side, a matrix of squares plotted the remainder of 1991—but red Xs defied the black-and-white of it all, drawn through sold-out dates like stitches safeguarding moments in time …

Beep-beep-beep.

"Yo! Who's hogging the elevator?" The swing-shift housekeeper was checking in.

"Hi, Lynn! It's VIP stuff. 'Rock stars on the way down!' Oops, phone's gettin'—"

"Uh, yeeeah. Joann, those dudes ain't rock stars. Heh! Later …"

The switchboard quieted after seven more calls, but lobby clatter droned on, vacillating between louder and softer as a tall saloon-style door swung open and closed. Outside PBX to the right, it squeaked on its hinges and separated reception from the back of the house. A short passageway connected the spaces and ended outside PBX to the left, opening into a larger office.

Beep-beep-beep!

The switchboard was ready for another round.

Fingers flying across the numbered panel, Joann sent calls to hotel rooms, sales offices, the restaurant, the bar, Housekeeping, Engineering, the concierge stand, and the valet booth. Then … reprieve.

Well, reprieve from the phones.

Reaching for the floor, she grabbed onto a miniature engraving press, roughly the size and shape of a microscope. Lift and … *thud!* Joann set the gizmo on the counter, parallel to the VIP list. Next, she flattened a Sylvan matchbox cover and positioned a papery square of pretend-gold ink. Now for the fiddly letters. Arranging a row of dainty metal plates, Joann lined up the first name, double-checked her spelling, and pulled down the press handle.

Smash!

And … success. Whew. No time for do-overs, especially on a night with flocks of VIPs and an extra-ornery switchboard. But there wasn't room for errors, either—or names that were too faint, too bold, or too smeared. You had to get it right. Just enough ink, just enough pressure, and, *voila*: just enough panache with a promise of preeminence.

You're the tops, Mister Slayton. You're one in a million, Missus Sherman. You're the utmost, Mister Williams.

Smash!

The high-flying crowd did love an extra frill—and the personalized matchboxes were particularly popular. They were always a …

Smash-smash-smash!

Joann clipped the matches to amenity forms and scooped up the packets. Perfectly *posh* packets for perfectly posh people. Tall and tan, rich and lovely. Clean and crisp in Armani, Chanel, Burberry, and Brooks Brothers; nary a crease in their khakis nor a scuff on their shoes.

Imagine actually *being* a VIP. Imagine being held in such high esteem that your name graced courtly tokens, chocolates were delivered in haste, and flowers were sent, straightaway, with cards announcing sweet somethings.

Pushing through the swinging door to reception, Joann dropped the matchboxes in the right-hand corner of the big desk, below the marble countertop. They'd sit there until rescued by Room Service, so she turned the bundle upside down. That way, the prized keepsakes were covered by their corresponding forms, safe from nosy nellies and *am-I-getting-one-of-those* types of questions.

The pile teetered precariously, like a posh house of cards.

Order up, Room Service!

Joann squinted at the kitchen door across the lobby. Then she turned the stack over again.

C. Jud Lillich.

A name glittered at the top of the matchbox heap.

The Sylvan Hotel

◆

What would it be like to get to the highest floor—hell, even the rooftop? What would it be like to get to your grown-up destiny? Was happily-ever-after a real thing? Did it last? Or did that kind of happiness have a catch? Maybe "epic" came with an extra side of scary—a greater chance of falling, after having climbed so far. And maybe the hardest-won wins were even easier to lose. One strike of a burning-hot match, and you'd be down in flames, buried in ashy depths after—

"The fire looks so *nice*. Should we wait over there until our room is ready?"

"Yes, ma'am. It will be just a few minutes."

A line of guests started to form, but Kathryn was already up to her neck in it.

"Yes, sir, I'll try to find you one with a bigger bathroom. And away from the elevator ... No, sir, we don't have ice machines ... A higher floor? Yes, sir ... I understand ..."

"I can help who's next!"

Following Kathryn's lead, Joann politely smiled but secretly marveled at her friend's ability to sound so concerned about Mister I-Deserve-It-All. She got two more parties squared away with keys—but a new barrage of beeps bombarded the switchboard.

"Kath, just holler if you need me!"

And back through the swinging door to PBX.

"Good afternoon, the Sylvan Hotel ..."

Then static scratched between the radios.

"Concierge to Security ... guest ... angry ... wants on elevator ... doesn't care about ... 'any VIP' ..."

"Ten-four. But no one's coming up 'til all the kids are down."

Static. Pop. Whiiine.

Joann adjusted the radio again.

There. All tuned in for boy—er, boy-band problems!

Kathryn pushed through the swinging door.

"Hey, can you call Room Service? The desk is a mess with all those matchboxes. Tell Finn to get-over-here-and-get-'em. Thanks!"

She hurried back to reception, and Joann dialed Finn. The room-service attendant was generally a good sport, but she knew he would bristle at the summons.

"Joann, I'll get to it as soon as I—"

Thanking him, she hung up before he launched into a lecture about the many other duties presently requiring his attention. Five calls were still holding!

When the phones slowed, it was time to tackle reservation forms. Joann's fingers now flew across the computer keyboard. *Careful-but-quick-careful-but-quick.* She didn't want to accidentally screw up someone's honeymoon night, birthday, or anniversary. Even if a guest hadn't mentioned it, there was always the chance that a booking was tied to a celebration. Given its exquisite setting, the Sylvan practically guaranteed a perfect memory. Understated grandeur, vintage accents, and a fireside ambiance created an unforgettable backdrop for unforgettable events. The four-star service also played a role. Plus, there was something special about adding your own entry to the story of a place steeped in history …

It had all begun with a treasure hunt—and a jewel in the making. A long-ago gold rush deep in northern wilds had left the Emerald City flush with possibility. Prospectors had passed through, and Seattle had cashed in on the whims of fortune hunters. But what was its *real* destiny? Surely, Seattle could be more than a pretty pit stop.

A decision was made to show off *all* the goods with a global get-to-know-you. So, one visionary staked his claim locally. He opened the Sylvan in time for Seattle's first world expo—then the rest was history. Fast-forward through a zillion years, world wars, a restoration … and old was new again, like the past waking up more beautiful than ever.

Beep!

Joann yawned and transferred a call. *She* needed to wake up! Minibar billing still needed doing, and there were four reservations to go. Getting the "chores" out of the way would also give Kathryn time for paper-correcting.

Joann eyed the stack of files shoved next to the typewriter. Her teammate had graduated from Seattle University and was now making inroads as a teacher, substituting around town. She would stay on at the hotel part time until Seattle Public Schools hired her full time. Currently, Kathryn was assigned to a long-term contract, which meant the job didn't end when the bell rang, so planning and prep often accompanied her to the Sylvan. Thankfully, their manager was fine with paper-correcting in PBX.

Oy. That mountain of folders looked like a pain in the ass. But Joann was facing challenges, too. She was interested in copywriting, but advertising

The Sylvan Hotel

♦

was an extremely competitive field. A communications degree from the University of Washington—and two internships—was a solid start, but she needed a portfolio. She also needed to make stronger connections, having spent the majority of her internships stuck at copy machines. Joann wanted to *write* the copy.

Joann wanted a grown-up job.

A grown-up job officially made you somebody: An important somebody. A respectable somebody. A somebody who mattered. A grown-up job also kept you safe. *Safe* under the kind of roof that a grown-up paycheck put over your head. It didn't have to be a big roof, but under those shingles—*your* shingles—you'd be happy and secure from any storm. There'd be rooms with character; flowers; candlelight. A book by the fire. Hot food on the table. *And* … maybe that grown-up paycheck would pay for an adventure, like a starry-night escapade in an exciting city, with exciting friends! Then you'd have a few pennies or even quarters left over for a rainy day.

Sloosh. Water doused the PBX window.

Okay, more like rainy *days*. Joann sighed. Then she sighed again, as a newly posted note yelled, "Calls must be answered within THREE rings."

Bleh. Hopefully, a grown-up job would free you from switchboards—and rules, rules, rules. Of course, there'd always be some rules, but you'd have more room to breathe and more money to do what you wanted! Your life. *Your* rules.

Tee hee—*your* answering machine.

There was just one catch: A lot of grown-up jobs seemed like they could get boring. Way too boring. And that wouldn't do for Joann. She wanted a bit of sparkle with her "safe."

Which had led her to the world of advertising. Plenty of sparkle there, and as a copywriter, she'd be paid to be creative! So she'd have "the big job" that would make her a real grown-up—but a grown-up who'd dodged the dreariness.

Beep!

And the damn switchboard.

Blink-blink-blink! Not yet, teased the row of red lights.

Static. Pop. Static. Not yet, scratched the radios.

"Concierge to Security. Please report to the lobby. We are under … teeny-bopper attack."

Frannie James

◆

"Valet to Security. Someone's *screaming*—"

Joann pushed through the swinging door. She and Kathryn watched Security head in, valets trailing behind. Finn emerged from the kitchen, also hoping to catch sight of …

New Kids on the run!

Just another day in hotel land.

Beep-beep-beep!

A perturbed switchboard beckoned. The desk extension could only access one call, so Joann high-tailed it back to PBX, where ten phone lines were also off and running. *Me-me-me,* they shouted. *Uh-oh, uh-oh,* they warned.

At the Sylvan, a lively chorus of callers was bound to keep you tethered.

⇒ ◆ ⇐

7:45 p.m.

Three check-ins to go. Kathryn had powered through the arrivals list! The pace was often non-stop, but on nights like tonight, the front of the house could take a break.

"Okay," said Joann. "Let the paper-correcting commence!"

Kathryn took a seat in PBX, and now Joann stood out front, but she leaned against the swinging door, holding it open. Standing at the threshold, she could monitor the desk *and* chit-chat with her friend.

Ahhh. Gotta love the lull. Once you finished check-ins, the lobby could mellow out significantly—sometimes for hours. But even on the craziest of nights, the swing shift was the best shift. Morning shifts started too early, and you were subject to surveillance by the entire management brigade. Graveyard shifts started too late and were too lonely. The swing shift was perfectly in between. You had the morning for errands, exercise, sleeping in, or whatever. Then work started at 3:00 p.m., management left at 5:00 p.m., and you clocked off at 11:00 p.m., just in time for a social life!

The crown jewel of Seattle's hotels also shined its brightest in the evening hours. Stepping through the doors … was like stepping into a fairy tale. For Joann, the Sylvan had cast its spell two months prior, when she'd stopped by with her boyfriend and his family.

Cozied up on a green-velvet sofa, she'd caught herself really warming to the place.

Joann had been there before, but that night, she'd started to see the Sylvan differently. Or maybe she'd started to *really* see it. Glimmering with the beauty of an old movie or a childhood storybook, the hotel had kindled something more than fireside cheer. There on a rainy hilltop, hidden in plain sight between hospitals, clinics, and concrete towers, Joann had found her once-upon-a-time.

She'd found a friend, too. Across the lobby, a pretty girl in navy blue had also shined brightly, welcoming guests as they passed by. Kathryn had looked so "proper-glamorous" at the marble desk, and yet there'd been such a warmth to her, too.

Joann giggled. She'd been smitten with the Sylvan. And her mind had raced with possibility: Imagine having a job far from the beige trappings of a sterile office. Going to work would be like … going home! So she'd approached her future teammate, and they'd struck up a conversation. Then Joann had applied, head-over-high-heels enchanted with the hotel.

And it did feel like home. But not home where you had to walk on eggshells. Not home with a leaky basement or a too-loud TV. More like home where a tweedy grandpa waited, with tobacco pipe lit and wisdom for the taking. Home where a worldly nana clucked, "Tell me *all* the stories!" and settled you into a fortress of a chair. Home where a pocket watch glinted, stopped atop an heirloom desk next to an alabaster bust and a vase of yesterday's cuttings. Home where you curled up hearthside in a patina of bright embers, dog-eared chapters, waxy wood, and softly dropping petals—perhaps a little old fashioned, but timeless, artful, and true.

The Sylvan was a real-life fairy tale.

Beep-beep-beep!

Wake up, Sleeping Beauty!

The switchboard was back at it. Kathryn took the call, and Joann walked all the way out to the front.

Thump! Navy jackets jostled behind a big window to her right. Set above a wide ledge, it separated the valet booth from reception and could open like a door. Cloudy white panes blocked the boys from view, but sounds of laughter signaled a courtyard slow-down as well,

then gave way to more muffled tones.

What did they talk about out there? Joann unhooked the latch, then hesitated. For the most part, Sylvan valets liked that "door" to stay closed. So it would, she thought. At least, until *he* was working again.

Robert was her favorite of their navy-and-gray-clad cohorts, and another reason the middle shift was the place to be. Work just didn't feel like work when he was around. It was something better—and working the swing shift meant that they were usually scheduled together. Just the thought of him brought a smile to her face. Other than Kathryn and Lynnie, there was no one whose company Joann preferred more. Well, and she liked her boyfriend, Grady, of course!

8:00 p.m.

Joann pushed through the swinging door and propped it open. In PBX, a tired teacher picked up a stack of homework papers. The clock was ticking—

Beep!

But the switchboard wasn't giving up the fight.

Kathryn set down the schoolwork and started across the panel. Then the toll-free line was beeping, too. She glanced at the clock. Hopefully, that was *her* boyfriend calling from Oregon. It was the agreed-upon time, and the one chance they'd have to talk this week. Scott was temporarily living in Portland to help his sister run a new restaurant. He was also interested in a teaching career but wanted a break from Seattle. Kathryn wasn't sure how long her guy would be gone, but they'd been together five years, and she was set on a future with him. Joann had been with her own boyfriend for two years; otherwise, she was in the same boat. Grady had recently taken a sales gig in California, but how long he was staying there was up in the air.

Beep! Five calls now holding.

Just like us, mused Joann. It was all on hold while the boys figured things out and the girls waited them out, suspended between now and what came next. She gazed at the lobby. Even at the Sylvan, they were "in-between." Like any hotel, it was a temporary stop; shelter for people on their way to somewhere else. Two guests waved as they exited the lounge, and Joann wondered ... how long would *she* be staying?

Kathryn answered the toll-free line, and Joann could hear Scott's voice:

"You're so friendly. Did you know it was me, or are you that polite to everyone?"

"Haha," his girlfriend replied. "Okay, just give me one sec!"

She routed the other calls to room 306, the concierge, the bar, and room 402. Free long-distance phone calls were a lucky luxury and well worth the interruptions.

Joann moved all the way out to the desk so her friend could have some privacy. Kathryn managed to get about fifteen minutes in, then said a quick goodbye to Scott as the switchboard went ballistic. When the beeping dwindled, Joann propped the PBX door open again.

Click.

She turned, her eyes searching a far corner of the office behind them. Another valet was opening another door. Todd stepped through, and—

"Excuse me, Miss? Is this where we check in?"

Joann returned to the front, registered the guests—then the switchboard kicked in with all its fury. She took a call at the desk extension, and Kathryn chased down seven more in back. The phone lines finally slowed, but, suddenly, there was a lot to talk about. Todd grabbed a chair in PBX, and now two souls sat at a hotel switchboard, happily chatting between the lines.

Paper-correcting would have to wait a little longer.

SYLVANS IN THE HOUSE

Joann checked the time: 11:00 a.m. She and Kathryn had been out until 3:30 a.m., and her head hadn't hit the pillow until 4:15 a.m. The girls weren't big drinkers, but they were night owls—and even more so now that they worked at a hotel.

After clocking off, many of the Sylvans were just too wired for bed. So Kay's, a bar located one block away, had become an almost-nightly ritual. If Kathryn didn't have to teach the next day, she joined, too—and when Kay's closed, the girls often found themselves sitting in one of their cars, talking for another hour or more.

Autumn chill snaked through old plaster walls, and Joann turned over, swaddled in a heap of blankets. Work was just a few hours away, but the mattress wasn't letting go. What bliss to be able to sleep in—no racing to get to class; no early commute! Maybe … just ten more minutes …

Crap! How was it already 1:00 p.m.? Joann threw back the covers, shuffled to the kitchen, and opened the fridge: One jar of mayo. One can of Bud Light. Yeesh. That granola bar on the counter would have to do.

Next up: She brushed her teeth and jumped in the shower. Then on with some makeup, the blow dryer, and … run a quick comb: Side part. Ship-shape. Sylvan-ready. Now for some navy nylons that weren't full of snags … the uniform blouse, skirt, and blazer.

Joann often suited up before getting to work, because finding a parking space could take who-knows-how-many minutes, and the locker room was extra-crowded at shift change.

Tick-tock—2:20! Aaack! Where the hell were her shoes?

I spy navy heels. She groaned, digging through the closet.

Tick-tock—2:25! And the car was half a block away. Joann lived in one of the quieter stretches of Capitol Hill, but a late-night return meant that you wouldn't be parking right out front. Heels clicking along the pavement, she walked briskly but breathed easy, grateful to live in such a place. Seattle had a relatively small downtown core, but it showed its stuff via a myriad of wonderful neighborhoods with distinct personalities—like this one.

The Sylvan Hotel

♦

Capitol Hill was a proudly eclectic community and another local gem, located just east of downtown. "The Hill" buzzed with vibrant commercial zones interspersed with regal manors, funky city shanties, and a handful of apartments. An old-money echelon anchored the mix, content to reside near the likes of peasants and punk rockers. The Hill was a true melting pot, and its residents liked it that way. Artists, musicians, teachers, students, retirees, professionals, gay, straight, old, young, black, and brown were making the best of it, together.

Joann's introduction to the neighborhood had been in high school, when she attended an academy there. Recently, on a drive back through her old stomping grounds, she'd spotted a "Vacancy" sign in front of a brick building with blue trim. The quaint complex was well-kept and nicely situated next to tree-lined streets with historic homes—but at $300 a month, the price is what sealed the deal. Her Lake Union studio had been very peaceful, but rent hikes were starting to happen too regularly. So, she signed for the keys and had *new* stomping grounds on the Hill!

It was the best part of the Hill, too. The busier Broadway area had been fun in her teenage years, but now she preferred the more bucolic side, around the Academy or Volunteer Park—and downtown was still just minutes away. Even so, she was pushing it today.

Yay! There was her ride: a charcoal-gray Jetta she'd scored for under $8,000! Used, but the best thing she'd ever driven, courtesy of some leftover money in the college fund from her uncle.

Joann envisioned him lifting her up as a child: up, up, up to peek into Grandma's kitchen cabinets. He'd passed a couple summers ago but was still lifting her up with an education, a few last dollars in savings, and a decent car.

Turning the key, she said a prayer:

Thank you, Uncle.

And Joann was off, hopeful that the traffic lights would be flashing in her favor. Sadly, they were not, so it was 2:53 p.m. when she reached the Sylvan. Barely enough time to find a meter space—but her favorite valet was in the circular drive!

"Hi, Robert! Please, please, please, can you park my car?"

"I got you, Jo."

"Thank you!"

Hurray for favorite valets. She wouldn't be late! She wouldn't have to feed a meter on her break, either. Joann hustled to the hotel entrance, and Robert took the wheel.

Sylvan employees *were* allowed to park on the garage roof, but only after 5:00 p.m. Until then, you were at the mercy of the meters—unless the right valet was in the circle. A valet friend who might be willing to sneak your car *into* the garage and eventually move it up top. Space was limited, but the guys found ways to make things work. You just couldn't make a habit of it, and you couldn't get caught.

Swish! Joann stepped through the lobby doors. Staff members were supposed to use the alley entrance and clock in at basement level, but it would've taken too long to go around and back up today. The concierge frowned, but she ignored him. Jed's moods were constantly shifting, so he'd be over it, give or take a minute—and she could adjust her timecard later.

Right before the elevator, Joann turned the corner and walked into a large hall. She stopped at a door on the left, then punched in the code, and … *click!* She was in. A few paces ahead, the front-office manager sat at a steely desk.

"Hello," Joann called out.

Type-type-type. Alicia barely looked up as reservations flowed from her tidy keyboard into the Sylvan database. Not a surprise, as the interoffice vibe was different—even deflated—without Kathryn. It almost felt like Joann was more "legit" when her friend was by her side. Their manager did make a point to treat people fairly, but … maybe Joann hadn't been her first choice for the job. *Maybe* the only reason Joann was there was because Kathryn had insisted—and Alicia would do anything to keep her favorite employee happy. Because Alicia *loved* Kathryn. But what manager wouldn't love the Sylvan superstar?

Kathryn Emerson was a brilliant, curious, confident, let's-get-it-done kinda gal. She was super-competent, super-reliable, and super-responsible—the ultimate find in a minimum-wage employee. She was also quite the stunner, and behind the front desk, she was easily the face of the boutique hotel. She belonged there. You could practically read their boss's mind: *Such a natural beauty. And what a vision of tradition in Sylvan navy. Utter … perfection.*

Joann giggled. Miss Emerson was rocking a Sylvan disguise! Truth: A Bohemian streak was utterly hidden, safely tucked beneath the prissy uniform her friend wore so well. Like a flight attendant of yesteryear, Kathryn's slender build cut a classy figure in the fitted skirt and blazer. A just-high-enough ponytail topped everything off, reigning in carefree tresses to swing in step with just-high-enough heels. Head to toe, she'd spun Sylvan navy into gold. But underneath the Pan Am veneer, Kathryn was still Kathryn, and that's what Joann admired most. Either way, their manager was very fond of her number-one agent. Kathryn was an exceptional hire—and, well, she probably reminded Alicia of home.

Hailing from the north end of town, Alicia Jones was the picture of country-club Seattle.

On loan from a world of white skirts and well-groomed greens, the winsome tennis player sported the beauty of clean living—but was more than willing to get her hands dirty. She could always be found in the "trenches" with the lobby crew, and even on her most harried days, the Front Desk lead hit it down the line. Hardworking and level-headed, she aced her game both on *and* off the court.

Still, Alicia would not be at the Sylvan for long. Married to a doctor and aiming to start a family, their boss was on the fast track to motherhood, PTA boards, and charities awaiting a champion. For now, though, Alicia could make good use of her degree, and the gig provided leadership experience for everything that lay ahead—although she'd already proven herself to be more than capable.

Alicia really was the best boss a person could hope for. She ran a tight ship and treated everyone with respect—but Joann couldn't shake the feeling that she wouldn't have been her manager's first pick. In fact, things might have turned out very differently without Kathryn.

On the night Joann applied, Miss Emerson had really gone to bat for her, insisting that she fill out an application right then and there. She'd also bypassed Human Resources and handed the paperwork directly to Alicia. Kathryn later explained that she'd had a good feeling: Something was different about Joann! Weeks later, they were standing side-by-side behind the big desk, and a friendship was born between check-ins and a busy switchboard.

Quickly passing her boss, Joann retrieved a cash box from the bank of lockers on the far wall. Then she made a beeline for the desk, trying to hurry through the awkwardness. But … maybe she was imagining it? Or maybe it boiled down to the same old problem. As in, maybe their manager didn't know *what* to think about Kathryn's sidekick.

Frannie James

◆

Miss Joann MacIntosh was somewhat preppy, but her Caucasian, Seattle-born father and Asian, Hawai'i-raised mother had bestowed her with a mix of Irish, German, and Filipino features. So, while she "dressed the part," Joann didn't look like your typical Seattle sorority girl. Black-ish brown, shoulder-length hair. Fair-olive skin. Sort-of-Asian eyes. And that constellation of freckles lightly dusting her face—a stubborn holdout from childhood. If you got close enough, you could see the faint "map" not-so-hidden under makeup, and ... gasp! It might throw you off track. The whole combination was, apparently, unsettling. Which prompted the what-are-yous. Followed by the guessing: *Part-Thai? Part-Italian? Part-Japanese? Part-French? Part-Chinese?* There was always an eagerness to name whatever "it" was. Not knowing seemed to make people nervous.

Even worse, Joann had been raised in the not-so-affluent Genesee Park neighborhood, in Seattle's South End. But she'd attended the "right" schools with classmates from Capitol Hill, the North End, and Queen Anne—most of whom had never heard of Genesee Park.

It was kind of like a one-foot-accidentally-on-the-inside situation, because Joann's parents had been determined to give their kids a Catholic education. Private school was more affordable then, and her father hadn't had a mortgage payment. He'd lived with his mother until he'd saved enough for a house, then paid $20,000 cash. But mortgage or not, tuition for four children had added up, especially for a teacher and a homemaker. Growing up, it was scrimp, scavenge, save, all the time. Not exactly superstar material. Not exactly ... Kathryn.

Then again, the girls had more in common than one might think—starting with their humble upbringings. After abandoning the stuffy ranks of upper-crust Boston, Kathryn's parents had found happily-ever-after on Vashon, one of Puget Sound's islands. Just a ferry ride away from Seattle, the Emersons had embraced the simple life, and they'd raised a beautiful daughter who was beautifully down-to-earth.

Ha! thought Joann. *Agent Emerson and Agent MacIntosh. Secret Sylvan twins!*

Beep! The switchboard had no time for secrets. Back-to-business-back-to-business.

Alicia grabbed the call, and Joann pushed through the swinging door, past PBX, and out to the front desk. After saying goodbye to the morning-shift agent, she began her tasks:

The Sylvan Hotel

•

Organize cash drawer. Straighten brochures. Now for the check-in lists. She printed Robert's first and placed a newspaper on top. He appreciated the report being ready to go at the beginning of the shift, along with a copy of *The Seattle Times*. Breezing in from the circle, the valet peered over the marble counter: List. Newspaper. And he didn't even have to ask.

"Thanks, Jo. Hey, guess what?"

"What?"

"Chicken butt!" he blurted with a "gotcha" smile.

"How old are you, again?" she joked.

Heading back to the circle, the valet made a serious effort to put on a serious face.

Hired shortly before Joann, Robert Bailey was twenty-four and also navigating the in-between. The guy was pure decency and funny as hell: a gentleman with a massive streak of mischievous. His easygoing ways complemented wholesome good looks—and he was a better, newer kind of "boy-next-door." Her friend was considerate, hilarious, outdoorsy, and athletic, with a dash of rebel in there for good measure. And as a fellow valet once said, he was also a bit of a "hippy."

Joann very much fancied Robert's congeniality and his sense of humor. Most importantly, she could count on him. Hotel life was often stressful, but Mister Bailey had her back. He was actually quite vigilant about looking out for her—and he was good company. Robert was upbeat but not in an annoying way, and always angling for a laugh. When work slowed, he'd come in from the circle with some goofy comment, eager for a reaction. He could be shy, then gradually braver, heckling her more as the night progressed, and when guests were safely out of earshot. The valet teased the desk agent to no end, but encouragement was never far behind. It was all in good fun—and it was purely friendship.

Outside the hotel, each of them was in a serious relationship. Joann was dating Grady, and Robert was dating the glamorous Tricia, a stylish Filipino girl with long dark hair and big brown eyes. She was also starting a career, employed at another hotel as a marketing manager. Tricia had stopped by the Sylvan a few times, but Joann didn't know much about her other than that she played soccer, like Robert. From the looks of it, Tricia seemed smart and perfectly pleasant. She and the valet also appeared to be a good match. They'd been together two-ish years—about the same as Joann and Grady.

"Jo!"

Across the lobby, Finn opened the kitchen door, waved, and made one of his silly faces.

Though he was surprisingly serious about Room Service protocol, Finn could also be quite a rascal. However, visitors never saw anything less than professional, as he could snap back to yes-sir-stoic in a split second. From head to toe, Finn was fully committed to the part he played.

Mister Room Service was, in fact, all about presentation, starting with himself.

The twenty-something Sylvan expertly channeled old-Hollywood suave and was particularly personable. Tall, blond, and chatty, Finn resembled a young Richard Chamberlain in a tuxedo shirt, black slacks, and black shoes. Just add hair gel, a white apron, and ta-da! *Thorn-Birds*-meets-Clark-Gable, at your service. He was like a younger, rascally kind of butler—and a most convivial charm was his superpower.

"Jo!" he called out again.

"*Yes,* Finn, I can see you!"

She stifled a laugh, and he pretended to be pulled into the kitchen, cartoonishly ducking behind the door.

Just inside that door and to the left, Stan Fontane, a cool-headed pastry chef, stirred up warm layers of tasty goodness. Mixers mixing and whisks whisking, the pâtissier was stationed in a cave-like alcove, up to his elbows in marzipan and meringue. The baking nook made for close quarters as it also provided a home base for Room Service—but when Stan did his thing, it was a sweet place to be.

Swish. The kitchen door opened again.

Speak of the ... devil's food cake! Carrying a dessert tray, Stan waved at Joann en route to the restaurant.

"Jo!" Finn quickly reclaimed the spotlight, appearing and disappearing once more.

God forbid Joann had missed any part of his schtick the first time.

Swish. Now the front doors were opening. Navy jacket, incoming.

Todd Barnes folded his arms on the marble countertop, his face expressionless. He was Kathryn's favorite valet, but Joann found him intimidating. Todd was like the valet king—or a golden boy, in a fiercer kind of way—with no time to mess around. He'd also graduated with a communications degree, but remained undecided when it came to building a career.

The Sylvan Hotel

◆

Regardless, the guy had built a life. Friends ... family ... music ... Todd was always out and about, *and* well-traveled for someone their age. Well-liked, too. Everyone at the hotel was a fan—guests included. He'd even partied with Guns N' Roses. And he was popular with the ladies.

"What's up?" the valet asked, his voice low and flat.

"Oh, the usual—waiting for check-ins. We've got about ten more."

Joann braced herself, not quite sure what to expect. She and Todd hadn't ever talked much, and he was obviously uncertain about who, exactly, Kathryn was hanging out with these days.

He looked into her eyes, his own flecked with skepticism—and she held her breath.

Please-don't-ask-me-something-I-don't-know-the-answer-to-I-get-that-you're-cool-but-I'm-not-cool-and-Kathryn-thinks-so-highly-of-you-and-she's-my-best-friend-so-I-don't-want-to-say-the-wrong-thing-that-will-make-you-think-I'm-an-idiot-and-make-her-embarrassed—

"Hmm." Todd pulled a wool beret over defiant, sunny-blond hair.

"Whaaat?" stammered Joann.

"You look more like a 'Margaret.'" He telepathically dared her to flinch.

"Alrighty then," she breathed out.

Satisfied, Todd patted the marble countertop. Well, at least he didn't hate her guts!

Swish. In walked Mister Bailey. Under the watchful eye of Mister Barnes, he pulled a stack of tip money from his pocket and started counting, holding up each dollar—his way of requesting a trade for bigger bills.

"One, ah-ah-ah. Two, ah-ah-ah. Three, ah-ah-ah."

Robert continued to count in a Sesame-Street voice, undeterred by the presence of Mister Too-Cool-for-School.

Todd's eyebrows started to rise. "Yeeeeeah, okay, Margaret. Check you later," and he flew off to help a guest. Robert stayed put, but the boy's routine was reaching new heights. Tucking in his upper lip above the gumline, Count Bailey "turned into" a bunny. Joann did her best to act unamused—but how was he so cute, even when he was being so ridiculous? They both broke into laughter and proceeded with the exchange.

Rrrrrrrrip. Robert pried open a well-worn Velcro wallet, and Joann handed him a twenty for his bundle of bills. Then they traded stories.

"I changed the last guy's room three times. None of 'em were good enough!"

"Yeah, I'm not surprised. He was totally condescending."

Swish. The stairway door opened across the lobby, adjacent to the kitchen door.

"Lynnnnieeeee!" Joann waved the housekeeper over.

The swing-shift "maid" was younger than them, but already the most cynical. Originally from Aberdeen, a battered old logging town outside of Seattle, Lynn had moved to the Emerald City for a new start. She'd gone through a lot of struggles early in life and didn't have much patience for snobby guests or asshole managers. Still, Lynn was unexpectedly endearing, her "attitude" was never bothersome, and she had the biggest heart on staff.

"What's up, Joann? Hey, Robert."

Lynn loosely tied her brownish-blonde waves into a low ponytail. Then she secured the white apron over her black uniform dress.

"I just talked to the rudest guest," she began in her stoner drawl.

"Room 201—" Joann and Robert replied in unison.

"That guy is such a *dick*," added Robert, and he returned to the circle as a car drove in.

"Aren't you two cute," Lynn slyly remarked.

"Stop, Lynnie. You know we're just friends." Heat tiptoed into Joann's face.

A door slammed, and the general manager rounded the corner. What was *he* still doing there? Straightening up, Lynn swiftly moved to the side, and Mr. Alexander threw a jangly key ring onto the desk, below the marble countertop.

"Okay, I'm going. Late day, today. A lot of stuff. Had to catch up."

Joann placed the keys in one of the key boxes behind her.

"Lynn, you shouldn't be out here," Mr. Alexander muttered in a haughty European accent. His face twisted scornfully under sharp yellow bangs.

Joann wanted to smack him. How dare he talk to Lynn like that. She was completely presentable—and maybe the hoity-toity guests *should* see who cleaned their toilets and made the beds.

Mr. Alexander turned to Joann, expecting her to concur. To his surprise, she smiled and waved at the retreating Lynn. The commander in chief cast a withering look at both of them and stomped off, his black trench coat flapping like it was having its own tantrum.

In befriending Lynn, Kathryn and Joann had seemingly puzzled some other Sylvans, but they paid no mind to any of it. *Screw 'em*, they'd agreed. "The maid" was better than anybody there would ever be.

Now by the elevator, Lynn mouthed the words, "call me," and held up an invisible phone.

Dammit. Joann knew Lynnie could take care of herself. She was from Aberdeen, for god's sake. But the way people treated her was very wrong. Where was the respect? Housekeeping was the hardest job at the hotel. Scrubbing. Vacuuming. Washing. Dusting. Scraping. Hauling. *Bring me this. Bring me that.* Just thinking about it was exhausting.

Joann could barely take care of her studio apartment. She did keep it extremely neat and tidy, but she wasn't so religious about the really deep cleans. Not after all those weekends at her grandmother's. As kids, Joann and her brother had earned a dollar here and there, wiping down walls, vacuuming top to bottom, dusting every staircase spindle, scouring countertops, spraying windows, polishing furniture, and putting the shine back into silverware. Jeezus, and the floors. Grandma would scold, "Use a little elbow grease," as her granddaughter went to war with the kitchen linoleum over and over and over again.

Housekeeping was hard work. Back-breaking work. The least you could do was be nice to the person who was mopping up your mess.

Ding.

Two gold doors opened. Kiet, another member of the housekeeping crew, waved to Joann from inside the elevator, then motioned for Lynn to get on. The kid didn't speak a lot of English—and just quietly saw to his tasks. Maybe he was Vietnamese? Chinese? Korean? Joann wasn't sure and didn't know if she should ask, especially given her own experience with that type of question. Also, most people at work ignored Kiet, so he suspected the worst when approached. He *did* seem to like Kathryn, Joann, and Robert, and he put up with Lynn, well, because she was Lynn. But for the most part, Kiet made a point of keeping to himself.

Joann held her breath. Those two were supposed to stay off the elevator as much as possible, giving guests priority. Clearly, it was shaping up to be a "fuck-it" kind of night.

Kiet waved to Joann again, and the housekeepers vanished as the doors closed.

Not a second later, Mr. Alexander blew back in.

Frannie James

◆

"I forgot my notebook—keys!" he loudly commanded.

Did you forget your manners, too? Joann silently retorted.

He headed to his office, and she watched the elevator lights. Four. Five. Six.

Stay up there, you guys.

Seconds later, Mr. Alexander returned, then blasted out the front doors again.

Joann exhaled. A storm had passed—and, hopefully, the rest of the shift would be smooth sailing.

"Hello, Miss? May I get some change?"

An Emerald City aristocrat neared the desk, dressed down but dressed up in an Oxford shirt, designer jeans, tasseled shoes, and a watch with too many time zones.

Behold, Mr. Wolf, the Sylvan's resident VIP. A financier who liked fast cars, Mr. Wolf frequented the hotel several times a month, zipping in and out of town on business. His two adult children still lived in Seattle and were regulars as well, often joining him for dinner in the lounge, bar, or restaurant. The Sylvan was their home away from home ... and they *definitely* belonged there. Loaded with Daddy Wolfbucks cachet, Ken and Khloe Wolf walked around like they owned the place.

The sibling sophisticates were half-Asian and Caucasian like Joann. They were a striking pair, although strikingly cold. Joann had tried her best to engage them, but the baby Wolfbucks were even above small talk.

It didn't add up. They were very cordial to Kathryn, but, in Joann's presence, they froze with disdain, taking cover under their overpriced Gore-Tex. Maybe the junior Wolfs felt a need to remind her that, despite any similarities between them, she was nothing like them. They were fancy-pants formidable ... and she was the help.

Papa Wolf pocketed his change, then was off, probably to dine with his pups.

≡ ◆ ≡

7:30 p.m.

Joann scanned the lobby. No one in sight, the switchboard had hushed, and the other desk agent on for the night was at dinner. Time ... for some research!

The Sylvan Hotel

•

The valet schedule was updated every Wednesday or Thursday, and Joann would check it against her own schedule, often trading shifts with other desk agents. The idea was to get her hours to match Robert's as closely as possible. It required some effort—but made a big difference.

Basically, a job where customers bitched at you for eight hours needed as much help as it could get. Other desk agents were your allies, but the valets were your partners in crime: accomplices in hijacking humdrum; co-conspirators in stealing laughs; henchmen who'd carry out (pizza) orders. Robert was the best at all of it and easily bounced back when things got frustrating. It was like you could breathe the moment he walked in, his grin lighting up the lobby. And he and Joann made a great team! Both of them appreciated a well-oiled routine, both were quite organized—and both were quick to anticipate what one or the other needed to get their jobs done. Work was just easier when they worked together, so they regularly checked in with each other about it at the end of the night when her friend would walk her to the car. "Will you be here tomorrow?" he'd ask, visibly relieved when the answer was yes.

Joann glanced at the concierge stand, just to the right of the desk. Could she get over there, check the schedule, and get back before the phones went crazy—or before anybody returned? Hmm. The concierge was safely out of the way, on break in the garage. As for the car-parking crew, it was probably haircut night, which meant they were also hunkered in the garage, awaiting their turn at the scissors …

Bryce wielded the blades every few weeks or so, during slower shifts. His Sylvan special was the cheapest trim around, and not having to sit through awkward salon conversation was an even better deal. Plus, Bryce had vision. He could see what was right for you. The valet had personally mastered the look of "downtown-artsy" with his casually coiffed locks, hipster glasses, vests, and very good shoes. Bottom line: Bryce knew what worked—so his teammates counted on him to keep those wild hairs in check.

Like Joann, Bryce had family ties to Hawai'i and some Filipino in him as well. He was also pursuing advertising and had recently started a business. Now a graphic designer by day, the young entrepreneur was the most "grown-up" of all of them. Bryce had an office! *And* he was engaged to his high-school sweetheart. Hot on the tail of success—and saving for a wedding—Bryce would be at the Sylvan a while longer, taking on shifts here and there. He was the most "respectable" valet, and one of Robert's best friends.

Frannie James

◆

They *must* be in the garage.

Joann pushed through the swinging door, past PBX, into the office, out to the hall, around the corner, and through the lobby to concierge territory. Stepping behind the lectern-style stand, she pulled a black binder from a built-in shelf located beneath the desktop. Then she flipped to the scheduling grid and quickly scanned the page:

Matt Heulin. Gorgeous badass who had nothing to say to anyone. He looked like he belonged in *The Outsiders*. His badass dark hair hung over badass blue eyes, and he wore badass black leather jackets. Matt was never insolent or rude, but he avoided "polite conversation," painfully mumbling obligatory pleasantries when trading in tip dollars.

The tongue-tied valet had not impressed management. But to Joann, Matt seemed more shy than anything. He also seemed to be perpetually embarrassed, flustered by the attentions of giddy guests and giddy Sylvans. Matt was a car-parking catch—with keys to a lot of hearts. But he only had eyes for his girlfriend Melody: also gorgeous and also a badass.

Whatever. Joann didn't mind Matt, but *her* eyes kept moving.

Lobby lighting rolled over the names in a fickle sheen. There he was! *Robert*. And they were aligned! Tuesday, Wednesday, Thursday, Friday … In sync for days to come, and they'd be joined by Matt, Bryce, or Todd. Just like the desk agents, valets worked in twos or threes.

"What's going on, Joann?"

Jed returned right as she pushed the binder back into its slot.

"Just enjoying a change of scenery!"

The concierge moved closer.

Yuck. Jed was a too-desperate type of a dude who grabbed at anything he could get. A squeeze; a graze; any opportunity that presented itself. His behavior was more dumbshit than malicious but gross, nevertheless. He couldn't keep his paws to himself, and he never hesitated to share thoughts about the hot girl in 208 or the babe in 412. But keep your mouth shut, nod, and smile … or Mister Yuck would find ways to poison your day. Because if he wasn't happy, then you couldn't be happy. Everyone else liked him, but Joann couldn't stand him. And why did *Kathryn* give him a pass, knowing how he could be?

Oh, that's just Jed.

No. That's just wrong, Joann thought, backing away. But … maybe Kathryn felt sorry for the guy. Or … her friend's efforts to see the good in people went too far sometimes. Or ... Kathryn just didn't like certain types of confrontation. Which was weird because she could be so fearless about so many other things. Then again, nobody wanted trouble at work. Jed was a manager, and saying something or "getting into it" with him could make all of their lives difficult. Well, maybe Joann had to give *Kathryn* a pass. Besides, no one was totally perfect.

And ... Jed's arm was around her. Ugh. Apparently, just standing next to him was an open invitation. In Jed's view (and as he'd repeatedly broadcasted), Kathryn was the ideal gal, but that didn't mean he'd turn down a chance at some gropity-grope with someone else. Gross. Why did guys do this? What gave them the right? It was a never-ending battle that no girl signed up for. Joann had been "drafted" at age thirteen, on a late-night ride back from babysitting: Black BMW. Hand on knee. And the fight had continued from there.

Beep.

"Oops, there goes the switchboard!" She slid out of Jed's grasp.

"Run, run, run!" he gleefully cried.

Eight lines blinked urgently in PBX. Picking up the receiver, Joann routed three calls to the restaurant, four to guestrooms, and one to Housekeeping. All quiet again, so she pushed through the swinging door and back to the desk, just as Brad was returning from the cafeteria. Smiling, her reception comrade pointed to an armload of finance magazines. That meant he wanted to sit at the switchboard. Joann nodded, smiling back.

When she wasn't working with Kathryn, Joann was (fortunately) paired up with Brad, the Sylvan's swing-shift "veteran." Brad was just a few years their senior, but he'd been with the hotel for about nine years. He knew all the ins and outs of the old bastion—and he'd seen a lot at that desk—so the lead agent could easily solve his way through anything. His ongoing work outside the hotel had also helped shape that infamous savvy. As a University of Washington (a.k.a. "UW") advisor, he'd become quite unflappable, having dealt with all sorts of "emergencies" and life's twists and turns. So, even in the face of the yellers, he could schmooze his way through whatever the meanest, rudest guests were being mean and rude about.

All in all, Brad was a course-corrector extraordinaire and kept everything on an even keel. But while he was "management material," Brad could surprise you. He was willing to break a small rule now and then and even turn a blind eye. He also enjoyed the company of his junior counterparts and took an interest in their lives. Not surprisingly, Brad was revered by the team—and he was captain of their nighttime world.

Beep! Captain Front Desk got settled into PBX.

Whoosh. Jed wheeled by with the bell cart, winking at her.

Swish. Ken and Khloe Wolf incoming.

"Hello," offered Joann—and they quickly turned for the restaurant.

She rolled her eyes.

"I saw that," a voice called from the lounge.

Joann waved to George, now smirking at her from under the weight of a loaded tray. Rounding out the evening roster, George was the Sylvan bar manager. The ninth of thirteen children, George was also a recovered-Catholic wiseass. So he served it up with a salty wit, a twist of sarcasm, and a big splash of truth. George was a little older than the girls but had crossed paths with Jed and Robert at school.

The barman carried on, and Joann took a seat on the window ledge next to a valet booth now empty of navy jackets. Still in the garage, she thought. Although, one of those navy jackets wouldn't be gone long—not when his favorite desk agent was working!

Robert and Joann had become fast friends just after her first week on the job. Jed and the valets had gathered out front while Alicia introduced "the latest Front Desk hire." Based on what Joann had learned at a restaurant gig, male employees saw new girls as "fresh meat," so she'd held her breath as another kind of interview began:

"Where-are-you-from; where-did-you-go-to-school; where-do-you-live; do-you-have-a-boyfriend?"

The grilling should have been over once she mentioned "my-boyfriend-Grady," but off-the-market hadn't computed … so the Sylvan inquisition had continued.

Meanwhile, one valet remained at the concierge stand, his eyes cast down—but when she told them the name of her high school, he'd looked up. The Academy was a sister school to *his* alma mater, as Jed had quickly explained.

"George, Robert, and I all graduated from the boys school."

Politely nodding, Joann had replied that her father and brothers were also alumni. It was then that Jed pointed to the bashful valet.

"This is Robert."

After a quick wave, the questions resumed, but Robert had looked up again when she'd named her elementary school. He'd attended a neighboring school, and coincidentally, they'd both loved an instructor who'd worked at both places.

Mrs. Rollins was the best!

Suddenly, it was like they'd grown up together—or like they'd known one another before, even though they'd just met.

Rat-tat-tat. A navy jacket knocked on the big window.

Joann unlatched it.

"Get to work, Mister!"

Laughing, Robert ran off to catch up with Matt.

Beep! The switchboard *sounded* off with an "on-hold" prompt.

Brad was likely stuck on another call in PBX, so Joann picked up at the desk.

"Good evening, the Sylvan Hotel …"

"Hi—Joann?"

"Hey, Tricia! How are ya? I'll put you through to him—just … hang on."

Joann dialed 116, and Robert, hearing the phone ring, jogged back to the valet booth.

"Bailey, let's go!" Matt flagged his teammate as more cars pulled into the circle.

Robert said his goodbyes and chucked the receiver onto the wall-mounted cradle.

Joann pushed the big window open and watched her friend approach a taxi. Tucking a pen behind his ear, he directed the driver forward.

Woosh. Wind gusted through the circle, blowing a strand of hair across his handsome face.

Joann realized her heart was racing. Startled, she turned away.

THE SEATTLE KIDS

Joann and Kathryn sloshed through Pioneer Square over slick cobblestones and grouted prism-glass sidewalks. Here and there, Victorian flourishes turned a pretty face to the rain, and turn-of-the-century lamps accented an architectural legacy. Terracotta, iron, stone, and 19th-century masonry held fast in a landmark ensemble of Romanesque Revival—one of the country's best surviving collections.

Also in the mix: A totem pole stretched toward the sky, honoring another legacy. Black, red, and blue-green carvings told of ancient tales: Raven. Frog. Seal. Sun. Stars. Moon. Daughter. Lake. And a voyage through depths inside the belly of a beast.

Puget Sound breezes began to blow, and whiffs of artisan bread tickled Joann's nose. Quickening their steps, the girls continued through Seattle's oldest neighborhood. The locale had seen its share of ups but a lot of downs, starting with "Skid Row": a strip of hill that would eventually be known as Yesler Way. Mill workers—often those who'd fallen on hard times—would skid or slide timber along that steep path, kicking off a journey through steam and water. Eventually, almost all of Pioneer Square went up in flames, lost to the Great Seattle Fire of 1889. Years later, a new version rose from the ashes, and by 1991, the hot zone had become home to offices, boutiques, Grand Central Bakery, galleries, bars … and a bibliophile's dream.

Set on the corner of 1st and Main, Elliott Bay Book Company was Seattle's most famous bookstore, and *the* spot to spend a blustery afternoon—or any afternoon. Shaking out umbrellas, Kathryn and Joann pushed through the doors, ready to hit the stacks.

Inside the shop, tall cedar shelves towered with tomes and stood rooted to creaky wood floors. Exposed brick walls were testament to the past, and the place hummed with possibility.

Just like the Sylvan, Elliott Bay Books was privately owned, independent—so you could always uncover something different, and in a uniquely inspired setting. For Kathryn and Joann, the children's section was an extra-favorite stop, as they loved the artistry that lived in the pages of picture books. Then onto other shelves as the lauded aisles were a sure thing for finds of all kinds.

An hour later, they rushed out of the bookstore and back to Capitol Hill for a quick bite at the Surrogate Hostess! Across from St. Joe's, the Surrogate Hostess was a Seattle institution. The unassuming café was just-enough "rustic," just-enough "urban," and home to the best lunch in town. Two made-from-scratch soups were ladled up daily, along with your choice of dressing on green salad. Mmm ... and a down-home slice of bread to boot. You simply grabbed a tray, lined up to order, then seated yourself at small or large wooden tables.

"I hope it's not *too* busy tonight." Joann dug into the homemade fare.

"Nah," responded Kathryn. "It's off-season for tourists, so we'll be slow at the desk.

But the dining room, lounge, and bar will be slammed with the start of the holiday season. We've probably got banquets happening, too. Oh, and the Dickens Carolers are singing tonight. Yikes. The boys will be running for hours."

"Bummer."

"Indeed. 'Tis the season for grouchy valets. Although, I think Todd told me they have a new guy starting tonight, so, hopefully ... then again, having to train someone in the middle—"

"We've got Robert, Todd, Matt, Bryce, *and* a new guy tonight?"

"Love how you're up on the schedule particulars, Jo."

"*What*? You know it makes a difference."

"True." Kathryn had no argument there. "And it will be good to see Bryce. We barely work with him anymore! We're losing that boy to yuppie world."

Joann crunched on herbed croutons. "I like Matt, too. I don't think he's rude—I think he just hates pretense. Um, and his unsolicited fan club!"

"Okay, but he has to learn how to play the game. He's not doing himself any favors—"

"Well, I've been told to be more 'perky,' and I think it's bullshit. Just because I don't talk like an over-caffeinated cheerleader doesn't make me any less competent, or friendly, or polite. And I can think of several people who are way worse, like those cocktail servers."

"Lee's nice," asserted Kathryn.

"Yeah, and Beth's never fake."

"And Lissa's okay. I dunno if she likes *us*, but she keeps it professional."

"But the other three glare too much. I hate how they act like we're their underlings—"

"Just do your job, and ignore their crap. Let's face it: There's always gonna be a bitch—

or three—in the bunch. Who knows what the problem is. Do the valets talk to us too much? Hello, that's the job. Do we suck because the bartender's our friend? Hello, he's not our boss. Are they pissed because Finn hangs out at the desk? Hello, the dude thinks we're freaks."

"And Finn loves himself a freak show!"

"Hey, is Lynn working tonight?"

"I hope so. But check this out: Alexander told her she shouldn't be seen at the front.

He thinks 'the help' should stay hidden."

"What did Lynnie do?"

"She just backed away from him. Then Kiet pulled up in the elevator and rescued her."

"Go, Kiet! Elevator extraction!"

The girls stood to bus their dishes. It was almost 2:20 p.m., and timecards would soon need punching.

⇒ ♦ ⇐

At the Sylvan, Joann and Kathryn pushed through the alley door, braved a crowded locker room, and clocked in. Lynn and Kiet prepped housekeeping carts in the hall, gearing up for the night ahead.

"Oh, look," Lynn said, assessing her friends. "It's the dynamic duo. My, Kathryn, but your ponytail sure is perky today."

"Haha, Lynnie." Kathryn tugged at the housekeeper's sleeve. "Hey, come see us after Alexander leaves, and plan on Kay's later!"

"Well, I'll just have to see if I can pencil you two in." Lynn tied on an apron, a smoke dangling precariously from her mouth.

"Whatever. Come visit when you get a break!" Joann yanked at the apron, untying it again.

"Jeezus Christ, you guys! Go to work. And go easy on those valets, dream team."

The Sylvan Hotel

•

Joann moved to playfully smack Lynn who ducked and ran off.

"You're in trouble now, Lynnie," Kathryn laughed.

With a quizzical frown, Kiet studied the three of them, then declared, "You-all crazy."

The girls hit the stairs and climbed to the lobby level, nearly running into Finn, who was passing by with tray in hand.

"Oh, look. It's the A-Team." Three, two, one … *evil giggle*.

"Yeah, yeah," Joann snarked brightly.

Finn strutted past and continued to giggle—but Cocktail Bitch One and Cocktail Bitch Two seethed from a nearby corner. Walking on through, Kathryn held her head high, that perky ponytail swinging with confidence. Joann avoided their disapproving eyes but felt less "perky" than ever. *Why did they have to be like that? She and Kathryn weren't at all interested in Finn!*

Click. The "A-team" stepped into the back office. Still on a call, Alicia waved, and assistant manager Leena flagged them down.

"Help, please!"

She pointed to a handful of forms.

"Got it, Leena," Kathryn replied. "Jo, I'll start in PBX so I can get these bookings done."

At the desk, Joann tended to a steady stream of holiday visitors. One after the other, she directed them to the bathrooms, bar, lounge, and restaurant. With a quick "thank you," Robert ran by for his arrivals list, then he was off to an already-busy circle.

Swish. A neatly suited and mustached concierge pushed through the stair door and into the lobby. Louis managed the bell staff and filled in on nights when Jed wasn't scheduled.

A stickler for procedure, he could often make the valets' lives miserable. There were also rumors of underhanded treatment—but Lou never harassed Joann or made her uncomfortable. Sure, he might call her out for sneaking a sitting break on the window ledge, but he wasn't a jerk about it. Sometimes, he even seemed reluctant to "lay down the law." So, yeah. The valets were more stressed when their boss was around, but Joann was relieved.

"Hi, Front Desk! We have someone new starting tonight. He's on his way up. Can I please get an extra check-in list to review with him?"

"Hi, Lou! I'll have it for you in just a sec."

Joann pushed through the swinging door to pull the list off the printer, and when she returned, a younger guy was also out front, zipping a navy jacket.

"Joann, this is Bill. Bill, this is Joann. You'll be working together quite often."

"Hello, Joann."

Bill stared as if he was star-struck. *Riiight*, she thought. More like he just wanted it to look that way.

Nice try, newbie.

"Hi, Bill. Welcome."

And he was off to the circle under Lou's wing, smiling hopefully at Joann.

"Checking in?" she asked for what seemed like the millionth time.

"Yes. We'd like a big room with a view."

Riiight. The Sylvan did not have a view, and it featured a European layout. There were no "big rooms."

Joann double-checked the availability and did a last-minute suite switcheroo. Winter meant low occupancy, so there was plenty of inventory to work with. Hopefully, they'd be happy with the upgrade.

Mr. and Mrs. We-Want-the-Impossible oohed and aahed at the holiday decor, then asked what the walls were made of.

"Honduran mahogany," Joann enthused for what probably *was* the millionth time.

7:00 p.m.

Swish. Navy jackets cruised through the front doors. Robert, Bryce, and Bill congregated at the desk, hands and faces red from the cold. Matt remained in the valet booth on the phone, and Todd assisted two guests outside.

"Hi, guys! How goes it?"

"Brutal. But good tips, at least." Bryce rezipped his jacket.

"We're going to Kay's tonight. You should join."

"I'm good with Kay's." Bill eagerly twirled a pen.

The older boys looked at him. Who was *this* guy, inviting himself to cocktails with *their* A-Team?

"Yeah, okay, we'll go," Robert glanced down at the desk.

The Sylvan Hotel

♦

Bryce turned to Robert with a surprised expression.

We will?

Joann was stoked. Robert didn't usually join them for Kay's—

Whoosh! Someone pulled into the circle. A big window flashed with illumination, as light blasted through frosted panes, the opaque glass no match for its might.

"Hi, valets!" Kathryn walked out of PBX, her eyes twinkling.

"Yo. *Valets.*" Todd walked in to round up his team, now lost to other things in motion.

The navy jackets grudgingly backed away from the desk, but the ever-so-cool Todd, having suddenly *lost* his cool, was slow to follow.

Beep!

The switchboard resumed holiday pace, sending Kathryn to PBX again. Joann prepared registration cards, and Robert radioed with a heads-up.

"Valet to Base. Corrigan party and Dworshak party checking in!"

The desk agent grabbed a radio.

"Ten-four," she replied, using the code for "affirmative."

Matt appeared with the Corrigans' bags, and Bill brought in the Dworshaks' bags.

Matt quickly returned to the circle, but the younger valet stopped midway, his eyes lingering on Joann.

Swish. The kitchen door opened, and Finn glided through with a trayful of culinary cargo hoisted high.

"Whoa, dude. Behind you."

Bill hastily turned, and Room Service made a "who-the-hell-is-that" face.

Joann tried not to laugh.

Look out, New Guy.

9:00 p.m.

Kathryn crossed her legs and adjusted the PBX chair. Leaning back, she sipped a tumbler of tea and kicked off her heels, grateful for a break. The only way to "legally" sit on the job was to work the switchboard. Out front, you were expected to stand straight and tall, perfectly poised behind the sleek façade. Regardless, either side of the swinging door could get tiring, so they took turns in each spot, unless two people were needed at the desk.

Kathryn re-clipped her beachy-brown ponytail, then spied a snag in her nylons.

"Fuck. I just bought these. And why in the hell can't I find a red pen around here?!?"

Ha! Kathryn was looking exceptionally proper in her Sylvan uniform, somewhere between Moneypenny and Mary Poppins—which made it all the more hilarious to hear that sailor's mouth let loose.

"Well, there's only one pen out front, and it's not red, either," answered Joann.

"Then I guess these papers are gonna get corrected in blue, goddammit."

Joann giggled. Kathryn Emerson was her own kind of charming. But despite the grumpiness and swearing, she was the staunchest of allies, a kick-ass confidant, and most surely the cleverest and coolest of co-pilots for an "in-between" adventure.

"Kay's is gonna be so fun tonight!" Joann grinned. "This shift needs to go faster!"

They *had* gotten through most of it. Twenty check-ins were all tucked in, parties were winding down, and restaurant servers cleared tables for tiramisu. A buzzy lounge still buzzed, but in a quieter way, as whispery voices melded into a low murmur. So at reception, two desk agents could now enjoy some calm before the last shift-storm. During that final bout of hustle-bustle, hotel patrons would swarm, requesting tabs, checks, and change. Next came the tallying of receipts, while last-minute housekeeping calls and commands for cars traveled between walkie-talkies. Then servers and valets would stop by to exchange tip dollars for larger bills … and another night would be in the books.

11:00 p.m.

Joann shut the cash drawer and finalized her paperwork.

"What's up, Miss MacIntosh?"

Bill was back. He'd changed out of his uniform into a T-shirt, jeans, and suede coat.

The Sylvan Hotel

•

The valet reminded her of someone. Maybe ... Ethan Hawke ... or ... Patrick Swayze? Yeah! Sort of an Ethan Hawke vibe—or sort-of-Patrick-Swayze, but with skater hair.

Tee hee. Another "Outsider" was in the house.

"May I get a pack of Marlboros?"

Balancing a stack of papers, the cashbox, and her cash-out envelope, Joann opened the cigarette drawer.

"How was your first night?" she asked.

"Good. So, I'll see you at Kay's?" He handed her three dollars for the cigarettes.

"Yeah. I just have to change—oh, and call in a cannelloni order!"

Cannelloni was Kay's specialty, but only regulars were privy because it wasn't on the menu. It also took its time in the oven. Luckily, Sylvans were allowed to call in requests toward the end of their shifts. When they clocked out, Italian deliciousness would be just about ready.

"Joann, we're gonna go change. See you at the bar!"

Bryce waved as he, Robert, and Todd neared the stair door.

Bill joined the other boys, and Joann greeted the graveyard shift.

"Hi, Ollie!"

"Well, hey there, Swing Shift."

The auditor signed into the computer and pushed his glasses up.

"Headed to Kay's? Now you girls be safe—"

"Don't worry! The valets are going with us."

"Ahhh, it's one of *those* nights," he teased.

"Ollie. We're getting *dinner*. Jeez!"

"Yeah, I see how it is. Well, have fun ..."

In the locker room, Joann peeled off navy nylons and rummaged through her bag.

"Aw, man. I brought two different socks."

"Oh my god, Jo. Who cares! You're not at Catholic school anymore!"

"Maybe I just won't wear them."

"Um, it's rather cold out, missy. And dark. Just fucking wear the socks. No one will see, and no one gives a shit."

Kathryn was all cares to the wind about clothes. But Joann had learned otherwise, and very early on. From kindergarten through fourth grade, she'd been a glasses-headgear-braces-homemade-pants kind of girl—and a meanie magnet.

Being mixed hadn't helped her case, either. The other kids were clearly Caucasian, Black, Asian, Latino, or Samoan, and they hadn't known *what* to make of her. On top of that, too many good grades had added up to too nerdy. The worst of it was when a teacher started reading Joann's stories to her classmates. One day, almost all of them chased her across the playfield.

Thankfully, Joann's father was transferred for work, and he enrolled his kids at a different school, close to the new job. He'd hoped it would solve the bullying problems—and it made for easy carpooling. So, Joann started fifth grade and started over. She no longer wrote stories, but she faked outgoing 'til she *was* outgoing—and worked hard to win favor with the junior leagues of Laurelhurst, Windermere, Sandpoint, Bryant, Montlake, and Ravenna.

The right look had also been key to survival, so assimilation was on the syllabus.

Roll-on lip gloss. Maybelline blush. Feathered hair. Upturned collars. Then cardigans when it was cool, pullovers when it wasn't—and always, always, always, the right kind of white-nylon knee socks. Babysitting money had helped her complete the "makeover," along with uniform sales on second-hand items like wavy-soled shoes and pants from a store called Saturdays.

Academically, Joann had blended in, too. And she'd started *fitting in*—and having fun. Foursquare. Dodgeball. Flag football. Touchdown … MacIntosh for the win! It had been a new life with new everything. She'd discovered the Rolling Stones, Rick Springfield, the Go-Gos, and Nancy Drew. She'd sneaked *General Hospital*, giggled about boys, and bubbled up her cursive. There'd been roller-skating at Skoochies, her first real campfire, Mad Libs mania … and invites to addresses with *upstairs* bedrooms—and where Barbies lived in townhouses!

You're-the-one-that-they-want-ooo-ooo-ooo-honey.

Greased lightnin' had taken Joann by storm, as she danced with her north-end chums to the soundtrack of another outsider story—and a tale of square-girl metamorphosis. She'd just hoped *her* square-girl past would stay secret.

Badass good girls were the future.

When she got to the Academy, Joann had been schooled by another well-heeled student body. She'd studied their carefully coordinated togs, mastering the ropes of pearls and penny loafers. Name brands hadn't been affordable, but she'd pulled "good-enough" together with sales finds and a growing eye for fashion. She'd also shelved books on weekends for Seattle Public Library—and for contact lenses. Pushing the carts, Joann would count dollars in her mind by the hour and set goals: *I am going to look normal. I am going to be normal. I am going—*

"Let's get going!"

Kathryn pulled on a baggy jacket over Levi's, a sweatshirt, and sneakers. Joann pulled on corduroys, a turtleneck, a sweater, and a parka. Then she slid her feet into one purple sock, one blue sock, and those old penny loafers. Back to dorkhood, she thought. But it *was* cold. And the days of elementary brutes and prep-school princesses were behind her.

They shut their lockers, then—

"Well, well, well. What do we have here?" A weary housekeeper advanced.

"Lynnie! Are you coming with us?"

"Fiiine," she replied.

"Woo-hoo!" they shouted. Work was over, but the fun was just beginning.

Stubborn air challenged the girls to a fight as they shoved against the basement door, pushing into the alley.

Roar. Rattle-rattle-rattle. Vroom.

Ahead of them, badass Matt drove out of the garage on his badass motorcycle with badass Melody, her arms wrapped tightly around him. Then they turned into the street.

Right out of a movie, thought Joann. Where was the twosome off to? Pioneer Square? The waterfront?

"Dammit, where are my smokes?"

Coughing, Lynn searched her pockets to the tune of two friends yelling about lung destruction. Immune to their diatribe, she kept digging, then cupped hands around a cigarette and a smirk.

At the top of the next block, white letters backlit over maroon-red squares vertically spelled out "KAY'S," like a lighthouse marking the shore between uptown and downtown.

Joann excitedly barreled sideways into Lynn, then hip-checked Kathryn.

Frannie James

◆

"Quit it, Jo!" Kathryn shoved her back.

"Yeah, Joaaanna. Relax. Don't get your panties in a twist because you-know-who is joining us. Haha—that's right. I heard your *boyfriends* talking by the locker rooms."

Lynn cried for mercy as both of them swatted her—but soon she was laughing and blowing smoke in their faces.

"Eww ... stop, Lynnie!" Kathryn moved to swat her again.

Joann thought her smile would freeze in place. Yeah, she was "stuck" in a kind of limbo for now, and it was hard to tell when she'd move ahead with her life—but she was far from alone. *How* was she so lucky to have found these people? Cynically sweet Lynn in cargos, flannel, and Doc Martens. Forthright. Spirited. Comical. Skeptical. Resilient. Rough-around-the-edges wise. Then there was Kathryn: The small-town island girl turned Emerald City girl. Fiercely loyal. Fiercely intelligent. Fiercely opinionated. Fiercely caring. Big hearted and bravehearted but hiding under swear words and oversized layers.

Both of them were becoming the besties of her dreams.

Before the Sylvan, Joann wasn't sure she'd ever have "besties." She'd made fairly strong friendships in middle school, but those girls had lived further away, and they'd gone on to different high schools. Then everyone had moved on.

At the Academy, Joann had crisscrossed cliques and class levels, but there was no taking up residence in any group. Not rich enough. Not smart enough. Not hot enough. Not cool enough. Not average enough. Not weird enough. Not good-girl enough. Not bad-girl enough.

For the most part, she'd safely skated down the middle. No invites to Arboretum keggers—or to smoke lunch-time cloves on Bruce Lee's grave—but she'd made it to houseboat bashes, Metro games, Genesee barbeques, Godfather's pizza parties, "all-city" dances, and Alki bonfires.

When she got to college, Joann had struggled in a friendship wasteland. UW was huge—and connecting with people had been near to impossible. Living on her own hadn't helped, but sororities and dorms had been a no-go after four years of all-girl cattiness. From lecture halls to study halls, Miss MacIntosh had been alone in the crowds.

Outside of school, Joann had worked with older women at the library and at the law firm. She'd enjoyed their company, liked their stories, and appreciated their wisdom, but outside of nine-to-five, they'd been busy grown-ups with busy lives. At her hostess job, most of the girls had belonged to sororities and kept to their own—or they'd been hellbent on bad drugs and bad boys. Joann, of course, had not been a part of Greek Row, and she hadn't been interested in scary substances or scary dudes. But now, here she was, a part of something better!

The Sylvans crossed the street to Kay's, and just inside a small foyer, Bill stood at the payphone. Seeing them, he finished his call.

"Yo. Front Desk!"

His expression was funny, daring, and shameless, all mixed up between ballsy and bravado.

Lynn hesitated, and Joann could practically hear her thoughts:
Who the hell was this?

"Lynn, this is Bill, our newest valet."

"Nice to meet you, Lynn."

"Hey," she said cautiously.

Bill held the second door open, and they stepped forward, past a deserted hostess desk.

Straight ahead, a closing restaurant was dim and hazy, but polished settings glinted, and fresh white linens were incandescent in the shadows. At the back, a pair of diners lingered, their plates still half-full. Quietly talking and rotating a hot votive, they tried to keep the last flame afloat. In a side station, waiters sipped chianti and cashed out, ready for bed—but just around the corner, another scene was waking up.

The Sylvans made the turn, then it all went almost black. Blinded by barely-there lighting, they grabbed on to one another and waited. Seconds later, eyes adjusted, and a classic Seattle haunt came into focus …

The infamous room was red, red, red, and a real-life time machine. Naugahyde booths had seen it all for decades, a jukebox spun oldies, and mirror-tiled walls reflected a time when mobsters and priests shared martinis and meatballs.

In the middle, small globes of scorched crimson topped a maze of tables and cradled tiny fires. Holding their own, the candles burned low but twitched in pulses, like hollowed-out hearts still doggedly beating. Ashtrays glowed with cinders, and on the far wall, an abstract Roman Colosseum dripped in muted golds and blues, as if melting.

Joann slowly moved inward through a fogbank of nicotine—but around her, the night was picking up speed. Seasoned waitresses shouted orders, a kitchen hollered, and a crotchety bartender was not in the mood. Parked on stools in front of him, cabbies drove up tabs, chatting shoulder-to-shoulder with other crusty characters, many on leave from apartments above. Down to raise spirits, the embattled regulars limped *in* on the regular, slowed by invisible injuries. But they took their seats like clockwork, not willing to bleed out dry.

"Kath! Jo!" Spotting them, Bryce waved.

The boys had claimed a tall, round table favored by Sylvan employees. It stood at the center of an almost-private nook, slightly partitioned off in a cylindrical space encapsulated by high walls. Bill pulled out chairs, and the girls sighed with relief after eight hours on their feet. Quietly observing the group, Lynn took long cigarette drags. Bill lit up too, and Kathryn admonished them both.

"Hi, kids. How was work?" Their favorite waitress balanced a beverage-filled tray.

"Kay!" exclaimed Joann. "How are you?"

"Fine, hon, fine. You know. Fa-la-la and all that."

She pushed a pen into slightly bee-hived, brassy-blond hair and planted practical shoes.

"Alrighty, here we go."

Resting her tray on the table, Kay set a sea breeze next to Robert, a vodka cranberry next to Bryce, and a beer next to Todd. Then she adjusted a pink grandma sweater and white blouse above a black skirt snugly zipped over nude nylons. Picking up the tray again, Kay tucked it under an arm, and plucked another pen from her pocket.

"What can I get you girls? Rum and cokes … and a Bud Light?"

Now Todd sighed. Obviously, "the girls" were there too often.

Kay nodded at Bill next. Grinning—and quite happy to be there—he ordered a shot of Jägermeister.

"Who's this?" Kay looked at the group.

Lynn exhaled a breath loaded with smoke—and the same question.

"Goin' for the Jäger," Bryce chuckled.

"Well, at least I'm not drinking fucking Bud Light!"

Okay, Mister Marlboro Boy. Already with the teasing.

"I can't drink the hardcore stuff. I've got allergies—"

"That's too bad," taunted Bill.

Lynn rolled her eyes.

The Sylvan Hotel

•

Kay returned to the well and called out their order:

"Joe! Two rum and cokes, a Bud Light, and a shot of Jäger."

The bartender began to sass her about this or that, and, lighting a cigarette, the waitress sassed him right back. Folding his arms, Joe paused, somewhere between annoyed and impressed. Then that scowl slowly turned into a smile—and he started to pour.

Click. A jukebox started to play, and Kathryn started the post-shift vent with tales of an evil switchboard:

"… So, I transfer them to the lounge, but nobody's answering. And the call keeps coming back, and the guy's just getting more pissed, and I say they don't take reservations for the lounge, anyway, and he keeps saying, 'Look if I could just speak with someone,' and I'm like, 'I'm sorry—it's a crazy night over there,' as in hello, it's fucking Christmas, and this is the Christmas *hotel*, and, by the way, I have nine other calls coming in, and, jeezus god, where is the fucking bar staff, so I send it back over again, and—"

"Easy, tiger. What's all this bitchin' about my bar?" Another Sylvan rounded the corner.

"Hi, George! How the hell did you get out of there?" Joann leaped up to hug him.

"There was a mass exodus right after you guys left, *and* my shit was done. Beth said she'd close out. Move over, Lynnie, and blow that fucking smokestack the other way."

"So, can you people start picking up your damn phone?" yelled Kathryn.

The music grew louder, and hordes of flannel shirts filed in.

"Sorry, I can't heeear you!" George laughed. "What do you kids want on the jukebox?"

"The Doors!" shouted Joann.

Todd looked at Kathryn. "Your friend's a weirdo."

"Todd Barnes, you take that back. Joann is the best." Kathryn lightly punched him.

"Just kidding, Margaret."

"Why are you calling her *Margaret*?" Kathryn frowned.

"She looks like a Margaret."

"What?!? She does *not!*"

Giggling, Joann crumpled her napkin and threw it at Todd.

Then the jukebox pressed on as did he and Kathryn.

"... She does, too ..."

"... Does not ..."

Across from Joann, Robert and Bryce began to debate what a prick Lou was or wasn't. George and Lynn were deciding how much Christmas sucked, and Bill was drinking it all in.

Tick-tock.

More libations—and more night owls—arrived. Each crew stopped momentarily before proceeding, their bleary eyes blinking and adjusting. Joann could just hear her father:

Stay outta the joints!

No way, Dad. No *way*. I wouldn't miss this for anything, she thought.

George and Lynn were now arguing about brands of rum, and Todd was getting political with Kathryn. Bryce was explaining some valet procedure to Bill—and Joann caught Robert's eye.

"Are you working tomorrow?" He sat forward.

"Yeah, you?" She sat forward.

"Yeah, 4:00 p.m. Then another three days scheduled for 3:00 p.m. What about you?"

"Same, 3:00 p.m. start."

"Hey, break it up, you two. Why so serious over there?"

George snickered with Lynn, and the valet jumped up.

"I was just telling Joann about my amazing strength!" Grinning, he flexed his arms in a superhero pose.

Lynn didn't miss a beat.

"Wow. I bet that impresses all the girls, Robert."

He and George laughed.

Lynn lit another smoke, and Joann excused herself to the ladies room. Bill slammed another shot and followed closely behind.

"Hey, Joann. You've seen the naked-lady painting in the men's room, right?"

"Yes, Bill. We've all seen her."

"Just checking. Wouldn't want you to miss—"

Robert appeared out of nowhere, informing them that he "needed to get in there" to have another look at the artwork.

"Yeah, okay," Joann responded, her face saying the rest.

Laughing again, the senior valet corralled the junior valet past her and into the bathroom.

11:58 p.m.

A chef announced, "Cannelloni up!" and the midnight meal was served. Then the Sylvans talked for about another hour until Todd said he was heading to The Saloon, a bar in Pioneer Square. It sounded a little dangerous—like him! Did you have to be extra-badass to be Saloon-worthy? Was that where Matt and Melody hung out?

"Why would you go *there*?" Kathryn quizzed.

"Because there's more to life than Kay's, Miss Emerson."

"How old do you think Kay is?" asked Joann.

"She's been here forever. She's probably Seattle's coolest two-hundred-year-old!" professed George.

"Todd, you should stay here with us. We're more fun," Kathryn proclaimed sweetly.

Lynn looked at Joann. *Uh, oh.*

Joann kicked Lynn under the table.

For a moment, Todd looked like he'd never leave, but—

"I gotta go. I got people waitin'. You comin', Bill?"

Mister Too-Cool-for-School was outta there.

New Guy nodded. "*Aw*, yeah. But … uh, should we walk the girls to their cars?"

"I'm by the cathedral," Kathryn stood and tied her scarf.

"We'll go with you." Todd stood and helped his friend with her jacket.

Bill turned to Joann, but Robert promptly chimed in.

"Don't you worry, Bill. We've got Joann. I won't let her out of my *sight*."

Lynn coughed behind an almost-empty glass, and ice cubes smacked her in the face. George tried to hide another snicker, and Joann narrowed her eyes at them. Then Kathryn, Todd, Bill, and George disappeared into the smoke.

Digging for keys, Bryce and Robert continued to joke with each other, and Joann fastened her parka, watching them with reverence. Low-key steadiness; clean-cut dependability—like the boys who carried your books in old TV shows. Unfailingly upstanding and effortlessly funny, Bryce and

Robert made any gathering complete in the best sense. It was like nothing bad could happen if they were in the room.

Buddies since college, the valets had played soccer together for Western University. These days, Bryce was further down the field, having scored a grown-up job, but Joann could see that he very much believed in Robert and had full confidence that his friend was on the path to *something*. In the meantime, Robert had a nice gig at the Sylvan, and he was dating Tricia, who was also on the road to success.

Bryce and Robert were both going places.

"Let's go, kids," said Lynn. "Uh, Joann, can I bum a ride?"

"Sure, Lynnie. You got it."

Minutes later, the group reached the hotel garage. Guest cars rested inside, securely parked behind an automatic door on the left. Straight ahead, a cement ramp tunneled up to a rooftop lot. Their own cars were parked there, scattered like islands in a sea of gray between cracks, bumps, and layers of grit laid bare in the after hours.

Robert teased Joann as they made the climb, Bryce and Lynn alongside.

City lights. Seattle skies. The night was almost over, but Joann didn't ever want it to end.

HOLIDAY BREAKS

The Sylvan was awhirl with Christmas. High tea in the lounge was a Seattle tradition, then Earl Grey and scones turned into cocktails, come evening. Yuletide tunes played on a loop, and live music was featured almost nightly.

At the center, a fireplace softly flickered. Blue-hot sparks ignited golden currents, fueling a slow-fast burn. Ornamental carvings framed the famous flames, and an old-world mosaic showcased old-world craftsmanship. Next to the hearth, the green-velvet sofa was the best seat in the house. Everything else was appointed just so, amid a beguiling montage of patterns, color, and contrast.

At the perimeter, pine garlands adorned the storied room, draped across panels of polished mahogany. A baby grand piano anchored the far corner, and in the lobby, all the trimmings festooned a ten-foot tree. Outside, strings of white bulbs cascaded from the roof to the top of the entrance in a Bethlehem formation that would rival the stars.

Joann loved the hotel at this time of year. Before working there, she'd often visited as a guest of her boyfriend's parents. The Lissemans were European, so the Italian Renaissance-inspired venue was much to their liking. Long-time residents of Capitol Hill, they also lived close by and attended mass at the cathedral, one street over. After church, a brisk walk to the Sylvan for coffee was customary—especially during winter and into the Christmas season.

Now, standing behind the marble desk, Joann could watch the pageantry all December long: The razzle. The dazzle. The putting on the glitz—wrapped up with a gracious nod to history. She was right in the middle of *Auld Lang Syne*, along with generations of in-city denizens patiently and impatiently waiting in lines past the doors. Out-of-town visitors joined the foray as well—many of whom assembled at the concierge stand, hoping for a ride to the theater, ballet, or other nearby attractions, courtesy of the hotel Town Car.

Holiday time at the Sylvan was always a hot ticket. However, as an employee, the Christmas chaos bordered on insanity. Cranky phone lines, pissed-off walkie-talkies, grouchy valets, frazzled cocktail servers, drunken merrymakers, special-request-this, and special-request-that could really wear you down by the end of an eight-hour shift.

On one such night, Joann clocked out, then rested her tired legs in the locker room. Kathryn had already left—and Robert and Lynn hadn't been scheduled—so she was on her own.

Tick-tock.

Finally standing up, she tossed the navy uniform skirt and blazer into a Sylvan dry-cleaning bag. Last on the night's list was a quick stop to drop her laundry in the bell closet, then time for bed and two days off. Although she wasn't *quite* ready to leave.

Her stomach twisted. The 25th was a few days away, and Grady was headed to Seattle.

He was also considering a permanent move to California, so ... it was time for an update. Actually, it was time for a big update. Joann hadn't heard much of anything from her boyfriend lately, because he'd been too busy.

Was he staying? Going?

Was she going with him if that was the case?

Did she *want* to go with him? Was it okay to say that she wasn't sure?

Joann dragged herself up the stairs, over to the bell closet, then back through the lobby. She'd been sitting in the locker room for more than an hour, so it was well past midnight. On her left, the lounge was empty, and to her right, the bar was almost vacant as well.

"What's goin' on, Jo?" George called out, then pointed at a liquor bottle.

She eased into a seat, and he set a drink in front of her. Mmm. Kahlúa over ice. She found herself discussing Grady's return and what it would mean. Is this how it always was with bartenders? Were they experts at getting you to talk? Or maybe it was the alcohol, already romping around in her brain.

George was rational, funny, insightful, smart—and he fearlessly bypassed the small talk. How awesome to find yet *another* good friend at work. She and the barman had talked before, but not like this. Ha—it was a Sylvan Christmas miracle! George was turning into a big brother, right before her eyes.

"Are you liking it at the Sylvan, Jo?"

"*Yes.*"

And the stories started to pour out. Stories about Kathryn, Lynn, Todd, Robert—

George was smirking again with the mention of Mister Bailey, and she demanded to know what was so funny.

"Oh, you two are interesting, together, out there," he said.

"Oh my god. We're just *friends*!" Joann sat back, having practically lunged out of her chair.

"Okay, okay. Relax. Just callin' it like I see it. Ya know, Robert's a good dude."

"I *have* a boyfriend. And Robert *has* a girlfriend."

George smiled, rinsed some glassware, and steam began to rise.

"It's getting late, Joann. Lemme walk you to your car … seeing as *Robert* ain't around."

Joann threw a bar towel at him. He spun around, caught it before it dropped, and motioned for her to follow.

"That was such a bartender move."

"Yeah, well, I'm a bartender."

Morning came quickly, and soon the phone was ringing. Grady had made it to town but called to say that he couldn't see Joann until Christmas Eve.

"Okay, but I have to work that night."

"No problem, I'll be there around noon."

Hours later, darkness took hold outside and seemed to be pushing its way inside.

And inside, Joann was on edge. Grabbing her keys, she got in the car and drove sixteen minutes through Madison Valley, along streets peppered with clapboard cottages and shingled bungalows. Then up a leafy lane that curved toward the lake. On the boulevard, she passed Madrona Beach, Leschi Marina, and Mt. Baker Beach. One last turn, a few numbers in … and there was the family home. Nothing fancy; rather nondescript. But her father *loved* it.

By 1967, Jack MacIntosh had wrangled with his mother's Madrona Victorian for twenty-plus years—and declared himself done with "high-maintenance." He no longer saw any charm in an old house, *and* he was ready to move out. So he *set* out to find something "modern," daring to venture south of more established neighborhoods.

Eventually, he found a modest rambler with "straight-forward-plumbing-and-electric," just paces from Lake Washington. The Stan Sayres boat launch was literally out the front door—a no-brainer for a fisherman. You could catch dinner at the end of the street! The fields across from the house (the future Genesee Park) had also been a big draw, versus neighborhoods with typical city streets and tightly-clustered homes.

Joann slowed the Jetta, peering through a window at her parents' windows. Tree lights blinked at a front corner, sending tiny surges of color spinning like rogue pinwheels. A tinsel star cast shadows on the ceiling, and jewel-toned ornaments pressed against panes—like gifts that didn't fit in a box.

She turned toward the driveway where several cars were parked, each within the lines of a paved square. Mom, Dad, both brothers, and her sister. Well, looks like I'll get to see everyone, thought Joann. The siblings were local, but there'd been limited time or energy for much of anything during the extra-hectic hotel season. Braking in the gravel behind the other vehicles, she turned off the engine. Then Miss MacIntosh fastened her parka and stepped into the night.

Ooof—the chilly air was already biting at her.

Laughter escaped the backyard. A ball began to bounce, and beyond a smudgy rooftop, the grainy white motes of a lone floodlight rose like a spirit fighting to keep its shape.

Joann turned her key in the door. Sarah, Mark, and Thomas were shooting hoops, but a chat with Mom was more her thing tonight.

First stop: the living room. Jack sat reading a magazine and flipping through TV channels. A *Fawlty Towers* rerun was competing for screen time with a bickering news panel.

"Hi, parents! I finally got a day off!"

Her father opened another magazine and remained silent—a typical reaction when it came to discussing his eldest child's employer. Jack had worked at a hotel in his younger years, and he'd hated it. Maybe it had been a seedier place than the Sylvan? At any rate, he'd been strongly opposed to Joann's employment there. Still, she'd insisted on giving it a shot. Working as a restaurant hostess had spiraled into a Greek-Row shitshow, and most everyone at the law firm had been nice, but being a receptionist had somehow made her feel antsy—and trapped.

"Dad, the hotel is *so* pretty at Christmas time."

Setting aside the magazine, Jack picked up his newspaper.

"Um, I've made a lot of friends, and at night, we run the whole thing!"

"Hhhhmpf." Lowering the newspaper, he grumbled at the TV.

How was it that she instantly turned into a suspect teenager again, just by walking through the door?

Daddy, I'm good at my job! I'm responsible! They like me!

Better to just keep quiet. She'd barely survived an era of full-scale war with him—

And if you couldn't "go home," where did you go?

In the kitchen, KIXI crackled through an AM radio, and Bernadette MacIntosh prepped dinner. Chop, chop, scrape. She accompanied the old-school soundtrack with her own rhythms. Joann had always liked hearing those rhythms—especially from their childhood bedrooms downstairs. The cooking-puttering-slipper-shuffling nighttime cacophony let you know that she was still there—that she was still close by.

Chop, chop, scrape. Mama MacIntosh sliced into Uwajimaya winnings as her daughter reported the latest Sylvan scoop: Quirky characters! Snooty guests! Funny friends! Bernadette listened quietly, although she had, on occasion, shared stories about her own adventures as a twenty-something. Joann would imagine herself looking through another window: a window that rarely opened—a window into another life. Her mother had been a MASH-camp nurse, stationed in the middle of duty, adventure, dances, dates, gal pals, guy pals, and a boy. *The* boy. Phillip. But Phillip had been divorced—a no-no in the eyes of the church. Phillip … was a sin.

Joann handed Bernadette the salt and pepper. Did her mother miss that time? What would her life have been like, minus a few rules?

"Jo!" Her sister rapped a knuckle on the glass slider. "Come outside!"

Opening the door, Joann readied herself for a hard pass. Bernadette sliced on, softly humming.

"Que sera, sera … whatever will be, will be …"

That night, Joann lay in bed, the knots in her stomach tightening. Christmas had been kind of a bust for a while now. Would this year be different?

Frannie James

Grady rang Joann's apartment at noon on December 24th. She buzzed him in and nervously set the call-box receiver back on the phone cradle.

"How are you, Joann?"

Her boyfriend took a seat on the gray roll-arm sofa, patted a corduroy pillow, then pushed the floral one aside. He complimented the tree she'd decorated, asked about her family, how she'd been, and how she was liking her job. Joann excitedly described her co-workers and her first December as a Sylvan employee. A couple minutes later, an odd expression overtook Grady's face, and Joann felt like she needed to hang onto something.

"I've met someone," he said.

"Huh?" answered Joann.

"I met someone in church, in California."

Joann no longer went to church.

"And she's taller, like me."

Grady was basketball-player tall, and—without high heels—Joann was five foot four.

"You're … you're dumping me on Christmas Eve because you met a tall girl who goes to church?"

"I'm so sorry, but this is for the best. I'm staying in California, and I think I'm supposed to be with her."

Grady stood to leave, his eyes just short of misty.

"No! Grady, please. Don't leave me. Please. I'll do anything!"

She was ashamed to hear those words come out. Where was her pride? But all she could think was that she'd be alone.

"I have to go," he said.

"No, we can make it work. Please!"

The room felt far away—and Joann was falling down, down, down, somewhere inside of herself. Grady walked out, and she watched at the window as he descended the front steps. Then she sank to the floor and pulled the phone close.

In moments, Kathryn's chipper voice broke through, along with the beeping sounds of a switchboard.

"Kathryn," Joann cried.

"Hey! What's wrong? What happened? Oops, one sec—"

Christmas music blared.

"I'm back. Sorry. The phone's been—"

"He's gone. He's moving to California, and he met a tall girl in church."

There was a pause.

"Kathryn?"

"Joann, come to the hotel. You'll be early for your shift, but just hang out with me."

"I can't."

"Yes, you can. We're all here, and we're all here for you. Fuck it. You don't need him."

"But, I'm going to be alone—"

"No, you're not. Okay, hang up and get in the car. Or should I send … someone to pick you up?"

Oh, *god*, no. She didn't want anyone seeing her like this. Besides, it wouldn't be fair to the valets. They had enough to worry about. It was Christmas.

"No, I'll be there soon. Thank you."

"It's gonna be okay, Jo. Breathe—and start driving. *We're waiting for you.*"

Joann cried as the traffic light turned to red.

Stop. Everything. Had. Stopped. What in the hell now? Who was this tall chick?

What was Grady thinking? Their families were friends. She was friends with his brothers.

His brothers were friends with her brothers. They'd all known each other since high school, and she'd started seeing Grady her last year of college. His interest had caught her by surprise, but the relationship was working, or … so she'd thought. And now he was blowing their lives up.

Goddammit. She'd been so tuned into the hotel lately. And *Robert*. But it wasn't like she'd done anything wrong. Sure, she "fixed" her schedule sometimes, because it made such a big difference to work with him versus without. And he made no secret of the fact that he preferred working when she was there. Was that bad? He *had* seemed disappointed when she didn't need him to walk her to the car the other night. She and Kathryn were going—

For crying out loud. Here she was again, paying attention to something else. And *so* there was a little chemistry. Big deal. People flirted all the time, and they'd barely been doing *that!* Still, she should have been paying attention to her *actual* relationship. She should have made more trips to California. Fuck, fuck, fuck. What a mess.

She was a mess. She had somehow managed to tank a perfectly respectable relationship, and now she was on her own.

Down Madison.

Up Madison.

Miss MacIntosh had arrived. Above her, fourteen lofty letters spelled out, "The Sylvan Hotel." But Joann couldn't see the signage through a fountain of tears.

Oh, thank goodness. There was a parking spot right across the street—how was that even possible in the midst of holiday central?

The valets didn't take their eyes off those spaces.

She fed the meter … then one foot in front of the other. And fuck the alley entrance. It was Christmas Eve.

Christmas Eve. How could Grady do this to her? And what in the hell was she doing *here* while her life was falling apart?

Nearing the circle, she hesitated, seeing Robert and Bill standing guard at the front. Seeing *her*, the boys straightened up, their expressions instantly somber.

"Hey, Joann." They each held a door open.

Kathryn had obviously broken the "news."

Robert searched her face, concern blanketing his own—but Joann could barely utter a hello. She continued through, and two sets of eyes followed. Two sets of eyes wondering what would happen next.

PARTY LIKE IT'S 1992

The Sylvan's pastry chef set a golden custard on the marble countertop. Crème brûlée—a dollop of bruised sunshine, securely nestled in a circle of porcelain following a dose of flame.

Joann loved watching Stan torch the tops of these caramelized delicacies on slower nights that afforded her time to loiter in the kitchen. As long as she stood against the wall and away from the "line" or hid out in the baking nook, the crew was okay with her being there. When restaurant orders started to ramp up, she'd make a run for it, not wanting to piss off the head chef who never hesitated to scream at whoever to "get out!"

Exhale. That kind of crazy-busy would return on the 31st, but for now, all of the Sylvans could breathe—and a well-earned break was on the menu.

"How *are* you, sweetie?" Stan asked gently.

The handlebar-mustached strong-man produced a clean spoon from his apron pocket.

"We heard your Christmas was a bit of a bummer."

"I'm okay. And thank you, Chef!"

Nodding, Stan set the spoon on the marble countertop. Relieved to see that he didn't need details, Joann shifted the conversation to his gorgeous work.

Across the lobby, Finn pushed a cart through the kitchen door. French press, incoming! He stopped midway to straighten the linens. Finesse would not be forsaken, even for minor drop-offs.

Then Room Service spotted the crème brûlée. "Gee, Joann. What'd you do to deserve *that*? Oh, uh … sorry. Never mind."

Joann shook her head, and his evil giggle returned.

"Christ, Finn," Stan sighed in exasperation.

"What? I didn't say *anything*." Then as the elevator began to close, he quickly surveyed the lobby and yelled, "Penis!"

"That boy," grumbled the chef.

When he wasn't charming his way through something, Finn made it his personal goal to rattle the elder kitchen statesman. So far, he had not succeeded.

The chef now turned to Joann.

"So? Are you going to survive?"

"Yeah. I'll be fine. I'm just sad."

"Baby girl, give it time—and I bet you'll be on the mend sooner than you think."

"Thanks, Mister."

Kathryn pushed through the swinging door from PBX.

"*Stan!*"

"Hi, darlin.' How are you?"

"I'm good. How are *you*? Oooooo, did you bring treats?"

"I did, indeed. Sorry, only one spoon. When Finn comes down, tell him to bring you another."

"Yummy! Thank you so much!"

"You're most welcome."

Waving, the power-house pastry god retreated to the kitchen.

"Have a good night, you two."

Joann waved back.

"You hanging in there?" Kathryn nudged her friend.

"Yeah. I guess."

Beep-beep-beep.

The switchboard was also having a moment, so Kathryn disappeared into PBX again.

Swish. Barbara Reddings pushed through the stair door on wobbly stilettos. Her fuchsia-houndstooth suit defied ambient lighting, but a set of audacious earrings was giving the entire ensemble a run for its money. Bold but clingy, the precious pair glittered like big-little upstarts threatening to steal the show.

Joann took a deep breath as Ms. Reddings drew closer.

Babs Reddings was the Sylvan's matriarch-in-chief. At sixty-ish, she had persevered for years at the old hotel, and didn't have to answer to anyone— not even the general manager.

Mr. Alexander was the figurehead, but Babs was the math. She ran the numbers, balanced the budgets, curated clients, and knew every dime, coming and going. The Sylvan controller was very much the right-hand woman of the two Seattle proprietors—a couple of moneybag misters who were content to leave her ladyship (and her calculator) at the Honduran-Mahogany helm.

The Sylvan Hotel

♦

Babs was all about bookings and baubles, and she was, unabashedly, the boss.

"*Great* shoes, lady."

Two cocktail servers bubbled and fizzed.

"And is that ... Chanel!?!"

The gay boys were up next. Word was out about a lobby "code red," so three food servers took a break to bow down.

"Honey."

"Sweetie."

"Porkchop."

They held her hands, massaged, hugged, squeezed. Then big kisses, small kisses.

Here a smooch. There a smooch. Everywhere a smooch-smooch. Not one of Ms. Redding's cheeks was to be neglected. Joann couldn't help but think of Sr. Annette's English class.

This shit was right outta *Pride and Prejudice*.

Now for the straight boys. Jed oozed and aahed, while Todd quickly pulled Babs's car to the doors.

Turning to Joann, the dowager frowned.

"Make sure Mr. Alexander gives you an envelope for me before he leaves. Don't let him out the door until he does."

"Okay, will do!"

Dubious eyes fixed on Joann through diamond-encrusted spectacles.

Likely too swift of a reply. And a major deficit in the brown-nosing department.

Damn you, Jane Austen!

Leaning over the marble, Madame Boss Lady searched for incriminating evidence of ... something.

"How are things up here, tonight? What's occupancy looking like?"

Joann rotated a list so that Babs could see the expected volumes and VIP specifics.

Adjusting her glasses, she inspected the print-out.

Swish. Stan pushed through the stair door, now in a black-leather cap, black-leather vest, T-shirt, jeans, and black-leather chaps.

Whoa! The tall muscle man looked so different out of his kitchen whites. Where was *he* going?

"Bell-closet keys, please, Joann."

Stan had finished his work week, and a flour-covered uniform was ready for cleaning.

"Look at *this* handsome devil!"

Babs fluffed her silver perm, having lost all interest in check-ins.

A full audit of the chef began, and Joann backed away, hoping to blend in with the key boxes behind her.

"Hello, Babs." Stan tipped his hat. "How are you?"

"Doin' fine, cowboy. Just about to leave. Off to dinner and a big glass of wine."

"That sounds very nice. Enjoy yourself, Ms. Barbara."

"Todd," the controller commanded, "I'm ready to go, now."

"Car's right out front, Babs."

"Love you, my boy."

"Aw, it's the job. No problem at all."

Exhale. Joann would live to see another day. She handed Stan the keys, and—

Kathryn pushed through the swinging door.

"Hey, do you know where Finn is? The kitchen's calling—they're trying to track him down."

"Well, he was at the elevator a few minutes ago."

Jed approached with bags and introduced the Howells party. Kathryn checked them in, and Joann took a seat in PBX.

Minutes later … laughter out front.

Peeking through slats in the swinging door, Joann spied Todd, Kathryn, Bill, and Bryce. Sigh. She didn't feel up for hotel humor. But … talking to people was probably the healthy thing to do.

Joann pushed through.

"We found Finn," Todd said, lowering his voice.

Kathryn giggled.

"He was upstairs getting stoned with Mary Ann."

"Who the hell is Mary Ann?"

"*Mary Ann*. From *Gilligan's Island*. Dawn Wells!"

"Okaaay … that is definitely one for the books."

The valets nodded in approval. Finn and Mary Ann. *Respect.*

The Sylvan Hotel

More guests arrived, so the Sylvans took their posts. Joann wrestled with three room switches, and 602 called to complain that his hot water wasn't working. Kathryn promptly paged Engineering, and, minutes later, Tim emerged from the bowels of the boiler room. Swaying across the lobby, he made his way to the desk, then steadied himself at the marble countertop.

"I checked, and the hot wwwater's fine," he slurred. "Tell the peeeople to bbbeee patient. Sometimes it … it takes a while for … for things to heat up."

"Yessir. Thank you."

Staggering back across the lobby, he left a boozy bouquet in his wake.

Jeezus, thought Joann. They were off to a head start with the New Year's shenanigans.

Five days later, it was officially shenanigans eve. At the front of the house, Joann, Kathryn, Robert, Todd, Jed, and Bryce welcomed droves of overnight revelers. George poured non-stop in the bar, and Cocktail Bitches One, Two, and Three ran back and forth with orders.

The restaurant was also hitting capacity, and a jazz quartet warmed up in an already-crowded lounge.

Lynn and Kiet were busy in housekeeping land, but found the time to make a few "drive-bys." Even so, they kept their visits brief, lest they be caught by Mr. Alexander, who was manager on duty—or "MOD"—for the night.

On his third lobby drive-by, Kiet delivered about a pound of turndown chocolates, usually reserved for guest pillows. The housekeeper proudly plopped the contraband candy on the desk, and *swish*—back through the stair door. Kiet had his own rebellious ways, and sometimes he swiped gold-wrapped goodies for his favorite desk agents.

"Well, I guess we've got our fuel for tonight," Joann laughed.

"No kidding," replied Kathryn. "Oh, and we have three rooms left."

"Great. Alexander's gonna have a conniption."

"Well, it's not like we're empty, and everyone's paying rack rate. Plus, you just *know* there'll be some stragglers who are too tipsy to drive. Hey, and maybe our 'fearless leader' will do us all a favor and stay in the bar."

"Yeah. Hopefully, George can get him sloshed. Then Mr. MOD can go upstairs—and pass out 'til next year!"

Beep-beep-beep.

Kathryn ran to PBX where a switchboard was under siege. More pillows! Too many pillows! Another blanket! Extra towels! Safety pins! Bobby pins! Irons! Ironing boards! Hairdryers! Sewing kits!

Mr. Alexander, incoming.

"Have you seen my wife?"

"I don't think she's here, yet," answered Joann.

"Well, we have dinner reservations!" he shouted.

Swish. His date veered through the front door looking like she was already three high-thread-count sheets to the wind.

"Where have you been? The restaurant is *waiting* for us. Our reservation was for ten minutes ago!" The general manager was spoiling for a fight.

And Joann was fighting the giggles. Mrs. Alexander was wearing what looked like an aluminum Christmas tree. Tufted layers of "foil" rustled on a tinny—and tiny—outfit that looked high-fashioned out of Reynolds Wrap.

Turning toward the restaurant, Mr. Alexander monologued about fine-dining decorum while his wife uttered apologies, unraveling behind.

Swish. Captain Front Desk pushed through the stair door, back from his dinner break—New Year's Eve was one of the busiest nights of the year, so it was all hands on deck—and everyone breathed with relief. Nothing could go wrong with Brad at the helm!

The band started up again, and guests continued to flow through. At reception, three desk agents crowded in as a sheet of paper was discreetly ripped into fourths, then eighths.

"Looks like the show's about to start!"

Kathryn scrutinized the crowd, all dressed up for the big countdown. Velvet, satin, and silks paraded in, escorted by tuxes, tails, and dapper dinner jackets.

Holding up ratings below the countertop, Brad voted each time an outfit made an entrance: FOUR. NEGATIVE TWO. SIX. EIGHT. FIVE.

A Sylvan fashion show was always fun—and just wait 'til the aluminum Christmas tree walked by!

A few minutes later, there was a break in the parade. Kathryn returned to PBX, and Joann approached the big window. Undoing the latch, she opened it ever-so-slightly.

"Hey, Robert."

"Hey, Jo."

"Good luck tonight."

"Thanks. You, too."

Then Kathryn radioed for Kiet to bring someone a toothbrush, and Lynn radioed back to say that they were on strike.

"Base to Housekeeping. That is not an acceptable answer," Kathryn sassed.

Mister Bailey joined in—and tried not to laugh.

"Valet to Housekeeping and Base. Please do not abuse this channel."

"Housekeeping to Valet. Go park some cars."

"Ten-forty."

Joann smiled. What the heck was "ten-forty?" Was that even a real radio code? Regardless, Robert had recently started to switch up "ten-four." She smiled again. Only Mister Bailey could make a radio code sound cute.

Eleven o'clock at last—and the girls were free to go. They'd intended to wait for the boys, but realistically, the valets would be dealing with vehicles until 3:00 a.m.—and there were likely no seats left at Kay's.

Brad had a plan.

"You two should stick around! Just wait until the Alexanders head out. Wifey's already wasted, so they'll be leaving soon. Then you can grab a key for one of the empty rooms—and treat yourselves to a little New Year's Eve on the Sylvan!"

"Aw, thanks, Brad! You rock!" Joann gushed.

"Well now, you two worked hard tonight," he gushed back.

"We all did, dammit!" laughed Kathryn.

The desk agents headed downstairs to clock off and change, then returned to PBX. It was going to be an extra-long night for Brad, so they'd volunteered to help answer calls until the coast was "all-clear."

Static. Pop. Whiiine.

Kathryn reached for a radio.

"Base to Valet, we can't hear you. Please repeat."

"Valet to Base."

"Go ahead, Valet. We can hear you, now."

"Uh, Base? Mrs. Alexander has …"

"Base to Valet. What did you say?"

"Valet to Base. Mrs. Alexander is down."

Miss Emerson looked at Miss MacIntosh. Miss MacIntosh looked at Miss Emerson.

"Valet to Base. Mrs. Alexander is in the circle. She … she has fallen into the hedge!"

Static.

"Base, how … what should we—"

Kathryn pushed hard on the walkie-talkie button.

"Base to Valet! Pull. Her. Out."

Both girls shoved up against the small PBX window, trying to see into the circle.

Who wanted to miss the upside-down aluminum Christmas tree? *Dammit.* Too much bramble!

Beep! Incoming call from the valet booth.

"What?!?" Joann demanded.

"Her legs … sticking … straight up!"

The line went dead, and Kathryn pressed even harder on the walkie-talkie button.

"Base to Valet. Come in, Valet."

More static.

"Base to Valet—"

"Valet to Base—"

Static. Pop. Static.

"Valet to Base. We have got this situation *so* under control," said Robert, his voice cracking.

Beep. Beep. Beep. Even the switchboard was laughing.

Static. Pop. Static. But the radios—

"Yeeeah. This is Housekeeping. What the hell is going on, up there?"

"Happy New Year, Lynnie!"

And they rang in 1992, Sylvan-style.

IT WAS A DARK AND STORMY NIGHT

The big window was open, despite wintry temperatures. On the other side of it, Robert untied a long, heavy, green-velvet drape. Curtaining off the valet booth from the driveway, he created a small shelter between the desk and the elements.

Across the lobby, faint notes of instrumental music underscored the clinking of glass and cutlery. A fire steadily burned in the lounge, and Joann rubbed her hands together, coveting the cozy scene. Then she glanced at her friend on the other side of the ledge. That window was going to stay open for as long as she could stand it.

These quiet nights at the hotel had been some of the best nights at the hotel. All the check-ins arrived by 7:30 p.m., and the MOD tended to stay holed up in an office downstairs. It was slow season at the Sylvan—and Joann and Robert were the only two people at the front of the house.

Miss MacIntosh took a seat at the window and opened a copy of *The Seattle Times*. Hunched forward on a wooden stool, Mister Bailey watched a game. The boys kept a small television hidden in the bell closet, and after management left (and tasks were completed), the prized possession brought basketball to you, live from the valet booth.

"And the Sonics score!"

Robert cheered as his favorite team set up on defense.

"Come on, buddy," he coaxed.

How nice that someone *wasn't* yelling at the TV.

Joann turned the newspaper pages and breathed out, feeling safe from any storms.

"Hey, Front Desk."

Curt, a newer food server, was on a search mission for late dinner guests. There were only five reservations, and in the world of fine dining, the loss of just one table could severely impact the night's earnings.

"No cancellation calls as of yet," Joann assured him. "The weather is most likely delaying arrivals."

Food-server counseling was a regular part of the job this time of year. But Joann didn't mind. She'd dealt with far worse—and she'd had plenty of lessons in waiter diplomacy at the restaurant job. The servers had often blamed or berated the hostesses if they ended up with rude tables, bad-tip tables, kid tables, salad tables, dessert tables, or iced-tea tables. *As if we had any control over that,* she thought. But you had to learn to talk your way around them. You learned to survive.

"Thanks, Joann. You're probably right."

Curt pushed through the front doors, out to the circle, and into the valet booth to check on the Sonics. A couple minutes later, he headed off to see George.

Commercial break.

Standing up, Robert slowly kicked the stool aside. Then he took a seat on the length of sill that lined his side of the window.

"How's the job search going, Jo?"

She turned toward him as far as she could. It was impossible to sit on that ledge and fully face each other, so they were back-to-back and sideways.

"It's going. I think I've sent out fifty cover letters so far with resumes and writing samples, but I need to pull together a more professional-looking portfolio."

"You can do it."

"I just wanna know: How long is this going to *take*???"

"Well, Joann, it builds character."

She could hear the grin in his voice.

"If you say so."

Robert chortled in response.

The game was back on—but the sound of car brakes interrupted the next play. Robert jumped to his feet, grabbed an umbrella, and tucked a pen behind his ear. Then he stepped around the velvet curtain and into the rain. Joann stood, and an adrenaline-like sensation catapulted inside her. What the hell? She looked at the valet booth, and—

Ding.

The elevator doors opened.

Kiet nodded her way, hands in black pants pockets, white shirt loosened at the top.

"Quiet tonight," he said haltingly.

"Hi, Kiet. Yeah. Are the guests being good to you?"

"Ha!" And his body language added, *What a notion.*

Kiet pushed through the front doors and waited for *his* favorite valet. When Robert returned from the garage, he began to school the housekeeper like a sibling, going on about the Sonics ... and how to best "keep an eye on Joann."

"Now, it's very important to track the number of personal phone calls she makes—"

"No, more like it's very important to ignore that advice!" Joann pretended to start closing the big window.

Both boys burst into laughter, and she pushed through the swinging door as the switchboard rang out. After transferring three calls, Joann realized she was still smiling. But that was Robert for you. He just tended to have that effect, despite any winter gloom. She could sit next to him for hours and never tire of it. The feeling was strangely wonderful, like ...

You were right where you were supposed to be.

Light flashed through the PBX window as another car pulled into the circle. Kiet made himself scarce, and Robert appeared, his ash-brown hair blowing in the wind. It wasn't light brown, but it wasn't dark brown, either. It was somewhere in the middle, almost as if it was trying to blend in—trying to be unremarkable. A shade of under-the-radar, just like Robert. Joann suspected that sometimes he was hiding behind all that humor ... and all that hair.

Whatever the case, Robert Bailey was far from unremarkable.

"Hello?"

And back out to the desk!

"Hey, Anna."

The food and beverage executive worked standard office hours but took on a fair share of MOD shifts. Anna *could* be fussy about department-related issues—however, she was one of the better managers who left you alone as long as you did your job.

"How's it going up here," she asked in a silky European accent. "My god, Joann, why is that window open? Aren't you freezing?"

"Yeah, I'll close it soon. Just wanted some fresh air."

Robert swooshed through the velvet curtain again and into the valet booth. Pushing rainy-night hair out of his face, he greeted the manager, eyes twinkling.

"Hey, Anna. How's it going? Are you keeping the front desk in line?"

"Okay, Bailey. That's about enough out of you," giggled Joann.

Giggling back, Robert pulled the big window shut.

Anna smiled.

"What?" asked Joann.

Rapping her keys on the marble counter, the manager continued to smile.

"Maybe it's not as cold as I thought."

Joann protested with a look, but Anna protested back with an even bigger smile.

"Call me if you need anything. I'm off to the restaurant for my MOD dinner."

Robert re-opened the big window and took a seat on his side of the ledge. Basketball was over, so he picked up the newspaper. Joann returned to the window and sat down as well. They were less than an inch apart—

The valet shifted, his back brushing hers.

Joann breathed in. It was so cold with the window open, but so ... warm. She fought the urge to rest against her friend. What a peaceful feeling—and so powerful. It could make a person not want to go anywhere.

Well, that was silly. The goal was to leave. To start their lives.

Joann frowned. How long *would* she be at the Sylvan? Where would she find actual career work? How would she break into such a competitive field? She was the daughter of a teacher who made a point to *not* rub shoulders with "movers and shakers." Joann had no prominent business contacts, save for the attorney she'd worked for, but that was an entirely different arena.

And what about Robert? What were his dreams? He was so outgoing but so guarded; it felt like she wasn't supposed to ask. Her friend rarely said anything about himself, and every time she'd gotten close to bringing up *his* situation, he'd turned the conversation back to something about her, made a joke, or ran for the garage. Maybe he didn't know what he wanted to do—or he was sick of worrying about it and didn't want to talk about it.

The same thing could probably be said for a lot of Sylvans. The hotel was work, of course, but it was probably also a safe harbor of sorts; somewhere you didn't have to explain or reveal too much; a safe haven somewhere between too-in-your-business and stone-cold-all-business.

The Sylvan Hotel

◆

Headlights out front. And ... Robert was up and running. Businessmen with no reservations. Joann got them registered, checked in, and on their way with room keys.

Then two restaurant parties approached.

"Young lady, we'd like our car, please."

"Same goes for us!"

"Where's the valet?" asked Mister I'm-Very-Important.

"We're in a rush," added Missus I'm-In-A-Hurry.

"No problem, folks. It will be just a minute or so."

Joann handed their tickets to Robert through the big window. Zipping his jacket, he ran down the hill to get the first car.

"You'd think they'd have the sense to schedule more than one person," declared Mister I'm-Very-Important.

Missus I'm-In-A-Hurry nodded in agreement.

"It *is* raaather ridiculous," she said.

"I appreciate your patience." Joann tried extra-hard to sound sincere. "We only had a few check-ins tonight, so there's less staff on. He's a fast runner, though. He'll be right back!"

Mister I'm-Very-Important ignored Joann. He'd obviously heard her but wanted the desk agent to know she had no voice in the matter.

Two more people exited the lounge and looked expectantly at the concierge stand. It was pouring out there, and they were *not* about to go searching for a valet.

They looked all around them and at each other.

How could a valet not be there, right when you needed one?

Joann let them carry on with a few more rounds of how-could-this-be-happening showboating, hoping to buy time before they joined the Mister I'm-Very-Important team—

Splash! Robert pulled into the drive and opened the car doors for Mister I'm-Very-Important. Then he ran down the hill again with the next ticket.

The show-boaters shook their heads in amazement. The valet had been *right* there in the driveway. Why hadn't he asked to help them?

Time to step in.

"Sir? Ma'am? He's got one other car to bring up." Joann gestured to Missus I'm-In-A-Hurry. "Then he'll be able to assist *you*."

Missus Showboater shook her head, and Mister Showboater overtly checked his watch.

Assholes. Joann thanked them again for their patience but flipped them off under the desk. Minutes later, the guests were gone, and a soaking-wet Robert caught his breath in the valet booth.

"Sorry, Robert. That sucked."

"Ah, hell. Another night, a few more dollars. Speaking of which …"

Swoosh. Around the velvet curtain; out to the circle; in through the front doors; up to the desk.

"What's up, Mister Bailey?"

Robert tucked a pen behind his ear once more, and those green-gray eyes crinkled with mock seriousness.

"Joann, the key is to always make sure your dollar bills are facing the same direction. As you will see, mine are in perfect order, and I am ready to trade them for twenties. One-ah-ah-ah. Two-ah-ah-ah."

The Count was back, sweepin' the clouds away.

The desk agent opened her cash drawer and traded the valet two twenties for his bundles of bills—damp and creased but definitely all facing the same direction.

11:00 p.m.

"Robert to Base! Walk you to your car?"

"Yes, please. Ready in five minutes. Just finishing some paperwork in PBX."

"Ten-forty—I got you!"

And … tally the receipts … lock up the cash … fix her face—

Wait. *What?* They weren't going on a date—

Commotion out front.

And … push through the swinging door.

In the lobby, fine woolen suits and Liz Claiborne bags stood staring at leather pants, tall ebony hair, deep-red lipstick, and winged eyeliner. Eyes flashing and hands on hips, a majestic creature groused to her companions:

"I'm not gonna wait for that damn elevatah!"

Joann was intrigued. Cracking good accent. And that *outfit!*

Taken aback, a few other guests slowly retreated, practically hugging the polished walls. They'd just wanted to return to their rooms after a nightcap.

And now … this. Even their shadows balked with contempt. You could practically hear their minds shrieking.

What in the—? Wasn't this a respectable place?

Ding.

As if on cue, the elevator arrived. Lissa and another cocktail server rushed into the lobby, their eyes transfixed on the punk princess disappearing behind golden doors.

Lissa's painstakingly penciled eyebrows breached in thin arcs of astonishment.

"That was Siouxsie and the Banshees! Seriously, Joann? Why didn't you tell us?"

"I didn't know they were here!"

The normally standoffish Lissa had, in one instant, thawed, her doll face come to life.

Miss MacIntosh even got a high-five. Then a happy cocktail server exclaimed, "*Whoa!*" and returned to the lounge.

Whoa, agreed Joann. *Siouxsie and the Banshees!* She knew a couple of their songs.

There was a really good one about being face-to-face, not telling lies, and someone torn between—

Aaack—Robert was waiting!

Ca-clunk. Ca-clunk. They were clocked off, and it was on. The walk to the car was one of the best parts of the night.

"Joann, it's still coming down out there. Stay put, and I'll go get the Town Car."

It was a fairly short distance to the garage, but Mister Ever-the-Gentleman wasn't about to let one drop of rain land on his favorite Sylvan gal.

"Well … if you're sure it's okay."

"Be right back," he promised.

Joann nodded. Then her legs went all wobbly. What in the world was wrong with her?

Minutes later, she heard a low rumbling—and stepped into darkness ablaze with light.

Robert had arrived.

In the alley, a navy car purred, its headlights burning through drizzly shadows. Between the beams, raindrops shimmered and danced before giving way to gravity.

Frannie James

♦

Click. Miss MacIntosh secured herself in the cushy passenger seat. Then her rainy-knight-in-shining-Town-Car hit the locks. They coasted through the watery alley, up the hill, and around the block, their navy raft softly bouncing and bobbing. The Sylvans were floating on four-star suspension, as if the clouds were now beneath them. Beads of water bubbled across the windshield, and Joann wished the garage was further away—or that he'd just keep driving.

Uh, what? Oh, *no*. She could not start crushing on Robert Bailey. He was with someone else! Surely there were kind, cute boys in the world who were actually available?

Robert slowly braked before taking the corner, and they rolled smoothly past the Sylvan. String lights winked from dark palm trees, and Joann tried to ignore the gears shifting in her stomach. What madness was this? She was losing her mind … because a boy was being chivalrous? That's what valets did. They opened doors; held umbrellas; carried bags. Courtesy was their *job*.

Her heart was flapping all over the place.

Pull it together! Don't be so desperate. You're carpooling with a co-worker.

But Robert wasn't just a co-worker. He was … Robert.

His hands are pretty.

For god's sake!

Her favorite valet carefully maneuvered the luxury sedan up the ramp. Reaching the garage roof, he slowed the car even more.

"See you tomorrow?"

Stopping alongside the Jetta, he quickly looked at his friend, then down.

"Yeah." She could hardly get the words out.

"All right, now."

He turned toward her again. Steady, strong, good, sweet, kind, handsome Robert.

They were almost face-to-face.

Joann could barely look at him.

And then she did.

JANUARY DARLINGS

An apprehensive Kathryn watched Joann shove "everyday" clothing to the left on a straining closet rod. To the right, a small selection of sleeker silhouettes came to light. Resting on hangers under garment bags, the "someday" dresses awaited their moment, suspended like velvety shadow-selves.

Cocktail attire was rarely required in Seattle, but tonight was an exception. They'd be attending the Sylvan's annual staff Christmas party, traditionally held in the month of January at one of the downtown restaurants. This year, Kaspar's was hosting. And Miss MacIntosh was ready to get out of the house! So, she'd cajoled Miss Emerson into going.

"Okay," Joann unzipped a garment bag and pulled out two dresses. "Choose."

Her friend was more petite than she, but they wore the same-size Sylvan uniform and could probably make this work.

Kathryn hesitated. "Well, which one are *you* gonna wear?"

"No, pick the one *you* want, first. Come on, Kath. Any of 'em would look great on you."

Joann held up another.

Kathryn couldn't stand this stuff. Ha! The gorgeous girl who hated anything but Levi's.

And there was the frown. And three, two … one:

"Why does it have to be a big thing? Why can't we all just go to Kay's and hang out? Or why can't we just—"

"Kathryn!" interrupted Joann. "Stop *freaking* out. Dresses make it easy. Throw one on over your head, add heels, and done."

"Gawd, Jo. These are fancy."

"Nordstrom Rack, Take Two, and a Bon Marché sale? Not that fancy. You can do it!"

Joann lived in jeans, too, but she also loved the transformational power of a little glamour; like art—and armor—on your own personal canvas. The right fabrics with the right lines; a bit of lipstick, maybe a dramatic eye, and suddenly, there was someone else in the mirror ... or just a clearer picture. A picture that said, *Darling, you, too, belong at the ball.*

Joann held up the dresses again. Not so long ago, she wouldn't have dreamed that she'd get to wear stuff like this. Outside of uniforms, her mother had knitted, crocheted, and sewed; making and mending their childhood clothing, most of which did double and sometimes triple duty as hand-me-downs. The same went for costumes, first-communion dresses, confirmation dresses—even Barbie doll clothes Joann had kept safe in her uncle's old cigar boxes. Anything else had been a basement bargain or a blue-light special.

But Kathryn was not interested in a Cinderella switch-up.

"I don't get this shit. I don't know the rules."

"Oh, my *god*. It doesn't have to be that difficult. Like my mom says, go with the Audrey Hepburn formula: simple, but with a small twist to keep things interesting."

Joann's mother had been a fashionista in her younger years, attending finishing school and dressing like classic film stars. She, too, had aimed to assimilate, taking cues from Audrey and the Donna Reeds of her day. That girl was long gone, but every so often, clues surfaced.

A pale-blue scarf with pale-white dots. A mysterious perfume bottle. A shiny flash of brocade from the back of the closet—and a faraway smile when Glenn Miller drifted through the radio. Scraps of a chic and happy Bernadette could also be found in photo albums, sealed beneath gloss-covered pages.

"Uh ..." Kathryn reluctantly stepped forward, then back.

"Okay, here. Just try!" Joann held out a black dress with a sweetheart neckline.

Accepting her fate, Kathryn grabbed the garb and shut herself in the bathroom where she could safely assess the outcome.

Joann's turn, and four choices remained. One seemed especially "grown-up." Sheer white ruffles topped black velvet in layers that *weren't* so transparent. It reminded Joann of her favorite movie dress: The Baroness's ball gown in *The Sound of Music*—and maybe the Baroness herself! Elsa von Schraeder was foxy, bitchy, and always in control ... but had another Elsa been hiding under those frills? Had she *not* been so sure of herself?

Nope—not for tonight. Instead, Joann chose a black, sleeveless, empire-waisted number that just skirted her knees. At the top, an overlay of clear sequins had been sewn into a black-and-white argyle bodice. *Like a secret shield,* thought Joann. *And like Holly-Golightly-meets-punk-rock*! Somewhere between class act, sex bomb, and girl next door, Ms. Hepburn had always been the right kind of stylish. The golden gamine had also been the right kind of human—and her kindness had made her iconic.

The bathroom doorknob turned squeakily. Please let her like it. Please let her—

It fit! She was smiling!

Joann grinned at her friend. "Wow, Miss Emerson. Oh, and the dress is okay, too."

"I dunno about this."

"I *swear*. You look fantastic. Now ... necklace ..."

"For fuck's sake. We gotta figure out *accessories*?" Rolling her eyes, Kathryn rummaged through the options. Then it was on with their coats and into the car.

First stop: The Sylvan, where Brad, Todd, Lynn, and Robert were all scheduled to work that evening. Hotel business was twenty-four hours a day, and unfortunately, some people would have to miss out on the festivities. In a gesture of solidarity, Kathryn and Joann had put together an assortment of treats to drop off for their friends on the way downtown.

Joann pulled into the load zone, and Kathryn clapped her hands.

"Oooh! Circle's empty, and there's no concierge on tonight. It's just the guys. Drive right up to the front. I'm not walking around in this soggy mess if I don't have to."

"Okay, but if they yell at me, I'm saying it was your idea."

"There's Todd. He won't care! Robert's on, too!"

Joann eased forward, then braked under the green canopy.

Swish! Two valets were at their service.

"Is this okay? Just for a few minutes?"

"No problem, Margaret. I'll put it right over there."

Todd moved the Jetta, and Robert moved to open a hotel door. As Joann walked through, her coat grazed his jacket, and—oof! Her heart did that flapping thing again.

Get a hold of yourself. That is your very taken, very good friend.

He smiled shyly.

Oh, god. Very taken, very cute, very sweet friend.

Brad smiled as Kathryn presented him with the care package. "Thanks, girls!"

Robert leaned forward on the concierge stand, and Joann's coat started to feel too warm.

Swish. Todd returned through the front doors.

"Hey," he said, staring at Kathryn.

Uh-oh, thought Joann.

Ding.

Lynn exited the elevator.

"Well good evening, A-Team. You're looking so … spiffy. On your way to the par-tay? What brings you *here*?"

The girl looked like she was on the verge of laughter. Was she stoned? Chances were high during a slow night in Housekeeping.

"Ohhh, I think I know why—" began Lynn.

"Yes," Joann interrupted, "We brought *treats* for you guys since you're missing out tonight."

"Awww. *And* we all get a chance to take in your finery—"

"Hey, Lynnie, could you come with me for a sec?"

Joann pulled her friend into the hall, punched the combination lock, and pushed her into the back office.

"What the hell, Lynn!"

The girls collapsed onto chairs laughing.

"Pure comedy. But hey, I get it. Can't waste a good dress—gotta make sure all the right people see ya." The housekeeper slapped the desktop in front of her.

Joann threw an eraser at her friend, then Kathryn walked in.

"What's so goddamn funny?"

"Oh, Kathryn. I'm just having a good time. You know how I am. I'm just glad *I* don't have to go to that thing."

"*Awww,* come on, Lynn." Kathryn made a pouty face. "If I have to—"

"No way, ma'am. No thanks. I'm gonna enjoy a stiff drink at Kay's when I'm off work, and in an old flannel shirt and ripped jeans, thank you very much."

"So when we're done at the restaurant, how about we meet you there? Pleeeaze?" asked Kathryn.

"*Now* you're talking," answered Lynn. "Well, some of us have to work around here, so …"

The Sylvan Hotel

♦

Kathryn and Joann followed her out of the office to a just-arriving elevator.

"Chicas, my chariot awaits." The housekeeper stepped in and flashed them a peace sign.

"See ya later, Lynnie!" The girls waved back, then rejoined the valets.

Todd escorted Kathryn to the circle and went to retrieve the car. Turning to Robert, Joann realized that she wanted to forget the party. She wanted to stay with him.

"Have a good night, Mister Bailey."

"Yeah, you too, Jo. Now, remember, don't do anything I wouldn't do."

"And that would be—?" She grinned.

He laughed, then opened the door again, his eyes carefully washing over her. Flushing, Joann walked through, but she felt as if she could barely pull away from him. What was happening?

Whoosh. Todd brought the Jetta around, hopped out, and walked to the other side to open the car door for Kathryn. Robert waited as Joann got in, then secured her door. Rolling down the window, she told him to meet them later at Kay's if he wanted to. The valet nodded, and she drove through the circle.

"So ... *someone* was stoked to see you," Joann said cautiously.

"I know."

Kathryn sank into the passenger seat—and Joann just about hit the brakes.

They were finally going to talk about this?

"I care about Todd. He's my best friend there, besides you. But I have a *partner*," said an emphatic Kathryn. "He is quite aware and just has to accept that. And he has a million girlfriends! 'Bettys and Wilmas' as he calls them."

"Yeah, but ... they're not you," Joann reasoned.

"I'm 'unattainable,' so it's a challenge. That's all it is."

"I think it might be more than—"

"No, it's not. He just has to meet the next girlfriend, and things will normalize again.

Then he'll be in PBX, telling me the story. He's Mister Adventure, and there are always stories. And girls. And someday, he will meet 'the one.' Trust me. It will be fine."

But ... had things ever been "normal" for Todd in the way he saw Kathryn? And lately, it seemed like it was getting trickier for him to pretend—

"Come on, you've seen him back there. Every week, there's a drama about whoever he met this time around. Then he gives me the report. Maybe he gets mixed up once in a while, but—"

"But *maybe* he's found someone he connects with, and who he cares about. A lot."

"It's a phase. It will pass. He will get over it. Everything-will-be-fine."

Kathryn turned up the radio.

Joann darted a glance at her friend. Had she pushed too hard? *Sigh.* Well, Kathryn *had* been clear with Todd. She was with Scott—and the two teachers-to-be were well matched. They'd built a life together, and they were set on building a future together. Plus, Scott was a cute, funny, all-around good person. The only big issue seemed to be this in-between time.

It was like they were all docked in speedboats, trying to get stubborn motors all-the-way started. Fast-idling and ready to fly, the Sylvans were marooned in the waters of wait-and-see—and confusion swirled around them. Ugh. The "middle" was great when it came to the swing shift, but maybe *not* so great when it came to life. The in-between was messing with people.

Kathryn was probably right, though, and Todd would get past whatever confusion was happening. Scott's absence had simply led him to believe that there might be a chance. But the valet was smart. He'd figure it out.

And Joann would also get it together. Robert was her friend. Period.

At Kaspar's, the girls found George and Finn just inside the door.

"Joann, Kathryn. How the hell are ya?" Room Service giggled his trademark giggle, and Joann giggled back. Finn looked so weird without a tray or cart attached to him!

The group walked into a big room of circular tables set with white linens and candles.

"Whattya drinkin'?" asked George as he pulled out chairs.

"*Dude.* You're not at work. We can get our own drinks!" Joann took off her coat.

"Hey," said a new voice.

Joann turned around.

Matt?

Now this was unexpected.

"Well ... hi! Um ... glad you made it!"

Oh, god. *Now* who was shy? Or even worse, did she sound like an airhead?

"Yeah," the valet replied. "You guys look good."

An entire sentence from Mister Aloof?

Okaaay ... uh ... what should she say now? Should she ask if Melody was coming?

Wait. That might seem too nosy—like a million other questions she had.

Who are you, Mister Badass?

"Jo, did you guys see Melissa Gilbert?" asked Finn.

"What? She's at the Sylvan?"

"Maybe you'll catch her tomorrow. I don't know what she's in town for, but she's supposed to be here a couple days."

"Don't let me down, Half Pint! Please be a nice VIP," Joann jokingly pleaded.

Back in the day, Joann had been a big *Little House on the Prairie* fan. She'd loved the homespun log-cabin dramas, starring a young Melissa Gilbert: A family safe and warm by the fire; a sweet father who played the fiddle; the wildflowers and windblown plains; the planting, the harvests, and the unquenchable pioneer spirit. Before that, she'd read the Ingalls books over and over, enamored with the writings about getting to the next destination, finding home, and making the best of it along the way.

Looking around the table, Joann basked in the warmth of candlelight, friendship, and happy chatter. Outside, rain pummeled darkness, but the restaurant lit up from within, like a huge lantern.

"How 'bout those boy bands, Kathryn," said George. "You know those are your favorite kinds of celebrities."

Kathryn grimaced. "Yeah. Pretend 'rock stars' who vandalize minibars ... fun."

"When was that?" asked Joann.

"Last summer. One of the bands broke into the booze, and their tour manager tried to blame us for *their* behavior. Then the brats told all the groupies where they were staying, so the lobby turned into a teenage-girl invasion. The switchboard got jammed up, too. And the boys were registered under alias names that were—surprise—nasty word combinations."

Joann wondered if *she'd* ever meet a "real" rock star. The closest she'd ever come to that was when Def Leppard stepped out of a limo at Seafair. The band had made a quick appearance to sign the KISW boat, right across the street from the house. Joann was not a fan of the hydro "soundtrack" that ripped through their neighborhood every summer—but British metal had been an acceptable change of pace.

The conversation stalled, so she offered, "I met Kenny Rogers and Kenny Loggins during their stays. Oh, and I think some of the 90210 kids were on property the other night. But Gregory Hines was the best: amazingly polite—as if he was honored to meet *us*."

Matt listened but remained silent as the conversation continued. Then Stan joined with their favorite cocktail servers, Lissa, Beth, and Lee. A few minutes later, Lou joined as well.

Matt had taken a seat next to Joann, and she could feel him shifting with his boss's arrival.

Breathe, Matt. You can do it.

Lou was never going to be a valet favorite, but Joann still preferred his company to Jed.

"So, Joann, what were the Kennys like?" prodded George.

"Rather impressed with themselves," she chuckled.

"Oh, snap! Hopefully you aren't scarred for life," he teased.

"Yeeeaaah … no. I don't keep track of the Kennys."

Everyone laughed, and Matt breathed out.

Ding-ding-ding! Mr. Alexander rose to give his toast.

"A big thanks to everyone for your hard work this year and for service excellence throughout the holiday season."

"Here, here," agreed Babs. "Let's eat! Merry Christmas, Sylvans."

Joann and Matt clinked a water glass and a beer can together. Then his silver-ringed fingers tapped the table, and he pushed dark long bangs out of light, restless eyes.

Joann tried not to stare. All of him was restless. And badass—

"Hi, Maaaatt …"

Cocktail Bitch One and Cocktail Bitch Two flounced by, their eyes locking on the valet, then the desk agent.

Great. Now I'm in trouble because I'm sitting with Heulin.

The Sylvan Hotel

Mumbling a low "hey," Matt escaped into a gulp of Miller.

The girls glowered at Joann, then found seats two tables over.

"Hey, Jo. Looks like your fan club's here," teased Kathryn.

Robert???

Seconds later, a hand was on her chair, and another on the back of Matt's chair.

"Good evening, Joann. What's up, man." Bill eyed the other valet suspiciously.

As if too wise to it all, Matt grinned and pretended to scuffle with his junior teammate before getting up to get more beer. Then Bill pushed an extra chair from another table next to Joann.

"So ... are we sticking around the party ... or?"

New Guy was ready to make a plan.

"*We* are enjoying our dinner, then *we* are meeting up with Lynn," replied Kathryn.

"Where are you meeting Lynn?" he asked. "Hold on ... let me guess. It's a very tough question."

Touché, New Guy.

"Kay's!" shouted their fellow diners.

"Girls. What is your *obsession* with that dive bar?" asked Stan.

"We looooove Kay's!" Kathryn enthused.

"Uh, no shit," Bill replied.

The table laughed, and he headed to the bar. A restaurant manager turned up the music, and someone asked Babs to dance. Two cocktail servers joined in, along with Sylvan executives and their significant others.

Joann looked at Kathryn. "What is this, a wedding?"

"I dunno, but I'm guessing you'll be out there soon, yourself."

"I think not," Joann sassed.

George and Kathryn elbowed each other as the junior valet returned with beverages.

"Wine, Joann?"

"Oh, thank you!"

She took a sip and, over the top of her glass, spied Matt sneaking out.

"He has to go get *Melody*," Bill explained.

"Cool. Well, nice that he could join ..."

"So, Joann, would you like to—"

"Jo, let's take off." Kathryn was staging an intervention. "George, see you later at Kay's? Lynn will be there—maybe Todd and Robert, too."

"Coolio!"

Mister Social had more tables to visit before bailing—and a dessert cart was making the rounds—but Kathryn was ready for immediate departure.

"Bill, do you want to join us at Kay's?" Joann added politely.

"Kay's it is," he sighed.

Lynn was arriving just as the "A-Team" rolled up to an open spot right in front.

"Rock-star parking!" Kathryn laughed.

Climbing out of the car, the girls waved to their friend. "Lynnie!"

"Yo. How was it?"

"Not bad. Free food and free drinks. Can't beat that!" Joann hugged her fellow Sylvan.

"Oh, my god. Joann's fan club showed up," Kathryn flipped her ponytail.

"Wasn't Robert working tonight?" Their friend fired up a cigarette.

"No, the *other* one."

Lynn's eyebrows shot up. "Joaaanna, you are out of control—"

"Okay, knock it off, you two! I'm not doing anything!"

"Relax, Joann. Kidding!" Lynn coughed out a laugh.

They made their way inside and found Todd waiting for them with Captain Front Desk.

"Brad! What!?! What are *you* doing here?" Kathryn hugged him.

"Oh, you know. I just thought it was a Kay's kinda night, I guess."

He began the post-swing-shift litany: 406, too loud; 310, too drunk; the Wilsons, too creepy; the Smiths, too bitchy …

"Order up!"

Kay headed for a corner where some old-timers huddled over regrets, what had been, and what could still be. Waves of sadness moved through Joann as she envisioned her godfather having those conversations. In his later years, Uncle John had reportedly frequented a dive bar in Lower Queen Anne. His poisons had been nicotine and coffee, but he'd enjoyed the company of some other regulars there.

The Sylvan Hotel

♦

The grizzled men nodded at each other, exchanging stories. Joann wished she'd been more aware during her uncle's last years of life. She hadn't understood how lonely he was. And she never imagined he'd be gone so soon. If only there was a way, even for one night, to sit with him for a while—to hear *his* stories. Uncle John had been there for so much of her not-so-easy childhood. But then he'd started fading. And she'd gotten caught up in school, work—

"Earth to Joanna. You gotta catch up!"

Lynn placed a Bud Light in front of her.

11:20 p.m.

Robert would probably be there any second.

11:30.

Maybe there were a lot of late dinner guests.

11:45.

He could be—

"Hey, Brad. Did you see Melissa Gilbert?" queried Kathryn.

"Half Pint's at the hotel?"

"Yeah!"

"What's up, Todd?" A junior valet bounded through the smoke.

Bill had arrived.

"Hey. You comin' to the Saloon tonight?" Todd pushed a chair toward him.

"No. Showbox and a house party after."

"Cool."

Maybe they should go easier on New Guy, thought Joann. Todd had a vastly low tolerance for bullshit, and he obviously didn't mind hanging out with the kid.

"We need music!" she declared. "I'm so ready for some Doors and Patsy Cline!"

"Does anyone have quarters?" asked Bill.

Lynn pushed a few in his direction, but the youngest valet began to see that he was trapped in an increasingly impossible configuration. Tables were being turned in *every* direction. Even the mirror-tiled walls were hazy with reflections of a twisty situation.

"Oh, well. Maybe later." Joann waved him back.

But the gauntlet—er, quarters had been thrown down. And Bill was down to twist.

He grabbed the coins, and Lynn's eyes grew wide as he dove beneath the maze, crawling on all fours.

"What the …" she craned her neck, watching him.

Soon a jukebox was cranking away, and Bill triumphantly returned with shots of Jägermeister in hand.

"Drink up, Joann," he dared.

"What the hell is that?" asked George walking in behind him.

"Jäger, dude. I'm trying to get Miss MacIntosh to expand her horizons."

Feeling herself blushing, Joann said a thanks-be-to-god for the dark room.

Lynn was once again choking on ice cubes, and George tilted his head to one side.

"Oh, boooy."

Joann excused herself, and George followed, razzing her as she reached the restrooms.

"Word on the street is you've got a bit of an admiration club, going on, young lady."

She stopped in her tracks, exasperated.

"Hey, I'm just sayin' …"

"Word on the street is everyone needs to chill."

George hip-checked her.

"Outta my way, sista. I gotta take a leak."

"Lovely." Joann hip-checked him back.

"Hey, at least I ain't trying to pour Jäger down your throat," he winked.

She laughed, then turned her attention to the opposite end of the room.

Tick-tock.

Smoke hovered around a dark entrance. Behind the bar, courage gleamed in a library of bottles shaped like giant perfume decanters wrapped in cigar bands. Overhead, the clock struck midnight, but Jim Morrison was still trying to set the night on fire. Three candles waned, and Kay struck a match, lighting three more. Sparks turned to flames, and a new chapter began.

FAITH AND LOVE, HIJINKS AND HOT PEPPERS

Valentine's Day, 1992. The night was cold but warm as Cupid checked into the Sylvan, along with a storm of Seattle sweethearts. Joann, Brad, Bryce, Bill, Todd, Jed, and Robert were also on target, catering to the deluge of guests. Behind the bar, George blended, mixed, and crushed as a love-struck crowd lined up for liquid confections.

Brad was MOD, so he invited the lobby crew to share his manager dinner: a hodgepodge of à la carte dishes ordered off the restaurant menu. The valets popped in when time permitted, and the desk agents snacked between check-ins and switchboard duty. Brad was always generous with his gourmet perks, and they'd stretch the allotted dollar amount as far as possible. Otherwise, the going fare was an unidentifiable staff meal dumped into cafeteria warming trays. Another option was a food run courtesy of the Town Car—and a willing valet—but only on slow nights.

Sprinting up and down the hill, the valets could barely stop to catch a breath. Overnight cars. Dinner cars. Lounge cars. Bar cars. In PBX, Joann sparred with a relentless switchboard. Out front, Brad cranked through check-ins, and the big window stayed open. It *did* make for easier communication, and Brad also enjoyed the company of the car-parking crew.

Click. Kiet, incoming. Waving to Joann, he set a pile of chocolates alongside the switchboard. Waving "thank you," she answered the next call, and he fled the scene.

The housekeeper was still leery of Brad, who to him probably seemed more like a manager from the "grown-up" team. Then again, Kiet was leery of most people. He was also an enigma. And sometimes it felt like the boy was holding on by an invisible thread, even though he was performing his own version of too-cool-for-school.

Joann looked at the chocolate. Where was Kiet from? Was Seattle his home, or had he recently moved to town? Did he have family here? Was he on his own? Well, unless Kiet volunteered the information, those topics were probably off-limits.

She thought back to the seventies, when a wave of Asian refugees swept into her church and Sunday mass. Many in the largely Italian parish had resented this "invasion." But the newcomers were just trying to survive. Forced to flee their homes, they'd become outsiders; souls in need of asylum. And god knows how they'd coped. Coming from places like Laos and Cambodia, Seattle must have seemed like another planet. Then a monsignor had begun to translate services …

"This is an *Italian* parish," congregation members griped.

But wasn't it supposed to be an "everybody" parish? One could only imagine what they thought about the mixed-up MacIntoshes. And what was wrong with Asian people, anyway? Was it bad to be even part Asian? The question followed Joann all the way to high school. Freshman year at the academy, itchy allergies started bothering her eyes, and sometimes she'd rub them even harder—because the puffiness brought out her eyelids, making her look less "in-between."

She shuddered. Religion had led to all kinds of conundrums as a kid. And how had hate been okay around the pulpit, while the stuff she'd loved was a sin? Starting with Judy Blume—banned. No perusing pages on puberty! *Wonder Woman* had been wrong, too. No worshiping false gods!

So church with bigots was good, but good books and good guys were bad. It defied logic! And how could you not like superheroes? People who'd often gained powers through pain, who then used those powers for good. Joann smiled, remembering her playground wish about wanting to *be* a superhero. Girl superheroes were especially badass. They were intelligent, stunning, gutsy, compassionate, strong, sensitive, and fierce, all at the same time. In the end, they made the story more interesting. How could you possibly find evil in that?

Are you there, God? It's me … "Margaret." Where in the hell is the love?

Valentine's-schmalentines. Joann picked up a pen—and a chocolate. Hopefully, Kiet was faring okay outside the hotel. His life inside the Sylvan was hard enough.

Beep.

"Hi, Lynnie. What's up! Oh, crap. Hang on … another call's coming in."

Click. Click.

"Yes, this is 408. I'd like a dozen roses sent up, please."

"Sir, I think our flower shop might be closed, but I'll transfer you, just in case."

The Sylvan Hotel

Click. Click.

"Lynn! What's going on? Are you here all night?"

"Why, yes. I'm a housekeeping-dream-come-true, at your service."

"Haha. Wanna go out, after?"

"Dude. I hate Valentine's Day."

"Uh, yeah. Not exactly a fan of it, right now, myself."

"Oh, Joann. Something tells me there's sweetness in store for you, this evening."

"Whatever. Hang on … I've got another call—"

Click. Click.

"Yes, this is 408 again. The florist isn't answering the phone."

Uh, because it was 7:00 p.m.? Julia often stayed late on special-occasion days, but come on. Why so last-minute with the flowers?

"One moment, sir."

Click. Click.

"Lynnie, I gotta go. There's a floral crisis in 408, and Julia's already gone for the day."

"See, girl? Valentine's Day is the friggin' worst."

"Call me later, and thank Kiet again for the candy, okay?"

Joann pushed through the swinging door to reception.

"Brad, 408 wants roses, and Julia left an hour ago. What should we do?"

"Hmm. All right, tell him we're checking our florist's office. I'll try to figure something out."

Miss MacIntosh updated the guest as Brad took off with the master key ring.

Beep! And there went the switchboard.

She turned to the concierge stand.

"Jed, I'm by myself up here because Brad's handling a flower emergency. Can you keep an eye on the desk for a sec?"

But the request bounced right off him.

"Kinda busy over here."

Aren't we all.

"Okay, but could you just radio me if someone needs help—"

Call routed, call routed, call routed, and call routed.

She rushed back to the front.

Hurry up, Brad.

One person at reception on a night like tonight would not serve for long.

Beep! Florist office, incoming.

"Hey, did you find anything?"

"Yeah. I think I can put twelve roses together. There's a bunch left in the fridge. Give me a second to throw in a few greens, wrap 'em up …"

And Captain Front Desk saves the day—er, night!

"*Awesome.* I'll let him know."

Joann quickly dialed 408. Then Lissa blew a kiss from the bar, having dropped off a kiddy-style valentine.

"For you," the cocktail server announced, pointing at the desktop with a wink.

"Thanks, lady!" Joann opened the card.

Swish. Junior valet, incoming.

"Hi, Bill!"

"Happy Valentine's, Joann."

He placed another card on the marble countertop. Bill had crossed out the signature of a sales executive who'd distributed them earlier—then he'd re-addressed it to her.

Giggling, Joann accepted the card and returned the sentiment.

Swish. Other valet, incoming.

"Happy Valentine's, Jo." Robert charged through the front doors and pulled a card from his pocket. "I just wanted to make sure you didn't have to go through today without getting one of these," he teased.

"Oh, she *got* a valentine," said Bill.

Laughing, Robert scribbled something on the card, then slid it across the marble.

The Minnie Mouse greeting had also first been signed by a nine-to-fiver. Now Robert's name was written on it, and the small envelope was re-addressed to "Jo."

"Gee. Thanks, I think?" Joann teased back.

"Yeah. That was lame," added Bill.

Both boys laughed and hustled off as the next round of headlights flashed in.

Joann's face suddenly felt hot. Was she some kind of joke now?

Marching into PBX, the desk agent picked up a radio.

"Base to Housekeeping. Come in, Housekeeping."

The phone beeped. Internal call.

"Joaaanna, what's your damage?"

"Lynnie. We are going *out* tonight. Um, please?"

"Whoa. What the hell happened to you?"

"I'll tell you later. I'm just—"

"Okaaay, I think you need some alcohol, and ... uh ... maybe something other than a Bud Light."

"Wait for me in the cafeteria after you're done."

"Ten-four. See ya then."

Lynn hung up, and Joann returned to the desk.

Come on, Brad. She was ready to hide in PBX.

Swish. Todd Barnes, incoming.

Folding his hands, the valet propped his elbows on the marble countertop, and thin black bracelets slid down defined forearms.

"Hey," Joann said gingerly.

"Margaret, do you believe in god?"

What was with everyone tonight?

Well, Todd, I'm from a world where superheroes are sacrilege but racists are righteous.

So ... not sure where I'm at with "God." Happy Valentine's Day!

"I dunno what I believe in, anymore, Todd. If *you* figure out the answer, please share it with me."

He nodded, zipped his jacket, and returned to the valet booth.

Swish. Brad was back.

Joann escaped to PBX. For once, she was glad to see the switchboard.

Minutes later, the lobby slowed down, and conversation picked up. Peeking through slats in the swinging door, she saw Jed, Todd, and Bryce heading for the circle while Robert and Bill lingered expectantly. Joann quietly stepped away and took her seat.

7:45 p.m.

Beep! Internal call, extension 116—the valet booth.

"Operator—"

"Jo, you have allergies, right?" Robert sounded worried.

"Yeah, why? What's wrong?"

"It's Bryce. He's getting hives on his neck and chin. It just hit him out of nowhere!"

"Is his throat swelling, or anything like that?"

"No. But huge hives, and they seem to be spreading!"

"Do you think it was the MOD dinner? Does he have any food allergies?"

"None he's aware of. Hey, do you have something we could give him?"

"Not on me. I have a cortisone cream at my place—"

"Can we go get it?"

"Right now? I don't know if I can leave Brad alone up here."

"It'll be fast. We should have about twenty-five minutes before the next round of dinner guests arrives, and your place is just a few minutes—"

"Well, if you clear it with Brad …"

"Thanks!"

Peeking through the slatted door again, Joann watched Robert confer with Captain Front Desk. Bryce was Brad's favorite valet, so, not surprisingly, he agreed to the plan. Bryce would not suffer on *his* watch.

Miss MacIntosh made a run for the circle, and Robert started the Town Car. Todd opened the passenger door for her, then jumped into the back, leaving Bill and Jed to hold down the fort.

"Let's go. So … what's Kathryn up to, tonight?" Todd pulled himself forward.

Ah. Kathryn had recently moved into the building behind Joann's—and someone wanted intel.

"Dinner with Scott … he's here for a visit."

"What do you think she's wearing?" he replied.

Oh, boooy.

Robert quickly shared *his* take.

"Aw, they're both sitting there in flannel shirts and long johns. They've been together how many years? Trust me. There's nothing to get excited about."

Joann looked at him, her expression saying, "Um … what?"

Todd persisted. "No lingerie?"

"Okaaay, next subject!" warned Joann.

"Sorry, Margaret," said Todd.

Robert proceeded with his Valentine commentary.

"You know, on Valentine's Day, my girlfriend and I don't get into that sappy shit. We just tell each other what we can't stand about one another."

Todd's eyes moved to Robert, then Joann, then back to Robert.

"Yeah, okay, Bailey. That sounds like a winner. Happy fucking Valentine's Day."

Now rolling his eyes, he retreated to the back.

Sheesh. Who knew the tough guy was a romantic? Turning around, Joann looked at Todd, who looked back at her. His face was tired. And ... *sad*? But not defeated. Then it was like he was looking *into* her. Like he recognized something—

She turned away.

"Where's Kathryn's—?" Todd rolled down the window as the Town Car slowed.

"There." Joann pointed to her friend's apartment.

"All right, Jo. We'll wait while you grab the stuff." Robert flipped the locks.

"Just give me a minute!"

Up the stairs. Into the studio. Joann paused in the dark, glancing through a window at the shiny car in front. There was Todd, forever wishing on Kathryn. There was Robert, oblivious to what *she* could have sworn had been happening over the last few weeks, and boyfriend to someone he protested Valentine's Day with.

Get over it, she thought. "What was happening" was probably happening in her imagination—and Bryce was probably itching for them to get back.

⁓ ♦ ⁓

At the Sylvan, Robert dropped off Joann, and she made a dash for it. *Whew!* Just in time. Guest cars were queuing up, and in PBX, the switchboard looked like it was having a seizure. She swiftly put eight lines on hold, then worked her way across the board until all the calls had been transferred.

When the panel quieted, she called to her teammate.

"Thanks for covering, Brad. Wanna take a break?"

"Yeah, thanks!"

Joann took her post out front, then picked up the desk phone and dialed the garage.

"Hey, Jo."

"Robert, how's Bryce? Did it work?"

"Yeah! Whatever it was seems to be calming down. Thank you so much!"

"No prob. Ooops, gotta go. Phone's ringing."

She quickly hung up. Where were all these ... feelings coming from? Why did he matter so much, all the time? How had she grown so attached? How had she thought that he was even remotely interested in her?

Ugh. Her brain had gone haywire.

Don't be so desperate! Pull yourself together. He is with someone else.

Beep!

"Hey, Jo," said Bryce.

"Hey! Feeling better?"

"Yeah, thanks. Never experienced anything like that, before."

"No problem, Bryce. Take it easy tonight ..."

10:55 p.m.

A familiar-looking, long-haired chap slowly pushed his hand across the marble countertop.

"Hi, there. Here's the key to my room."

"Okay, thank you."

Joann tossed it in the key box.

Anthony Kiedis stared into her eyes for a few more seconds. Then the fur-clad frontman tossed his Pantene mane and sauntered off.

Robert opened the big window. "Ready, Jo? I'll walk you to your car."

"Thanks, but I'm goin' to Kay's with Lynnie."

"Be safe. I'll see you tomorrow."

"See you tomorrow."

Joann closed the big window, re-addressed Lissa's card, and pinned it in PBX for the morning shift. Then she walked through the back office with two other valentines rustling in her blazer pocket. Out in the lobby, she stopped momentarily, watching Mr. Kiedis and company climb into taxis. No doubt, they were off to exciting adventures to see exciting people in exciting places, far from the Sylvan ... and far from the in-between.

The Sylvan Hotel

◆

Would she ever get beyond those doors? And *did* she still believe in a god or an all-powerful "universe?" Did she still believe in herself? And what about love? Would she find it? Would it find her?

The taxis drove through the circle.

Ladies and gentleman, the Red Hot Chili Peppers have left the building. Thank you, and—

"Good lord," Joann said to herself. Sure, she had questions, but life could be so much worse. She needed to stop worrying—to have faith that things would sort themselves out.

Still, she couldn't help but wonder ... where was this story headed?

Miss MacIntosh retrieved two valentines from her pocket and lightly shuffled them.

Come on Universe, don't hide the answer.

Give it away.

She cradled the hearts in her hands.

Give it away.

Dear Jo—

Give it away now!

"Ha. My brain *is* haywire."

Joann repocketed her Sylvan tokens. Then she hurried to the stairs as Cupid shuffled his own cards.

OF BLOSSOMS AND BOOGERS

What a glorious April afternoon. Resting on the front steps of her building, Joann breathed deeply after a run through the neighborhood. Two robins chirped at her, and flower stars rustled from papery dogwoods. Crocuses cuddled in grassy sidewalk clusters, tulips popped around sunny porches, and late daffodils unfurled in golden tufts beneath cherry trees frothy with bloom. Ancestral pines overlooked the perennial spectacle, patiently waiting for it all to unfold.

The robins chirped louder.

"Okay, okay, I'm going."

Shower. Makeup. Hair. Nylons. Uniform. *Where. Are. My. Shoes.*

And ... she was at the hotel again.

"Robert! Sorry, would you mind?"

"No prob, Jo—I got you!"

Hopping out of the car, she followed a crowd of guests through the front door and across the lobby. By the elevator, women in lab coats milled about, chatting and exchanging business cards.

"Lancôme. Spring-color event," Jed explained, running past.

Click. Joann walked into the back office and out to the desk.

Swish. More cosmetic reps swept through the doors.

Looking down their extra-exfoliated noses, two of them fake-smiled at Alicia, who cordially directed them to the seventh floor.

"We've been here before."

Fake-Smile One and Fake-Smile Two now turned *up* their noses. They were palette *professionals.*

Well, you still need to work on your tone, thought Joann. But her manager's feathers remained unruffled. Instead, just one amused smile laced with pity, and—*whack!* Alicia returned that serve and sent them running. For the elevator, of course. Then, to Joann's surprise, her bemused boss whispered, "They sure told me!"

Um, what? Alicia was a badass! A badass who didn't need *any* makeup. Her manager also seemed so much warmer these days. Maybe ... maybe

Alicia'd had a change of heart—or Joann had just misread something. Whatever the case, she was liking this new vibe.

Watching the powdered participants shove into the elevator, Alicia dusted off a dress with gold buttons and smoothed her chestnut hair. Then, adjusting a lightly-draped sweater, the cashmere-caped crusader winked and returned to her ... station.

Talk about too-cool-for-school.

Swish. Kathryn pushed through the swinging door.

"Why are the check-ins so early today?" she whispered.

"Dunno. But it's going to piss off Housekeeping. I don't think all the rooms are ready."

Beep-beep-beep!

Joann ran to the switchboard.

"Yo. What's with the chicks in science costumes?"

"Hi, Lynnie! It's a Lancôme thing. Some big meeting about colors."

"They booked a hotel to talk about lipstick?"

A Housekeeping manager screeched orders in the background.

"Uh—later, dude."

Beep. The switchboard was also on task.

"Good afternoon, the Sylvan Hotel. How may I help you?"

And ... the calls kept on coming: Concierge. Kitchen. Catering. Valets. Sales.

Then back to the desk to help with check-ins.

"What's up, Joann?"

"Hi, Bill."

"May I please get a list and a *Wall Street Journal*?"

Why couldn't he look at Robert's list? But the valet was waiting—and apparently not interested in sharing.

Turning to the computer, Joann hit a few keys, then retrieved the print-out.

"Here you go."

Tap-tap-tap. The big window opened. Bryce waved to Joann and Kathryn, then called to his teammate.

"Hey, Short Pants. Get out here, would ya?"

Kathryn stifled a guffaw. The older boys enjoyed reminding their younger teammate of his junior status—and made a point of doing so regularly.

An unfazed Bill retreated. "See you later," he promised.

The swinging door opened, and Alicia returned with a new desk agent in tow.

"Kathryn, Joann, meet Tory. She'll mostly be working mornings, but I wanted her to do a little shadowing with you two, to get a sense of how the evening shift goes."

"Hello," they said, shaking her hand.

Replying with an extremely high-pitched, "Hiiiiii!" Tory practically levitated.

Oh, brother. This was not good. Babs had once encouraged Joann to "perk up," but if this is what they had in mind …

The reception newbie followed Joann to the switchboard. Tory was quick to learn and, in between calls, rambled away with enthusiasm. Well, at least she wasn't bitchy. The front-office team had evolved quite nicely, and Joann wanted it to stay that way—especially compared to where things had been on her own first day. One guy had repeatedly thrown pencils at her head and punched her in the arm while she learned the switchboard. Another agent wouldn't stop with the sexual innuendos, and it was exhausting for everyone, hour after hour. Tory was over-the-top bouncy but harmless and capable.

Joann re-joined Kathryn at the desk.

"Well, New Girl's got the hang of the switchboard."

"She's very … peppy."

"Yeah, well, at least she's nice, and it will be an easy shift with three of us on."

Swish. Todd incoming—and ready to switch out ones for twenties.

Right then, Tory pushed through the door from PBX, so Kathryn made introductions.

"Tory, this is Todd, one of our valets. Todd, this is Tory. She's training with us tonight."

"Hi, doood!" The newbie hit a new octave.

Todd's fingers froze, mid-count.

Joann held her breath, and Kathryn stifled another guffaw.

"What's up, Squeaky?" The valet thinly smiled.

Thrilled with *her* new name, Tory bubbled on about the hotel and how great it was to be there.

"Cool." Todd resumed counting.

The Sylvan Hotel

Pleased with having made her acquaintance with one of the "infamous valets," the desk agent in-training bounced back to PBX.

Todd finished the exchange, then tucked his bills away. With a slow-motion salute, he turned for the valet booth.

"Well, that was painful," said Kathryn.

Now Joann was trying not to laugh.

Check-ins were lining up again, so the girls made haste to get room keys assigned. Arriving dinner guests also filled the lobby, along with executive staff now materializing from offices to leave for the night. Tory was acing the switchboard, so Joann and Kathryn kept watch at the desk. When everything cleared, Todd and Jed approached.

"Dinner?" they asked Kathryn.

"Go," said Joann. "I'll eat after you."

Miss Emerson walked around to meet the boys, and they left for the cafeteria.

"Hey, Jo." Robert incoming.

The valet rested his arms on the marble countertop, and—

Dammit! There went her stomach. She quickly pulled out one of the front-desk binders and opened it, pretending to study—

"Is that the schedule?" He leaned forward.

"Um, yeah. Sooo, having a good shift?"

Jeezus, now *she* sounded peppy. Maybe Tory was rubbing off on her.

"Kinda hectic, but things are settling down. We might have Bryce do haircuts."

"Are all the execs gone?"

"Yeah. Man, that one bookkeeper lady is so rude. She's always bitchy. For no reason! But, you know … she should watch it, or *else.*"

The valet rubbed his hands together with a cryptic smile.

"Or else …???"

"Or else we'll wipe boogers on her steering wheel."

"*Robert Bailey*! That's disgusting!"

Laughing at her horrified expression, he bolted for the garage to check on Bill.

The lobby grew still. Tory had the switchboard under control; Kathryn, Jed, and Todd were downstairs, and Joann was trying not to be bored.

"Only boring people get bored," Robert's voice chuckled in her mind. "Eat some chocolate. It will make you feel like you're in love."

Where did he get this stuff? Get out of my head, she thought. *Robert, Robert, Robert.* This had to stop. He *wasn't* interested in her. She was a teammate. For crying out loud—how had things gotten this far? Maybe she'd developed a harmless crush after Grady dumped her, but now she was getting too tangled up in the valet's kindness and attention. This must be some sort of rebound thing.

Snap out of it, she thought. *He has a girlfriend. I'm just an entertaining way to pass the time during swing-shift hours.*

Joann had been so irritated with both Bill and Robert after the valentine-card "competition." But Robert was just being his silly self. And Bill was just ... Bill. She'd overreacted. There was no reason to get bent out of shape, and it was time to get over her valet "problem."

It's just that she could have sworn ... some of those walks to her car ... or those rainy-night rides to the roof ...

Okay, timeout. She was looking for something that didn't exist, or something she'd conjured out of ... something?

Aaack. Stop it, Joann!

Swish. Todd and Jed returned to the valet booth, and Kathryn returned to the desk.

"Anything happen while we were at dinner?"

"Just talking with Robert about work stuff."

"You okay, Jo?"

"Yeah. But I think I've gotten a little too attached to him."

"Well, he seems a little attached, himself."

"He has a girlfriend," Joann replied dismissively.

Kathryn tightened her ponytail.

"Then maybe he should act like it."

Finn crossed the lobby with a tray.

"Are you behaving out here, A-Team?"

"Whatever, Room Service," Joann chided. "Try not to get lost on any *three-hour tours*."

Finn giggled and flew onto the elevator. Thorn Birds was on the move.

Joann turned to Kathryn. "So ... how was dinner?"

"Oh, fine," said Kathryn. "Todd's got a new girl, so he was telling me aaaaaall about it."

"Aha. Progress!"

"See? Everything's back to normal. Yes, Todd and I connect on stuff, but *I have a boyfriend*. And no matter what, he knows that."

Well, Todd had gotten the message. So why couldn't Joann? Robert was not available.

Maybe she just needed a couple days off from this place. Tomorrow was Easter—and a gathering at the parents' house. But no church on *her* schedule, so she'd sleep in, enjoy a lazy drive ...

Swish. Ken and Khloe Wolf pushed through the front doors.

Yep. Time for a break—from snotty guests, check-ins, lists, valets—

"What's up, Joann?" Bill incoming.

"Hi! Nice hair."

"A Bryce special." He ran his fingers through golden-brown layers of light and dark. "Anyway, you girls have a happy Easter. I'm outta here."

"Thanks. You, too."

Swish. And Bill was on his way.

"Someone wanted to show off his new 'do," teased Kathryn.

"It *does* look good on him. It's like cleaned-up-skater-boy. It's ... cute."

Miss Emerson's eyebrows started to elevate.

"Oh, come on. Now you think ... me and *Bill*?"

Ding.

Housekeeping and Room Service walked out of the elevator. The lobby was still empty, so they stopped at the desk.

"What up?" asked Lynn, looking around. "Hold on. Something's missing. Oh, I know—where are your, I mean, *the* valets?"

"Haha," replied Joann.

And cue the evil giggle.

"Not funny, Finn!" added Kathryn.

Still giggling, he escaped into the kitchen.

Then Tory pushed through the door from PBX.

"Hi, doods! Um, the guest in 206 wants more pillows, but Housekeeping isn't answering their phone!"

"Oh, that's when you have to use the radio—er walkie talkie," said Joann. "And, Tory, this is Lynn. She's on for Housekeeping tonight."

"Hi, Lynn! So, yeah ... 206 wants more pillows!"

"Well, tell 206 they can—"

"Thanks, Tory. We'll make sure they get the pillows," interrupted Joann.

"Cool! Thanks, doods!" Giggling, she pushed back through the PBX door.

Lynn smacked the marble countertop. "I just *brought* that guy pillows. How many fucking pillows does one person need? And what's up with your new friend ... doods?"

"Oh my god, Lynn. Can you please just bring him some more pillows?" Kathryn pleaded. "He's gonna call down here and yell at us!"

The housekeeper sighed. "For you, I'll do it."

Lynn went to find pillows, Kathryn went to check on Tory, and Joann waited at the desk, staring into the polished depths of Honduran Mahogany.

Ding! Finn exited the elevator once again and disappeared around the corner into the back hallway. Then he reappeared. First his head, then his shoulders, then his torso. Ha! Someone else was battling boredom. Room Service so easily amused himself, and Joann couldn't help but laugh as she watched him climb up and down imaginary stairs on the other side of the desk. The guy could be such a kid brother—even though he was *older* than her!

"What's up, Finn?"

Just returning from the garage, the valets eyed him suspiciously.

"Oh, hey there." Mister Room Service pretended to be embarrassed, but evil giggles prevailed. Then he turned back to Joann. When he wasn't delivering Sylvan cuisine (or pestering the pastry chef), Finn loved to dish about whatever needed dishing. Her friend would make the rounds during slower hours, enjoying the company of cocktail servers between orders; food servers between courses; valets between cars—and desk agents between check-ins.

"So how's occupancy tonight? Hey, and did you hear ..."

Room Service exchanged the latest "news" with Joann, then talked basketball with the valets. When he proceeded to the bar for his next stop, Joann took a seat on the ledge.

Tap-tap-tap. Robert pushed at the big window.

"Jo, I've moved your car into the circle. Just come get the keys when you're ready."

"Thank you!"

Hopefully, her steering wheel was booger-free.

"And now it's time for a commercial break," announced the valet TV.

The next afternoon, Joann steered the Jetta south onto Rainier Avenue. In the distance, snow-capped Tahoma ruled blue skies. On the sidewalks, gnarled trees with hints of green stood like upturned broom sticks ready to dust off any clouds and give silver linings their say. The sun was making a rare Easter appearance, and the view was unmatched.

Just add a choir of ten … and it was tantamount to church.

At least, it was Joann's idea of church. Not that she didn't believe in the possibility of a higher power, but she'd fallen away from the Catholic faith.

And it was a relief.

Relief from the regimens: Mass on Sunday. Holy Days of Obligation. Confession. Penance. Repent. Repeat. The rosary on the ride to school. The Hail Mary. The Our Father. The Joyful Mysteries. The Sorrowful Mysteries. Skipping mysteries (hoping their father was too tired to notice).

Relief from sin. Sin was here, there, and everywhere. Joann remembered wincing as her uncle struck his chest during a church prayer: an apology for "offending God." Back then, Mommy even wore "My Sin" perfume. And you really had to watch yourself, because the guy in the dining-room painting wasn't doing very well. Cursed to wear a crown of thorns, he suffered if you were bad, because misbehavior made that prickly halo tighter. *Look closely—more blood!* They're drinking Jesus' blood. Sunday vampires. Everyday demons. The devil, the devil, the devil.

Relief from the strain. Her dad may not have had a house payment, but Catholic-school tuition for four had mortgaged him to the Vatican. As a result, he'd lived on a shoestring budget, and the self-inflicted hardship had taken a toll. Too militant. Too temperamental. Too angry.

Relief from the hurt. Joann still wouldn't wear belts and cringed at the tinkling sound of a buckle. The sound of a god-fearing father. A short-tempered father. A fatherless father.

The sound of a strap that hadn't stopped. Seven. Eight. Nine. Ten. *Any more sass, and we'll wash your mouth with soap.*

Relief from the absurdity.

You-know-who had the stigmata—and the doc saw Satan in the corner.

Stop watching Bewitched. It's witchcraft.

No sex before marriage. No birth control. Women can't be priests. Priests can't marry. Homosexuality? Just don't act on it. Unbaptized babies go to "limbo" if they perish. Marry a Catholic—but not a divorced Catholic. Wear a scapular—if you die, you'll go up. When Grandma washes church vestments, the water can't go down.

Camelias baptized. Raspberries blessed. If only Eve hadn't wrecked the garden—but …

Women are the root of men's evil.

Oh, yeah. Joann had left it all behind. On the run from the pope and her parents, she'd moved out and started a new life … which had also resulted in relief from other wounds.

Bernadette Salvador MacIntosh had been one of the world's most dedicated mommies.

In her world, children were a gift—not trophies or checkboxes on life's list. Joann had watched other parents faking interest in her friends' day-to-day doings, but Bernadette had been all in. She'd listened. Comforted. Nurtured. Read to them for hours on end. Sung to them. Played with them. Tucked flowers in their hair and made teddy bears talk. Fixed the homework. Pulled the teeth. Cut the bangs. Sewed the costumes. Drove the carpools. Cooked the casseroles. Planted the veggies. Baked the birthday cakes. Said the I-love-yous.

Then seventh grade happened, and Joann's mother sort of disappeared. It was like a piece of her slipped away; like she was there, then she wasn't, except that—she was. One afternoon, Bernadette picked up the kids from school, and her sugary disposition was suddenly hard-edged. She'd become a stranger overnight. Sitting back, Joann had leaned her head against the car door, waiting for her *mom* to return. Outside, a wind blew past, taking something with it.

Then gifts … became burdens.

The Sylvan Hotel

We've made sacrifices for you.

Maybe the challenges of an extremely frugal lifestyle had finally worn her mother down. Or the abuses she'd witnessed were suddenly too heavy to carry. Or had Bernadette just lost herself somewhere along the way? She'd always put family first—even before herself—and she'd had a small say in most matters. Maybe Mommy had been running on empty. Or an emptiness had begun to spill over.

Then the real struggle began. From seventh grade on, the MacIntosh household grew increasingly volatile ... and Bernadette feared for her daughter's soul. By sophomore year, Joann wanted out of the house at every turn. But the parties started at 10:00 p.m., and she was due back at midnight. Basically, it became an impossible situation. Because out there, Joann *belonged*. She belonged to people with new ideas; people who asked questions about the world; people who made her laugh; people who made her feel wanted. So she started missing curfew and, if grounded, she sneaked out again.

Basement door. Yellow camper van. Headlights off! Running, running, free.

As a teen, Miss MacIntosh had never been falling-down-drunk, and most of the time, she'd barely been buzzed. Joann had also drawn the line at drugs, and she hadn't really dated—but the clock was her nemesis. Even if she called or was just a few minutes late, a rational discussion had been impossible.

We will lock you up, Joann MacIntosh. We will put you away.

Round and round and round. Joann had never been good at "playing along," so the cycles went in circles. And since she'd fought back hard, the punishments were hard.

"Take the bus!" Her father would snap as he drove off with her sister to the Academy.

Then, holding her breath, Joann navigated a dicey route, walking to and from the Rainier Avenue Metro stop. One afternoon, a teenage boy crossed from the other side of Andover, pushed up alongside, and grabbed her arm. The kid looked somewhat younger—but he was bigger than Joann.

"Hey!" she'd angrily exclaimed.

But anger soon turned to fear. She couldn't wrestle free, and two older guys stood jeering on a nearby porch. As the kid dragged her closer to that house, Joann had pulled with all her might, yelling at him to get off of her.

Thankfully, he'd let go, either because she'd made enough noise—or he'd chickened out of some dare, settling for a good laugh instead.

Keeping her eyes down, Joann had continued up the hill, trying to walk calmly but quickly. Shaking under her coat, she'd resisted the urge to check behind her. What if they changed their minds? There were three of them and one of her. At 43rd, she'd practically broken into a run, then slowed again as she saw her father in the driveway. It had taken every ounce of strength to get away from those boys, and it would take even more strength to get back in good graces—so she could get back in the car.

Even then, the battle for control waged on. Convinced she needed reform, her parents had threatened to take their daughter far from her friends. They double-locked the basement door and shut other doors to freedom, like driver's ed. But Joann made it through high school … and got a license! Then her parents demanded rent, so she got the restaurant job—and some car privileges. Soon, however, she was in trouble again. Hostess shifts ended at 11:00 p.m., and staying to talk with a cast of characters resulted in more broken curfews, even at age twenty.

But Joann had been captivated. Salty line cooks! Sassy bartenders! Bantering between golden pints, the fish-and-chip mongers would often turn the front of the house into their house after the last guest had gone. Inked with the stains of hard work and hard truths, they'd held midnight office hours, like street-smart professors in not-so-white kitchen whites.

Then there was the ad man in-the-making: a waiter who, by day, had been breaking into the biz. Joann had been desperate for wisdom—and he'd happily shared his thoughts, desperate to feel wise.

Last but never least was Tammy, a Mercer Island beauty who'd fallen for the ad man. One night, the hostess told Joann her story: a grown-up tale about a grown-up game of Chutes and Ladders. There'd been a torrid affair and a lot of happiness, but a last-minute hitch was sending Tammy down the hatch. The ad man had places to go, and another player could help him climb higher. So, weeks later, Tammy finished her last shift and slipped out. After all, a classy girl kept quiet. Meanwhile, a not-so-wise guy closed out, counting his wins and burying his losses. Joann had wanted to say something. But who was she to say anything. Especially to someone … caught up with everything.

"Dad, I was just talking with people! About career stuff and life—"

"You've *lost* your privileges!"

The Sylvan Hotel
•

The keys to the Ford were confiscated—but rent was still due.

So, Joann had hoped for safe passage once more, carpooling with hopeful male co-workers. It had been another dicey commute, but Metro service to Leschi was spotty in those days—and she hadn't shaken that earlier transit trauma. *No more hillside draggings*, she'd vowed. Biking wasn't an option either, having been clipped by a car on her mother's one-speed as a kid. *Are you okay?* And they'd zoomed off, leaving her a no-speed, nervous wreck.

Eventually, Joann saved enough to buy her own cheap Ford, but money was short, otherwise, and freedom was slipping even further out of reach. Then Uncle John died and left her a college fund. Losing her godfather had been devastating, but Joann had vowed to do right by him. She got her own place, got a degree—and things got better with everyone living apart. These days, her parents scarcely started arguments with kids who could *all* drive away.

Joann breathed out. The relationship with them would always be tricky, but time and space were helping. And they *were* trying. Bernadette was always telling her that she could do anything she put her mind to. Jack would tell her that she "needed to get sanctified," and she'd roll her eyes. But he'd check her oil, and they'd move on to other topics, starting with his watch-those-tires-and-fluid-levels speech. Sometimes, they even took walks through the Mount Baker streets a few blocks up; Joann extolling the beauty of the historic mansions—and her father rattling on about the one he could have bought, but-who-would-want-those-property-taxes.

Common ground was an ongoing challenge, but in the driveway, they'd managed to find neutral ground—between her new life, her old life, a piece of flattened cardboard, a toolbox, and a couple old cars. Jack had also retired, and Bernadette was beginning dialysis, so new perspectives were coming into focus.

Joann looked at the mountain again. She was glad not to be in a church—to be alive and on her own in the Northwest. God was in the rivers, lakes, forests, and snowy slopes; in Puget Sound waters full of Orcas; in landscapes abundant with evergreens. And to think all of that was just minutes from downtown! Seattle wasn't a glut of concrete or high-rises like so many other places on the map—and natural beauty was everywhere. The city had also evolved past its "podunk" beginnings, but its soul was intact. Not *totally* cosmopolitan ... but not the boonies, either.

Seattle was perfectly in the middle.

Turning into her parents' driveway, Joann parked, then pulled at the visor. What the—valet hair clippings tumbled into her lap and onto the seat and floor.

Robert Bailey, are you kidding me?!?

She climbed out of the car and marched into the house.

I am going to throttle him.

"Happy Easter to you, too," her brothers said as she hurtled past.

They were discussing a security gig that Mark had worked almost a year prior—a "ten release," whatever that was. Something about "Mookie Blaylock" and how "Ed was pissed about not enough fans being allowed through …"

In the kitchen, Joann picked up the phone and dialed the numbers.

"Good afternoon, the Sylvan Hotel, how may I help you?"

"Hi, Tory. Will you please transfer me to the valet booth?"

"Hi, dood! Sure, one sec—"

"Valet," answered Robert.

"What the hell?" demanded Joann. "Seriously, Robert?"

"S-s-sorry, Jo. I'll make it up to you."

But that laugh was hopelessly infectious, and she found herself joining in. Truth be told, Joann couldn't imagine an instance where she'd be mad at him for very long. Because underneath the jokes and a zipped-up navy jacket, Robert Bailey was as good as gold. Yes, he heckled her, but he'd also shown her tremendous kindness, the likes of which she hadn't seen in a long time. The likes of which was changing her life.

"Hey, are you working on Tuesday?" he asked in the most melty valet voice ever.

"Yeah."

"All right, now. Happy Easter."

Joann hung up, slid the glass door open, and breathed in a backyard infused with spring. Sunshine warmed her face, and pollen swirled like Pacific pixie dust in slivers of light streaming between leafy branches and buds. Throughout the grass, honeybees swooned on sweet clover, and buttercups nuzzled dandelions. Steller's Jays chased squirrels through the fig tree and, toward the garden, a goldfinch flitted midair with monarchs.

Miss MacIntosh closed her eyes. Just two days, something inside her whispered. Just two days until she'd be back at the hotel.

The Sylvan Hotel
◆

She opened her eyes. And back with him.

A breeze blew by as she looked at the world. *Was* it warm, or did she feel a chill?

Which way would it go? Window—

Dad at the windowsill. "Hey!" shouted her father. "What's with all the hair in the driveway?"

CAR TALK

Water droplets covered Kathryn's Volkswagen Fox in a patchwork of sparkling polka dots.

It was 2:30 a.m., and the late-night world was dark but glistening. Kay's had closed, but nobody wanted to go anywhere.

"How did you think to grab forks?" Kathryn reopened the Carolyn's Cakes box.

"Well, I had a feeling more sugar would be in order, and it's not like we can't return 'em the next time we're here!" Joann laughed.

"Now *that* is good," Miss Emerson mumbled.

"So good," Miss MacIntosh agreed.

"Don't eat all … the … cake …"

The "A-team" looked at their semi-conscious friend stretched across the back seat.

"How many beers did she have tonight?" Kathryn took another bite.

"I think it was more like vodka crans. You okay, Lynnie?"

"Mmmmm. I … happy … birth …"

"Just let her sleep, Jo."

"Yeah, nighty night, Lynn. We'll be right here pigging down aaaall the yumminess! Thanks, by the way, Kath. This is *delish*."

"You're welcome, birthday queen."

"And *that* was a fun party!"

"Our junior valet was certainly attentive."

"Hilarious, Kathryn."

"*He's* hilarious. Jeezus Christ, that boy is not giving up on the Joann quest anytime soon."

"Oh, he's just … young."

"I'd say he's more *determined* than anything."

"Actually, I think he's started seeing someone."

"And, clearly, he's keeping his options open."

Joann pushed her fork around in the frosting. She was now twenty-four years old. What, exactly, was she doing with her life? She looked at Lynn, breathing peacefully, then over at Kathryn. The hotel had brought them together. But where was it all leading? And was she ever going to start her career?

What if the universe was trapping her in the in-between? What if she was stuck for real?

Stuck like dollar bills on the ceiling of the Comet Tavern—or the webs of gum on that wall in Post Alley. Stuck ... in the swing shift of life! Would Joann be left behind? Kathryn was already on her way, and the resourceful Lynn was sure to find her path. There was also a valet who probably wasn't going to be a valet for much longer. Jeezus. She'd been so bummed when he said that he couldn't go to her party. How was she going to cope when he left the hotel?

"Hey, you. What's up?" Kathryn tapped her arm.

"Nothing. Er ... well, I wish Robert—"

"I'm sure Robert wanted to be there. He must have had ... other plans. And what the hell is going on with him? I'm seeing a lot of mixed messages happening, which pisses me off because I don't want you to get hurt."

"But he's not ... it's just ... well ... like the way he smiles at me, some nights—"

"You mean the way he smiles at you *most* nights?"

"Oh, gawd. Don't *say* that. I'm already too far gone. But it just feels like all is right with the world, the *second* he walks in. It's intense. He seems happy to see me, too. Then the shift ends, we say goodbye, and I convince myself that I'm imagining stuff. Because he's with someone else, right? Then, the next day, it starts all over again. I don't get it. But he's sooo sweet to me. And did I mention that he's cute? And funny? And we're a great team."

"Well, okay—Robert's not a sleazy guy. And nobody's married, yet, so I think it's fair to say that we're all trying to figure shit out. But maybe he should back off until he *does* figure his shit out."

"Well, it's not like he's in my face or being gross or anything like that—"

"Yeah, but come *on*. The guy is obviously conflicted."

"Um, we've almost eaten all the cake."

"Well, sometimes you just gotta have cake. Besides, it will soak up my rum and cokes and your Bud Lights, so we can drive!"

They'd only had a couple drinks each, but the after-Kay's car conferences were now routine, regardless.

Tick-tock.

Frannie James

◆

The "A-Team" spent so many hours together! Of course, they couldn't talk about everything at work, and Kay's also involved visiting with other Sylvans. But they never strayed too far from one another. Then, between closing time and bedtime, they covered the important stuff.

"So what about you, Kath? What's happening with Scott? Will he be back soon?"

Kathryn looked down at her lap.

"Oh, he's figuring it out, too. I don't know when he'll be leaving Oregon, but we're okay. He really did want a break from Seattle. And he's still interested in teaching here. We're good partners, so I'm sure it's going to be fine."

"Well, I'm rooting for you guys. Sorry if I stressed you out about Todd."

"There's no stress. And, yeah, I *do* have a nice connection with him, but it's purely friendship—I'm supposed to be with Scott! Also, *I'm* sorry. It probably wasn't great to hear me talk about all that when a lot of it might apply to what's happening on the other side of your situation … although … it *does* seem like Robert is a lot less sure about … something."

"I dunno." Joann slouched in the seat.

Kathryn continued. "Maybe … hmm. Well, there's not just one human for every human in this world, so … maybe there's some weird coincidence happening. As in, how often do we find ourselves face-to-face with two really good matches? But even if Robert's torn, he and Tricia … well, they have history. Which he's for sure gonna weigh against whatever's going on with you. Or maybe there's just something going on with *him*, or … oh, who even knows."

Ugh. Joann was *totally* stuck. Stuck between college and career. Stuck between being a grown-up and a kid. Stuck between frustration and love for her parents. Stuck between a boy and a girl he met first.

Stuck between everything.

"You're going to find the right person, someday, Jo."

But what if Robert's the right person?

The right person at the wrong damn time.

Someone knocked on the window, and Joann rolled it down.

"Hi, doods! What are you still doing here?"

A rain-soaked Tory was more perky than ever. Sam, a newer valet, had an arm around her shoulder.

"Hey, guys. You okay to drive home?"

"Yeah, but we're going to Thirteen Coins first. Join us if you want!"

"Thanks, but we've just stuffed our faces with leftover cake."

"Tee hee! Well, happy birthday, dood. See ya!"

Joann rolled up the window, and Kathryn laughed, flipping her ponytail.

"That girl is a strange bird."

"Yeah, she's kind of a freak. But I stand by my original verdict. At least she's not a beeeyotch. God knows we've got enough of those—"

"Looks like she and Sam are together. That's a good balance. He's kinda introverted, and she's big-time bubbly. It might just work!"

Joann watched the rain bounce on the hood of the car.

Just like Tory. Bounce, bounce, bounce. Why was it so easy for some people? How was it so impossible for *her* to get it right?

"You ready to go?" asked Kathryn.

"Yeah. Thank-you-thank-you-thank-you. It was a great night."

"Of course! I love you, Joanna-banana!"

"Awwwwww," Lynn slurred. "You guys are cute."

"Lynnie, were you awake the whole time?" Joann searched the rearview mirror.

"That's for me to know and you two to find out."

―――◆―――

Kathryn and Lynn headed to the Hill, and Joann drove her own car back to the hotel.

Swish. She waved to Ollie, but then George pushed through the PBX door.

"Jo! What are you doing here? It's almost 3:45!"

"I was talking with the girls after Kay's—and I need to pee! Why are you still here?"

"I forgot my keys and got talking with Ollie. Hurry up—I'll walk out with ya."

Joann continued through, but momentarily slowed her steps. To the right, an empty lounge was picture-perfect; a piece of art in itself. It looked like a still life—or another life that you could step right into, even if just for a moment. And it was all theirs in the after hours. Sometimes, she'd return and stay a while after Kay's closed. The coveted green-velvet sofa became *her* sofa, and she'd curl up while Ollie ran calculations, like a night-owl roommate.

Frannie James

◆

Tick-tock.

Joann imagined an invisible grandfather clock presiding over a living room that ran on its own time. Firelight slowly inched past the hearth, casting brilliance onto ghosted furnishings and revealing textures beneath textures in finely crafted threads. On the ceiling, shadows trembled, pulled, and pushed while conversation embers burned in the dust below.

⇒ ◆ ⇐

"Be right there, Jo!"

As the barman said goodnight to the auditor, Joann searched her purse for the new cassette, a birthday gift from Bill. She turned the tape around in her hands: *Louder Than Love*. Framed between yellow-gold strips, a shirtless dude swung mermaid-worthy hair. Fists gripping microphone wire, he raged in black, white, and shades of gray. Giggling, Joann unwrapped it.

"Did you enjoy your party?" George met her at the doors.

"Yeah!"

"Where was Robert tonight?"

"I think he had … plans."

"Oh, boooy."

"Whatever, George. Jeezus."

"Jeezus ain't got nuthin' to do with it."

"Robert Bailey has a *girlfriend*."

"Yeah, well, maybe he's not sure if he belongs with that girlfriend."

"Or maybe it's just really bad timing. He met her first."

"He met you second, and he's not married, yet!" winked George.

"Don't say that! I'm sure she's a nice person. It's just that *he's* so—"

"Okay, okay. I got it. And you've got it bad for that boy. Just remember, Joann.

Don't put people on pedestals."

"What do you mean?"

"Robert's just a guy. A good guy, but he isn't perfect."

"Ten-four." She hugged him. "And thanks, George. I'll see you soon!"

Joann climbed into the Jetta, put on her seatbelt, and turned the key.

Outside the car, string lights impatiently flickered on palm trees, the fountain trickled faster, and a tenacious rain was not letting up.

Inside the car, Joann shoved *Louder Than Love* into the cassette player.

The Sylvan Hotel

◆

Holy—*wow*. That voice! A voice singing about ugly truths and people hiding their eyes.

Well, right now, Joann needed to close her eyes.

Let's go, mermaid dude.

And she shifted into drive.

PLEATLESS IN SEATTLE

It was summertime in the city. Groaning, Joann and Kathryn reluctantly pulled on their polyester-wool-blend uniforms. The hotel had air conditioning, but it was a dinosaur at the core—and old-school innerworkings often struggled when it came to moving things in the right direction.

Whew. Just a few hours to go, and the heat would start to subside. Everyone lived for the sunny months in Seattle, but this year was unusually hot and dry. The city had even declared a drought. Still, the Sylvan busy season hummed along, and the tourists joked about "where's the rain." Wedding guests also lined up, as the Sylvan was a go-to for Emerald City nuptials and honeymooners.

"Checking in?"

Brad and Kathryn sweated it out in front, and Joann sweated it out in PBX. One tired fan was doing its best, but the smell of cooking is what blew in. Saucy essences were on the lam! Clinging to breezes, they drifted from the restaurant, circled through the courtyard, then made their way through the window.

Smash! The matches were taking forever. *Six* VIP parties, *four* honeymoons—

Beep! The switchboard was also on a tear.

Incoming call. Room 408 was all wound up.

"Ma'am, I can't—please—can you slow down?"

"Put. Your. Manager. On. Now."

Walking out to the desk, Joann whispered to Brad that he was needed on the phone. She had no idea if he was actually scheduled as a manager that night, but whatever.

Without blinking, Brad finished his check-in and directed Joann to transfer the call.

Turning around to pull keys for a check-in, Kathryn scrunched up her face with a what's-wrong expression. Joann shrugged her shoulders and ran back to the switchboard.

The Sylvan Hotel

•

A minute later, Brad asked her to assist out in front, saying something about a steamy emergency.

"Kathryn! What happened?"

"The cleaners ruined a mother-of-the-bride dress. They were supposed to press it and ended up pressing out all the pleats."

"So ... *Brad's* gonna fix it?"

"Yeah! He radioed Kiet to meet him in the hall outside 408 for a garment-steamer hand-off. I guess he's gonna perform pleat surgery whilst schmoozing the upset mama."

"Is there anything Brad can't do?" asked Joann.

"I know! I couldn't steam anything back into anything!"

Slam! The valet phone was taking the brunt of something.

Joann listened in at the ledge.

"What the fuck," griped Todd. "How the hell are we supposed to deal with cars in this mess?"

In the circle, important-looking headsets talked to other important-looking headsets, and water hoses lay strewn about under mechanical contraptions on stands.

Joann closed the big window.

"What's the deal with all *that*?" she asked Kathryn.

"Some movie crew's filming a scene and hogging the driveway with rain machines. I guess they have to, well, 'make it rain.'"

"How's that gonna work with valets and cars?"

"Well, the hotel's making money off of it, so you know how that goes. Hollywood's our VIP, tonight."

Across the lobby, a man in a baseball cap picked up the house phone. Wait, was that ... Tom Hanks was in the house! The movie star stood in plain sight, but under his hat and out of context, he was just another guest.

Mr. Hanks finished his call, then returned to the circle.

"Kathryn, what movie is it?"

"I have no idea."

"I just saw Tom Hanks talking on the house phone!"

"Yeah, I think Meg Ryan is here, too."

"No *way*!"

A new line of check-ins formed, and the switchboard started up again. Joann rushed back to PBX and answered calls non-stop for twenty minutes.

Click. The combination lock turned in the back-office door. Captain Front Desk had completed his mission! He proceeded to reception, and Joann proceeded with minibar billing. She glared at the clipboard. Brad never had to deal with the detestable chore, but he handled angry guests—and runaway pleats—so a silent understanding excused him. They really were supposed to take turns, but everyone bent the rules from time to time. So Brad was exempt from booze balances, Kathryn took toll-free calls, the concierge smoked weed in the garage, two valets parked desk-agent cars, Room Service was always up to something … and Housekeeping was battling everything.

Joann's misdemeanor of choice was using the main entrance, but Mr. Alexander didn't seem to mind. Besides, that guy broke rules, too—like using her for free nanny service. Sometimes, she watched his kid for an hour or more on shift. Ha! At the Sylvan, baby-sitting was the price for front-door privileges.

If only she could get out of minibar math, too.

Brad pushed back through the swinging door.

"Meg Ryan's on set right now, just outside the restaurant!"

"Can I go see? Please? I'll only be a second!"

"Sure!"

Joann exited the back office, crossed the lobby, then turned into the far hall. Pushing through a side door, she found kitchen staff and cocktail servers on cigarette breaks, sitting by a tall wooden gate.

Unfazed by the Hollywood hullabaloo, they were content to watch Joann do the jumping.

"Well?" asked a server.

"I saw Meg's braid!!! Do you guys know what movie this is?"

"Probably a rom-com. Because … Tom Hanks and Meg Ryan, right?"

One more jump, then it was back to the lobby.

"Is Brad still in PBX?"

"Nope. He's up in 408 again," said Kathryn.

"What? Why? Hang on—I'm coming around …"

Click. Joann entered the combination and unlocked the back-office door.

Beep! Five calls needed answering, then she joined Kathryn at the desk.

"What the hell happened with 408? I thought Brad saved the pleats!"

"Oh, we're way past pleats."

"Huh?"

"So, there's a guest staying here under the name of Art Deco, and Art Deco is one of the guys in KISS."

"The band?"

"Yeah, and Art Deco got busy with some groupie girl last night who left him a note thanking him for 'the great sex.'"

"What does that have to do with 408?"

"Well, someone put Art Deco's note in the wrong message box."

"Whose message—oh, no … the lady in 408 got it?"

"But that's not all. The lady in 408 had a husband named Art who *recently passed away*, and now she thinks someone in the wedding party is playing a mean prank. That's why Brad's upstairs again. He steamed the dress, but now he's trying to explain the … uh, steamy message."

Joann looked at Kathryn. Kathryn looked at Joann. You could not make this shit up.

"Just another night in the ol' motel."

"Yeah," laughed Kathryn. "Oh, and did you see Meg?"

"Only the back of her hair," said Joann.

"I wonder what the movie is."

They opened the big window and watched a dramatic downpour.

Robert-to-Todd.

Todd-to-Bryce.

Housekeeping-to-Concierge.

Concierge-to-Housekeeping.

The walkie-talkies kept shouting, so Joann returned to PBX and turned them down.

"Robert to Base."

And … volume back up.

"This is Base. Go ahead, Robert."

"Base, just checking in to make sure you're staying on top of the situation back there."

"Base to Valet. We've got it covered. You have yourself a good time in the fake rain."

"Ten-forty. Over," he chuckled.

Splat. More water hit the PBX panes. Lights. Camera. Shower. Who would have thought: Pretend rain in Seattle! The window cleared, and

Joann took another look. Out by the circle, she saw an annoyed and drenched Bryce skirting the middle.

Click.

Two other valets cut through the back office, then into the PBX passageway.

"Hey, Jo," Robert smiled.

"Margaret," Todd nodded.

"You guys are soaked!"

Pushing through the swinging door, Kathryn almost crashed into Todd.

"Easy there." The valet steadied her, but now it looked like *he* might fall over.

"Ahem. Okay, we need Housekeeping!" Joann grabbed a radio. "Base to Lynn! Will you please bring some towels to reception?"

"On it—just give me a minute."

"Thank you!"

"It's too crowded in here!" Miss Emerson returned to the desk with Mister Barnes.

"How are you, Jo?" Mister Bailey stepped into PBX with Miss MacIntosh.

Robert leaned against the doorway, wet hair falling in oh-so-earnest eyes. There went her stomach. Again. How *did* he do that, just by entering a room? Eeek—a very small room.

So much for "taking space." She'd been trying to avoid him for a couple weeks, finding reasons to leave the desk when he was in proximity—and walking to Kay's most nights with Kathryn. The hotel had also been busy, so she'd managed to pull it off ... until now.

"I'm good, Mister Valet. How are you?"

"Aw, it's a crap night out there. I wish they'd take their cameras and leave."

"Yeah, it does look kinda miserable."

"Anything with your job stuff? Did Arlene let you edit some PR?"

Arlene was the Sylvan's PR "department" and something of a local celebrity. Bubbling with super-human enthusiasm, she'd set a new gold standard for the art of creating buzz. Arlene was the best a smaller hotel could hope for—and one of their favorite grown-ups. The tiny maven had a huge heart, and she'd recently given Joann a shot at some writing projects.

"Yeah, she did. So I can cite that as experience, but I'm still figuring out how to put together a portfolio of—"

The Sylvan Hotel

◆

"Did somebody call for towels?" Lynn stepped through the back office and into the PBX passage. "I brought—*oh*. Hello, Robert. Did you get caught in some movie rain, or what?"

"Lynnie!"

Raising his arms, Robert pretended he was going to hug her, wet jacket and all. She ducked and tossed him a towel.

"Thanks, Lynn," giggled Joann.

"You know me ... here to make sure your—er, *our* valets are taken care of."

Robert laughed, and heat coursed through Joann's face.

The walkie-talkies started to whine. "Concierge to valets, please report to the circle."

"Valet to Concierge. We're on our way." Robert zipped his jacket. "Now, Jo, I'll be back to check on you later. And please don't make more than two personal phone calls while I'm gone."

She threw a pen at him, but he dodged it with a jubilant grin.

"Bailey, wait up—" Todd pushed back through from reception.

Joann answered another call, then joined Kathryn at the desk, followed by Lynn. Brazenly seating herself on the ledge, the housekeeper pulled at the big window and peeked around it.

"Joaaanna, look at all the waaater!"

But the boys were crossing the lobby, and Miss MacIntosh couldn't take her eyes off Mister Bailey.

Gawd. She needed to get *past* this.

"Helloooo," whispered the housekeeper. "I'm guessing we should hit Kay's tonight?"

"Yeah. I'm kinda—well, it's been a weird night."

"Sure, Joann. 'Cause it's a weird night. Truth: You are sprung on that boy."

"Well, it doesn't matter 'cause he's not available. I just can't seem to get that through my damn mind."

"Are you *sure* he's not available? Because he's looking like he is."

No, Joann reminded herself. Robert was an especially nice guy in a world overrun with not-so-nice guys, so his actions could easily be read the wrong way—or imagined the wrong way. His interest in her was *friendship*. Pure and simple.

Lynn hopped off the ledge. "Kiet probably thinks I abandoned him. See ya at eleven!"

Joann hopped onto the ledge, and Kathryn finished a guest registration. Then she took a seat at the window as well.

"That about does it for check-ins. And Brad's in the cafeteria taking a break. He calmed down the 408 lady, so the Art Deco case is closed."

"Sheesh. What would we do without Brad? Oh, and Lynn's up for drinks."

Joann re-latched the big window. It was definitely a Kay's night. Otherwise, the whole world would be asleep, and she'd be lying awake, thinking about that boy ... and never-ever counting sheep.

She'd be sleepless in Seattle.

EVERYTHING'S COMING UP ROSES

The Sylvan was oversold. Joann and Kathryn *dreaded* nights like this. You'd have to review the check-in list with Alicia or Leena, then come to a decision about who to "walk." Walking a guest meant sending someone with a reservation to another hotel. Alicia would put rooms on hold at bigger properties, and once an unlucky party arrived, they'd find themselves right back out the door. Then the Town Car would deliver them elsewhere. In return for their trouble, the Sylvan would cover room, tax, and, depending on how important the person was—or how much they bitched—maybe even dinner.

The key was in guessing who was less likely to throw a fit. Business travelers were generally a safe bet. They didn't care where they slept, as long as the alternate accommodations were on par with what they'd reserved at the Sylvan. That said, you weren't supposed to mess with reservations made by your very best clients. The same went for honeymoons, birthdays, and anniversaries. Those parties had specifically selected the Sylvan for its atmosphere or a special significance. Transferring them to hotels like the Sheraton—even for free—was not going to fly.

Walking guests was risky business. Even with a free room (or without a special occasion), many people did not find a sudden change of plans to be acceptable. So you had to buck up, brace yourself for the yelling, get through the interaction fast, emphasize how it would all be on the house, and assure them that everything would be fine.

Joann and Kathryn reviewed the updated check-in list. Four names were highlighted in pink, which meant four walks.

"I'll take the first two," Kathryn shrugged. "I want to get my share of the yelling over with."

"Fine with me. I've gotta get mentally prepared," replied Joann.

Alicia appeared with a list of hotels that knew to expect the Sylvan castoffs and instructions on which guests were to be sent where.

"Sorry, team. But you can do it! You're the bees' knees! Order some dessert on me tonight …"

Joann loved how their boss trusted them to do their jobs. If only they didn't have to oversell! But that's how it worked throughout the industry. Unfortunately, the swing shift had to deal with the worst of it, because they handled the majority of the check-ins—but it still beat excruciatingly early morning shifts with managers underfoot all day.

Tick-tock, four o'clock!

Swish. Three valets pushed past the stair door, ready to report for duty. Robert immediately looked toward the desk, grinning at Joann. The swing shift had some minuses, but it did have its pluses. Golden hour indeed, she giggled to herself.

Robert struck his superhero pose, and those giggles turned to laughter as he stopped right in Todd's path.

"Bailey. *Dude.* Come *on.*"

The car-parking crew continued to the circle, and Matt waved to the girls.

"Did Matt Heulin just manage to crack a smile?" Kathryn looked at Joann in disbelief.

"Yeah, and last week, he cracked a *joke*. Then he came right up to the desk to ask if I wanted to try this weird drink. It looked like it had tadpoles in it. I grossed out, and he thought it was sooo hilarious. I was like, who are *you*, and what did you do with Mister Badass?"

Joining them out front again, Alicia uncapped a green highlighter.

"One more thing: We've got some important new business coming through tonight, and I want to make sure that they do *not* get walked, under any circumstances. Microsoft has contracted an Ogilvy & Mather team out of Los Angeles that will be staying here regularly." She began to draw green lines. "This guy, right here, is a VIP. He's the head of the group."

Ogilvy & Mather?!? It was too good to be true! Joann had started to consider a copywriting career after reading *Ogilvy on Advertising*. She studied the check-in list. Mr. Conner Mann was the VIP, and there were six green lines beneath him. Lizzy, Josh, Nancy, Eileen, Mike, and Ted. Maybe she could make some contacts and catch a break!

Smash!

Conner Mann.

She triple- and quadruple-checked the matchbox lettering. Would he be friendly? Snooty? How often would they be staying at the Sylvan? Could she *really* "network" on the job? What was appropriate? Would she even *have* a chance to talk to any of them?

The Sylvan Hotel

♦

"What do you mean, you're oversold?"

Joann peered through the PBX door.

"I am so sorry about that, sir," Kathryn said in her walk voice. "I don't know how this happened, but ..."

"Base to Valet."

"Go ahead, Margaret," Todd responded.

"Valet, first walk is here. Please pull the car around."

Static.

They hated walks, too. Whoever was driving tonight would have the joy of listening to four different parties lamenting about the gross injustice, all the way to a destination not-of-their-choice.

"Ten-forty, Base. Ready when you guys are," Robert's voice crackled.

"Base to Valet, thank you."

"No, Base. Thank *you*."

Well, if there was one person who could find any fun in this, it was Robert.

Joann pushed through the swinging door as the guest began to lecture Kathryn.

"Young lady, you need to tell your superiors ... not a good way to conduct business ... my travel manager ... going to hear about this ... I can't believe ... oh, dinner is free, too?"

"Yes, sir ... the valet is ready to take you ..."

One down. Three to go. Jed walked that baggage right out the door, and Robert pulled right in with the Town Car.

Kathryn took a sip of her ice water. "Well, that could have been worse. One more for me, then it's your turn, Jo!"

"Okay. I'm almost done with matches, and the other stuff isn't looking too bad, so we should be in good shape."

⇌ ♦ ⇋

Seven o'clock. In the lounge, a jazz singer was heating things up with an Édith Piaf improvisation. At the desk, Kathryn was getting through her next walk, and in PBX, Joann was getting tired of minibar billing. She finally traded places with her friend—then moments later, Jed rolled through the doors with a beleaguered bell cart.

"Joann, this is the Ogilvy & Mather party."

They were here! Kathryn returned to the front to help, and six O&M associates pulled out IDs. Then registration ... pleasantries ... keys ... restaurant information ... and ... where was the VIP?

As if reading her mind, Lizzy announced that "Mr. Mann will be arriving in a few minutes."

Gathering outside the lounge, the ad execs strategized a dinner plan. Heading to the elevator, Jed pushed on with their luggage and winked at the desk agents. Mister Concierge looked exceptionally pleased, so the O&M team had obviously been generous. Hopefully, they'd be willing to provide career tips, too.

Kathryn went back to the phones, and Joann waited for Mr. Mann.

Opening the big window, Todd called to her from the valet booth.

"Yo. Margaret. Is Kathryn in PBX?"

"Yeah. Also, we've got two walks to go—just fyi."

"Ten-four. Thanks, Margaret. Oh, and one more Ogilvy dude just got here."

Swish. The front doors opened, and a sharply dressed executive appeared—maybe in his late thirties? Regardless, the guy moved like top brass—or another kind of captain, looking right and left as if to locate the gold. Then the marble desk was in his crosshairs.

Flying through the lobby, Todd carefully maneuvered around and past him.

"Good evening." Mister Expensive Suit was extremely stylish; mostly sharkish.

"Good evening. How may I help you?" Joann tried to sound professional with just enough "perky."

"I'm Conner Mann. And you are ... Joann?" he asked, examining her name tag.

Do not sound like a bimbo. Do not sound like a bimbo. Do not sound like a bimbo.

"Yes. Welcome to the Sylvan, Mr. Mann."

"Hello, Joann. Call me Conner."

Swish. Robert and Matt sailed through the front door and parked themselves behind the concierge stand, listening as Joann checked him in.

"Here's your key, and I'll have Jed bring up the bags for you. Just dial extension two for room service or four if I can help you with anything else. Would you like a wake-up call—"

"Cooonnner!" Eileen and Nancy waved from the lobby. "Come have a driiink …"

Quickly moving to join him, they flattered, flirted, and fawned.

"Joann, what do you suggest I try for dinner? Ladies, this is Joann."

The Mann minions froze, then …

"Come ooon, Conner. Driiinks!"

"Well, Joann? Dinner suggestion?"

Swish. An uninterested Matt exited the scene. Robert wasn't going anywhere, and two pairs of O&M eyes aimed daggers at Joann.

"You know, I love the crab cakes that our restaurant makes. A must-try."

"Okay. Crab cakes it is, then. Thank you." Mr. Mann retreated, escorted by his companions.

Hopefully, she'd sounded assertive enough. Good grief. *I love the crab cakes. It's a must-try.* If only her father could hear her now.

Many of Joann's childhood dinners had come from beaches in Edmonds, a bit north of Seattle. Her mom would supervise clam digging just below the train tracks while her dad hit the shallows with a three-tipped rake and a patched, pink bucket.

White shirt. Red cap. A man half-above and half-below. Joann would watch from rocky kelp beds as the water got too close to the top of his waders. He'd sift and scoop, capturing Dungeness crab, red rock crab, and every so often, a golf ball or two.

At the house, Jack would hose off his catch in the yard. Then he'd clean up the gear, and Joann would keep an eye on the doomed creatures, following along as they clawed their way through one last shore expedition. Those fiery pinchers had grasped, pushed, and pulled so hard, only to end up in hot water.

"Who are those guys?" Robert neared the desk.

"Ogilvy & Mather, an LA team for Microsoft stuff. That was the boss. He seemed cool. Maybe he can give me some advice about breaking into copywriting!"

"Yeah. Maybe." Frowning, the valet moved closer to her side.

Why was his face saying something different? What was wrong?

Ding.

"What's goin' on, you two?" Jed rolled a now-empty bell cart off the elevator.

Robert slid a pen behind his ear.

"I've been monitoring Joann's personal phone calls. *Someone's* got to keep her in line."

Joann shooed them away. Five more check-ins, two of which were walks. Time to get this over with.

Beep! Kathryn got the switchboard under control, then Todd was dragging the other PBX chair across the floor. When he could, Mister Barnes still spent his breaks alongside Miss Emerson, discussing life in the windows between calls.

Joann missed the slow season, and *her* "window shifts" with Robert. But even on busier nights, she felt happy and safe when he was there. Somehow, that boy made it all better, all the time—and she was beginning to wonder how she'd ever get along without him.

The combination lock clicked in the back-office door. Shortly after, Todd walked around the corner. Nodding at Joann, he continued through the lobby.

Was Todd feeling the same way about Kathryn? Had he really fallen for her? Or *was* she just a challenge? Had he reached the point of no return? Or *did* he just get confused from time to time? Joann wished she had the guts to talk to the guy. But guts or no guts, that would never actually happen. Kathryn was her best friend, and—just like the boys with their bro code—she couldn't violate girl code.

8:00 p.m.

Mr. Mann returned to the desk.

"Thank you again for the dinner suggestion. May I put in an order for a wake-up call?"

"Of course." She noted his request.

"So, Joann. What's your story? How long have you been here at the Sylvan?"

This was her chance!

"Almost a year. I'm hoping to get into copywriting, so the hotel job pays the bills while I work on putting a portfolio together."

"Is that right? Hmm. We should talk. Perhaps next time you'll join me for crab cakes."

No. Way. Mister Big Shot was inviting her to dinner? Maybe she'd actually make some career progress! Except, there was a rule about fraternizing. But this wouldn't count, would it? It was just … crab cakes!?!

"Thank you. I'd love to. I just don't think they'd allow me to sit in the lounge with a guest."

"Who is 'they?'" Mr. Mann loosened his tie.

"Oh, you know: management."

"Well, don't you worry about that. The next time I'm here, I'll get you all cleared, and we'll enjoy some dinner. What time are you off?"

Holy shit.

"Not 'til eleven."

"See if you can make it 10:30, and it's a date."

"Okay, sounds like a plan!"

Mr. Mann stepped into the elevator, and Joann stepped into PBX. She had news!

"That's *amazing*, Jo."

"I'm so excited! I can't wait to hear what he has to say! Uh … I hope Alicia and Babs are okay with me eating in the lounge."

"It sounds like they won't have a choice." Kathryn giggled.

"Valet to Base! We've got the Perisich party checking in."

And … walk time.

Whatever. She would not let a couple cranky guests spoil the night. Things were *happening*!

9:00 p.m.

An extra-annoyed Kathryn called to Joann from PBX.

"Someone just fucking cancelled, and we're gonna be left with an empty room because we already walked all the walk people."

"So much for our 'perfect sell.'"

"Yikes. Babs is gonna be mad. We're charging them for the last-minute change, but she was reeeally set on a perfectly full house."

"Valet to Base. We've got a romance package checking in—name is Gannon."

Kathryn put down her pen.

"Hang on. I thought all the special-occasion parties were checked in."

Uh, oh. Joann returned to the front and checked the computer. No Gannon party listed anywhere. What to do? These people thought they had a reservation—and for a special occasion, no less. This was going to be ugly without some quick thinking.

"Kath! I'll round up the amenities, and you check 'em in. We'll use the room from the cancellation. Just stall them as long as possible. Now, what goes in a romance package?"

Kathryn read from the brochure.

"'Champagne delivered to your room, rose petals on the bed, yada yada, chocolates.' Okay, tell Finn to get the champagne and candy up there, ASAP. We can skip the matches, but what about the flowers?"

"George is MOD! I'll ask him to unlock the florist office."

The Gannons were through the front doors. Kathryn took her post out front, and Joann dialed Finn. Then she dialed the bar.

"George! Manager-on-duty emergency! We've got a romance package arriving *right now* with no notice, and we need rose petals. Help!"

"On it, Jo. What room?"

"402!"

"Okay, I'll check the florist fridge, then meet you up there!"

She dialed Jed next. He would need to slooowly escort the guests through the hotel in order for this to work.

"Yes?" asked the concierge.

"Jed, please stall this check-in as long as possible. There's no record or reservation, and we're trying to get all the amenities upstairs."

"Okaaay." Predictably, he prickled at the request.

Joann ignored him and hung up. It wasn't like any of them had planned this. She snagged a radio, then a 402 key, and ... Kathryn greeted the Gannons.

Sprint through back office. Casually fast-walk to elevator. Jeezus. The swing shift was a never-ending mess of surprises.

Ding.

For once, the elevator wasn't delayed. Thank god. She wouldn't have to run up the stairs in heels.

Second floor. Third floor. Fourth floor. And there was George, just in from the stairs, and rushing at her with a plastic bag in hand.

"You got 'em?" Joann whisper-shrieked.

"Yeah! The last one!" George whisper-shrieked back. "Hurry up. Open the effing door!"

Giggling, Joann nearly dropped the key.

Her friend cautiously stepped in.

"So ... whatta we do?"

"Oh my *god*, George! Throw them on the damn bed!" Joann swiped at the petals and almost fell over.

"Jaaayzus Christ. Give me those."

George pulled back the duvet. He swept his hand over the sheets, and Joann let the giggles fly as a pack of fleurs flew.

"Base to ... Base." Kathryn's voice scratched through the airwaves and gritted teeth. "Is. It. Ready."

"George, hurry up!"

"Hold on! You gotta do this right!" He raced to the other side.

Talk about pure comedy. Joann spun giddily as bursts of pink and red rained down in the honeyed lamplight.

"Base to Front Desk, please send them up."

Joann threw a last handful of roses at her friend, and they exited 402 in tears. She couldn't remember when she'd laughed so hard.

Ding.

Finn bolted out of the elevator.

"What the hell is going on around here?"

"No reservation ... Kathryn ... stalling ..."

Ding.

"Shit, here they come!" Joann was in stitches.

"Get *out* of here, you guys. Go!" Now Finn was whisper-shrieking.

Running for the stairs, his teammates cackled their way back to the lobby.

And ... *swish*!

"Well, I'm glad someone is having fun around here," Kathryn crossed her arms.

"Oh, my god, Kath. You should've seen George with the flinging. Skills, I tell you!"

"All right, you two. Miss MacIntosh, *back* to the switchboard! And George, *back* to the bar!"

"Up top, Joann!" The MOD high-fived the flower girl.

Then she returned to PBX, where "perfect sell" was now written on the calendar.

10:00 p.m.

Internal call, Housekeeping.

"Joaaanna, it's almost that time. You going to Kay's tonight?"

"Yeah! Let's meet in the cafeteria."

"Ten-four."

Out in front, the lobby had settled, and things were—hopefully—back on track. Kathryn was changing bills for Todd, Matt had left, Jed was signing off, and Robert was tidying up the valet booth.

Swish. Room Service pushed through the stair door.

"Yo. Front Desk. Any more surprises I should know about?"

"Sorry, Finn! I swear, the romance-package people just showed up without a reservation. We don't know if they ever really had one, or what—but thanks for getting the champagne and stuff up there."

"Okay, but you need to work on your rose-petal technique."

Three, two, one ... *evil giggle.*

"Wanna join us for Kay's, tonight?"

"Nope, Zoo Tavern for me. Later, dudes." And Thorn Birds was outta there.

"Todd, you up for Kay's?" asked Joann.

"Nope, Off Ramp. Kathryn, you goin' with Margaret?"

"Yeah, I'm waiting for her, but I'll walk downstairs with you. Jo, see ya in the cafeteria when you're done!"

Robert incoming. "Well, Joann. Looks like it's you and me."

Oh, lord.

She watched him run a hand through his hair. The valet wore it somewhere between long and short but struggled to keep a wild strand at bay. It was always falling by the end of their shifts.

What it would be like to push back that hair; to kiss that adorable smile; to—

"Walk you to your car?"

"No thanks. It's a Kay's night. I'll be okay with Lynnie and Kath."

Did he seem disappointed?

The Sylvan Hotel

Well, come with us!

But why bother asking. They both knew the answer.

"All right, be good now. I'll see you tomorrow."

"*You* be good! And yeah—see you tomorrow."

The valet laughed and headed for the locker room.

Stopping by the bar on her way out, Joann thanked George again for his help.

"No problem! What a night, huh? It's all comin' up roses, baby!"

Downstairs, she caught a flash of a navy jacket. Robert was almost through the alley door—then he paused for just a second.

Then Joann paused, but her heart skipped.

Hold me close, and hold me fast, the magic spell you—

What *was* this spell he cast?

In the locker room, her face flushed in the mirror.

La vie en rose, whispered her soul.

PLANES, TRAINS, AND AUTOMOBILES

Two mallards paddled in circles, doing their best to splash off the heat—then dove for cooler depths. Right above them, two MacIntosh kids lay soaking up the duck days of summer, stretched across towels on a Stan Sayres dock. Three hours from now, Joann would be in nylons and a uniform, but *right* now, it was bikini-hour on team sun-worship. Seattle rays were shining brightly, and …

Her thoughts drifted. It was kind of nice to be away from hotel world. Maybe she should take a vacation. There were enough desk agents on staff at the moment, so covering her shifts would be easy. Yeah, a trip to Oʻahu might just be the ticket—and she could stay with Uncle Domingo. Maybe he'd let her borrow the truck! She could drive around the island … hit the beach … read books … get tan—no work, no lists, and no boys.

"Wanna go to Hawaiʻi?" she asked her sister.

"I gotta get back to Pullman. Semester is starting …"

"Right. Okay, WSU chick. Well, looks like I'm goin' solo!"

Wait—that would be almost two weeks without Kathryn, Lynn, George, or Robert.

Oh, don't be a baby, she thought. Besides, when had she ever taken a trip alone? It was time—and it would be healthy to be away from it all. To be away from him. She was tired of the confusion, tired of feeling she was past it, then getting sucked back in.

"Let's go," Sarah yawned. "You got work, and I gotta pack."

"Awww. I don't wanna. It's so nice out here!"

Lake Washington rippled with light, and the dock softly swayed. Motor boats buzzed, and an eagle chased a seaplane. Somewhere, dogs were barking. In the distance, cars zoomed along I-90, east to west, west to east. Woozy from the heat, Joann watched the steady stream of ant-sized autos flying across the floating bridge. Three. Four. Five. Six. Like tiny cartridges of time, speedily creeping by. A passing sailboat broke the trance, and the siblings stepped into flip-flops. Then … back across the dock, out through a sizzling parking lot, and over the grassy bank.

The Sylvan Hotel
◆

Just up the street, their father puttered in a hot driveway where ragged onion rows wafted at the border—his idea of landscaping. Opposite the onion garden, an aging rowboat rested against a wall of Roman brick, and at the front of the house, calla lilies and dahlias skirmished for space under dusty picture windows.

Whiiiiiiiiiiiine! The newer sound of jet skis pierced the air, and Joann's eyes moved to the skiff, "docked" inside the garage.

Would *they* ever get out on the water again? How long had it been since Jack had gone to Linc's Fishing Tackle for licenses? She couldn't remember the last time any of them had cast for trout or pulled lines out for salmon. But her dad was older now. Hauling boats had become less appealing ... and change was in the air.

In summers past, Jack had always been determined to nab his limit on the daily. So, for MacIntosh kids, school vacation meant fishing—and 3:00 a.m. "wake-up calls" from the top of the basement stairs! Each of the kids (as well as their mother) would take turns joining him to increase the total allowance. His daughter shook her head, remembering the fishing rotations. Then she grimaced, remembering his fear about the Native Americans "getting it all" before anyone else had a chance.

One year, a very young Joann had looked through living-room windows toward Stan Sayres and spotted something magical: Torch lights punctured the darkness, and swaths of gillnets opened midair, as if to chase stars before falling. Indigenous communities had been making a big catch, days before the fishing season opened. The tribes had been granted "permission" as a truly honorable judge had restored their treaty rights—and some of this had played out right at the end of her street! Okay, well, at that time it had been a dirt road, but nevertheless, why hadn't the family walked over to watch? Instead, her father had paced inside the house, agonizing about how "there's gonna be nothing left." But ... hadn't it all been taken from the First Peoples to begin with? How had he forgotten?

Years later, a UW professor untangled it for her. Fired up at his podium, the poly-sci preacher had beseeched his Kane Hall congregation: "Take note: There always has to be an enemy to keep people divided, because keeping people divided keeps them powerless. How do you create an enemy? By demonizing difference."

Miss MacIntosh had never been good with equations, but in this case, things were adding up. And clearing up: like in third grade when she'd put on her first pair of glasses. Why hadn't her *dad* been able to see what was happening? He was a teacher. He taught math! And history. Where was the logic?

Eventually, she found some answers in another story.

From an early age, Jack had spent many years scraping for scraps: scraps of a father he couldn't remember and scraps he barely survived on. The Depression had been the worst of it. Starving, he and his brothers would lick cream off the top of milk deliveries on neighboring Madrona porches. Then the famished boy grew into a scared man. To this day, he seemed worried about someone taking something away—and the angry news shows weren't helping. Jack seemed to be getting … lost, bit-by-bit-by-bit. Joann thought of the cold mornings she'd watched him walk off to work when he was still teaching close to home. Daddy would vanish into the fog, but for a few seconds, his black hat and long black umbrella remained visible—and she'd hold on with her eyes until he totally disappeared.

"Now, where did I put that wrench …"

Joann turned down her father's transistor radio as he rummaged through an aging toolbox. Hopefully, his *kids* could be a different kind of influence.

Jack pointed to his bottle of sunscreen.

"You two need to be careful—or you're gonna burn up out there," he warned.

Then he pretended to tickle Sarah's face with his grease-covered hand. The youngest MacIntosh girl ran off and around to the backyard, sassing him about "minding his own business."

Joann watched them in disbelief. A *lot* of things were changing.

Having completed his checklist, her dad grunted an approval and told her to "get going."

"Yeah, I don't want to miss out on my free dinner!"

Well, not really. But she knew her father would like hearing that they—

"They give you a free dinner?"

Her father was all about free. Joann had no memory of him wasting a drop of anything, nor had he squandered a good deal or what was there for the taking. When they hadn't been fishing, clamming, crabbing, or oystering, Jack would turn the car east through Cascade passes for even more foraging. Three hours later, they'd arrive in Wenatchee, a real homesteading town on the other side of the mountains. Then it was down another dusty road to a farmhouse shaded by walnut trees—and where their Uncle Leo's orchards awaited! Commercial pickers always left fruit behind, and her dad had always been first to follow. Meanwhile, Joann's mother and Auntie Gloria would work late into the night, preserving all of those harvests. In that sweltering country kitchen, everything from cherries and pears to peaches to plums was cooked and canned. Even watermelon rinds were made into pickles and tomatoes turned into jam. Then other months brought other harvests, like deer, duck, and pheasant. So Jack would be off to Eastern Washington again, on the hunt for weekend adventure with all their boy cousins.

In town, her father had hunted for bargains—one of the best being the day-old-loaf deals at Gai's Bakery. He'd put a dime in each child's hand, then line 'em up to ensure they caught their bread limits, too. With cars, it was catch and release. Jack had frequented auctions: scoring, fixing, selling; scoring, fixing, selling. A weary classified-ads operator would jot down the terms, called in from a black rotary phone. Cash only! Eight-hundred-or-best-offer!

The memories kept pushing forth, and the sun pushed down harder as Joann turned her eyes to the street. Just across 43rd, Genesee Park was a dry panorama of light browns, pale golds, and a few die-hard greens. A gravel trail meandered through the grassy vista, and at the far end, patches of brambles formed thorny walls. Leafy trees also stood tall at the edge, listless in the afternoon hours. Waves of warm air shimmied, and in between, childhood reappeared, then disappeared.

Genesee Park *was* her childhood. Jump over the logs, and run, run, run …

Pensive geese, giant ponds, water bugs, and speckled eggs. Red wagon. Orange frisbee. Blue kite. Cartwheels. Johnny-Appleseed cousins and daisy crowns … flower girls and flower power. He loves me. He loves me not. He loves me.

Genesee Park was also the seasons. Marshy fields. Icy fields. Dewy fields. Parched fields. Best of all, Genesee Park was blackberry summers. Long green canes bending with fruit; straw hats … white pails … Then running through the sprinkler—and red-purple preserves sweetly simmering by nightfall.

Slam! Jack secured the hood of her car and slowly headed for the garage. He barely ever said goodbye. It used to bug her, but now she saw something different. He hated goodbyes.

Joann climbed into the Jetta. "See ya, Dad!"

He didn't reply, but raised both arms in the Jack MacIntosh version of a wave, his long white sleeves torn and stained, unbuttoned and falling like tattered wings.

⇒ ♦ ⇐

Click. The back-office door opened. Who would that be? All the valets were in the circle.

"Joann?" a little voice called.

Oh, no. Nicky Alexander was on the loose. Mr. Alexander's eight-year-old son had been spending even more time at the hotel and was turning into their very own "Eloise." Running into PBX, he shoved himself between Joann and the switchboard.

"Lemme answer one! Please? Lemme do it!"

"Nicky, you know what your father said. No answering the phones. If you're going to be here, you have to sit at one of the big desks in back, and you can't touch anything!"

Then that look that said, *I'll-pester-you-forever-unless—*

"Two calls, kid." She stood as the beeping started.

Quickly taking a seat, Nicky held tightly to the receiver. "Good ... evening. Uh, the Sylvan."

His feet swung in the chair, and—

"Joann, what's the number for the restaurant?"

"Hit the 'transfer' button—"

And ... disconnected.

"Okay, now pay attention: hit transfer, then ..."

Nicky gave up on the switchboard, but there was much more fun to be had. The boy ran to his father's office, retrieved a toy train, then returned to the office behind PBX. *Clickety-clack, clickety-clack, clickety-clack.* The desks had become train tracks.

This was going to be a long night.

"Valet to Base."

Nicky darted into PBX and grabbed the radio.

"Go ahead, Valet."

"Uh ... Base?"

The Sylvan Hotel

◆

Joann grabbed the radio from Nicky.

"Go ahead, Valet. Sorry 'bout that."

"Hey, Jo, can you look up the room number for Mr. Martin?"

"Sure, one sec ... Okay, it's 302."

"Thanks, Base."

"No problem, Robert."

"*Oh*, is Robert outside?" Dropping his train, Nicky was out the door.

"Base to Valet."

"Go ahead, Base."

"Small dude, incoming."

"Ah, jeez. Okay, thanks, Base."

"Good luck, Valet."

"Ten-forty."

Joann peeked through the PBX window. Nicky had located Robert and was tailing him like a puppy in the circle. Then he pounced into the Town Car, eager for a ride-along. *Uh oh.* Give the boy an inch, and he'd drive with you for two miles.

Twenty minutes later, Nicky was done with the circle (more like Jed had told Robert to kick him out). Returning to PBX, he unleashed a stapler on some paper. *Ca-clunk. Ca-clunk. Ca-clunk*—

Joann routed fifteen calls, then reached her limit.

"Nicky, let's find your dad. Come on, it's almost time to go. I'm sure he's wondering where you are."

That probably *wasn't* the case—but it was too busy, and Joann couldn't watch an eight-year-old, run the switchboard, and help in front all at the same time.

She guided Nicky into the hall, where they found Mr. Alexander locking up his office.

"Young man, I've been looking for you!"

Yeah, right.

"Joann, I've got to check on one more thing. Can he stay back there—?"

"Sure, Mr. Alexander." The desk agent and her charge returned to PBX.

And ... switchboard beeping.

And ... people lining up out front.

Joann routed eight calls, then joined Kathryn at the desk to assist. Nicky followed and paced behind them. Two visitors looked at him curiously, and Joann explained that the youngest "team member" was the manager's son.

"Oh … yes … what a cutie …"

The newly arrived guests tottered away with Jed, and the cutie began to play with the credit-card machine.

An exhausted Kathryn retreated to PBX. She dealt with classrooms full of kids all day and had hit her limit.

"Nicky, you need to stop messing with that." Joann tried her best to be firm.

"What? I'm not doing anything."

"Yes, you are. I've asked you to stop. One, two, three …"

But that didn't work with Junior.

Joann moved the credit-card machine, and Nicky slapped her on the arm. "Whoa!"

Robert was at the big window—and wasn't having it. Marching out of the valet booth, he pushed through the front doors, crossed the lobby, then into the back office and past PBX.

"Nicky, come with me. Right now," he instructed, calmly but firmly.

Busted. Junior sheepishly followed Robert to the valet booth.

"You do not ever hit Joann. Is that understood? You do exactly what she tells you to do, and you do not lay a hand on her. *Ever.* Got it?"

The poor kid looked shell-shocked. But it was fair. You couldn't just run around smacking people. Jeezus, thought Joann. Life at the Sylvan: practice parenting between parking cars.

Swish. Mr. Alexander, incoming.

"Where's my kid?"

"With Robert."

"He should not be in the circle!"

No shit, Sherlock.

Swish. Mr. Alexander, outgoing.

"I swear to god, why can I never find …"

Miss Emerson incoming—and once again in search of the elusive red pen. Then muttering to herself about a lack of proper office supplies, she returned to PBX.

Beep!

"Front Desk—how may I help you?"

"Jo. It's Danny."

"Well, hello!"

"Hey. I got in yesterday. Was hoping to come by your hotel to see you."

"*Oh!* Okay, yeah! And maybe I can clock out early …"

Joann's stomach jumped through time. Danny was another alumnus of the nearby boys school. They'd met sophomore year, and by senior year, they were dancing at prom—but it had never quite happened for them. Danny had been a rising star in the drama department and a refreshingly cynical, funny *and* cute guy who, by junior year, was Joann's true-blue ally. They should have been more, but Joann had been too scared to lose the best thing in her life. His "dating" history had been the topic of a lot of gossip, and she didn't want to become another casualty. High school's leading man had reportedly caused several off-stage scenes with his leading actresses *and* a fervent female following. He'd sworn the stories *were* gossip, but Joann hadn't been sure. What if she and Danny took things further than friendship and he vanished? So the not-a-couple couple had gone on to college and to date other people. However, Joann had agreed to "marry him at 40 and adopt a bunch of kids" if, at that age, they found themselves unattached.

"So what's with Danny?" Kathryn asked. "Is he here? Is he coming by? Oh man, and Robert's on, too."

"Okay, can we just change the subject?"

"Housekeeping to Base." Lynn's voice danced across the airwaves.

Kathryn grinned. *Don't tell her,* Joann pleaded with her eyes. Merrily objecting with her own eyes, Kathryn picked up a radio.

"Housekeeping, could you please call me at zero?" and she returned to PBX.

Swish. Kiet was through the stair door.

Without uttering a word, the housekeeper crossed the lobby and placed a handful of turndown chocolates on the marble countertop. Next stop? The valet booth where, hopefully, he'd keep Robert occupied.

8:00 p.m.

Joann was sitting on the ledge at the big window. It was closed, but the outlines of navy jackets were visible from the other side. All at once, they stood. Then the hotel doors opened, and there was Danny.

"Hey, Jo."

Navy jackets now hovered at the concierge stand. Who was *this* interloper?

"Wanna hang out after work?" Danny smiled with confidence, despite the audience to his left.

This was so weird. High school was colliding with the hotel.

Danny was waiting. The valets were waiting.

"Hey! Yeah, sure! Uh, so … my friends and I usually hit Kay's after work! Wanna go?"

"Well, why don't we get some food first and catch up? I haven't seen you in a while."

He was looking at her like … but … she wasn't feeling like …

Maybe she just needed a moment. It had been some time, but maybe now it was *their* time. Maybe it wasn't supposed to work with Grady—or Robert—because she *was* supposed to be with Danny.

Kathryn pushed through the PBX door.

"Danny, this is my friend Kathryn. And guys, this is Danny, an old friend from high school."

Nice-to-meet-yous were exchanged, and Kathryn propped herself on the window ledge, not wanting to miss out on tonight's episode of *All My Sylvans*.

"Kath, I'm gonna leave early if that's okay—then meet everyone at Kay's after."

Ding.

Lynn strolled through the elevator doors.

"Hey, Lynn, this is Danny."

"Hi, Danny! Nice to meet you!"

Lynn leaned on the concierge stand and looked at Robert, while Robert looked at some papers.

"So, Dan, I can clock out at ten, and I've got my car here. Maybe swing back around then?"

"Sounds good. See ya at ten!"

Joann and Kathryn retreated to PBX, and Lynn beelined through the lobby to the back hallway.

Click. The combination lock turned, and she joined them by the switchboard.

"Lynnie, don't even—"

"Joanna! Driving *all* the boys crazy."

The Sylvan Hotel

•

Having clearly just smoked something, the housekeeper was highly amused. She ducked, expecting a smack, and just about knocked both radios off the counter.

"Would you cut it out? He's just a friend."

"A hot friend," Kathryn replied.

"Dude, Robert's looking a little rattled out there," Lynn added.

Beep! Incoming call from the valet booth.

"I think it's for you," giggled Kathryn.

Joann shushed her and took the receiver.

"Operator."

"Hey, Jo—got a hot date tonight?"

"Robert, just because I'm meeting Danny after—"

"Joaaaaaaaaaaaan!"

"No, it's not like that. I mean … well—"

"JoAAAAAAAAAAAAAAAAAAAAN!"

"Oh, my god! Just forget it."

She disconnected the call, then turned to her friends, both of whom were now giggling.

"Listen up, goofballs: I'm leaving at ten, and I'll see you at Kay's."

"Oh, we'll be there, don't you worry about that," teased Lynn. "Hahaha. Now this is—"

"Yeah, yeah, I know. Pure comedy."

"Jo?" Robert called to her from the front.

"Someone *is* rattled," whispered Lynn. She ran out of PBX before anyone could swat her for real, and Miss MacIntosh pushed through the swinging door.

"So, are you going to be at Kay's tonight?" Robert started counting out his bills.

"Yeah, I'm grabbing dinner with Danny first, then we'll head back over."

"Okay, I'll see you there."

What. The.

How many nights had she practically developed a neck cramp, looking across the bar, hoping that maybe, just maybe, he'd walk through the door. And now she had a date. And now he was going.

Frannie James

10:00 p.m.

Joann clocked out, then it was back up the stairs, past the circle, and into the arms of her old partner in crime.

Okay. *Focus.* Wait—why did she need to "focus?" What was going on with her?

There was a time when being with Danny had been everything. They'd been high-school soulmates, clicking together like two puzzle pieces in the middle of a bigger puzzle: family issues, friend issues, hopes, dreams, and what it was all supposed to be about.

The south-enders had been introduced at a basketball game their sophomore year. After an awkward tolo date, they'd reconnected the following year amid a teenage sea of drama and rebellion. He'd performed in all the plays, and she'd worked backstage, happily waiting in the wings. Offstage—and in between girl problems and math problems—Joann had helped him learn his lines. She could still see them, sitting in the golden-green Genesee meadows, Camelot scripts in hand:

If ever he would leave her, it wouldn't be in summer …

Joann had taken care of Danny, and he'd taken care of her, especially during a junior year filled with turbulence. Parents shouting; threatening. Siblings baffled by her inability to "just go along with things." Evisceration; isolation. At times, it had felt like the hurt was going to push Joann right out of her body. Danny had kept her sane, and he'd probably kept her alive—although … Joann had also learned a new way to survive. She'd figured out how to turn part of herself off—to flip a switch in her mind. It was like that part went somewhere else for a while. Somewhere far below the surface; somewhere safe in icy depths; somewhere safe beneath a ship in flames. Somewhere she could pack away the pain.

Joann had packed her bags a couple times, too. She'd never forget that twin-sized mattress almost bending off the porch, thrown out by an enraged Jack MacIntosh—along with the contents of her bedroom. Minutes later, Danny had pulled into the driveway. For the youngest of nine in a Catholic family, that type of situation hadn't been anything new. He'd looked at Jack with casual bravery, then looked at Joann.

Let's go.

The Sylvan Hotel

•

The boy had been Lancelot on stage—and in real life. Luckily, Lancelot's parents had been traveling that summer, so Joann moved in with him at the house in Columbia City. Then the new roomies went to work while waiting out her father's temper. Danny spent long hours welding for his brother's business and frosting fluffy cakes at Borracchini's, while Joann covered shifts at Columbia Library nearby. Jack did, eventually, cool off, and Joann returned home. But she and Danny began to spend even more time together.

Throughout senior year, the pair teamed up for parties, Metro League games, and dances, always circling back to one another. Best of all, Friday nights had been *their* nights. Like clockwork, they'd commiserate over candlelight at B&O Espresso, off Broadway. Then, before they knew it, prom season arrived. Both were set on "boycotting the bullshit," but Danny eventually hinted, and Joann asked him to hers. So in May of 1986, they were dancing at the Space Needle, where Joann had been over the city *and* over the moon. During one slow song, her friend had protectively pulled on her strapless dress, securing it gently, proudly—and like they'd always been together. Like they belonged together. Still, she'd remained hesitant about taking things further. She didn't want to lose her best friend.

But why hesitate now? Come on! He was the reason you lived through high school!

They decided on Piecora's and cozied up like old times, surrounded by a comfortable collage of green walls, posters, vinyl booths, and red- and white-checkered tablecloths. It was such a warm, familiar space—but drafts were getting antsy under high ceilings.

Danny began to describe an interesting class he'd taken at his fancy East Coast college, but Joann found her mind wandering and sneaked a look at her watch. *Shit.* They were all at Kay's. *Robert* was at Kay's!

"So … ya having fun with all the hotel homies?" Danny smirked.

Although she was right next to him, Joann suddenly felt as if she'd floated far away. At one point in time, they would have giggled in cahoots at the world outside of themselves. But she belonged to another world now—a world he was … laughing at? Her face burned. He didn't even know the Sylvans, and she *was* a Sylvan. For the first time, it felt like … he wasn't seeing her.

Oh, get over yourself, and give the guy a break. You're probably just tired—and are you really seeing **him**? *He's been away for a while and had lots of experiences that didn't involve you, yet here he is. Where's your damn loyalty—*

"Jo, I'm kinda tired. Can we … can I just crash at your place?"

Oh, boooy. She had not been expecting that. Ugh. He'd been her best friend *and* the boy responsible for all those high-school butterflies—but she just wasn't feeling it. They were the same *and* different.

At the apartment, Joann sat on her twin bed, back against the wall. Across the room, Danny sat on the sofa.

"Jo, why don't you come over here with me?"

"Um … Danny, I think I'm going to go meet my friends. They're waiting, and—"

"Yeah, okay."

Welp, she knew that tone. Danny had been her hero, but he could also be sort of temperamental, which sometimes put her on edge. She'd always managed to tiptoe around that stuff—and the spark between them had always managed to outshine anything else. But it had gone dark.

Joann fought the urge to cross the room and wrap her arms around her friend. She still loved him, and hopefully, he still loved her enough to maybe, one day, understand. She looked at Danny once more, then looked away. It was time to go.

Five, six … down the front stairs. Into the car. Nineteenth to Madison!

Ten minutes later, Miss MacIntosh threw open the glass door and waited for her eyes to adjust. Kathryn. Lynnie. George. Kiet. Finn and Stan had made it, too.

The smoke cleared. These were her people, now—her partners on the path to wherever. And tonight, they had the bar to themselves.

Gulp. There was Robert.

And *he* was looking for *her*. The valet crossed the room, his face lighting up.

"Now, Jo, I just wanna make sure you weren't doing anything out there that I wouldn't do."

Putting his arm around Joann, Robert guided her to the table.

Lynn quickly chimed in.

"Where's yer friend?"

"Yeah, where's Danny?" added Kathryn.

"I left him crashed out on my sofa."

"What did you do to him?" Lynn snickered.

With a mischievous giggle, Robert pulled out a chair for *his* friend.

Joann tried not to stare. He was faith and goodness in flannel, a Hendrix T-shirt, and jeans.

He was … home.

The splash of an oar on a still morning.

A rush of river water.

Wood smoke and flame; freshly hewn fir.

Sunday tides.

Moonlit evergreens.

Okaaay. This had to stop. She didn't want it to stop, but she would make it stop.

Miss MacIntosh turned toward Mister Bailey.

"I think I'm gonna take a trip—Hawai'i. I need to be away for a while."

"Well, if your soul's asking for a break, you should do it." Now serious, he looked at his drink.

"Yeah." She looked at her drink.

"Hey, so, a guy walks into a bar," shouted George.

Despite a tableful of boos, he continued with the joke. In the corner, a woeful jukebox continued to croon about a boy who would give his heart gladly and a girl who has no clue.

A girl who just can't see and who keeps walking toward the sea.

Lynn's eyebrows arched.

"Who put this song in?"

"Yo, Bailey!" Finn shouted. "Dude, 501 saw one of you guys peeling around the corner in his Jag and bitched *me* out about it. Fucking go easy on the guest cars, man."

He tried to sound authoritative, but the evil giggle had already returned.

"I dunno what you're talking about," Robert shouted back.

"501 should just be happy he didn't get boogers on his steering wheel," announced Joann.

Now the table was shouting.

"Ewwwwww!"

Frannie James

◆

"Bailey, what the—!" George stood up, hands-on-hips, in mock disgust.

Stan rolled his eyes, Kathryn rolled *her* eyes, and Lynnie choked on her ice.

But Frank Sinatra was tuned in, and he was all for staying young at heart.

Sliding her elbow over to nudge Robert's, Joann shyly looked down as Old Blue Eyes ramped up. If she should survive to a hundred and five, she'd be so grateful for all of these moments—these moments of being alive.

THERE'S NO PLACE
LIKE HOME

Joann finished packing the blue Eddie Bauer duffle bag. Then she changed into a white tank top over a dark plaid mini-skirt and a light chambray shirt on top of that, the ends tied at her waist. Stepping into sandals, she looked in the mirror. Tropical too-cool-for-school!

The flight was scheduled to arrive into Seattle at 10:00 p.m. With no delays, she could get through baggage claim, call for a ride, and get in a quick visit with her parents. Then she'd hop in her own car and hopefully meet Kathryn and Lynn at Kay's.

It was day twelve of her Hawaiian hiatus. For almost two weeks, Miss MacIntosh had done nothing but bury herself in beaches, books, long walks, and long drives. There'd been a dinner or two with Uncle Domingo, but he was barely ever home, working night and day at the family autobody shop. He was also tired a lot of the time. His wife had died young, and without Auntie Maria, it was like the whole house had fallen into a deep sleep. Things just grew quieter and quieter—and you never really knew what to talk about, or what was okay to talk about. Joann and Domingo had done their best, but for the most part, she'd been on her own. Then her youngest brother decided to fly out for a quick break, and …

Volume up! They hit the road with Soundgarden, driving from Mililani to the North Shore, and farther. Windows down and wind in their hair, they'd sung about Jesus Christ poses, Jesus Christ arms, and Jesus Christ crowns. Tee hee. A '90s rosary, thought Joann. The Seattle sound had, in fact, looped with them all over the island. However, any thoughts of the Pacific Northwest faded as red-dirt fields, pineapple, sugar cane, turquoise waters, and velvety green mountains whizzed by. After Thomas left, Joann had been solo once more, but it was one of the best trips she'd ever taken.

—◆—

A trade wind skimmed sheer curtains, and red-crested cardinals sang through an open window. Breathing deeply, Joann inhaled fragrances of banana, orchid, mango, and plumeria. O'ahu was other-worldly, but now she needed to get *back*. She no longer wanted to be away.

Check in. Board. Cruising altitude. Baggage claim. Quarters. And … payphone!

"Kath! I'm at the airport!"

"Oh, my gosh, we've missed you! Welcome home! Can we go to Kay's tonight?"

"Yeah! Dad's picking me up, then I'm gonna say hi to Mom and get my car. I'll see you right after!"

—◆—

The Ford Taurus exited north from Sea-Tac onto I-5, and Joann described the trip to her father. He was gruff as ever but relieved that she'd returned. He, too, appreciated Hawai'i, but Joann's father was a Seattle boy, through-and-through. He also preferred his kids to be within spitting distance—and, of course, he saw no need for "the spending."

"There's so much you haven't seen in your own backyard."

As a family, they'd done *some* traveling, starting with a U.S. station-wagon tour when Joann was eleven. School was out, and they were off. It had been a red-blooded, red-upholstered American odyssey. Sunny Delight … bologna sandwiches … creepy motels … kitschy souvenirs … giant redwoods … pink canyons … green pastures … gold horizons … Kodak faces … Dear Uncle John … postcard places … Dear Grandma.

Hawai'i had come next. In the late '70s, Wardair Canada whisked the MacIntosh kids out of Vancouver B.C. to the island of O'ahu. They were hooked for life, but Jack would join in less and less. He'd done his fair share of travel to the islands and clocked "plenty" of U.S. travel in the army. Jack had also checked off Europe through a university program and again on honeymoon—so he'd pretty much retired the ol' suitcase. Now, watching the junior MacIntoshes make annual or even bi-annual visits to Hawai'i gave him a headache, as he found it frivolous.

There's plenty to do at home!

During Joann's childhood, "entertainment" had been Seward Park, Genesee Park, Stan Sayres, Madrona Beach, Coulon Beach, Renton Park, and watching Jack fly fish the Cedar River. He'd also taken them to parish bingo nights and high-school basketball games at his alma mater.

The Seattle Public Library and the (free) Frye Art Museum made the list as well, and eateries like Royal Fork, Burgermaster, The Old Spaghetti Factory, and IHOP had been *special* treats. Occasionally, the kids scored birthday invites to Farrell's or Pizza and Pipes—or bus rides downtown with Grandma for ice cream at Woolworth's. Then in September, the family would head to Puyallup for the state fair: Games! Goldfish prizes! Hatching chicks! Fisher scones!

During those years, the MacIntosh crew also dove into swimming lessons (and free lunches!) at the Rainier Beach community pool. Later in the afternoon, dips at Madrona Beach were followed by Lawrence Welk, Star Trek, and dinner at Grandma's. Road trips had ruled the warmer months, too. In addition to the Wenatchee excursions, Joann's family had harvested the rocky shores of Hood Canal, Scenic Beach, Potlatch, and Long Beach. On a Bremerton beach, they'd watched a cousin scuba dive, exploring constellations shining below. He'd surface with sea stars, borrowed from shy clusters of red, violet, and tangerine. Back in the day, that was exciting stuff.

"Joann, you need to be calm. There are places to explore right here in—"

"But, Dad, there's a lot to see out *there*, too. I can't wait 'til I'm old. You never know—"

They pulled into the driveway.

"Aloha, Mommy!"

Joann hugged Bernadette and recapped all things Hawai'i. Then she handed over boxes of macadamia-nut chocolates while Jack excitedly lugged a case of pineapple from the car. The gift was an Uncle Domingo tradition, as he and Bernadette had grown up on a Del Monte plantation. Located on O'ahu, Kunia Village had been their first home-away-from-home after leaving the Philippines. The siblings had immigrated to the U.S. as children, then labored as migrant workers alongside their parents. Years later, Bernadette enrolled in nursing school and said goodbye to those fields forever, but amazingly, she still loved the taste of Hawai'i's famous fruit. As grownups, the Kunia kids now lived very separate lives, but Domingo always sent his *sister's* kids packing with an extra-sweet supply of what still connected her to Hawai'i—and to him.

"Honey, you just got here." Bernadette inspected the juicy haul. "Why don't you rest—?"

"Mom, I miss my friends sooo much. I haven't seen them in twelve days. They're all at work tonight, and everyone's off soon, so we're gonna meet up at Kay's."

"Stay outta the joints!" her dad shouted.

He chopped up a pineapple and slurped it over the kitchen sink. Then on to the freezer where a stockpile of "just-sixty-eight-cents-on-sale" pizzas awaited pillaging. No need to call Pagliacci in this house.

"Oh, Dad. Kay's isn't 'mafia' like it was in your day."

"You're just looking for trouble hanging out all hours of the night in those places. You need to be calm. Be calm, Joann. *Be calm.*"

"Daddy! It's not like I'm there by myself. *Kathryn* goes, too."

Harumpf. Her father loaded up the oven with his Totino's extravaganza, now piled high with a fruity golden topping. Then he turned for the living room and turned on the news. Both parents highly approved of Kathryn, so just the mention of her name could neutralize a situation. Joann's best friend was pragmatic, polite, *and* becoming a teacher. She'd even taken shop in high school, attended their university, and her first job had been working the desk for a car mechanic.

They understood that Kathryn wasn't religious, but miraculously, Miss Emerson had cred.

"Goodnight, parents!"

Joann drove north on Lake Washington Boulevard. Overhead, the trees looked startled in the headlights, their darkened leaves turning a lighter green. On her right, a glassy, shadowy portal overflowed with the past: Rainbow trout. Sockeye salmon. Bundled-up mornings in 3:00 a.m. air. Net. Oars. Poles. Letting the lines out: "Sixty pulls!" The sun rising as they rowed back. Baked fish. Fried fish. Grilled fish. Smoked fish. Salt-and-brown-sugar summers gone by.

Whoosh. She moved forward through her childhood route. Time to move forward with life. Twelve days off had given her new energy and new motivation. Being away had helped her get past the Robert stuff, too. Clearly, it had all been in her head. Clearly, he was a nice guy who'd been kind to her after the break-up with Grady. Clearly, she'd been vulnerable.

Their shared and similar school history had also created an imagined "familiarity."

Yikes, and Danny. It was no surprise that he'd been disgusted with her behavior.

Her friend had made a special effort to see her, only to be ditched while she chased a mirage. Realistically, though, leaving him on his own was the better plan that night, regardless of whether Robert was waiting. Besides, she hadn't felt comfortable in a studio apartment with someone who was very in the "mood," when she was not.

Sadly, Danny had left early the next morning, and there hadn't been a word since. Hopefully, he could forgive her. Joann would always love him, but things had changed—and they were still changing.

Yes. This was more like it. Head-on-straight. And maybe she could try to date someone *outside* the Sylvan. Meeting new people could be good. She just needed to figure out how. But there was more to life than boys—like getting serious about her career, for starters. She would keep going with cover letters and ad concepts. She'd also be more aggressive during Mr. Mann's next stay. But tonight ... it was time to be with friends!

She wondered about Kathryn. Maybe there'd been an update on Scott? Joann just didn't know how much to push her bestie to talk. For the most part, Miss Emerson seemed very in control and quite sure of herself, but once in a while, Joann could swear she saw something ... Even so, that something, if it even existed, was buttoned up tight—and there was no point in risking the wrong question—or their friendship.

Boren Avenue! Left on Madison! Almost there!

Eleven thirty-five—and the smoky stench of home.

"Look who's here!" Kathryn and Lynn spotted her first.

"Welcome back, dood!" Tory exclaimed.

"Nice tan." Finn was already giggling.

Kiet waved, and Brad nodded her way, engrossed in conversation with Sam and Jed.

"Hey, Joann!" Bill smiled and began his hike to the jukebox.

"*Jo.*"

She turned around.

"Well, hello, Mister Bailey!"

The valet looked stunned. And stoked. And ... mysteriously overwhelmed.

"I was *just* saying a few hours ago, 'If Jo got on a plane right now, she'd be here in time to make it to Kay's.' Then Kathryn said you *were* on a plane and that you *would* be here! Wow! When ... when did you get in?"

What was ... his eyes ...

Be calm, Joann. Be calm.

"I got in at ten and called Kathryn from the airport. The trip was fantastic, but I was ready to um ... well ... anyway, hi! How *are* you?"

And just like that, his arms were around her.

Somewhere, the moon was shining on golden sands, but Joann MacIntosh was in another paradise. Cigarette smoke swirled. Patsy Cline ... Frank Sinatra ... checking in ... Valet to Base.

Please don't let go—

"Excuse me, kids," said Kay.

The boy let go, and the girl sat down slowly, worried that she might lose her footing.

A sudden weakness gripped her at the core, and she tried to focus, pretending to be listening to George. Or Lynn—

"You okay?" Kathryn whispered.

"I ... uh ..."

"You need a drink!" Kathryn motioned to their favorite waitress. "Kay, can we please get a Kahlúa with ice over here?"

"Sure thing, hon. Comin' right up."

Be calm, Joann. Be calm.

"How was Hawai'i?" Kathryn pushed at her under the table. "Lots of fun at the beach?"

"Yeah. Uh, I drove ... all around the island. North Shore, Sunset, Waimea ..."

He was sitting so close *and* too far away. Dammit! Where was all the control she'd had just minutes ago? Twelve days of talking sense to herself was out the window in seconds.

And that *hug*. That was not—no. She would not get sucked back into this. Not again.

"Oh, look. Here's your drink. *Drink it.*" Kathryn pushed a cold glass in front of her.

The Sylvan Hotel

•

Syrupy ice cubes sweetly clinked and separated. Fighting a flood of heat, Joann took a sip. Then she reached under the table for her bag.

"Lynn, I got a T-shirt for you—Kathryn, you, too."

"Wait, where's mine?" Robert inspected the tote.

Rummaging around, he found a skirt and put it on like a hat. Miss MacIntosh grabbed her camera. Time for a Kay's candid, and just enough film. She snapped away, and the valet smiled victoriously, his arms outstretched in a (jeezus christ!) pose.

"So, Joann—how does that tropical lipstick not get all over your glass?" he teased.

How is it not all over you, right now.

"Magic, Mister Bailey. Pure … magic."

Robert and Kathryn laughed, and Joann excused herself to the restroom.

Okay. Breathe. Perhaps it was time to leave the Sylvan. There were other hotels; other front desks. And distance had been good. It had worked in Hawaiʻi—or at least she'd thought it had. *Ugh.* Maybe a more permanent distance was what needed to happen.

Leaning into the mirror, Joann inhaled and exhaled, fogging up the already-blurry glass.

The problem was, she could no longer see herself without him. It was like she was breathing through him. Hell, she was breathing through *all* of them.

"Hey, Joann." Lynnie pushed through the bathroom door.

"Hey! It's really great to be back!" Joann hugged her friend. "Uh, I'm just … uh …"

"Yeah, I know."

"God, Lynn. I had twelve days away. *Twelve days* to … to forget …"

"Joann, it doesn't work like that. You're not just going to—" she took a drag. "I dunno what to tell you. Someone out there can't make up his mind, and you're caught right in the middle. It's not your imagination. Come on. No point in hiding."

"Last call, kids." Kay made the rounds, and they closed down the bar.

At 2:00 a.m., the Sylvans filed into the street: some off to late-night meals; some off to retrieve stuff out of hotel lockers—and everyone else to cars and cabs.

"So … 3:00 p.m. tomorrow?" Robert knew the answer, but he asked anyway.

"Yeah, I'll be there." Joann knew that he knew, but she answered anyway.

"Come on, Bailey, let's boogie," said George.

"You good to walk to your car?" Mister Bailey wasn't budging.

"It's okay. Kath and Lynn are going with me, and we're not parked on side streets."

"*Bailey*. Let's go!"

"All right, now. Be safe."

The Sylvan trio walked toward Kathryn's car, which was parked the closest.

"Well, it's not Hawai'i, but we're glad you're back, Jo."

Miss Emerson breathed in the marine air as it rose up from the waterfront. She always said that in the late-night hours, the smell of Puget Sound made her feel more at home.

Miss MacIntosh breathed out. She was back in the Northwest but surprisingly warm, even as trade-wind memories were fading.

Kathryn unlocked the Volkswagen, and the girls climbed in.

"Fuck." The teacher frowned. "We don't have any cake."

"Ha! So … what's *up*, you two? Anything exciting happen while I was away?"

"Not much. The Gipsy Kings played in the lounge with Frank, Nicky's still terrorizing everyone—as you heard—Lancôme meetings are picking up, Mr. Mann was asking about you …"

3:00 a.m.

Someone was knocking on the car window.

"Yo! You gals okay?"

"Georgie!" The housekeeper smiled, lighting a cigarette.

"Goddammit, Lynn. I don't want that smell in my car. GROSS!"

"Okay, okay. Take it *easy*, Kathryn. Uh, lemme just step out of my office for a second."

"Hey, I'm thinkin' Thirteen Coins for Eggs Benedict!"

Kathryn declined.

"I need sleep, but maybe … Jo?"

"Yeah, George, sounds good!"

"Kathryn, I'm with you. I need sleep, too." Lynn put out her smoke and climbed back in.

Up Madison, left on Boren ... and 3:15 a.m. at the 'Coins! Thirteen Coins was a 60's throwback and another time machine. Somewhere between west-coast retro and east-coast classic, the restaurant was like a posher cousin of Kay's. Open 24 hours, the late-night hotspot was moody but bright, and radiated a different kind of insider vibe—like a cigar club ... but one with no rules.

A sleepy hostess led the Sylvans along a windowed wall of booths that stretched to the ceiling. Vestiges of an era gone by, the tall, dark-brown Naugahyde cocoons had been witness to many secrets and stories whispered over hash browns, toast, sandwiches, and antipasti. Owls carved into wood kept watch from above, and on the tables, a mix of monies from different countries shined beneath clear resin like treasure through a looking glass. Across from the booths, a row of high-backed captain's chairs swiveled at a long counter fronting an open kitchen. Grilling, flipping, and frying, an army of chefs shouted their way through orders while blue flames crept back and forth.

"You're in for some good grub, sister. Eggs Benedict is famous in these parts!"

"*Yum.*" Joann closed her menu. "Now tell me what's goin' on with *you!*"

The conversation turned to George's ex-girlfriend. Joann so appreciated his openness—and it was interesting to hear a nice guy's side of the story. Listening intently, she tried to support him the same way he'd always supported her. Aw, and George was so not over his ex. It sounded like the ex wasn't over him, either. But for some reason, they couldn't make it work.

Love was complicated.

Or maybe people just *made* it complicated.

Or growing up made it complicated.

"What about you, Jo? I saw that hug. What's goin' on with you and Bailey?"

"I was gone for twelve days. I thought I'd put all that out of my mind—"

"He ain't outta your mind, and you sure as hell ain't outta his!"

"Yeah, well. I'm mad at myself. The guy walks into a room, and I just …"
"Oh, boooy." George laughed. "You'll figure this out. It's all good."

Tick-tock.

Joann's head hit the pillow. She was floating along the Nile, past pyramids, sunrises, owls, and tropical isles. But not forgetting all the while … not forgetting home sweet home.

GRUNGE CITY

September marked one year at the Sylvan. So much had changed. And so much had stayed the same …

"Hi, Front Desk!" Finn pushed a loaded cart across the lobby. "Hey, I'm thinkin' about a run to Tai Tung later. You want in?"

"Sure," Joann nodded excitedly. "My parents used to go there! It's got vintage cobwebs!"

"Yeah, but their potstickers rule. I'm bringin' back a *grocery-bag* full."

"Yay!"

"Just remember that the next time you holler at me about picking up matchboxes."

Room Service rolled onto the elevator, giggling as the gold doors closed around him.

The big window was closing as well and would likely stay that way. The car-parking crew had *boy* business to catch up on. Bryce was there tonight with Robert and Bill. Todd and Matt too, as they'd started earlier and still had an hour to go. Everyone was in the house! A rare occasion, as of late, because Bryce was down to two shifts a month … because Bryce's business was booming! All that hard work was paying off, and the ad man no longer needed Sylvan tip dollars. At this point, staying on the roster was probably old habit and a chance to see friends—before he was totally buried with clients.

Laughter filled the valet booth, along with loud opinions on Bill Clinton, George H.W. Bush, and basketball. Then things quieted, and Robert was talking—most likely about Tricia.

Joann moved away from the window. Two shifts ago, the valet's girlfriend had called from a Manhattan payphone in tears. She'd recently moved there for medical school, and life was upside down.

Joann had visited the Big Apple once with Grady and remembered feeling very small—and very trapped. Looking down any street, all she could see was an endless hallway of skyscrapers.

Such a busy, congested, dog-eat-dog place. And Tricia was there all alone.

"Joann! Can you ... Robert ... can you get Robert ... please—"

"Don't cry, Tricia. Just ... hang on ... he's right here."

Later, Joann had asked her friend if everything was okay, but he'd just mumbled about an "adjustment." Since then, she and the valet had barely spoken—although that was probably a good thing for everyone. Maybe Tricia leaving had finally helped end any previous confusion.

Guilt. Sadness. Shame. It was a chilly night, but Joann was boiling over. How stupid could she be? She'd simply crossed paths with Robert at a time when he'd been figuring out whatever needed figuring out. And if something *had* happened between them, well, it was over. Fact: Robert and Tricia were a couple. Fact: Robert and Joann were colleagues.

"Hello, Joann." Bill picked up his check-in list and *The Wall Street Journal*. "All mine?"

"Hey, Bill. Yes, all yours."

"And can I—"

She opened the drawer and handed him the Marlboros.

"Thanks!"

He left three dollars on the marble counter and headed to the circle.

"Joann, Kelly will be shadowing you tonight." Alicia pushed through from PBX with her latest hire in tow.

The Sylvan's newest desk agent grinned from ear to ear. Kelly had earned a degree in hospitality management and was eager to put that knowledge to use. The girl was also seeking a fresh start, having declared herself "done with the sorority thing." Kelly was looking for something different.

Kelly, like Tory, was mainly working morning shifts, but Alicia wanted her to try evenings for a little while. It was good to have agents who could cross over as needed, especially with Kathryn having started the school year.

"What's with the lists and newspapers?" Kelly asked.

"We print check-in lists for Housekeeping, the restaurant, the concierge, and the valets. It helps them have an idea what to expect, to track progress as we get through the shift."

"And the newspapers?"

"They're for the valets. *Seattle Times* for Robert—*Wall Street Journal* for Bill."

"Aren't *you* nice."

Joann laughed.

"We help them out—they help us out. Keeps things running smoothly around here."

"Hello, Joann." Captain Advertising was checking in.

"Hi, Conner! How are you?"

"Fine, thanks. Hey, so, I haven't seen you—"

"I was in Hawai'i for a while. I must have been off the last time you were here …"

"Well, I've got a late conference call tonight, but I'm available afterward. Can you meet around 10:45? We could get an order of those crab cakes."

"Okay! The night auditor is usually early, so that should—oh, but, um … I've gotta get permission."

"Right. Well, let me talk to your supervisor."

Joann pushed through the swinging door to the back office.

"Alicia? Mr. Mann is out front. He wants to speak to a manager about letting me join him for a drink after my shift."

Alicia's eyebrows were begging to differ.

"–About *career* stuff! He said we could meet in the lounge and talk about working in advertising."

Alicia went to confer with Mr. Mann and was agreeable to Joann sitting in the lounge after the VIP very politely made the request—although it sounded more like a command. Bottom line: Nobody said "no" to him.

Ding.

Mr. Mann waved from the elevator.

"What was *that*?" demanded a wide-eyed Kelly.

"Well, we got to chatting one night when he first started staying here, and I told him that I'm interested in advertising. So he said we should talk and that he'd like to get to know me better—"

"I'll bet he wants to get to know you better. I bet he—"

"Stop, Kelly! You're embarrassing me. That's not how it is."

"What's so embarrassing?"

Bill crossed the lobby. At the desk, he stared at Joann and twirled a pen. Around, and around, and around.

The other desk agent made a coughing sound which quickly turned into laughter.

"Nothing, Bill. Kelly's just being her hilarious self."

"Okay, then. Um, Joann, have you eaten dinner yet?"

"Yeah. You going to the cafeteria?"

"Yep. Wish me luck!"

Swish.

Kelly was cough-laughing again.

"It's like the Joann fan club around here tonight."

"Whatever, Kell. As if you don't have your own fans."

Swish. Jed incoming. Then Ken and Khloe Wolf followed. Joann attempted a hello, and they promptly ignored her. So she threw Kelly to all of the wolves, as the girl seemed more than capable of fending for herself.

Studying the PBX calendars, Miss MacIntosh breathed out. Not as many red Xs—which meant the "sold-out" nights were dwindling. What a relief. Summer had been crazy, and they were all looking forward to the slow-down.

"Are you going to be okay with Mr. Mann?" Alicia stood in the doorway.

"Yeah, Allie. No worries. It's all on the up-and-up. I *swear*."

How lucky to have such a good boss. These days, Alicia almost seemed like a big sister!

"I trust your judgment but wanted to make sure—"

"I know—I totally appreciate it! Thank you."

9:00 p.m.

It was quiet time at the Sylvan Hotel. Jed was in the bar visiting with George, and Kelly had clocked out.

Joann leaned on the marble desk. A few feet ahead, an East Indian gentleman leaned against Honduran Mahogany.

"Can I help …" but she stopped herself.

The guest's eyes were locked on the hotel entrance, as if he was being extra-vigilant—or

waiting for a chance to escape! Such an intense energy—and curiously covert underneath that cool hat and long, dark hair. Well, it *did* seem like he didn't want to be noticed. So … probably best to leave him alone. Wait—did the dude just need a taxi? Yellow Cab wasn't always reliable. Maybe she should offer to call Farwest …

The Sylvan Hotel

◆

The gentleman's eyes remained fixed on the entrance, and a couple minutes later, he moved toward it. Just then, Jed emerged from the bar. *Look out, Mystery Man.* But, alas—hunted down! The concierge excitedly greeted him. Mister Someone was polite, then quickly left.

"Do you know who that *was*?" Jed exclaimed. "Kim Thayil, Soundgarden!"

Well, that outshined your average night on the job!

Joann loved Soundgarden. Thundering but melodic, feral but poetic, dark but uplifting, and rich in texture. Like a museum painting of a soul screaming—one of those colossal pieces that could stop you in your tracks. A rendering so vivid that it transported you right into the belly of the beast, as if a portal or window had opened. And in the middle of it all, Chris Cornell's unyielding vocal cords conquered primal highs and lows, the scales no match to his might.

Brawny. Wounded. Unbending. Ornate. Soundgarden was a rock phenomenon and her favorite of the "grunge" music she'd been learning about.

She was also learning that grunge had been a game-changer—and, these days, you never knew who'd pop up at the Sylvan. Because *Seattle* was starting to pop. The city was reportedly churning out bands—or maybe they were just getting noticed. Either way, Seattle was on the map and catching the eyes of music and entertainment types. One of the hotel managers had also dated a guy in the biz ... "Geffen" someone. So apparently, word was getting around. Everyone was checking out the town—and checking into the hotel.

There were obviously other accommodations in the city, but Joann figured the musicians liked the Sylvan for the same reasons she did. The European motif was artful and the place had way more character than a corporate hotel. It was also well located, just outside the downtown core: close, but not too close. And of course, the dark corners and low-lit lobby spaces made it easier to fly under the radar.

Swish. The stair door opened—and an off-duty desk agent strode through in bootcut jeans over a black bodysuit.

"Kelly! What are you still doing here?"

"I got to talking with one of the cocktail servers in the locker room and thought I'd check up on you since it's almost eleven!"

"I'm waiting for Mr. Mann—he should be down soon. Are you ... going out?"

"Yeah! Come with me, sista. We're young, single, and we should be having *fun*. I can wait in the back office while you have your drink with the Ogilvy dude, then let's go! And I don't mean Bud Lights. I wanna dance!"

Pulling some lipstick out of a pocket, Kelly bolded up her lips in brownish-red.

Then she tightened a pair of gold earrings and released long, amber curls from a scrunchie.

Joann grinned. Why the hell not? Lynnie was off tonight, and it was a school night for Kathryn …maybe …

"You know what? You're on."

"Woot! Time for something new!"

Ding.

Mr. Mann stepped out of the elevator, and Kelly disappeared down the hall.

"You ready?" he asked.

Be calm, Joann. Be calm.

"Give me five minutes!"

Ollie pushed through the swinging door.

"Good evening, Mr. Mann. How are you?"

"Just fine, sir. Just fine. Joann has permission to join me in the lounge, so we'll get out of your hair."

Ollie tried to pretend that he hadn't been caught off guard.

"Oh, uh … Enjoy!"

"Thank you. We shall." Curtly smiling, Mister VIP was off to hail a cocktail server.

The night auditor swerved, his Sylvan spidey senses taking full account.

"Joann, what is—"

"It's okay, Ollie, Alicia cleared it."

"Are you sure about this?"

"Yes! I'm trying to get advice about getting into advertising!"

But Ollie wasn't buying it.

"Well, I'm right here if you need me."

Miss MacIntosh unpinned her nametag and rushed out of the back office. No time to change. It was already 10:50 p.m., and a VIP was waiting! Reaching the corner, she slowed down, then continued toward the lounge—and Mr. Mann.

The Sylvan Hotel

◆

The ad executive looked like he *was* a commercial. Seated hearthside, the Ogilvy director reminded Joann of one of those debonair dudes in a 1960s whiskey ad. Smiling nervously, she took a seat across from the executive. Smiling back, he studied her through glasses plucked straight from the pages of a GQ Magazine. Then Mr. Mann loosened a silk tie under a suit that screamed all kinds of currency—but in the smoothest possible way—almost as if he was a sparkly … mobster.

The fire quietly burned, but the room seemed to crackle with high voltage.

Jeezus god. Hopefully, she wouldn't make a fool of herself.

Then George appeared.

"Here's your order, sir—"

Seeing Joann, the bar manager almost dropped a plate of crispy crustaceans.

"Hi, George. Mr. Mann has invited me to interrogate him about advertising!"

The bartender backed away. "How nice," he said formally.

Oh, boooy. She was going to hear about this later. But right now, she needed to get down to business. Breathing in, Joann readied herself for an "interview."

Mister Mann asked about life at the Sylvan, her trip to Hawaiʻi, and life in Seattle. In turn, Joann asked him about Microsoft and the agency world. She also told him how she'd read and found inspiration in David Ogilvy's book.

Before she knew it, it was 11:20 p.m., and the VIP had to call it a night.

"Thanks for the company, Joann. I hope we can do this the next time I'm here."

◆

"Let's do this!" Kelly was fired up.

"What should I wear?" Joann rifled through the clothes in her locker.

T-shirt, jeans, sneakers—then she borrowed a sweatshirt hanging from Tory's locker and tied it around her hips.

"Yeah! Layer up! Look, now you're a grunge goddess!" her buddy declared.

They headed to the roof, and Joann started the car.

Frannie James

◆

"Where to?"

"Belltown, baby. I wanna check out the Vogue!"

From Madison, they headed across 1st Ave, past dimmed storefronts and businesses.

The area was all but deserted until 1st and Blanchard, where an expanse of street corner stealthily blinked. Charged with promise, thinly spelled names in green, gold, and red tavern typefaces pulled at souls in the dark.

They had arrived.

Joann slowed the car, not totally convinced she should stop. Dive bars were pretty much the extent of *her* "nightlife experience." Even in college, it had been pinball and beers at Red Onion; drinks with the restaurant-job team at The Attic … uh… yikes. The list was not very long. She couldn't think of much else, other than a couple stops at the kitschy Nitelite, one visit to the Comet, and after-hours commiseration in the bar at the lakeside café. Ah yes, and there was a short phase spent at Sorry Charlies, where a play-anything piano man obliged drunks, divas, and … well, drunk divas.

There was the Vogue—an obscure, low-rise building, kitty-corner from Queen City Grill and something "Frontier." At the front, a span of windows oscillated like fast-motion movie screens as light strobed across bodies covered in T-shirts, leather, fishnet, and tattoos.

They parked a few paces away, then lined up behind five other people. Joann fidgeted with her sweatshirt. Even the rain was jittery! Inside the door, glowing lipstick instructed them to hold out their wrists. After two quick stamps, someone else pointed to a room packed with all kinds of night owls. The floor vibrated under a human sea, and two girls in black vinyl vamped on high, dancing and gyrating atop two large speakers. A short pause was followed by guttural guitar riffs and a beat that prompted cheers all around.

Then a powerful voice was singing about eyes being sewn shut.

And it was compelling Jesus to fight back.

"What is this?" Joann yelled.

"Alice In Chains!" Kelly yelled back.

Joann liked it here.

Between work and sleep.

Between reality and a dream.

Between rock, metal, and punk.

High school and college had introduced her to Duran Duran, the Police, the Cure, Squeeze, Depeche Mode, Adam Ant, Erasure, the Thompson Twins, the Psychedelic Furs ... And she still loved Tom Petty, The Doors, the Kinks, the Stones, Foreigner, Elvis Costello—Tom Waits, too. But this was incredible.

Kelly was yelling again.

"Don't go in the bathroom! They're doing drugs!"

Christ. Maybe they shouldn't be here. Joann started to panic. Somewhere, her father was panicking even louder: *Stay outta the joints!*

Miss MacIntosh zoomed in on two dizzy zombies spinning near a hall. Holding onto each other, the friends were finding their way, stumbling through beams of purple light. *Aaack.* Was this okay? On her right, two goth chicks just grinned and gave her a thumbs-up.

Fuck it. She'd stumbled into some kind of Seattle underbelly, but joy was the real "crime" here. Joann kept scanning. Between dance-floor flashes, she could see a space blooming with life, safely sealed away from the watery world outside. Near the far wall, a slow-moving man leaned down to adjust his oxygen tank. Ha! The Vogue was an underbelly submarine—where everyone breathed easier.

Double fuck-it. She'd just steer clear of the can.

Now the powerful voice was asking to be saved.

It was like ... a different kind of church—

"Woo-hoo!" Kelly tugged on Joann's arm, dragging her to the center.

They jumped, swayed, stomped, and let go, awake and alive with lightness after dark.

— ◆ —

"Jo!" Kelly motioned for her to follow, and they cooled off in front of the club.

"Let's check out that place!" She pointed to "The Frontier Room."

Last call. A tired I'm-on-to-you bartender was on the brink of over it. Kelly had heard that "Nina" kept a shotgun behind the bar, and that no one ever messed with her. Joann timidly asked for a beer, but her friend wanted to test out additional scoop about "strong-ass drinks."

Gulp. The scoop checked out.

The girls found a table, and Joann drank in the scene:

Frannie James

◆

The "joint" was a '90s diorama—ragged but shining with the mottled luster of a long-lost painting on a canvas buried in someone's basement. Scraps of torn posters clung to a wall, and ashtrays littered the table along with highball glasses and the dregs of fiery spirits. Her eyes kept traveling: torn-up black booths; worn-out wood paneling; nicotine veil. Even the room was soused, yet totally at peace in its grimy stupor.

Ethereal. Coarse. Pure. Stained. No place. Someplace.

Joann was lost and found, all at the same time. She wanted to stay. She wanted to go.

She wanted more Vogue. She wanted more Alice In Chains. She wanted—

"Shit! Joann, can you get me to the ferry? I gotta make the last boat to Bainbridge!"

They ran for the car, shrieking with excitement.

"Kelly, we *have* to do that again next week!"

"Easy there, big thunder. Haha. What are your friends going to say when they find out you're playing in grunge land?"

"I don't care. I love it!"

"Word, mama!"

Joann waved goodnight, turned the wheel, and turned on Soundgarden.

At 3:15 a.m., she threw herself on the bed, ears still ringing with adventure. She'd met with Mr. Mann, and she'd stood by Kim Thayil! Then she'd danced at the Vogue, found the Frontier Room, and hadn't been shot by Nina. What would happen next? It was all so ... new ... and ... exciting ...

Joann's eyes were closing but open—and Soundgarden's *Birth Ritual* pushed on in her mind.

Goodnight, room. Goodnight, moon.

Goodnight, grunge boy with that badass tune.

CHANGING WINDS AND WEATHERED WALLS

"*What's with you?*" Babs asked suspiciously.

"Wh ... what do you mean?" Faltering, Miss MacIntosh took a step back.

Then Tory pushed through the PBX door.

"Hi, Babs, How *are* you???"

She practically hurled herself over the desk.

The big boss smugly patted Tory's hand.

"Now you see that, Joann? Take a lesson from young Tory, here. You really do need to perk up."

Oh, my fucking god. You have got to be kidding me.

And Babs was off to see what else needed fixing.

"Okay, dood, just let me know if you need ..." Tory bounced back to PBX.

What I need is for you to stop—

"Hey, Margaret." Todd began to count his dollar bills.

"Hi! How's the circle tonight?" Joann opened her cash drawer.

"Oh, you know. Just another night. How 'bout up here?"

"I miss Kathryn."

Todd glanced at PBX. "Squeaky on with you?"

"Yeah," Joann muttered.

"Don't be judgy, Margaret." He smiled wryly.

"I know. But Kathryn's the best."

"Well, she'll be here tomorrow, right?"

"Yeah."

I know you miss her, too.

Todd finished the exchange and headed back out.

"Hey ... Barnes."

"Yeah?"

"Do you like the Vogue?"

"*Margaret.* Did you go to the Vogue?" His steps slowed.

"Yeah. I've been going Thursdays with Kelly. It's so fun!"

Was he smiling? Oh, god. Maybe he was laughing at her.

"Good for you, Margaret. Yeah, the Vogue is cool."

Swish. The valet updated Bill, passing him at the doors.

"Yo. Margaret went to the Vogue."

Bill turned for the desk.

"Joann. You're branching out."

"Okay, Bill. Haha."

He raised both eyebrows.

"I'll go to the Vogue with you. *Any* time."

"I ... I'll keep that in mind."

"You should." Twirling a pen, he twirled back to the valet booth.

What a dork. Although he *was* kind of growing on her. In an adorable kind of way—

Beep!

"What's up, lady?"

"Hey, Kelly! You in town tonight?"

"Yeah. But let's hit a new place—a club called The Weathered Wall!"

"Okay! Maybe Tory will let me clock off early."

"Sweet—I'll be there at 10:20."

Swish. Robert, incoming. Wait, there were already two valets on, and it wasn't that busy.

What was he doing there? Dammit, all that boy had to do was walk in the door, and—

"Hey, Jo."

"Hi, Robert! How goes it? Are there three of you on tonight?"

"Bill's leaving early, so I'm covering for him."

"Got it. I'll print a list for you. And here's a newspaper."

Bill called to him from the big window.

"Hey, Bailey. Joann went to the Vogue."

"Okay, *jeez*," she sighed.

Whoosh. Headlights in the driveway.

Tackling the check-ins, Joann methodically assigned registration cards and keys. *Did* she need to be more perky? *Had* she gotten too icy after too many nights of too many guests bitching at her? Couldn't a person be helpful or do her job without sounding jacked up on helium?

She couldn't be alone in thinking this. Joann had seen many a guest step back when Tory lurched out at them from behind the counter. Although, for the most part, Babs was probably right. They were living in a "cheerleader" culture, and you'd best be serving it up sweetly—but with not-too-loud pom-poms and an extra side of gooey.

It was like the whole volleyball thing—a high-school experience that had served up hard lessons. After a first few weeks of klutzing through it, something had clicked, and Joann could suddenly bump, spike, and slide her way to victory, all over the court. She made varsity sophomore year, and her parents had been thrilled at this unexpected skill. Showing up to every game, they'd applauded her with great enthusiasm in a rare moment of approval.

Playing with all her might, Joann had passionately encouraged her teammates while doing whatever it took to keep that ball from hitting the floor. It had been a total blast, and she'd given it her all. Win or lose, volleyball had been everything, on *and* off the court.

After one big game, Joann scored a sweet-sixteen kiss. One of her brother's buddies had been a super fan with a super-secret crush—and he'd smooched her in the rainy parking lot before running off.

There were travel adventures, too! When it came time for tournaments, Joann was allowed to accompany the older girls on a few excursions. At Lake Crescent, there'd been cabin chats, cooking lessons … and boat rides without fishing poles! Wobbly canoes had been a revelation, but the stunningly clear water was *really* something to behold. As if bewitched, the lake was like a giant window that could show you what was down in the depths.

Exhilaration. Elation. Joann had lived for volleyball. She was a force on the court, a favorite in the stands, a mentor to junior players …

Cut to three years later. The older girls were gone, and new teammates were making new ripples. They also tended to mentally forfeit the moment their side fell behind.

But Joann was all about the rally.

"Don't give up girls—we got this! Fight-fight-fight! Let's get it … let's goooo!"

But the new teammates were *not* about the rally—and Joann was netting resentment.

Despite the sideline smears, she'd continued to play and cheer her heart out, a warrior on the court with her body *and* her voice. Then, senior year, a classmate joined on who was very ... bouncy—and, as Joann roared, "Yeah!" Bouncy peeped out, "*Yay.*"

Bouncy's game had been decent, but no better than Joann's. However, when it was time to vote for MVP, Miss MacIntosh was at a loss, and Miss Bouncy bounced off with everything.

Not gooey enough. Not cutie-pie enough. Not good enough. Not ... quiet enough.

Swish. Jed pulled a packed bell cart through the doors and across the lobby.

"Follow me, folks."

Joann made a point to smile extra-sweetly at the guests, and they glared back. Ha. She couldn't win. At least Mister Concierge looked happy. Perhaps a big tip was in order. Or maybe he and Bill had been smoking things in the garage. Well, at least he wasn't being pissy.

8:00 p.m.

Joann looked at a very-closed window. The weather was getting colder, and the valet booth had become even more of a boys-only domain. *It's for the best*, she thought, and secured the latch. Then she thought about all those nights during the previous winter, back-to-back with Robert. They'd been a good team, and at one point, it probably had been more than that. Even so, everything was now resolved with Tricia out of town. She and Robert had obviously re-committed to making things work.

"Hey, Margaret. I need another twenty, please."

"Sure, no prob." She hopped off the ledge and exchanged Todd's bills.

"So, Kathryn's at home?"

"Yeah, school night."

"Well, tell your buddy I said hello." His poker face seemed to waver, just for a moment.

"Barnes—"

Then she stopped herself.

Keep your mouth shut, Joann. It's none of your business. Don't make trouble.

She didn't want to send him down the wrong road.

"Nothing. Never mind."

10:20 p.m.

Swish. The stair door opened.

"Hiii, Robert." Kelly skipped through the lobby.

The valet listened from the concierge stand as she hurried Joann along.

"Come *on*, Jo. The Weathered Wall awaits, babeeeeeeeee!"

"Just hang on! I'm going as fast as I can!"

Swish. The stair door opened again.

"Lynnie! You're not on the elevator. What happened?" teased Joann.

"Alexander bitched me out. Maaan, this is cramping my style."

"Aw, just forget about him!" Kelly pulled her into a hug.

"So you're looking extra-hot, tonight, Kell. Where are you two off to?" Lynn pulled out a cigarette pack and smacked it.

"The Weathered Wall!" Kelly threw up her hands. "If someone would step on it!"

"Joanna, you're … branching out. *Another* dance club?" Lynn was trying not to laugh.

Robert was already laughing and added, "Jo—do you wanna dance with somebody? Do you wanna feel the heat with somebody?" He fist-pumped the air in slow motion while clicking his tongue.

"Okay, whatever, you guys. And it's not that funny, Whitney Houston."

"Lyyynnn, come with us," Kelly begged.

"Yeeeah, no. I am not Weathered Wall material."

The housekeeper backed away from the desk.

"Um, Lynnie … why don't *you* branch out?" Joann smiled.

"Oh, I've got branches. They just don't involve weathered walls. Call me later if you want …"

Shortly after 11:00 p.m., Joann waved to Robert and headed out with Kelly.

"Now, be safe, Jo."

"Don't worry, '80s boy."

Midnight. The ol' Weathered Wall was trying seriously hard to be a scene. Gross, thought Joann. Too meat-markety. Her friend was digging it, though, so best to keep quiet.

"Jo, that guy is looking at you!" Kelly laughed and dashed off.

Eddie Vedderish face. Chris Cornell hair. Chris Cornell height. Yeah, he was cute.

But Joann had never been swept away by lust-at-first-sight. There had to be *some* kind of connection. Without it, there wasn't going to be much chemistry, at least for her. And this didn't seem like a place you met boys who wanted to know you, even a little bit. So the only thing she'd score *here* was waking up feeling bad about herself. It's not that she expected a marriage proposal, but signing up to be used and discarded by some stranger wasn't her thing. How could it be anyone's thing? A person was not disposable.

Joann frowned. How did people end up on that path? Screw someone who threw you out with the garbage. Screw yourself by betraying yourself, then numb yourself to numb it all out. She didn't want to go through life like that. She also knew better than to pick up boys in bars—another hard lesson learned years ago.

In 1984, Kenzie O'Brien's widowed mom decided to go out for a drink—and brought home company. Then she and Kenzie both lost their lives.

When they were fifth graders, Kenzie and Joann ran in different circles. Kenzie had been super-cool, and Joann had been medium-cool. But they'd discovered a shared love of Nancy Drew, and a friendship was born. Kenzie even agreed to try something different, and one day, she ventured south, joining the MacIntosh family for a crowded kitchen-table dinner. Later, the girls laughed as Kenzie held up a pair of Joann's jeans to a pair of very long Irish-dancer legs.

Not a fit.

In the end, Kenzie realized that she and Joann were from worlds that were just *too* different, but they read those mysteries for as long as possible. A smart girl sleuth who was brave and beautiful! The search for truth! The small-town suspense! Best friends! Boyfriends! Adventures in a blue car! Joann and Kenzie *loved* their mysteries. Then, at age sixteen, Kenzie disappeared in the worst kind of mystery.

The Sylvan Hotel

◆

The Nancy Drew book club had disbanded by seventh grade, and its two members had gone on to different schools—but the loss left Joann reeling all the same. Best to not bring up the subject, though. The grisly events had gone down in a neighborhood where nothing bad ever happened, and to a very respectable family.

You weren't supposed to talk about it.

"Hey, girlie, look what *I* got!" Kelly pressed a piece of paper into Joann's hand.

Eddie Cornell's phone number.

"Kelly! Why would you do that? *Christ!*"

They ended up back at Kay's with Lynn.

"Jo, you need to lighten up. And Lynnie, you need to go with us next time!"

"Okay, Kell. I'll go with you if Joann has two drinks tonight instead of one!"

"Deal!" Joann threw back her Bud Light and ordered up a Kahlúa.

Her friends high-fived each other, and Joann shook her head. Those two were going to get her into trouble—but at least she wasn't jonesing about valets.

The next day, Robert was parking cars, and Todd was parked in PBX. The driveway started to fill up, but Todd wasn't budging. What was going on back there? Jed hustled out to help get the circle cleared, and luckily, nobody needed assistance with luggage.

Click. Joann heard the combination lock turn in the back hall. She grabbed a stack of registration cards, pretending to be organizing paperwork. Arriving in front, Todd paused and stared at the lounge. A few seconds later, he proceeded to the doors.

Joann pushed through the swinging door to PBX.

"Hey. Is everything okay?"

Beep-beep-beep! Kathryn … wasn't looking like Kathryn.

"I'll get it." Joann picked up the desk extension out front.

Beep-beep-beep-beep-beep! PBX was a sea of alarms. Then two more check-ins; then three. Joann assigned keys, filed the paperwork, and pushed through the door again.

Frannie James

◆

"What happened?"

"I can't be what he wants me to be. Sure, Todd and I connect. I don't deny that. And I care about him. But he doesn't want to be just friends anymore. *But I have a partner.*"

"I thought he was seeing someone?"

"They never last very long, Jo."

"Well, they're not *you*."

Kathryn angrily spun the chair away from her friend.

"Sorry, Kath. Not trying to make it worse. I'm just being honest. I think Todd has real feelings for you, and it might take him a while to get over it."

"The whole thing's giving me a stomach ache. I admit: It's worse than I thought. And I feel bad for him. But that doesn't—I'm … I'm with Scott."

Joann nodded. Kathryn and Todd had been strong allies. They'd viewed a lot of the world through the same lens. But now that lens was splintering—like a windshield cracking—

and things were getting distorted, making it dangerous for everyone. Time … to pull over.

Joann picked up a radio and paged Lynn from the desk.

"Base to Housekeeping. Lynn, please call me at extension four."

Beep.

"Um … I think it's a Kay's night."

"Dude. Is it ever *not* a Kay's night?"

"Okay, but seriously. Meet us in the cafeteria when you're done."

"Is everything all right, Joann?"

"Ahem."

"I guess that's a 'no.' Wait, is it Kathryn? I swung by PBX earlier, but it was *ocupado*—"

"Yep. See you at eleven!"

≡ ◆ ≡

Midnight. Kathryn was on her second rum and coke, and Joann was nursing a Bud Light.

Sitting between the Sylvan A-Team, Lynn nervously lit a smoke. It seemed that the trio was crossing into new territory.

Meanwhile, Frank Sinatra was gearing up for the moon and stars.

But first he wanted a kiss.

The Sylvan Hotel

◆

"Why is this song playing. He wants to kiiiss ... But I *can't* ..."

Kathryn was buzzed. And Lynn's eyebrows were reaching new heights.

"Wow, girl. I'm liking this. Might I interest you in another beverage?"

She pushed her own drink toward Kathryn.

"What's goin' on over here. You gals all right?"

The world's best waitress was checking in.

"It was just a long night up there," Joann answered. "You know how it is, Kay."

"Are those boys botherin' you?"

Lynn retrieved her drink and chugged almost all of it. Then Kathryn slid down in the booth.

"Alrighty. Come get me if you need more."

Kathryn laughed, and Joann breathed out. *Whew.* Thanks-be-to-Kay. Because Kathryn falling apart was too scary. She was the one who held everyone together.

"Boys are ... boooooys are ..." Kathryn sighed.

"And ... I think that's enough for *you*." Joann pushed her friend's glass away.

Lynnie pushed it back.

"Joanna, maybe Kathryn *needs* to get drunk."

"Um, she's *driving*?!?"

"Doesn't she live right next to you?"

"Yeah, but she'll be extra-grumpy tomorrow if she doesn't have her car, and she hates being hung over."

"I can drive it and follow you. Oh, but ... I'm already drunk, too."

Kathryn and Lynn both giggled, and Miss MacIntosh rolled her eyes.

◆

12:50 a.m.

Joann dropped off Lynn, then continued to Broadway with Kathryn.

"Let's get food. I wanna wait an hour before we go back for your car."

"I'm *fine*, Jo."

"Well, I just want to be sure. How about cheeseburgers?"

"Lynn's gonna kill us for missing out on cheeseburgers."

"We'll make it up to her."

Frannie James

◆

At Dick's Drive-In, they parked, ordered, then ate in the Jetta. Outside, a late-night crowd swarmed. Drag queens, druggies, gangsters, good girls, bad boys, coeds, rockers, and rappers gorged side by side, gabbing between bites of greasy goodness.

When they started back, Joann turned on the radio, and Huey Lewis took them to task:

Did they believe in love?

She was being haunted by '80s boys.

Not now, Huey. Not the time.

Joann turned off the radio, but the rain fell hard and loud.

"Are you okay, Kath?"

Please don't be mad at me for asking you that.

"I'm just gonna miss my friend. But … time to take space, I guess."

What the hell, thought Joann. Why did things have to be so difficult? Why was this happening? *This* was "the joy of youth?" Come on, Universe. Stop toying with us.

It was Thursday again, and Kelly was ready to party. Even Lynn was joining, so as not to break her promise. Tory was willing to close, and right around 10:30 p.m., Joann was free to go.

The desk agent tallied her cash drawer and told the girls to wait in the circle. Then Robert brought her car around. She just had to change, and they'd be off to the Weathered Wall.

Locker open. Locker shut. T-shirt. Thermal-textured tights under stringy denim cut-off shorts. Flannel. Sturdy boots. Thick socks bunched over the tops of the sturdy boots. And to keep her safe … Uncle John's WWII dog tags.

Goodnight, navy uniform. It was grunge-girl hour.

Joann glanced in the mirror. Whatever "grunge" was, she was into it. And you could check out Kay's on any given night to see that a lot of kids were. She'd also seen a few of the Sylvan servers dressed this way—Matt and Todd, too. It was like a mix of bike rider and hiker—or blue-collar-cool with hints of weekend-in-the-mountains and foggy-Northwest-beach. Sometimes, it looked like everyone was headed for a big bonfire.

The Sylvan Hotel

The working class was having a moment, and the people were dressed for it! Ripped this and that over long-john underlayers; leather, combat boots ... and who didn't love a little dad-flannel? The soft-but-strong shirts woven in muted plaids, stand-out shades, and solid patterns would always be her style.

Really, though, "grunge" was just the stuff you'd find in most Northwest closets. But somehow, all of it had a new edge. It was like Seattle was rocking a badass makeover—because everyday-practical had turned everyday-magical. And it wasn't so much dirty as it was messy—but an *organized* kind of messy. It could even be sexy if you weren't being a total slob. But gone were a lot of the "bodycon" outfits and strappy sandals. Even at the clubs, grunge was the dress code. And you could see why—especially as a girl. Grunge was empowering. It combined badass with beauty. It said "equal" versus "plaything." It said no-more-bullshit. Joann still loved a good dress, but grunge was real life. Grunge was truth. That was *her* idea of liberation.

Yeah! Babs could take her "perky," and shove it.

Jogging up the stairs, she grinned. Boots were the best after eight hours of standing in heels—and good for stomping to Soundgarden.

Robert was waiting at the concierge stand. He moved to get the door for her but—

Kelly whistled from inside the car.

"Joanna. Where is the preppy girl we used to know and love?"

A worried valet handed his friend her keys. "Now be safe, Jo, and—"

"I know, I know: don't do anything you wouldn't do," she recited, smiling.

"Where did you say you're headed?" A worried valet now leaned on the car.

"The Weathered Wall!" cried Kelly. "Someone's got people waiting! *Come on, Jo!*"

Joann waved, laughing off Kelly's comments. "See ya, Mister Bailey."

The Sylvans found parking close to the club and ... no line! Once inside, Lynn immediately threw back a drink and pointed out all the poseurs.

"Watch it, Lynnie. You're gonna get us in trouble," Joann cautioned.

"This is puuuuure comedy." She tried to simmer down but with no success.

Twenty minutes later, Joann was ready to leave. "Kelly, I'm honestly not into this place. I thought, well, give it another try, but—"

"Okay, *okay*. Jeezus, Joann! I just wanted to—Oh. My. God."

"What? Kelly, what's the matter?"

Then Lynn was laughing.

"Lynn, what the hell's so funny?"

Putting her hands on Joann's shoulders, Kelly spun her around. There, in the middle of the club, was Robert, still in uniform with walkie-talkie in hand. *What the ... ???*

"Robert!" Running over, Kelly latched onto his arm. "Yay-yay-yay! What are you doing here?"

"I just wanted to make sure you girls were okay. I had to drop off a guest one street over, so I figured ..."

The rainy-knight-in-shining-Town-Car—winning favor once again.

"I told you we wouldn't do anything you wouldn't do!" Joann pulled at his sleeve.

Kelly pulled at Lynn, who was looking like she might hyperventilate.

"Okay, have fun." Grinning, he turned to go.

"No, stay-stay-stay!" Kelly grabbed onto Robert again, but he gently peeled her off.

The valet was always so good with her. A lot of the hotel dudes could be too touchy-feely with the girl. Sure, Kelly could be overzealous at times—but that didn't give anyone the right to take liberties.

"I gotta get back to the hotel. The Town Car's in the load zone! Remember, I'm still on the clock!" Still grinning, he exited the club.

"Bahahahaha. Pure. Comedy." Lynn was now holding onto a weathered wall. "I cannot believe ... in his uniform ... with the Town Car ... *on the clock* ..."

"Lynnie. *Chill.*"

"Oh, my god, Joanna. I want to call Kathryn so bad."

"Yeah, well, Kathryn's sleeping because she has a million kids depending on her tomorrow. We are not waking her up to discuss Robert!"

"Joann, someone seems rather concerned about you." The housekeeper reached for her smokes.

Kelly "woo-hooed," and the next song started.

"He's. In. A. Relationship."

"Yeah," replied Lynnie. "With someone on the opposite coast!"

Kelly was jumping up and down again.

"Let's leave," said Joann. "I'm so not into—"

"Yeah we know what—er, *who* you're into!"

Outside, the Seattle drizzle washed everything clean, and Joann breathed in the coming season. Fall was such an amazing culmination of endings and beginnings. What would *this* autumn bring? Dare she even ask? There seemed to be more questions than ever, but it also felt like so much was possible. Her heart pounded with excitement. How was she going to get any sleep? This feeling …this *anticipation* … It was shaping up to be an all-night thing.

She started the car, and Temple of the Dog was right on track.

Joann did not know what was going on.

But she was starting to guess that nobody was gonna make it end.

THE VALET VORTEX

"*Valet to Base.*"

"Go ahead, Robert."

"Just checking on you, Base. Haven't seen you all night."

Joann had been sticking to PBX as the ol' hot-and-cold routine had—

Incoming call. Valet booth. And … the temperature was changing yet again.

"Hey, Jo. You okay back there?"

Just trying not to like you so damn much.

"Just tired, and the switchboard's been busy. How are you? Shift going smoothly?"

"Yeah. Be sure to wait for me when you're done. I'll walk you to your car. Hey, and how was the workout today? How many steps on the stair-stepper? We should run stairs sometime. We could race!"

Hilly Seattle had hundreds of outdoor stairways, many of which were remnants of the city's trolley days. The trolleys were long gone, but the steps endured. Hidden amid trees and pretty blossoms, the up-and-down groves were like secret wildflower paths, linking blocks and blooms of different elevations.

So … a race with Robert Bailey. It was a fun idea—although the valet's soccer-legs were sure to outpace hers in seconds. And she'd probably have an asthma attack trying to keep up, or she'd faint at the sight of him being all sporty with those eyes twinkling and those calf muscles muscling and that hair flying in the chilly air.

Hold on. Was he being serious? *No.* Just talk. And not a good idea, anyway. Meeting him for something like that was a sure-fire recipe for getting her hopes up, only to crash and burn. Her heart couldn't take it—or stairs at high speed!

Thankfully, he changed the subject.

"By the way, how many personal phone calls have you made so far tonight?"

"Robert, I assure you that Kathryn will be my only personal phone call."

"Alrighty. Just keepin' an eye on you."

"Ten-four. Talk to you later."

Joann hung up, then dialed Miss Emerson. No answer, so she left a message:

"Hey, Kath. Just callin' to say hi. We miss you! Hope school is going okay and that you're—"

"Joann, someone's asking for you." Brad looked concerned.

She hung up and followed him out to the desk.

"There she is." Captain Advertising sized up Joann.

"Hi, Conner! Checking in?"

"Yes. Can I count on you for crab cakes at 10:30? I've explained to Brad that your manager cleared it."

"Sure. Uh, Brad, are you okay with me leaving early?"

"Absolutely." Brad wasn't *really* sure what to make of this, but guests (especially VIP guests) called the shots.

"Okay, Joann. I'll meet you in the lounge at 10:30."

By now, Bill, Todd, and Robert had gathered at the concierge stand.

"See you at 10:30," she responded.

Avoiding all eyeballs to the right, the desk agent busied herself with cigarette inventory.

"What's up, Joann?" Bill continued to watch her.

"Oh, just finishing my stuff."

Who cared what they thought. It was time to get serious about her career. She didn't want to be left behind.

10:30 p.m.

Joann joined Mister Mann in the lounge while three valets and a desk agent looked on. Babs was MOD that night, and added another pair of peepers to the mix. Conner Mann wanted to have a drink ... with *who?*

Deciding to investigate, the controller started her "rounds" in the lounge—and practically curtsied for Ogilvy & Mather's finest. Her guest was currently one of the Sylvan's top five clients, which bought him the best rooms, the utmost respect—and whatever else he wanted. The VIP thanked Babs for allowing the crab-cake conference. Then he shook her hand, and she left them to their dinner.

"So how have you been, young lady?"

"Fine, thanks! How was Microsoft today?"

It was small-talk city—and it stayed that way for thirty minutes. Joann just couldn't find a way to bring up "next-step" advice for a copywriting career. Oh, god, and Robert was waiting for her in the lobby.

"Well," she lied, "I have an early doctor's appointment, tomorrow, so …"

Mr. Mann stood and instructed Beth to "put it on his room." Then he escorted Joann out of the lounge, and they stopped just short of the concierge stand.

"Shall I walk you to your car?" The executive straightened his tailored jacket.

"I got it." Robert forcefully zipped his navy jacket.

The executive did not acknowledge the valet but said his goodbyes to Joann.

"You have a nice evening, now. I'll see you soon."

Joann waved, and the elevator doors closed. Then she slowly pivoted to face an unsmiling Robert.

"Jo, do you know what you're doing?"

It wasn't really a question.

What the hell. She was just trying to get her career going.

Goddammit, Robert Bailey. What do you want from me?

They buckled themselves into the Town Car and sat in silence on the drive to the garage. Then Madonna's voice pierced the quiet, and Robert turned up the radio. The '80s diva dared to tell a tale—one that was hard to hide very well. A story about not being ready for a fall, secrets burning inside, and a truth that was never far behind.

Okay … what?

Was he—

Did he just …?

No. Joann sighed. She was losing her mind, as usual.

"See you tomorrow, Jo?"

"See you tomorrow, Robert."

When she got to the apartment, Joann searched her pockets for that small, crumpled piece of paper. Fuck it. They could do lunch in a crowded restaurant. She'd try it. Just this once. She was gonna call Eddie Cornell.

The Sylvan Hotel

Mr. Weathered Wall agreed to meet the next day. Standing in front of her mirror, Joann was undecided in a flowered baby-doll dress, denim jacket, and boots. What *did* one wear to lunch with a grunge god? Did grunge gods even ... lunch?

As it turned out, Max was a freelance photographer—fashion; industrial; real estate; art stuff. Okay, kinda interesting, and yeah, he was good-looking ... but sooo full of himself. He seemed impatient, too, like, can-we-just-get-on-with-it-already. Eww. He didn't even know her! But maybe that was the point.

Gross. Kelly would say to lighten up, but Joann couldn't get past the idea of being disposable. She'd never tell anyone else what to do but ... personally? The idea of being treated like a piece-of-ass-trash wasn't ever going to be a turn-on. And even if she wasn't "respectable," she was trying to respect *herself*. Or at least not hook up with a jerk. Then again, most people would probably say, "Who cares? He's hot!"

Maybe something was wrong with her. Maybe she *was* uptight. And maybe she wasn't feminist enough. But ... "giving it up" to whoever? Was that truly girl power? Or was it self-sabotage? Sure, women should be able to do what they wanted. But had feminism gotten twisted somewhere along the way? Why should she support asshole entitlement? Was that really being "empowered?" Why should she offer herself to whoever to be a throwaway toy? Was that living as an equal, or was "meeting" (so-called) men at that level actually *sinking* to that level? Maybe it was actually taking a step *backwards*. Maybe it was playing right into the bullshit. Maybe the patriarchy ... was pulling an even bigger con.

Aw, jeez. Maybe she was just old-fashioned. Wait. Could a person be feminist *and* a little old-fashioned? Or was it possible that being a little "old-fashioned" could actually be feminist? *Dammit.* She was overthinking again. Maybe she really did just need to go with it. But ... how? How did one ignore all the fuckery that women had been subjected to since the beginning of time? And it's not like the abuse and exploitation had stopped. Then there was that secret anger lurking under a lot of the smiles. As in, a girl's personality, heart, and brain were already *such* an annoyance—like barbed wire around the parts men wanted—and if you didn't play along, you were a bitch for making dudes jump through even more hoops. You were a bitch of an obstacle course.

So … wasn't it more feminist to *not* participate in this crap? Yeah, maybe she *was* overthinking it, but she was also over it. She was *sick* of it. And why should she risk putting herself in harm's way?

Joann looked at Max again. *Okay. Try to feel … anything.* Even if she *was* willing to risk it—*and* sneak past her own rules—there had to be at least a hint of a connection. Of course, you had to start somewhere—and there was always a chance of finding someone decent beyond hey-you're-kinda-cute—but … was this the right way to "start somewhere?" Instant douche-baggery was just making her miss her friends. It was making her feel lonely.

Good grief. She was supposed to be on a date to move past the hotel. But all she wanted to do was get *back* there. Instant douche-baggery … was a no-go.

Mr. Weathered Wall was getting bored.

Whatever, dude.

"Well, I've got work, so …" she said sweetly and pretended not to notice the annoyance on his face.

"See ya," he said as they left the restaurant. "Call me sometime. We'll do it again."

"We both know that's not happening," she muttered and drove straight to the hotel.

Swish. Robert and Bryce, incoming. She looked up, and Robert looked away.

What a surprise. Hot. Cold. Very hot. Very cold. It was hopeless. She was hopeless.

"Good evening, Joann." Bill twirled a cigarette.

"Hey. Here's your list and a *Wall Street Journal.*"

"Thank you. So, uh … wanna go out with me tonight?"

"Yes, Bill. I will go out with you tonight."

What had she just said?

The Sylvan Hotel

•

"Uh, okay. It's ... a date."

Slowly backing away, he tried not to run out the doors with the news.

Hearing commotion in the valet booth, Joann dialed Kathryn.

"Hello?"

"I said yes. I dunno if it's a good idea, but I said yes."

"Jo. What did you do."

"I told Bill I'd go out with him."

"*What?!?* Joann, are you sure about this?"

"No. But I'm ... I ... well, I went to lunch with the Weathered Wall guy, and I have to say, Bill has way more appeal than that—"

"But I think—"

"It's fine. It might even be fun."

"Jo, maybe you should just—"

"Oops—gotta go, Kathryn. We've got check-ins."

Joann hung up the phone, and Jed appeared with two guests.

Robert and Bryce appeared shortly after and stood behind the concierge stand, watching Joann check in the Ording party.

Eleven o'clock couldn't come fast enough.

But then it did.

Swish. The senior valets waved goodbye.

Miss MacIntosh stapled her receipts, dropped them in the safe, then took a deep breath.

What-am-I-doing-what-am-I-doing-what-am-I-doing-what-am-I-doing. Her heels noisily clicked on the stairs.

What *was* she doing? Bill wasn't a stranger, but they weren't buddies, either. Still, they at least shared a thread of connection. They worked alongside one another, and despite a few cocky comments, the junior valet had always been decent to her. Bill could be a dork, but he wasn't full of himself. He also wasn't an asshole, and he wasn't sketchy. If anything, Bill knew that if he messed with her ... well, he'd have an entire staff of older valets to deal with—and George.

How often could you take a risk with a safety net built in?

She pulled herself together in the locker room.

Come on, Joann. Be a big girl. Try something new. You don't have to do anything you don't want to do.

But was she about to do *this*? Good thing Lynn wasn't around.

Ha! This is your fault, Lynnie. If you'd been scheduled tonight, you would have talked me out of it. Either that, or you'd have smacked me upside the head.

Tick-tock.

Pulling open the locker-room door, Joann found the junior valet waiting right outside.

"Hey. Wanna take my car?"

"Sure." And … his arm around her.

Well, this was progressing rapidly.

After a slightly awkward drive, they ended up at some random bar downtown where his friends were hanging out.

"I want to show you off!"

Okaaay … no. She wasn't an object. *Bill, I had more faith in you.* Strike one.

The friends seemed curious but didn't stick around. Slapping him on the back, the crew told him to "have fun."

Blatant bro crap. Strike two. But … that one *was* more them than him.

Bill slammed a shot, and Joann sipped her drink, determined to keep things normal—whatever that meant.

He seemed determined to get wasted.

Okaaay.

Joann left him to the task and approached the bar for a glass of water.

"Excuse me—"

Then arms were wrapping around her waist, followed by hands sliding over her hips and thighs.

Well, *now* she had the bartender's attention.

"Bill—"

She turned, and his mouth met hers.

Whoa. What—

The bartender threw a towel over her shoulder and glared at the Sylvans.

Get a room.

Joann pulled back from Bill, but then …

God, the way he was looking at her. It was—

It was like a whole other story was unfolding.

But making out with the junior valet, like, ten seconds into their "date?"

Welp, there was no guessing about what *he* wanted.

Ha. Maybe they *should* get a room. Um, but that could be bad, work-wise. Still, it wasn't like Bill had to stand at the desk right next to her.

The Sylvan Hotel

Wait—wasn't he seeing someone? No, he wouldn't have asked her out if he had a girlfriend. Or maybe they'd recently broken up—or ... maybe it had never been that serious—

Over-thinking alert, Joann scolded herself. Besides, she'd never really had a one-night stand. But ... a one-night stand with Mister-Fucked-Up-Most-of-the-Time? Then again, she wasn't exactly a shining example of maturity at the moment. Who gets so attached to someone who's not even—

Nope! Don't even go there.

Joann put her arms around Bill, pulling him close.

Well, dude, it's your lucky night, I guess. We can be fuck-ups together.

The valet did not need convincing.

"Let's get out of here."

Joann tried to keep her hands steady at the wheel. His hands were everywhere.

Minutes later, they made it up the front steps to her building.

"Bill. Let me open the *door.*"

He laughed, and she fumbled for the key. Then a few more steps and ... the next key.

Door opened. Door slammed. Miss MacIntosh was up against a wall.

The call-box phone receiver crashed down, knocked off its cradle.

Jeezus, dude—can we get past the entryway?

More importantly, *was* she sure about this?

Well, he was safe enough—so ... maybe she didn't need to be sure. Maybe she just needed someone else to take charge for a moment. Although, that "someone else" could barely stand up straight.

No overthinking, dammit.

"Jeezus, Joann!" Laughing again, Bill pulled at her dress.

He was about to rip the thing, but now *she* was laughing.

Dress off. Boots off. Pants off.

How long had it been since she'd been held like—wait, had she *ever* been held like—?

Joann pulled away the sofa cushions, then ...

Click. The hide-a-bed locked into place.

Frannie James

Weeks later, Jed, Todd, and Kathryn sat across from Bill and Joann at Queen City Grill.

Bill was trying to keep his hands where they were supposed to be, and Kathryn looked ... well, she was not thrilled with this development. And Lynn had been horrified.

"Oh, Joanna. You and *Bill???*"

"Don't look at me like that, Lynn. It's not serious. Actually, it will probably be over very soon. The 'big challenge' is gone, and ... well, he'll be on to other fish in the sea."

"But ... *Bill???* What about—"

"That isn't happening, and ... it's kinda nice to be with someone, even for a moment ... who ... well, who knows what they want—"

"But ... does he?"

"Oh, for god's sake. It's just sex." She had tried to sound matter-of-fact.

"Aaagh. My ears! Stop it, Joann."

"Joann." Bill was asking her what she wanted to drink.

"Okay, I'll try your damn Jäger!"

Kathryn squirmed, then frowned.

"Aw, yeah!" The junior valet was off to order, disappearing through soupy, orange light.

Sitting back, Todd silently assessed the situation, a smile barely forming at the corner of his mouth.

Don't be judgy, Barnes.

And what was going on with him and Kathryn? Hadn't she planned on asking him for space? The senior valet looked too content. Like all was right with the world; like he was right where he was supposed to be. Joann recognized that look and quickly turned away.

Bill reappeared, and she took a sip of the infamous Jägermeister.

"That's disgusting!"

"I think you need *more*," the valet whispered in her ear. Then he downed the rest.

"Okaaay ... maybe it's time to call it a night. And I still need to get my car from the hotel. I'll grab the check." Kathryn stood, and Todd followed.

Jed grinned at Bill and Joann as if he was envisioning—

Yuck. Hurry up, Kathryn.

The Sylvan Hotel

•

A few minutes went by, and her friend hadn't returned.

"Guys, I'll be right back."

In a hall, Joann found two Sylvans in the middle of a quietly heated conversation.

"Everything okay over here?"

Miss Emerson looked at the floor.

Everything is not okay.

"Let's go. Kath, I'll take you to the hotel. Bill can get a ride with Jed."

―⁕―

At the Sylvan, Joann waited for Kathryn to start her car—but Miss Emerson wasn't shifting into gear.

Getting out of her own car, Miss MacIntosh zipped up and crossed the chilly rooftop. Climbing in with her friend, she pushed aside piles of Rush, Peter Gabriel, and Sade cassettes on the seat. Then she shoved her feet between *Weetzie Bat* books and school papers that littered the floor.

A cassette player kicked in, and the Indigo Girls began to play.

"Kath—"

"I did it."

She shut off the ignition.

"What happened?"

"I told him I care about him, but that we needed to take some space. I feel terrible."

"It's gonna be okay, Kathryn. And you did the right thing. You're protecting your friendship—and you're trying to protect him! And Todd ... well, Todd's discovered that there are other girls in the world besides 'Bettys and Wilmas.' He respects you. He can *talk t*o you—and he obviously finds you attractive. And ... well ... he might be in love with you."

"I'll miss him."

"I know."

A staccato downpour eased, and above them, hotel windows lit up like gold searchlights. Leaning back, Kathryn closed her eyes.

"I'm not ready yet."

"Okay."

Joann surveyed the gray lot. They were supposed to be adults, now, but sometimes it seemed like they were in over their heads. For starters, what the hell *was* she doing with Bill? She'd told herself that a date or two might be fun, but instead, they'd gone straight to ... something else. At first, she'd felt weird about it. Then she'd convinced herself that she *did* need to lighten up. She'd known Bill for over a year; he wouldn't treat her like garbage; it didn't have to be serious; he wasn't a bar psycho—and, hell, she liked his hands on her.

But she was having doubts again. Bill was funny and full of chutzpah, but he was also too reckless. Joann was long past bad-boy bullshit, and while Bill's determination could be charming, some of his antics could be tedious. And there was a reason she'd never had casual sex. Aside from the usual risks, that type of thing could too easily turn into disaster. They used protection, but there was no defense against bruised egos—or bruised hearts.

Joann had also been certain that, at minimum, the situation involved mutual respect, but ... maybe that wasn't the case, after all.

The former high-school wrestler was still fighting in some kind of match—still running in some kind of race. Who knows? Maybe the entire thing had been based on a bet made in the valet booth. She knew how guys could be. Joann had heard it all when she worked at the "Greek Row restaurant," aka the lakeside café, in college.

The sorority girls there had been one thing, but the frat boys were in a whole other league. One of the Greek gods had been quick to pursue her, but the "romance" was over before it began. Hopping off his motorcycle, Joann had watched her would-be beau size up the modest MacIntosh address. Then the one-second suitor kissed her good-bye—because there were bigger fish to fry. Another lad with brilliant blue eyes asked her out next, but he was brilliantly boring. He'd also seemed strangely upset when she hadn't been impressed with his ... brilliance.

Two bartenders tried next—one with anger issues and one with sleaze issues. Then some of the dudes who hadn't tried dating her confided in her, instead. She was safely outside their system, kept secrets, and was a great listener. *Joann MacIntosh, frat-boy priest.* She'd hung out at "the house" on summer nights while the bros drank blueberry vodka, agonized about the female population, and played favorite tunes. While Tracy Chapman sang of revolution through a Hi-Fi, Miss MacIntosh had been schooled about tradition on the down-low: Alpha Delts. Dee Gees. Tri Delts. Lambdas. Fijis. Gamma Phi. Joann had been a Zeta fly on the wall, learning about

185

The Sylvan Hotel

●

which houses were the "good houses" and which girls were the "right" girls: the respectable girls. But what camp did *she* fall into? The god squad hadn't been sure, either, as their friend was different—but she wasn't a *total* "random." Even then, her once would-be beau would look at his brothers in disbelief. What the hell were they doing with Joann MacIntosh? Didn't they know she was nobody? Heaven help 'em if they got attached.

Bill wasn't a frat boy, but he could see that Joann was well regarded at the hotel. Maybe hooking up with her was a way to say he was just as good as the other guys. And if that was the case, *did* he respect her? Then again, it's not like they were being public about anything. Although they weren't hiding it, either. So … maybe he just wanted to prove something to *himself*. Well, it's not like she'd ever know. She couldn't even ask him regular, every-day-type stuff. Bill was not interested in getting attached at any level, and he wasn't interested in answering—or asking—any questions.

From the little Joann did know, Bill's father had split early on, although he wasn't totally out of the picture. Mama, on the other hand, was quite close to her boy and seemed super-sweet. She'd visited the hotel on occasion and looked like one of those eternally devoted den mothers, always ready with an extra sandwich, a needle to sew that button, a new pair of socks. All-smiles all the time, and very proud of her clever, strong son. However, her son's shoulders were chiseled *and* chipped. Bill had also attended rich-kid schools, quickly learning what he didn't have—and what he wanted. Then there was an epic first love and an epic first break-up, which left Bill thrashing at the surface because he was stuck underneath.

Regardless, the valet was going to show everyone that he was above it—if he didn't kill himself first. Bill drank himself under all the tables, and weed was one thing, but coke? That was too scary. Joann never saw him do any of it, but she wasn't blind to "bowls" in the garage and "eight balls" in bar bathrooms. She'd heard him talking about it, too. Drugs were all over the place. *Bill* was all over the place. But he was old enough to make his own decisions—and he didn't need another mother. Not to mention, he would find her concern laughable.

Joann knew she was playing with fire. She'd stupidly gotten into the guy's car when he'd been too far gone. A couple times, he'd slammed on the brakes so hard that it felt like she'd been in an accident. Bill was never cruel, but he was trying to drown something out—so he was too willing to take chances. And now it was getting dicey for both of them. If she was honest with herself, it was like she'd learned to flip another kind of switch—as in selectively leaving safety by the wayside—because she wanted to drown something out, too.

So she kept seeing him. It was new to be desperately wanted, and her brain was desperate for distraction. But what, exactly, had she gotten herself into? Every time she thought whatever they were doing had played its course, it would start over.

It was like an accident that kept happening.

And there *was* a girlfriend, but the relationship was chronically on-and-off. Bill would return to her, then a week or so later, he'd meet up with Joann again. One night, she'd dared to ask, "You okay? What's going on?" His answer to that was more sex. But … they were casual, so should she care?

And how long did flings last? Was she getting stuck *again*? How did one get "stuck" in a fling? And would she ever have a chance at a real relationship? Would she ever be enough for someone? Where were the guys who wanted you at night *and* talked to you in the morning? The guys who'd take you on a proper date. The guys who liked looking at you *and* looking out for you. The guys who actually saw you. The guys that didn't have to be away from you to be with you. Uh, and the guys who didn't have to be bombed out of their mind to be with you.

Joann had been passed-out-drunk *once* in college. The boy with the muscle car had dropped her off, and she'd dropped down, down, down. Bacardi 151 had landed her on the kitchen floor, trying to stop the spinning. Other than that, her alcohol-fueled exploits had been on the fairly tame side. And she'd been stoned twice. Not that marijuana was a big deal, but what was up with being high before work, during work, after work … then loads of booze and whatever on top of that? Joann wanted to be *all the way* in her life. And she wanted someone who wanted to be all the way in it with her.

Why would a person be so willing to take a chance with hard drugs in the first place, she wondered. Perhaps some souls just had too many things to drown out. Or maybe healthy people didn't know how lucky they were. Like her dad, Joann had struggled with asthma and allergies, and like her mother, she'd been born with kidneys that could fail as she got older.

Joann did not have the luxury of chemical escape.

The Sylvan Hotel

♦

Her stomach started to hurt. She was still trying to figure out her own life, and now? Now she was only getting more lost in someone *else's* haze.

She and Bill had so much not-in-common, and the drug stuff was at the top of the list. It seemed like, for a *lot* of people, nothing was "fun" anymore, unless drugs were involved. At least Kathryn was on the same page—and Lynn liked her pot, but she wasn't out of control. Even Kelly had her limits. As for Todd? He'd probably done his share of dabbling but was too smart to be doing the hard stuff all the time. And, of course, Bryce and Robert played it pretty straight—or at least they weren't getting high *every* hour of the day—and they were definitely not doing the scary shit.

Robert. She'd been trying so hard to move on but was right back to thinking about him. Did he ever think about her? Maybe she'd finally proven she wasn't a "respectable girl." She wasn't any closer to finding a grown-up job, and she was hanging out all night in the "joints" with Bill. Although Robert never made mention of any of it. God, did he even care about her anymore? But really, what *could* he say?

Joann fought back tears. Things were getting so twisty.

"I think I'm ready now." A groggy Kathryn tightened her ponytail.

Joann nodded.

Then Miss Emerson started the car, rolled down a window, and gulped in the cold.

Click.

A cassette tape was spinning, and the Indigo Girls quietly roared to life, searching for insight between black and white. That duo had also stopped by a bar in the early a.m., seeking comfort in a drink or a friend. But there was probably more than one answer to these questions.

Joann returned to her own car, then followed Kathryn onto Madison and up to the Hill.

It was time for sleep—so they could wake up … and do it all over again.

DASHERS, DANCERS, PRANCERS, AND VIXENS

Christmas Eve, 1992. Brad, Joann, Todd, and Robert braced for a busy night. Surprisingly, the hotel grew quiet around 5:00 p.m. after most of the guests had left for parties and other events.

Only a few revelers lingered in the lounge, and one last check-in would be arriving late.

Brad was ready to do some Noel noshing, but Anna was MOD, so there were no restaurant privileges to be had. It was looking like cafeteria cuisine, unless the valets could be talked into another plan. Pizza? Burgers? Cannelloni-to-go?

Joann opened the big window to an empty valet booth.

"I think they're in the garage, Brad."

He turned up a radio.

"Base to Valet. Come in, Valet."

Reindeer were gonna fly before anyone went near the cafeteria dinner. It was Christmas Eve!

"Valet to Base. Go ahead, Base."

"Valet, I'm thinking Piecora's."

"Ten-forty, Base. Call in the order, and we'll pick it up."

Brad dialed their go-to pizzeria, and minutes later, the Sylvans feasted.

Mmmm. Pesto-vegetarian. Mmmm. Pepperoni.

Joann peeked through the slatted door to check on the desk. Not a creature was stirring, not even—

"Helloooo."

Shoot! Joann returned to the front.

"Hi Babs, what are *you* still doing here?"

"I'm meeting a friend for drinks, then I'll be heading out. Smells like pizza up here."

"Yeah, we ordered Piecora's."

"Oh, do they deliver?"

"Well …"

The Sylvan Hotel

"Joann, you guys better not make a habit of that. If Alexander catches—"

Click. The back-office door opened and closed. Then Todd flew around the corner.

"Hiya, Sweets!" Babs hugged the valet, her snowman earrings dangling and bangles bangling.

"You stickin' around, lady? Let's have a drink."

He offered his arm and steered her toward the bar.

Joann giggled.

Todd Barnes. Hotter than the flame on a figgy pudding. More powerful than a Christmas miracle. Able to transform grinchy grandes dames into giddy grandes dames.

Brad settled into PBX for a long winter's newspaper, and Robert joined Joann out front. Though on opposite sides of the desk, they stood side by side, waving to Frank as he smiled from the baby grand.

"Pizza!" mouthed Joann, gesturing to the office.

The musician waved back, then began to play.

And a piano began to make plans.

It was promising to be home for Christmas. Then it was begging for snow …

"I wish it would snow," Joann murmured.

But with or without white flurries, Christmas had once again come to the Sylvan. Outside, starry lights shined down on a fountain that barely trickled under layers of ice. All but suspended, the courtyard showpiece looked like a glassy sculpture or a cold cocoon—or a riff on that stopping-by-woods poem Joann had memorized in school:

The fountain's lovely, cold … and weeps.

The whole *scene* looked like a poem. A poem that was burning itself to memory.

Bittersweet pangs of nostalgia began to push at Joann from somewhere beneath. She still missed the Christmas Eves celebrated at her grandmother's. The Victorian house had been a quintessential setting for holiday visits by the hearth and carols around an old upright. There'd also been rare moments of peace as the fire crackled and candles flickered under frozen eaves. Sadly, after Grandma MacIntosh was moved to a nursing home, the "night before Christmas" felt lost—but here in the hotel, what had disappeared was returning.

Joann pointed to the festively decorated branches by the elevator.

"Well, that's one fancy Tannenbaum, but I *do* like my Chubby & Tubby tree at the apartment."

"Chubby & Tubby is the best!" a surprised Robert replied.

Joann wanted to tell him more Christmas-tree stories, like how her father once chopped them off the side of the road in Issaquah forests, east of the city. According to family lore, her grandfather had gambled away land out there. She didn't know much else about the man, other than that he'd installed some of the first phones in the Green Lake neighborhood. He'd also been a lighting and prop manager for The Paramount Theater and Pantages—maybe the Moore at one point, too. But no one really talked about Grandpa—mainly because he'd lived through only four of her dad's Christmases.

Joann could still see Jack behind the wheel of that old Plymouth station wagon. Perhaps those Eastside outings had been a way to keep his own father's spirit in the mix. That said, the December field trips did make for some odd memories.

Pull! Her brother would yank the chain, and their parents would unload shotguns. Clay pigeons cracked midway through the clearings while Joann cracked books—and cases—in the car. Huddled under blankets, she and Nancy Drew had chased all the clues. Another golden-backed book also went along for the ride, packed with Greek fairy tales about gods, goddesses, and a flying boy who aimed high-in-the-sky … but a little too close to flame.

Pull! Her dad had also aimed high—like he was firing off tidings to the heavens, letting a ghost know they were there. When he tired of shooting, a small saw wheezed across bark, "reclaiming" a bit of Grandpa. Then Jack MacIntosh tied his plunder to the car … and back to the city they'd go.

In later years, the tree hunt had taken them to Chubby & Tubby, a hardware store where you could buy anything from flashlights to five-dollar "Charlie-Brown" trees. Sometimes, her dad bought two and tied 'em together with fishing line. Then he'd hit Jack's Pay Less, west of Rainier Beach. The gritty shop was housed in a sort-of garage where you could get deals on Archway Christmas cookies—and whatever auto parts you needed. Ah, the smell of sugar sprinkles and motor oil …

Yeah, Joann wanted to tell Robert a lot of things. But maybe that would be too weird.

"Thanks for picking up the pizza." She patted his sleeve.

The Sylvan Hotel

Robert seized on the segue. "You're so *welcome*. Just another example of how we valets *consistently* go above and beyond—"

"Okaaay, Mister Bailey."

"Now, Jo, do you know about Beth's Cafe?"

"Where's that?"

"Aurora. Kind of a diner-trucker dive with twelve-egg omelets. Uh … but maybe you're not ready for Beth's, yet," he chortled.

"Haha, very funny."

A car pulled in, so Robert tucked a pen behind his ear and headed out.

Beep! She picked up the desk phone.

"Hey, George! You having a good Christmas Eve, so far?"

"Yo! I'm just chillin' in here. You want coffee or cocoa or somethin'?"

"No thanks. Not yet. Just calling to say hi. It's kinda quiet tonight."

"Yeah, I might get to leave early—gonna do some Christmas-Eve swing dancing!"

The barman had recently taken up Lindy Hop classes and was rock-stepping his way through the city with a whole new community of friends.

"Okay, Jo, just call if you change your mind. I'll be by later—gotta stick around for now, if you know what I mean."

"Don't worry—Babs is leaving soon. She's just meeting a friend for a drink."

"Coolio, sister. Have fun out there …"

Ding.

And what to her wondering eyes should appear, but Lynn!

"Feliz Navidad, Front Desk."

"Well, hello there, Lynnie. I see you're back on the elevator."

"You bet your ass I am, baby. It's Christmas Eve."

"Okay, but watch it. Babs is still here. She's meeting a friend in the bar."

"Thanks for the heads-up. Wouldn't wanna piss off the boss lady."

"You goin' to Aberdeen tomorrow?"

"Maaaybe. What's your action?"

"Oh, the usual, I guess. My family's into the open-presents-in-the-morning thing, and they'll start calling at nine, hollering about why am I not there yet."

Swish. The front doors opened, and a high-brow tuxedo escorted low-hanging sequins toward the desk.

"We'd like a table in the lounge."

"Sure! Go right in. One of the cocktail servers will be out to take your order."

"Thank you, Miss."

"You're welcome."

Lynn and Joann watched the couple glide away.

"Well aren't they purty," said Lynn.

"Yeah. Sheesh. Like movie stars."

"Kinda prancy if you ask me."

"Well, at least they weren't rude."

"Where's Brad? He's missing out on the fashion show. *Did you see that dress?*"

"He's reading newspapers in PBX. By the way, we ordered pizza, earlier, from Piecora's. Do you want some?"

"No thanks. I'm watching my figure."

Reaching into her apron pocket, Lynn pulled out a turndown chocolate and popped it in her mouth.

"Now that's good," she mumbled.

"Hey, is Kiet on tonight? He might want some pizza."

"It's slow. I told him to clock out."

"Why Lynn, that was so considerate of you," Joann teased.

"You know *me*. I'm a giver. In fact …"

Lynn reached into her apron pocket again.

"Merry Christmas, Joanna! I made you a mixtape! Don't say I don't do anything for y—"

"Oh my gosh! Whaaat?!?"

"Yeah, well, I know you like your grunge—and your girl bands."

The cassette case was covered in handwriting: Alice In Chains. Nirvana. Temple of the Dog. Mother Love Bone. Mudhoney. Jane's Addiction. The Cranberries. Sophie B. Hawkins …

"This is *awesome*, Lynnie. Thank you!"

Leaning over the countertop, a desk agent hugged a housekeeper.

"I love you, my friend. Merry Christmas."

"Aw, don't get me all teary now. Love you, too, Joann."

Ding.

The Sylvan Hotel

Lynn hurried to catch her ride.

Swish. Balancing a dessert tray, Finn crossed the lobby and made his funny faces at Joann. Then he spotted Lynn.

"Yo, Housekeeping. Hold up!" He stepped into the elevator. "Dude. Aren't you supposed to be taking the stairs?"

The gold doors closed as Housekeeping flipped Room Service a partridge in a pear tree.

"Valet to Base. We've got two parties without reservations."

"Plenty of room in the inn, Valet. Send 'em on through."

"That's a ten-forty, Base."

Joann welcomed the newcomers and upgraded them to suites in the spirit of Christmas Eve. Then Frank started the next tune, and a throng of locals arrived for their annual Sylvan pilgrimages. Springing into action, Todd and Robert ran up and down the hill for an hour straight, getting cars in and out of the garage.

Tick-tock. And time for a break.

"Hey there, Miss J." The piano player folded his elegant brown hands on the marble.

"Hi, Frank! Ready for dinner? There's pizza in back!"

"Nah, that's okay. George set me up with some food earlier."

"Well, thanks for all the music tonight."

"Sure thing. Any special requests?"

"You know what I want to hear."

"Goodness, Joann. Don't you and Kathryn get sick of that?"

"Never! Please-please-please?"

"All right. I'll see what I can do."

"Thanks, Santa Baby!"

"You're *welcome.*"

Minutes later, the boys finished parking all the cars, and George poured coffee to warm them up. Re-joining Joann, they stood in front of the desk, on either side of her. All three faced the lounge, taking in the jolly scene. Frank began to play, and the Charlie Brown Christmas music came to life.

Breathing out with contentment, Joann folded her arms on the marble countertop.

Todd turned to Joann.

"Margaret, how many times have you and Kathryn asked Frank to play—"

"I know, I know. But we love it!"

The valet had no argument.

This was Christmas Eve.

Raising a glass, the glamorous couple smiled at them from the lounge.

Joann waved. Maybe they had a movie-star life, but the desk agent was enjoying her own spotlight. Flanked by the Sylvan boys in blue, she was Christmas-too-cool-for-school. Standing between Todd and Robert, she felt safe but also powerful—like together, they were invincible.

If only she could freeze this moment in time, just like the icy fountain outside.

Inhaling the scent of evergreens, Joann watched ornaments quivering on the tree as people walked to and fro. Down the street, cathedral bells were ringing, and churchgoers

donned boots and scarves, making haste to welcome Christmas at midnight. It was all so magical.

"Miss, which way to the bathroom?" And … spell broken.

The guest was directed around the corner, and the boys returned to the valet booth.

8:30 p.m.

Kicking back in PBX, Brad kicked up his feet on the counter. Paging through magazines, he asked Joann if she wanted a break.

"Nope, it's okay. Nothing's really going on at the desk. It's the lounge that's—"

Then the radios started to scratch and pop.

"Valet to Base."

Robert, incoming.

Joann picked up one of the radios and peered through the PBX window. All was calm. All was bright.

"Go ahead, Valet."

The Sylvan Hotel

•

"Joann, I'd like to dedicate this song to you."

What was he up to …

"*Rudolph the—*"

And so began a Christmas-Eve serenade, featuring an endearing saga about an outsider with a nose for adventure who, one extra-foggy Yule, gets in good with Santa.

Brad looked up from his magazine.

"Well, it sounds like the Sylvan has two musical guests tonight."

Static. Pop. Static.

"Base to Valet."

"Go ahead, Base."

I will remember all of this forever. All of it. Even if we're not meant to be together. I just … will.

"Base to Valet. That was … *ahem* … lovely."

"Well, Base, we aim to please."

Chuckling, then more static.

"Housekeeping to Base."

Oh, boooy.

"Go ahead, Lynn—er—Housekeeping."

"Thank you so much for that. Room 301 thanks you as well … Delivering pillows … radio on … everyone … heard …"

"Valet to Housekeeping, you are *so* welcome."

"Hello?"

Joann peeked through the slatted door.

The senior engineer waited out front with Anna, radio in hand.

"Hi, guys. What's up?"

"Joann, you know that there are rules about how the radios are used."

Mitch tried to look stern, but that frown soon turned to laughter, and Anna rolled her eyes.

Great. Joann was going to end up with snags *and* coal in her stocking.

"It wasn't me! I didn't tell him to do that!"

"Seems like you've got your own personal Christmas caroler."

That heat was creeping into her face again.

"Sorry, Mitch. I'll be sure to remind our young valets as to the proper protocol."

"Ten … *forty*."

Winking, he headed to the bar with Anna, exchanging holiday greetings with Finn in passing.

The room-service rascal halted at the desk. Three, two, one, *evil giggle* ... and he was on his way.

A minute later, an agitated George walked out of the bar.

"What the hell, Jo?"

"What?"

"Your valet pal?"

"I swear, I had nothing to do with that!"

"Uh, huh. Well, I just so happen to have a radio in there, tonight. And it's kinda quiet.

And do you remember who's still around, getting her Christmas Eve on?"

Ohhh, shit. Babs!

"Sorry, George."

"So I'm pouring at one end of the bar, and suddenly, at the other end, Bailey's singing about reindeer."

Joann couldn't hold back the snickers. Her friend threw both hands in the air, then retied a loose apron while trying not to give in to his own snickers.

Swish. Robert re-appeared from the circle, smiled nonchalantly, and took his post at the concierge stand.

"BAILEY. What is the *matter* with you?" But George was already cracking up.

The valet burst into laughter, and George fully surrendered, face-palming as he returned to the bar.

Joann was so ... happy. They were a slightly dysfunctional family, but they were a family—and this was one of the best Christmas Eves she'd ever had. Robert pretended to organize papers at the concierge stand, and she wondered if he felt the same.

9:45 p.m.

Jingle Babs incoming.

"So, how was the bar?" Joann tried to sound as sugar-plum-perky as possible.

"Fine." The controller replied frostily.

The Sylvan Hotel

◆

Jeezus H. Claus.

"You going to be okay up here?" Babs wasn't budging.

"Yeah! Check-ins are finished, and the switchboard's not doing anything."

The earrings-in-chief slowly turned.

"Merry Christmas, Joann."

Whew.

Now dash away, dash away, dash away all!

Babs passed the concierge stand, then halted as a now solemn Robert moved to get the door. Holding it open, he stood at attention as Todd pulled her car around.

Joann held her breath, and—

"Goodnight, Elvis."

"Er … goodnight, Babs."

Somehow, Robert stayed composed, and Joann spun to face the key boxes, dangerously close to laughing out loud.

─══ ◆ ══─

10:00 p.m.

One wise pastry chef arrived bearing gifts.

"Merry, merry, children. Hope you're being nice *and* naughty." The baker extraordinaire presented two crème brûlées. "You can all share. One for the desk agents—one for the little boys."

Stan winked at Joann, and the Christmas tree star winked at Stan.

─══ ◆ ══─

10:40 p.m.

"Merry Christmas!" Captain Front Desk waved goodnight to his teammates.

"Ready?" asked Robert.

"Yes," replied Joann.

Ca-clunk. Ca-clunk. The timecards were nestled all snug in their beds—

And outside, the night was cold but warm.

Tick-tock.

"See you in a couple days?" Robert affectionately held out his arms.

Frannie James

◆

"See you, Robert."

Wrapped in a navy-jacket hug, Miss MacIntosh wished she could tell her friend that there was no better gift.

Then up on that rooftop, two Sylvans paused—but cathedral bells soon chimed, and rain began to fall.

Easing past the garage ramp, Joann turned her car onto Madison. At the top of the block, a red traffic light blinked through the mist, then swayed as if ready to take off in the wind.

On the left, palm trees twinkled, and holiday wishes hid beneath the gumdrop silhouettes of midnight umbrellas. Taxis splashed around a luminous fountain, the hillside glistened, and the love light gleamed.

Then red turned to green.

Joann slowly accelerated as Christmas sparkled in her rearview mirror.

TIMEOUTS AND TRUTHS

January 1993. Another year—and another Sylvan Christmas party!

Kathryn curled up on the sofa, and Joann pushed most of the clothes in the closet to the left. Then she unzipped the garment bags.

Three, two … one.

"I hate dressing up."

"Well, good thing you don't have to think about it, then," said Joann. "All you have to do is close your eyes and point."

Kathryn pouted in protest, so Joann chose for her, pulling out the fabulous "Baroness" dress. All those sheer-but-not-so-sheer ruffles were ready to go, perfectly layered over black velvet. It had never been worn, and now she knew why.

"Kathryn, this is *your* dress!"

Miss Emerson peeked out from under a blanket. "More like a puff pastry."

But Joann shoved the frock in her pretty face, and Kathryn marched off to the bathroom with it.

Joann chose the black-velvet floor-length halter dress she'd scored on clearance. And tonight, it was going to look like a million bucks.

Yessss. Two weeks of extra running and stair-climbing was also paying off! The thing fit like a glove. Wowza. If only the godmother could see her now …

Once upon a time, Joann's Aunt Mary had been entrusted with her niece's safekeeping—and a wand of fire. Named as godmother, she'd held the baptismal candle and committed to watch over Jack's first child. Far from her brother's idea of a role model, Aunt Mary was an unexpected choice. Most likely, it had happened through default, because Jack's other sister had nine kids of her own. So Mary stood at the altar and professed undying faith for her girl. Then the godmother passed the torch. To Jack's eventual chagrin, it was a good match—although Mary had been even more of a "rebel." Sadly, she'd kept her distance from the family, and cancer claimed her before Joann knew the story—a story later found in letters about another young Miss MacIntosh. Mary had also attended the Academy as a result of being pulled out of a different school. *You're associating with the wrong crowd!* But Mary never stopped being Mary. She dared to drink beer and smoke cigarettes, loved a good gown, and danced the nights away, all the while sassing her brother ... even if it meant he wouldn't drive her to school.

The biggest rule Mary broke was staying single until middle age. After all, she'd watched her mama barely scrape by, widowed early on with five children. Before that, Grandma had worked with Charlie Mayo as a lead surgical nurse—but marriage put an end to such things and marked the beginning of struggle. Clearly, Mary had wanted something different. So even as Jack berated Auntie for her "ways," the other Miss MacIntosh built a banking career, traveled, entertained many suitors, and refused to heed traditional expectations—or her brother.

Aunt Mary had been queen of her destiny.

Joann remembered her amazement at how both godparents could simply ignore her father. The keep-your-mouth-shut-mind-your-manners meals came to mind, where Uncle John had delighted in announcing that "a pea rolled on the floor!" Followed by his nephews and nieces giggling into the peas on their plates. Then there was the godmother, going on about adventures at sea, her love of a good ship, and starry-night capers. Joann had listened in awe, twisting an owl ring on her finger—a special gift from a special godmother. "On a cruise, one wears black at the captain's table, and you push peas onto the back of your fork," she'd wink.

But Jack had not been impressed. He'd just wanted everyone to *eat* their peas.

Here's to you, Godmother.

Joann stood tall in front of the mirror. Then she set the natural, brownish-toned lipstick aside—and on went the red one.

Bibbidi. Bobbidi. *Boom.*

Kathryn walked out of the bathroom, and both girls gasped.

"That is perfect on you, Kathryn!"

"Well, that getup is serious business on you, Jo."

"A girl's gotta do full-on black velvet at least once in her life, right?"

Kathryn shuddered. "Not me."

"Okay, I'll deliver Brad's care package, then meet you and Scott at the restaurant?"

Kathryn nodded. The boyfriend had returned and would be escorting her to the party!

The Sylvan Hotel

⬥

—⬧✦⬧—

Proceeding across 19th, Joann nervously turned onto Madison. The roads were icy, and she'd been in an accident a few weeks prior. Her father *had* said that a charcoal-gray vehicle blended too well with pavement in a perpetually overcast city, and sure enough—

Crash! A teenage driver had turned left onto Broadway, hitting the Jetta at the Madison intersection. Joann had spun out, then stopped by hitting a pole on that corner. Nobody had been hurt, and the damage had been fixed. Still, she couldn't help but feel shaky at the wheel.

—⬧✦⬧—

Silent night in the circle. Not a valet in sight.

Swish. Brad happily accepted the treat delivery.

Swish. Joann continued on her way.

At Il Terrazzo Carmine, Scott, Kathryn, and Kelly stood waiting at the doors, and—dressed in her best flannel shirt and jeans, Lynn was ready for anything! But first, she reached for her lighter. Walking in with Scott, they joined George, Finn, and Stan.

"So, Joanna, where are all your boyfriends?"

"Haha, Lynnie. We will have a good time, with or without valets!"

At the other end of the table, Scott and Kathryn didn't seem worried about any valets. Good for them, thought Joann. Things should work out right for *someone* around here.

Dinner was served, but her stomach … so … jumpy. She was still feeling shaky when the music got louder. Then someone was tapping her shoulder.

"Nicky! How are you?"

"Joann, will you dance with me?"

"I'd be honored, young sir." She took off her coat, and they hit the dance floor.

Several of the older women on staff gave her the thumbs up—even Babs!

The music stopped momentarily, and familiar arms encircled her waist.

"Yo, Nick. Mind if I get a dance?"

The kid willingly obliged and returned to his parents' table.

Joann turned, and Bill pulled her to him.

Raw determination. Pure moxie. Maybe this was the real reason she'd been feeling so nervous. And the way he *looked* at her.

Aaack. She could only imagine what the Sylvan grown-ups were thinking. The cocky kid ... and Joann? And since when was Bill okay with being so ... public? Recently, he'd attempted to actually express something, saying that she was "one of the coolest girls he knew," but if he did anything wrong or if things didn't go the right way, he'd be in trouble with everyone. So, what was *this*? Uh, and what, exactly, made her "so cool?" And were they actually going to try and navigate a social situation? This was just ... weird. Maybe he'd had a few drinks, or—

Joann turned toward the table. Lynn was aghast, and Scott was whispering to Kathryn. *Who's that?* Stan looked surprised, and Finn was fascinated— then giggling.

"Break it up, you two!"

An elated Kelly joined them on the dance floor, not wanting to miss out on whatever was happening.

1:00 a.m.

The black velvet dress lay in a rumpled heap. Bill was sleeping soundly, and Joann was not. How long could this go on? It was supposed to be a fling. So wasn't it supposed to end? Months later, he didn't seem to be tiring of the weirdness, and she was still allowing it to happen, because ... well, she didn't know why. And what was up with the mysterious girlfriend?

They'd literally gone too far. Joann liked Bill, but this was pointless. He was drugs, risk, questionable friends. He was interested in finance—good at political science. She didn't do drugs, preferred relatively straight-laced friends, knew nothing of finance, and was still learning politics.

Joann shifted on the sofa bed.

This thing was getting uncomfortable.

She looked at the clock: 3:30 a.m. Then, looking at Bill, she felt a surprising twinge of sadness. Joann gently pushed back his hair.

Someday, they would no longer know one another. Someday—

He opened his eyes.

What are we doing? What is this?

And Joann floated away.

The Sylvan Hotel

The following Tuesday, she returned to the hotel dreading after-party gossip, but thankfully, no one commented. Then Alicia joined her at the desk. They were reviewing the check-in list when Robert stopped by for his list and newspaper.

"Joann, you are *so* efficient," he gushed and ran off.

"So," Alicia whispered, "*Ahem* … if … if you … if you end up with anyone from the hotel, I … *ahem* … I think … well, Joann … um … you and Robert …"

Okaaaaaaay. Looks like her manager was going to make the comments.

"He has a girlfriend, Allie."

"Well, anyway … I've … probably said enough. Yeah, so … let me know if you have any questions. I'll be around for a few more minutes."

Joann straightened the freshly potted orchid on the desk. Arrrgh. She needed to straighten out her life. When was she going to get beyond this place? When was she going to grow up?

She was losing control. Of everything. And, yeah, she had questions. But none she should be asking her boss!

The extension phone beeped.

"Hi—Joann?"

"Nicky??? What's up?"

"Can you get my dad?"

Uh-oh. He sounded upset.

"Okay, hold on. I'm going to check across the hall before I transfer you to make sure someone's there."

Hurrying out the back-office door, Joann rushed to Mr. Alexander's office. He was in a meeting, but his assistant was all ears.

"Merril, Nicky's calling. I think it's important. I'm going to transfer him," she warned.

Moments later, Mr. Alexander threw his key ring at Joann and ran out the front door.

"What happened?" she asked Robert.

"Mrs. Alexander left the kid at Bellevue Square."

What the—how do you leave your child at a mall?

So much for grown-ups.

Frannie James

♦

Joann looked at the check-in list. Okay. Mr. Mann and crew were expected tonight. She needed to step on it with the career stuff. She needed to grab her chance. Maybe tonight he'd—

"Hey, Margaret."

"Hey, Todd. How goes it?"

"Good. I'm outta here soon. Can I get change?"

Joann opened the cash drawer.

"You majored in communications, too—advertising, right? Still thinking about it?"

The boy shrugged his shoulders.

"I'm thinking I've got some more traveling to do."

Translation: He *wasn't* that interested, anymore. But Todd was a tough person to read: so cucumber-cool … and that poker face barely faltered. You never knew exactly what—

"Valet to Base. Ogilvy & Mather is arriving."

Joann began the check-ins. One by one, a band of travelers from another "Madison Avenue" filed into the elevator, ready to raid minibars and hit the sheets. Then they'd wake up, head off to software land, seize the day, and even more Northwest treasure—er, agency billings.

"Mr. Mann will be arriving later." Lizzy eyed Joann.

"Can I help you with anything else?" An extra-attentive Bill eyed Lizzy.

"No thanks!" She snatched her bag from him and joined the others at the elevator.

Joann burned with embarrassment. Why did Bill have to do that right in front of her? Yes, they were "casual." But she hated his increasingly over-the-top and in-your-face display of appreciation for the ad agency girls. It left her feeling like dirt. And she'd agreed to "no-strings" with him because she thought he could (at least!) be respectful. Obviously, she was wrong. Instead, Joann had lowered herself to upholding the bullshit. She was a fucking hypocrite and had failed herself in the worst way.

The valet was now eyeing Miss MacIntosh, so she took shelter with Brad in PBX.

—◆—

8:00 p.m.

Mr. Mann, incoming.

"Well, there's my girl."

Robert, Jed, and Bill gathered at the concierge stand, and Joann checked him in. The VIP confirmed a 10:30 p.m. meet-up in the lounge and was off to his room. Bill looked like he was going to punch everything, and Robert looked disgusted.

Come on, ten-thirty. Let's get on with this.

"Housekeeping to Base."

"Go ahead, Housekeeping."

"Base, can I call you at extension four?"

"Yes, Housekeeping. I'm at the front."

Beep!

"Hi, Lynnie!"

"Hey, Joann. Can I please get a ride tonight?"

"Of course!"

She would never say no. Not after all the times she'd had to beg people for rides.

Not after being dragged up that hill. Joann would never put anyone in that position. Ever.

"I'm having a drink with the Ogilvy guy at 10:30-ish, so I'll be ready at 11:20-ish."

"Look out, girl. You know how those corporate types are."

"It's just job stuff! I'll meet you in the cafeteria afterwards."

"Ten-four."

And time for a break. Brad agreed to hold down the fort, so she wandered across the lobby toward the kitchen. Ken and Khloe Wolf passed her on the way, quickly turning their noses to the Sylvan stratosphere. Joann put *her* best poker face forward, but almost laughed at the thought of lurching out at them, Tory-style.

"What's up, darlin'?' Slow night?" Stan pulled and pushed at freshly made dough.

Nodding, Joann breathed in warm cooking smells that brought her grandmother's kitchen to mind. Rosemary MacIntosh could be so stern, but she'd tie on an apron over those mean-old-lady shoes and soften like creamed butter. Then flour and sugar were scooped out of big built-in pantry bins, ready for stirring into all kinds of deliciousness. Grandma had been well versed in everything from divinity to mousse, and at one time, she'd even baked for Frederick & Nelson. Fancy people could buy her cookies (and Frangos!) at the famous Seattle department store—and she could keep the basics on the table at home.

Joann breathed in again. Yum. All those pots, pans, and kettles rattling with goodness; like a taste of the past simmering in the present.

Stan continued with the dough, and Finn began to prep a cart. Joann watched as he arranged prim, linen-lined trays with chocolates, VIP matchboxes, petite flower vases, bottles of bubbly—

"Are your boyfriends working tonight?"

Finn ducked as she threw a dishrag at him.

"Give it a rest, kids. This is a small space. Room Service, keep your mouth shut, and Front Desk, no throwing shit." Wrapping up his ingredients, Stan began to clean the board.

"Hey, so ... what's goin' on with that Conner Mann guy?" Finn was back to serious.

"I'm hoping he can help me break into advertising."

Stan frowned. Pausing from his work, the flour-dusted defender struck a serious tone.

"Joann, keep in mind: not everyone has your best interests at heart."

"I know, but it's really just career stuff!"

"Penis-penis-penis." Room Service just couldn't resist.

"Dude. You need a new line." Joann swatted him and walked out.

"For fuck's sake, you two," Stan restarted the "this is a small space" lecture. Then he returned to his task, and Joann returned to the lobby.

At 10:25 p.m., she began to organize her receipts.

"Jo, can I get change?" Robert tucked a pen behind his ear and started counting.

"Sure." Looking at him, Joann tried to feel nothing. But ... it was hopeless. She knew she would always feel something—

Ding.

Mr. Mann, incoming.

Robert retreated from the desk.

"Ready?" Mr. Mann watched as Joann tidied the countertop.

"Yes—be right there."

The Sylvan Hotel

◆

She deposited her cash in the safe, then Robert radioed.

"Jo, do you want me to wait—"

"No, it's okay. I'll be fine!"

"Ten-forty, but have Ollie walk you to the car."

"Will do. See you tomorrow."

Joann hurried to meet Mr. Mann.

"Are you working on your portfolio?" The VIP sipped his drink. "A good starting point is a good book."

"Yes. I'm creating some fake, er—'spec' ads. One of the valets does graphic design, and he can help me put them into layout."

At least, she hoped Bryce would help her.

"Do you see yourself staying in Seattle?"

"If there's an opportunity elsewhere, I suppose I'd be open to leaving."

"Keep in mind, though, you gotta be *red-hot* to make it as a creative."

"Understood. But … I'm up for the challenge! I did well in my copy class, and I'm ready to try it in the real world. Also, I'm really interested in 'conceptual' copywriting—"

"How are we doing? Need anything else?" George was checking in.

"No, sir. I've got to call it a night. Joann, shall I walk you to your car?"

Now the bartender was frowning, but Joann ignored him.

"Sure, Conner. We can go out the front. Then it's just a few steps to the garage, where I'm parked on the roof."

"How exciting. I get to see some of your world: the behind-the-scenes of the Sylvan!"

If you only knew.

Out the front door and onto the hillside. Next stop? The ramp to the garage roof—where Joann traversed an even slipperier slope.

"Ah, Volkswagen. Cute."

"Yeah, thanks. I like it."

The ad man fell silent.

Um … this was starting to feel …

Was he waiting for her to say—?

This was feeling wrong.

Arrrrgh. Robert had *told* her to leave with Ollie. Why hadn't she listened to him? Was she just so determined to prove him wrong—and now … now she was—

Mr. Mann moved toward her, and she abruptly opened the car door.

"Thanks so much for the walk! See you next time!"

His lips curled. Was that a *sneer*?

"Goodnight, Joann. See you next time."

Oh, no. Had she messed this up? *Fuck!* Her imagination was working overtime. Again. Hopefully, she hadn't lost her chance at a career. What if he didn't talk to her anymore? This is how it worked, right? You got those kinds of jobs through knowing the right people. Ugh. She could just hear Lynnie … Oh, shoot! Lynnie was waiting!

After circling back to pick up her friend, Joann practically floored it to Kay's—where it was safe.

"What up, girlies?" Kelly was just getting out of a cab.

Standing in the entry, the Sylvans waited for their eyes to adjust, then moved forward. Bill was parked at a back table and—was Joann supposed to avoid eye contact or … what? He nodded, so she waved, trying not to cringe. This was beyond stupid. But he was with his friends, and she was with hers. Most of all, they were *not* a couple, which meant "shields up."

"I'm declaring girls' night!" Joann lifted her glass.

"Whatever, Joann," Kelly laughed. "I see him looking at you. He can't resist, and neither can you, you bad girl!"

That girl found humor in everything. Why couldn't Joann be more like—

"Lighten up, sista, I'm just kidding!" Kelly laughed again.

Then Lynn pulled out her cigarettes.

"Give me one of those!" Kelly begged.

"God, you guys. Can you give the cancer a rest for just one night?"

Marlboro smoke incoming.

"*Bill!* Woo-hoo!" Kelly was on a roll.

"What up, ladies?"

"Sit!" Kelly was also on a mission.

"Sorry, I've got plans." He stared at Joann.

Let the games begin.

But she wasn't playing.

"I'll sit with you, Kell." Their favorite bartender had arrived.

"George!" All three girls attacked their fellow Sylvan with hugs.

The valet left, and Joann breathed out, but then it felt like something was sinking—

The Sylvan Hotel

Oh, hell no! This night was not going to bring her down. She would make the best of it with her own buddies. But a heaviness kept pushing on her from somewhere. Pocketing a quarter, she headed to the payphone. School was out for winter break, so Kathryn would likely be up.

"Jo? What's wrong?"

"I think the stuff with Bill has gone too far. And, yeah, I still have unresolved feelings about Robert. And my career's going nowhere. And I got all paranoid tonight and thought Mr. Mann was gonna *kiss* me—so I probably destroyed my chances of further help from *him*. Um, and I miss you! God, I'm such a loser. Sorry. I …"

"Breathe, Jo. You didn't destroy anything, and if you did, well, you don't need Mr. Mann. And Bill's probably freaked out, too, because whatever you guys are doing—well, you're still doing it. As for Robert? He might be struggling with his own confusion—but he does need to stop with the hot-and-cold. And I miss *you!*"

Despite her friend's kindness, Joann was hot with shame. She had to learn how to handle this stuff by herself. She didn't want to become a burden. Also, Kathryn was moving on with her life and career. What if, someday, her friend just left for some reason? It's not like it hadn't happened before. Joann didn't have the best track record when it came to people sticking around.

A high-school memory surfaced: The Academy, circa 1985. Zoe Wendelson was looking for something different—something outside of her Queen Anne circle—and Joann MacIntosh was it. Soon they were teaming up for dances, football games, and off-campus lunches. Zoe had a car that could take them to Taco Time!

Joann was proud of her friendship with Zoe, and Zoe felt at ease around Joann. Even better, *Zoe's* new bestie was friends with the handsome Danny. At one point, Joann happily introduced the two. A super-popular girl and a super-sought-after guy? Surely, it was inevitable. But Zoe's expectations quickly clashed with Danny's reality. The south-end boy did not have the time, the right clothes, or the money required for dating a dream girl, and he broke it off two weeks in.

A month later, Zoe hit the floor, drunk and drowning in a puddle of disillusionment. Her parents' marriage was broken, and on top of that, she—who nobody ever dumped—had been dumped. Joann had never seen the golden girl look so … real.

"It's *all* bullshit," she sobbed.

Days later, the society princess was back to holding court in school halls. But Joann had seen too much, so that was the end of that. Then again, maybe the whole thing had just been an alliance of convenience ... or a novelty had worn off. Either way, Zoe moved on, and Joann became part of what needed forgetting. Most importantly, Miss MacIntosh was to keep her mouth shut. Period. The end.

Yep. You just never knew how long a friendship would last. Because ties could be cut. Severed by truths, lies, mistakes, secrets—and secrets behind secrets.

"Jo, you okay? I love you. I'm here for you. Always."

"Thanks, Kath. I'll let you get some sleep. Love you, too."

Back at the table, Kelly was flying high, and Lynn was falling over.

"Um ... George?!?" Joann threw up her hands.

"What, Jo? I'm not their babysitter!" Laughing, he pushed a beer toward her.

"Yeah! He's not our babysitter!" Kelly bounced up and down in the booth, and Lynnie looked like she needed a nap.

"So what happened with Mr. Crab Cakes?"

"Nothing. We just talked advertising, then he walked me to my car."

"Uh, huh."

"I swear! That was it!"

"And what's going on with your boyfriend? He looked wasted, but his little posse looked like they were just getting started."

"First: He's not my boyfriend. Second: I'm not *his* babysitter."

"I heard *that!*" George took a swig.

"Joanna, can we go? It's time to ... go ..." Lynn was now in a fetal position.

The Bainbridge ferry was docking, and Joann pushed Kelly out of the car.

"Don't miss your boat!"

Next stop: an apartment building on Belmont, between Downtown and Capitol Hill.

"We're here, Lynnie!" Joann nudged her drowsy friend.

The car idled, foggy with late-night temperatures.

"Bill's kinda growing on me," muttered Lynn.

"Okaaay … where did *that* come from?"

"But Joanna, I have to say something. Please don't freak out. I'm sorry, but I have to."

"Lynnie, you can say whatever you need to say to me. Seriously."

"Joann. I … I think I love you."

"Well, yeah. I love you, too."

"No, Joanna. I—oh, fuck."

*Oh, fuck. Joann, you idiot. She **loves** you.*

"Lynn, are you—?" Joann breathed in. How did one have *this* conversation? She couldn't hurt—or lose—her Sylvan sister.

"Yeah, I've started dating girls. But I have the biggest crush on *you*. Oh-my-god. I'm so embarrassed."

"*Lynnie*. Please don't be embarrassed. I'm flattered, and I'll always love you as my friend, no matter what. But I … uh … dig boys. I'm a total freak! I can't help it!"

The girls giggled.

"Look, we spend a lot of time together, and it makes sense that you might get a crush. I mean, we're hanging out, right when you're *figuring* it out. But I don't care, Lynn. I swear. Hey, if it makes you feel better, I can totally relate to crushing on someone who isn't available!"

"Oh, Joann. You're so tragic." She blew smoke out the window.

"And … *there* is the Lynn I know and love."

"You're really not mad at me?"

"Never."

"You're a jewel, Joann. Totally golden. I hope one of those boys figures that out."

"Aw, Lynnie. *You're* golden. And you're gonna make me cry."

"You're gonna make *me* cry. Hey, you wanna get stoned? We could listen to some 4 Non Blondes."

"Tempting as that is, I think what I need right now is a good night's sleep."

"Well, if you're sure."

"Yeah, I'm sure. And you could use some rest, too. But remember, I'm still your same old friend. I swear!"

"Word."

Wiping the window, Joann watched a tired Sylvan stumble up the stairs and waited 'til she got safely into her apartment. What the hell, Universe?

Frannie James

◆

Lynn wanted Joann. Joann wanted Robert. Robert wanted Tricia. Tricia was in New York. Todd wanted Kathryn. Kathryn wanted Scott. Bill … *sigh*.

The alarm clock was going off: *Time-for-work-time-for-work-time-for-work!* Joann was living in a Sylvan vacuum.

George zipped through the lobby, rushing out as she arrived.

"Later, skater! Me and Bailey are playing hoops tonight. Gotta go!"

Shoot. Work just wasn't the same without Robert—or George, for that matter.

Swish. The stair door opened, and Joann waved to three morning-shift housekeepers making final rounds for the day. Crossing the lobby, they hesitated, looking at her curiously.

Joann knew what that was about. She and Bryce were the only employees at the front of the house with the slightest hint of brown, other than Frank, who was hidden in a corner behind the piano, and Ollie, who worked the graveyard shift alone. It had been like that at the restaurant job, too. People of color were still at the back, along with the occasional white kid from the wrong side of the tracks.

Waving tepidly, the housekeepers hastily moved past. Guilt heated up inside Joann but quickly boiled over into frustration. The women could barely hide the suspicion on their faces.

Childhood scenes of Filipino potlucks rolled like scratchy film in her mind. She had dreaded them as much as church. Her mother had been trying to stay connected to the culture, but Joann always felt like a caged cat at those things—or a fish out of water. More scenes rolled through her mind:

Women in the kitchen. Men on the stoop. Fried rice. Plain rice. Rice, rice, rice.

"You don't know Ilocano? Not even Tagalog?"

The ladies would look at Joann, then around and through her. The girl wasn't all-the-way-white, but she wasn't really Asian, either. Nerdy, too. And—horrors! She liked mashed potatoes.

Auntie Lumpia. Auntie Pancit. Adobo bullies. Bibingka meanies.

"Say hello to the aunties, Joann."

They're not my aunties.

The Sylvan Hotel

Being mixed was mysteriously off-putting. Joann wasn't white enough, but she also wasn't brown enough. Somehow, she was always in-between. And this type of "in-between" was extra tricky. Because people needed to be able to put you in *one* box. It made them feel better. About what, exactly, she didn't know.

And she hated the who-do-you-think-you-are-trying-to-be-one-of-them stuff.

I'm me! I'm Joann MacIntosh! I'm just a girl from Seattle!

The phone rang, interrupting her thoughts.

"Hey, Jo."

"Hi, Robert! Heard you're playing basketball tonight. That sounds fun!"

"Yeah, a rec game. I could … pick you up."

"*Oh*. Uh, okay! Well, lemme call Kathryn. Maybe she can cover for me."

Joann could barely remember her best friend's number.

"Kath! Can you please cover … couple hours? Rec game … said he'd pick me up!"

He's picking me up.

At 5:30 p.m., one desk agent ran downstairs to change, and another quickly "subbed" in.

"Thank you, Kathryn!"

Both girls agreed to bypass the timeclock, and Joann would just pay her friend for the hours out of pocket. That way, Babs wouldn't suspect any funny business.

Out in the circle, Todd, Sam, and Jed watched in surprise as an off-duty Robert pulled forward. Yellow camper van. Headlights on! Joann giggled. She was sneaking out again.

The Sylvans were soon cruising across the Viaduct, and Volkswagen windows framed a fiery view. Hard glass edges dissolved on the tallest downtown buildings, burnished by the setting sun. Puget Sound skies stretched far and wide in a backdrop of orange-pink, and Robert also seemed to radiate light. Joann couldn't believe it. They weren't in a Town Car. They were in his car. And they were leaving the hotel. Together.

A boy switched gears, and a girl's heart jolted. Gawd, and those forearms—

Be calm, Joann. Be calm.

"Time out!"

Joann watched George and Robert commiserate, courtside.

The two boys were naturals. Their passing game was on point, and together, they owned the alley-oops. Best of all, they were having a blast. So different from the angry boys who lettered at school. No technicals; no tantrums; no posturing. Pretty graceful, actually.

The boys jumped back in, and the Sylvan spectator silently cheered. It was so nice being "kids" together, no matter how old they were, who they were, what they were, or where they were from. And good-old-fashioned fun ... was fun! Breathing out, she felt that feeling again—like she was right where she was supposed to be.

Back at the Sylvan, Robert dropped Joann off—but not before they discussed their work schedules. The pair promised to see one another the next day, then, walking into the lobby, Joann felt like the evening light had pierced her heart and was leaking out all over the place.

"Kath, just give me a sec to throw on my uniform!"

"Did you have a nice time?"

"Yes! Thanks so much for covering!"

"It's no big deal. Glad you could go."

"Thank-you-thank-you-thank-you."

"No prob."

Kathryn looked worried; skeptical; unconvinced. Joann knew her friend was being protective, but maybe Robert was rethinking things. On the other hand, maybe he was just being polite. Or maybe he was getting confused again. Or ... oh, screw it. Right now, Joann just wanted to put doubt in time out—because a Seattle girl liked a Seattle boy, and maybe, just maybe, he liked her, too.

Whew. Twenty-four years, and her life was still trying to get up a big ol' hill of hope—trying to get to *some* destination. What that was she wasn't exactly sure ... but she wasn't stopping now.

THE STARGAZERS

Captain Front Desk pushed aside the check-in list—down to three arrivals, and it was only 7:00 p.m.

Tick-tock.

The second-to-last Wednesday of January was going torturously slow.

Joann opened the big window. Todd and Bill were counting the hours, too, passing the time with newspapers and TV. Robert was off as Tricia was in town, but Joann was relieved.

The hot-and-cold routine had picked up yet again, and lately, temperatures were falling in a big way.

At times, Robert didn't talk to her. At times, Joann didn't talk to him. At times, he stayed in the garage. At times, she stayed in PBX. He still walked her to the car when they were scheduled together, but something was really shifting.

"Joann, you can sit in PBX for a while, if you want."

Brad took a seat on the window ledge, and Joann took the hint. Let the boy-bonding begin! She planted herself at the switchboard, but it was giving her the silent treatment, too.

Well, back to her novel. Kathryn had suggested a medieval fantasy, and Joann was enthralled, reading all about goddesses, pagans, priestesses, and writings in the stars.

Amazing that the book wasn't bursting into flames.

Bless me Father, for I have sinned. It's been a million years since my last confession, and I've been enjoying heathenish books—

"What's up, Joann?" Bill walked into PBX with a folder in his hand.

And heathenish nights.

"Hey! More poli-sci? Need an editor?"

He handed it over, relief on his face. "Thanks, Joann."

This was so bizarre. You'd never know that they'd been together the night before. But apparently, compartmentalization was how this worked. He *had* been much more respectful lately, but how did people do this kind of thing long-term? Or did they *not* usually—

Joann grabbed a pen. Bill was finishing up at UW and had recently asked her for editing help with his assignments. At first, she didn't know whether to be annoyed or flattered.

It was nice to share something other than partying and check-ins, although she was trying not to be paranoid about being used. But truthfully, it was a little late to start worrying about that.

And wasn't she using him, too? Just because she hadn't been casual with anyone before didn't mean she wasn't guilty of the same thing.

Page one. Page two. Page three.

Sigh. Quiet shifts just weren't the same without Robert.

For god's sake. She'd just been up all night with Bill—and she was editing his paper—but she was back to thinking about Robert. What was her *problem?* Clearly, she had two … and she needed to move on from both of them. One couldn't make up his mind. The other had too many issues. But she obviously had issues of her own and seemed stuck, unable to move past whatever all this was.

Maybe she should start working mornings. Badass Matt had recently done that, and he seemed … well, more badass than ever. Yeah! Time for her to be a badass, too—and finally get on track with the job thing. Time to focus on her career. *Not boys.* Sigh. Maybe it was just time to leave the Sylvan, once and for all.

Beep.

"Good evening, the Sylvan Hotel. How may I—"

"Hey, Jo."

"Kathryn! Hi! We miss you! What's happening in the outside world?"

"I miss you guys, too! Just tired from school and feeling blah."

"Come by if you want. Hang out in the back with me. We're done with check-ins, and I'm just working on Bill's poli-sci stuff."

"Now he's got his own personal editor? And who else is on with you tonight?"

"Well … Brad and Todd are here."

"So, do you think I should come by? You know, because—"

"Kath, I think it's okay. Todd can handle it."

"I haven't seen or talked to him in a while, and it's not like I've been working a lot at the hotel, and—"

"Just come by. Spend the night with your fellow Sylvans!"

"How about you, Jo? Are you spending the night with a fellow Sylvan?"

"Now you sound like Lynn. Get your butt in the car, and get over here. We can order pizza and catch up!"

"Okay."

Joann reached for a radio.

"Base to Valet."

"Come in, Base."

"Kathryn's on her way in. You guys up for pizza?"

"Todd to Margaret. Call it into Piecora's. We'll go get it."

"Ten-four. Thanks, Todd."

Buzz. Pop! Whine.

"Housekeeping to Base."

"Go ahead, Housekeeping."

"Did I hear someone say pizza?"

"Affirmative."

Internal call. Housekeeping.

"Joaaanna, what's going on?"

"Hey, Lynn! Kathryn's on her way in. She's not scheduled, but we're gonna get dinner because we're hungry and feeling blah. Hop on the ol' elevator, and join us!"

"Who's up there with you?"

"Just Brad, me, Todd, and Bill. No management. They're all gone for the night."

"Okay, well … unless you two wanna dine alone with your boyfr—"

"Bye, Lynn. See you in a few."

Click.

Bill walked through the back office and into PBX again.

"Joann, what kind of pizza are you ordering?"

"Our usual: pesto-vegetarian and a combo … Why? Any special requests?"

"*Come on*, Joann. You gotta get Canadian bacon and pineapple!"

"Okay, then. If you feel that strongly about it!"

"But *you* have to try it, too."

"I've had it before—it's good!"

"Cool. Me and Barnes will pick it up."

"Thank you!"

"Anytime." He leaned in closer, raising his eyebrows.

Joann tried not to laugh—or blush. Bill cracked her up when he tried to be "suggestive." It was way cuter than too-cool-for-school, better than any game, and sometimes, it was even … sweet. Then again, that was probably the effect he was going for.

Minutes later, the circle flooded with light, and Joann could hear a car pulling in.

Miss Emerson had arrived.

Miss MacIntosh held her breath. *Please let this go okay.*

Todd held all the doors open, Bill rounded up the Town Car, and Joann went back to editing.

"Hello, stranger!"

Brad caught up with Kathryn while Joann reviewed the rest of Bill's work. Flipping to the last page, she heard Todd's voice. Then, peeking through the PBX door, Joann saw a Kathryn who was shining brighter than ever. A girl who was happy to be with her crew again. A girl who was smiling up a storm.

"Barnes. Let's go. Pizza!" Bill held up the Town Car keys and shook them.

"Can you grab it, man?" Todd didn't want to go anywhere.

Bill's eyes were rolling, but he complied with a knowing smile, practically winking at Joann as she pushed through to the front. Whatever Todd asked you to do, well, you did it. And it didn't take a genius to see what—or who—the priority was at present.

Ding.

"Well good evening, Kathryn."

"Lynn! Oh, my gosh. I've missed you!"

The two girls hugged.

"Hey, kids, sounds like a party out here!" Joann took a seat on the window ledge.

"Hi, Jo!"

Kathryn was starting to look so grown-up, especially on the other side of the desk.

"Joann, there's no sitting on the ledge—no matter how high your heels are," Lynn joked.

Undeterred, Miss MacIntosh rested against the big window.

"Pizza should be here soon. I called it in earlier, and Bill—"

"Aw. Isn't that great? Bill can be *so* helpful." Lynn teased.

Joann telepathically swatted her, and Kathryn stifled a giggle. Then she and Todd headed to the bar to see George.

"Meet me around back!" Joann motioned to Lynn.

Click—and they sat in the office for a while, talking.

"So what's up with Todd? Didn't Kathryn put some space into that situation?"

"Yeah. It's weird. Not bad-weird, just … confusing-weird—and kinda sad. Like, okay, Kathryn and Scott seem totally solid. They're the whole package, right? They're 'everything.' But Todd … Todd's a very important *something*. I dunno. Maybe for Kathryn, he's a lifeline in the *middle* of everything."

"But … if 'everything' is so perfect, why do you need a lifeline?"

"Maybe everything isn't always so perfect. Or maybe it's not even about that. Maybe it's about needing a lifeline in the middle of ourselves. Or a map *back* to ourselves. Like a lifeline between who we're 'supposed' to be—or who we thought we'd be—and who we actually are."

—✦—

"Pizza!" Bill pushed through the back-office door, arms loaded with Piecora's boxes.

Click. Kathryn and Todd followed, then George and Brad joined.

Dinner was served, and in between slices, Lynn and Bill talked Fugazi, Brad and George talked Sonics, and Kathryn described some of her students to Todd. The room felt like a big hug, and Joann breathed it all in. Hopefully, this wouldn't be the last supper of the season.

Beep. The switchboard agreed.

"Good evening, the Sylvan Hotel—"

"Jo!"

"Hi, Kelly! Hey, what do you think about a fondue party? My apartment's small, but we could make it work, and I have my mom's old pots! Maybe … like on a Tuesday? The hotel should be quiet, so most of us will be off or out of here early."

"Yay-yay-yay!"

Frannie James

◆

⇒ ✦ ⇐

A week later, Joann made her way toward the hotel entrance, weaving around idling cars and valets. Palm leaves whispered, and strains of music escaped through the main doors, quickly lost beneath the whir of travel and transport.

"Margaret."

An anxious Todd stopped her between the fountain and the valet booth.

"Hey. You okay? What is it?"

To her surprise, the valet began to talk. To really talk. He began … to confess.

"I—what should I—I—don't know what to do—Kathryn. I—what should I do?

Should I—should I back off?"

A bell cart rolled by; car doors opened and closed; walkie-talkies shouted. But Joann heard none of it. Because a tidal wave was crashing in. A tidal wave of truth.

Todd's infamous "cool" was completely gone. No more bro code. No more girl code. Just … truth. A boy was in love with a girl. But the girl couldn't love him back in the same way. And he didn't know how to let go. He didn't know how to give up.

Joann was all at once stunned and devastated. The guy needed answers … from her?

And there was no sugar-coating any of it. He'd see right through any bullshit—but she didn't want to hurt him, either. She also had a responsibility to Kathryn.

Standing there, Todd waited for her to answer.

"Um …" she began.

Jeezus, god. What were the words? He had accidentally fallen for his friend. And it was not to be. Two paths had crossed, but the stars were not aligned.

Okaaay. It's not like she could say *that*.

Sigh. How to not drive the knife in further?

"I'm sorry, Todd," she continued. "But … *Kathryn is with someone else.* I know it's not fair. Trust me: I get it. I'm so sorry."

Last rites for an ill-fated love.

Joann touched his arm.

Should I hug him?

No. She knew that he wouldn't have it. They were in the middle of a driveway full of guests and Sylvan staff. It was not the place to make a scene.

Nodding, Todd backed away, but he held her gaze a moment longer as if to hold on for something. Anything.

Goddammit. *Why* did this have to happen? How could life be so unkind? If you weren't meant to be together, then why would the universe lead you down shiny avenues of possibility? It was like they were all being moved around on someone's chess board.

Fuck you, Universe.

The following Monday, Joann and Brad passed the time discussing life and fondue at the desk. Todd was in the garage, and Robert was in the valet booth reading his paper. Tricia was still visiting, so they'd both be at the party, but Joann refused to worry about any of that. She just wanted to have some fun with her friends. Winter in Seattle was exceptionally dreary—

And they could all use a break from the gray.

Brad retreated to PBX, then a valet quietly stopped by on his way out.

"You should come to the party, Todd. Please think about it."

Joann tried not to sound like she was pitying him. She was in awe of him. Mister Barnes had said the most honest thing she'd heard in a long time. He'd put it all on the line.

He'd put it all on the line for love.

"Yeah, okay. See you there. Later, Margaret."

A Sylvan rock star adjusted his beret, turned, and took off.

Todd Barnes. Always and forever, too-cool-for-school.

Tuesday arrived, and the clock was ticking. Joann swept and scrubbed, then Kathryn walked over to help cook. They also reminded Joann's neighbors about the party, promising to keep music levels and the number of guests within reason.

George showed up next, followed by Kelly and Lynn.

"Hey, Joann! Is this where it all happens?" Lynn pointed to the sofa.

Frannie James

◆

"Eww!" laughed Kelly.

"Thanks for that imagery." George made a grossed-out face and gulped his beer.

"Jooooo—I didn't hear an answer to that question," taunted Kelly.

"Oh, wouldn't you all just love to know!" shouted Joann from the kitchen.

"Not really," George sassed. "Is *he* stopping by?"

Nope. Bill had plans. Besides, something like that would probably be too boyfriend-ish.

"*He* is out with the guys." Joann turned on the stove.

"Holy cow, that's a lot of cheese!" Kathryn exclaimed.

"It's fondue, baby! Fire that shit uuuup!" Kelly woo-hooed and inspected the music selections.

"Christ, Kell. Chill out!" George threw back another gulp of beer while she laughed her way through the rest of Joann's cassettes.

"Hahaha. Faith No More. Soundgarden. Smashing Pumpkins. I know who *you've* been hanging out with! Wait—Sting?"

"What? I like Sting," Joann argued from the kitchen. "Gordon Sumner's a damn good writer!"

And a spiritual superhero, she thought.

Tory and Sam showed up next with cocktail servers Beth and Lee, followed by Jed and his new girlfriend Sadie. Recently hired by the Sylvan, Sadie was a more junior manager and a not-so-stuffy day-shift sophisticate. She made a big effort to be kind to the desk agents, and she brought out the best in an otherwise temperamental Jed.

Joann giggled. Sadie was changing *all* of their lives!

Then Finn was giggling, having just arrived with three of his kitchen buddies. Joann's apartment was bursting at the seams, but they were making it work. The Sylvans were safe and warm inside a giant bubble of belonging.

"Hey! There they are! What's up, Bailey?"

George slapped Robert on the back and shook Tricia's hand.

The couple waved through the kitchen door, and Joann pretended to be extremely busy stirring cheese. Tonight was a no-drama zone. Tonight was about being together—and friendships she hoped would last.

"You okay?" Kathryn wrapped an arm around her.

"It's all good." Miss MacIntosh kept stirring.

"And ... did you ... ahem ... is ... Todd ...?"

"Yeah. But just so you know, he asked me what he should do. And ... I ... well, I re-emphasized what you told him."

Kathryn nodded. And the cheese bubbled. And the chocolate melted. And a grater grated. And the knife—

11:50 p.m.

One batch of fondue to go.

"Ouch!" Blood seeped out of Joann's left index finger. She had sliced into the skin beneath her knuckle. "God, that hurts!"

Kathryn rushed over with a dishcloth. "What did you *do*?"

"I dunno. The blade just slipped—"

"Jo, that is seriously bleeding."

"What the hell's going on in here?" Lynn walked into the kitchen. "Oh, Christ. Injury!"

She slowly backed away.

"Yeah, but it's fine. Pass me that spatula, will you, Lynn?"

"Um, *no*," Kathryn protested. "Lynn, keep Jo away from the stove. I don't want blood in my fucking fondue!"

They pushed her into a corner chair, and Joann watched the dishcloth soak through again.

In the living room, most of the guests were on their way out.

Take-care. Catch-you-later. Adios. See-you-on-the-flip-side.

The goodbyes had begun.

Joann looked at the clock. Where was Todd?

"Well, Kath, he said he'd be here."

"Maybe ... maybe he found a way to put some ... space ..."

A drafty shadow hovered, and Kathryn shut the kitchen window.

Holding onto the towel, Joann applied more pressure.

But the Sylvan kept on bleeding.

Unstoppable red. Resolute red. Defiant red.

Using her free arm, Joann pushed the window open again, breathing in as a chilly wind blew past. The night skies were clear—and almost too bright.

Frannie James

♦

One mile away, he lay on the ground, looking at the stars. It was cold, but he didn't feel cold.

He made a wish that she would be happy, always. It was what he wanted. He knew she'd given him what she could. He knew she loved him. And he loved her. And nothing else mattered.

SILENT SCREAMS

He'd been gone a month and a half.

Joann hugged the covers. Sometimes, now, she couldn't handle the thought of work. And when she drove by that intersection, she wanted to wail.

On a late night in February of 1993, a fiercely golden Sylvan had turned for Capitol Hill, driving an International Scout. Seatbelt off. Roof off. Doors off. Soon the boy was flying. Flying, flying, flying. Flying through darkness, past the moon ... and into the stars.

Hours later, Tory spoke urgently from the answering machine.

"Joann. I—I'm so sorry. Todd Barnes ... drunk driver ... Broadway and Madison."

No. *No, no, no.* This could not be real. She dialed the hotel.

"Tory, has someone told Kath—"

"Yes."

Hanging up the phone, Joann carefully sank onto the sofa, as if to somehow slow all motion. She could feel the cushions giving way, but her body was somewhere else.

Tick-tock. The clock had sounded so loud.

Tick-tock. Throw pillows.

Tick-tock. Wood floors.

Tick-tock. A stray thread.

Tick-tock. The knife.

What should I do? Should I back off?

Tick-tock. The circle.

Tick-tock. The fountain.

Tick-tock. His eyes.

Eyes that had seen so much of the world—and not enough. Eyes that could see everything ... eyes looking for ... Oh, god. Joann couldn't call her. She knew not to. Not yet.

"Hello?"

"Robert."

"Jo? What's—what is it?"

"It's Todd. He was … killed." She heard herself say the word, but as it escaped her mouth, she wanted to erase it from the air—to stop what was about to be written into their story.

Both Sylvans froze on either side of the line, trying to suspend themselves somewhere safe. Somewhere safe between now and the next moment. Somewhere safe from the hurt. Somewhere safe from more blades slicing through.

Days later, the Sylvans attended Todd's memorial, along with what appeared to be the entire youth population of Seattle.

I got people waitin.'

You sure did, thought Joann. And you *lived*. Todd had squeezed a lot into the time he'd had. All those friends. All that travel. Family. Music. Love. He'd had a fuller life than many twice his age. She whispered a prayer of thanks that he hadn't been in a rush to sit in an office and that he'd made the most of the in-between.

The service began. A desk agent and a housekeeper sat one row ahead of Kathryn, trying not to turn around. They knew she wanted them close, but at a distance. Like everyone else in that room, her friends were now a reminder of what was—and it's not like any of them could really help.

Joann's thoughts drifted to childhood, when her cousin Luke had taken his own life.

After it happened, his sister, the youngest cousin, had been sent to stay with them regularly.

Same age, so same bedtime as Joann—which became a nightmare for both of them. Bridget would start to cry, and Joann would try to help, but the girl was inconsolable. Luke was gone, and pain had taken his place.

As the nightlight flickered, Joann had silently begged her cousin to fall asleep. Because she didn't know what to do. And the grown-ups remained mum on the matter, playing bridge upstairs—while pain festered below.

Joann was older now, but she still lacked answers.

And Kathryn …

The Sylvan Hotel

♦

Kathryn looked like she was vanishing. She continued to work weekend shifts at the Sylvan, but it was like she was there ... but not there. And every time the lock in the office door clicked, she probably wanted to scream.

Dear god. How could Kathryn possibly stand to be in that lobby? On the other hand, maybe she needed to be around people who understood at least part of her pain.

In losing someone, a chunk of yourself is ripped away. They're lost, so you're lost. It can feel like you're drowning; like someone's holding your head in a bucket of water. So you have to find a way to breathe differently. You have to learn how to breathe underneath—kind of like the girl in the lake.

When she'd been just a kid herself, Joann had looked over Stan Sayres dock, only to realize that a "doll" in the water was actually a child. Horrified, she could barely yell for help, staring at the small body, asleep ten feet down. How long had the little one been under? Thankfully, Joann had been with a quick-thinking neighbor, trained in CPR. A frantic father dove in, resuscitation worked, and the tot survived, unscathed. The paramedics had shaken their heads. A miracle? Timing?

Had she adapted?

It's said that cold temperatures can preserve your brain in the course of a drowning—that the cooling effect can delay severe damage. Eventually, though, you have to find a way to come up. But ... what if you didn't want to? What if you got good at "breathing" below?

Maybe that was a secret truth to grown-up life: A lot of folks were breathing underneath. And maybe a lot of them had gotten too good at it. But staying down there was dangerous in the long run. You might not come all the way back. So you had to figure something out. You had to learn how to survive up top again; how to swim *with* the injury—and through all the waves that followed. Hopefully, happiness would also find a way to roll in now and then. Or if you looked hard enough, you could find it somewhere between sinking, adapting, surviving, breathing, and surfacing.

Someone moved the second PBX chair out of sight—and the hotel became a house of whispers.

"So tragic ... and he was in love ... maybe ... someone up front ... and ... Frank ... tried to stop him that night ... on ... way out ... had a question ... Todd had to be ... somewhere ..."

But the swing-shift crew just carried on quietly. Lists. Newspapers. Check-ins. Base to Housekeeping. Here's your key. Do you need dinner reservations? Walk you to your car. Then Babs asked them to join Todd's sister in writing letters to the judge who would be mediating the case. Their assignment was to urge the court against throwing a kid in prison. Joann breathed in. Her father had said that "the killer should be locked up." But ... the Sylvans were asking for leniency? This was a new way of thinking.

Joann listened as her co-workers discussed the teen's plight. They agreed that no good would come of incarceration as opposed to rehab, therapy, and counseling. The kid was too young. No point in wasting two lives. Joann started to wonder ... what was *his* story? What circumstances had propelled him into Todd on that fateful night?

Joann also thought about her first year of college and some "acquaintances" she'd made.

Chills took hold, along with memories of nights in Discovery Park, scaling cliffs in the darkness, trying to "keep up" with people who could have easily brought her down. Why take the trail, when you could slide and climb through eroding dirt, trees, and brush? And why *not* wade, waist-level, through the nighttime sea water below? She'd even followed the same group into a pitch-black railroad tunnel. Joann was lucky that two legs full of stinging nettles was all she'd ended up with from that time. What in the world had she been thinking? And had she really grown up since then? Recently, she'd been in a car with someone who should not have been driving. Verdict: She was in no place to—

Don't be judgy, Margaret.

Writing the letters was the right thing to do. Joann edited them when everyone was done, and the missives were sent on their way. Sue, the other Sylvan bartender, spray-painted another message—a big red heart at the base of the pole marking that corner. A street-sign dedication followed, and the daylight was extra harsh as a smaller group gathered at Madison and Broadway. Kathryn didn't attend, but Joann accompanied Robert, Jed, Sam, and Bryce.

She stood there quietly, but her brain howled questions. Why had this intersection claimed his life and not hers? Why couldn't he have been spared as well? Everyone loved him; admired him. He was just a guy trying to make a living—and trying to live. He'd just wanted to spend time with his friends! And *why* did she have to throw that stupid party? But why had the universe even allowed this to happen? The boy had been robbed of his life and stolen from theirs.

His voice was moving through her.

The Sylvan Hotel

◆

You look more like a Margaret. Where's Kathryn ... Do you believe in God ... Should I ... What should I do?

Roses hung taped to the pole, and the Sylvans posted Todd's picture between the flowers and a starkly scribed epitaph: *Please don't drink and drive. Todd E Barnes. 1965 – 1993.*

Cars cruised by; lights changed; crosswalks filled and emptied.

Just another day.

Joann tried to slow her breathing. Even the air was suffocating with anguish, love, and so many unsaid things. She stared at the photo. Sealed beneath glossy plastic, a boy was now frozen in time.

Why, Universe? Why, why, why?

Then her grief ran out of words.

She looked up again. For now, a tall signpost would have to tell the story: a precious tale of a life that was lived—and a boy who was forever young.

Black T-shirt.

Black bracelets.

Jeans.

Wry smile.

Adventure seeker.

Truth seeker.

Dream chaser.

Star chaser.

Son.

Brother.

Soulmate.

Friend.

That night, Miss MacIntosh cried herself to sleep under the covers as Sting summoned more tales—tales about a time once spent in fields of gold.

─ ◆ ─

The weeks went on, and a new valet was hired. The first time Andrew asked Kathryn for change, Joann wanted to punch his leering lights out—to wipe that disgusting smirk off his face.

You will never know her. Not like he did. She will never even look at you.

The other valets looked at the floor, and Kathryn acted as if nothing had happened.

Frannie James

♦

But what was she supposed to do? What could anyone do? So they all pretended like everything was fine. Maybe you just had to keep moving; keep parking the cars; keep counting the change; keep checking 'em in. Anything to get through the day.

Because sometimes, you just wanted to go back to bed and cry. Because everything was not fine. And while the silence grew louder, Joann's memories screamed with visions of Kathryn and Todd—and one of Kathryn at the bookstore. Her friend had been paging through the last chapter of a novel, explaining that she "wouldn't read it if bad stuff happened." Flabbergasted, Joann had insisted.

You might miss something good in between.

But maybe the middle was just a set-up. Because at some point, you were gonna pay for any happiness. Christ, maybe everyone would have been better off had this Sylvan "adventure" never happened. Then death could have fucked right off. But ... what would *life* look like if none of them had met? And would fate just have broken hearts by way of a different road? Would it have found another path to Todd? Fuck. Fuck. Fuck. How could you *not* ask:

What was it all for?

You lived, and the price was loss. And trauma. And emptiness.

And silence.

Like when Uncle John died.

Following the Beaches of Normandy, John MacIntosh had survived a Nazi prison camp but greatly struggled for the rest of his life. Nevertheless, he'd been a star volunteer for the VA Hospital on Seattle's Beacon Hill—and he'd found joy in the birth of his niece.

"Ya came out squished up, but ya turned out okay!"

Cut to twenty-one years later and another goodbye. The veteran lay in the hospital, fighting a war with emphysema and delirium. His wrists secured to a bed, the soldier was a captive once more. Uncle John's heart gave out shortly after, but he made the most of the last few beats, declaring: "This is my girl. To hell with you if she's not good enough for you."

Joann thought of the time her dad had chastised her for buying a five-dollar shirt. He'd called her a "spender," but Uncle John had shushed him with laughter. Raising two bushy eyebrows, her godfather declared that she'd done it because "she was a relative."

That was Uncle John. He'd always been helping in some way. There were limits, given his health problems, and he couldn't overstep his brother too

231

The Sylvan Hotel

◆

far. But he'd jumped in when possible, with encouragement—and gifts for *his* gift. First desk. First reading lamp.

First camera. First alarm clock. First nail polish ...

Then there was that Catholic-school tuition. Even before the college fund, Uncle John had probably been helping her parents with their growing bills. He even bought all her Academy fundraiser candy, so she wouldn't be out in the cold, begging for money.

Joann reached for her parka and wrapped it around herself. Uncle John had provided that, too. During childhood winters, her mother would double their clothes, double their socks, then rubber-band plastic bread bags over their feet under leaky K-Mart boots. Their "outerwear" hadn't been much better. But then Uncle John's school money sent her to UW *and* to REI.

Son. Brother. Uncle. Godfather. Champion of extremely nerdy nieces. Photographer. Engineer. Hunter. Fisher. Butter on corn and rye. Car fixer. Everything fixer. Aqua-Velvet bookworm. Frère Jacques, fried-egg mornings, coffee, and raspberry jam. Tinkering man. Trekkie. Licorice, plaid, and silver lighters. Reading glasses and gold-boxed cigars. Charlie-Brown heart. Two purple hearts. Forever stole and broke our hearts.

When the crushing notes of *Taps* filled the cemetery air, Joann froze watching her father's shoulders quaking under their weight. Something was shattering all over the place. Uncle John had been a father to both his brother and his niece, and he'd been a bridge between them. Now silence and pain served in his stead.

The next day, Joann felt as if her insides had been carved out. But there was no talking about any of it.

"Housekeeping to Base."

Swiveling in the PBX chair, Joann turned up the radio.

"Go ahead, Housekeeping—or you can call me. I'm at the switchboard."

Beep! Lynnie incoming.

"One sec, Joann. I gotta turn down Temple of the Dog. Walkman break! So, you okay?"

"No. The new guy's gross, and everyone's acting like nothing happened."

"Dude, they're hurting. And sometimes people deal with stuff ... by not dealing with stuff."

"Everything's so horrible."

"Yep. I'm sad for Todd, his family, his friends ... Did you see all the kids in that church?"

"I know. God, I hope he didn't suffer."

"Joaaanna, he probably went straight into shock."

"Thank you for talking about it."

"I'm here for ya, girl."

"Lynnie, let's always be friends. *Please.* We've gotta stick together."

"Word."

"Hey, and … um …"

"Yeah?"

"Can you bring extra towels to 208?"

"Fuuuck meee. I was just on the second floor—"

"Thanks, Lynnie."

Out front, Miss Emerson faced the lobby as if paralyzed, and Joann slowly approached.

"I thought he was taking space."

"Aw, Kathryn. I'm so sorry."

Her friend gripped the desk, and Joann tried not to think about the night in PBX when Todd had steadied the girl he loved.

"Don't leave Jo. Don't leave me."

"I won't."

"Valet to Base, we've got the Uncer party checking in."

Joann took out the registration card and grabbed the key.

A serious Finn walked across the lobby and flashed them a peace sign.

Kathryn began to register the guests, and Joann opened the big window.

That fucker was staying open, no matter how cold it was.

"Hey, Bryce. Hey, Robert."

"Hey, Jo."

"I've got a list for you guys. Here's a paper, too."

Kathryn retreated to PBX, and the newly arrived guests followed Jed. Then Joann returned to the window.

"Kay's tonight?" asked Bryce.

"Yeah."

—⁂—

At 11:00 p.m., the Sylvans clocked out. They plodded through a cold alley, then processed along Madison. Joann wanted to hold onto Robert's arm as the hill got steeper, but she shoved both hands in her pockets and bargained with the universe instead.

Please. Do NOT take anyone else away. We're a family. We need each other. We're still too young. Do NOT let anyone else die. I'll be a good person. I'll get my shit together. Please.

"Guys, wait up!" Finn and George hustled after them.

Inside Kay's, a group of tables was quickly shoved together. Joann squeezed in next to Kathryn, and Lynnie squeezed in next to both of them.

The door kept opening: Sue, Lee, Lissa, Beth ... and someone had called the other three cocktail servers ... Brad, Jed, Bill, and Kiet, too. For the first time in months, everyone was together—and it was time to say their own goodbye.

Check it out, Barnes. Everyone's here. You belong to us. We belong to you.

George raised his glass, and they toasted to the life of their friend.

Kathryn put her head on Joann's shoulder.

Bill fired up the jukebox and high-fived Kiet.

Robert and Bryce told funny valet stories.

Kay hovered because, well, Kay knew when she was needed.

Finn and George debated beers with Brad.

Lynn smoked half a pack of cigarettes.

Jed, Beth, and Lee ordered the cannelloni.

Sue and Lissa sang along with the jukebox and cried.

Then three not-so-bitchy cocktail servers waved at two desk agents.

So two desk agents waved at three not-so-bitchy cocktail servers.

The night went on, and Joann once again begged the universe to leave them alone.

And a Sylvan silently wished her friend well.

Say hello to heaven, Todd. Mother mercy. I never wanted to write these words about you.

The music grew louder, the smoke grew thicker, and the love was stronger than ever.

OF MICE AND MANN

May 1993. Joann had scored an early check-in at The Inn at the Market. It was her birthday, and the girls were set on celebrating. Life was moving forward, and they were trying to, as well.

From the suite, she looked through a window past Pike Place and Seattle Aquarium to Elliott Bay. Seagulls circled, and below the birds, ferry boats stayed the course, well-past pilings and dock ropes. The barnacled vessels pushed on in gray waters, hulls wearing, green trim fading.

On shore, the sounds and smells of a market day filled the air. Such *good* medicine.

You couldn't help but feel better amid old-timey farmers; pretty produce; gigantic flower bouquets; quirky craft stalls; humbow, piroshky, bakeries, bistros, piano buskers, singing buskers, dancing buskers, a man playing spoons, and deep-sea hotties who sent fish flying!

Pike Place was the country's oldest continuously operating public market—and Seattle at its best. Alive with taste, smell, color, and sound, the rootsy cornucopia never failed to buoy the soul. Joann especially loved The Crumpet Shop, DeLaurenti, and Sur La Table, a culinary extravaganza stocked floor-to-ceiling with someday-kitchen supplies. Left Bank Books was also a marvel, stacked floor-to-ceiling with truths. First and Pike News was not to be missed, either. You could "read all about it" in newspapers and magazines galore!

"What I don't understand … is why we *work* at a hotel but we have to go to *another* hotel to have a party. And what the hell is wrong with Kay's?" Lynn opened a beer.

"It's a change of scenery, Lynnie." Joann tugged at her friend's hair.

"Joanna, don't mess with my 'do. You know I've spent hours primping for your shindig."

Straightening her Nirvana T-shirt, Lynn jumped onto the sofa.

"Don't wreck the throw pillows with your Docs. I don't wanna get charged!"

The Sylvan Hotel

◆

"Dude, *relax*. I'm in the housekeeping business. The Inn's decor is in good hands."

"Jo, I've made room in the fridge. We've gotta keep the beer away from Lynn."

"Oh, like *I'm* the lush around here. Whatever, Kathryn. I've seen you with your rum and cokes." Lynn tossed the pillows at her.

"Joann, come check out your birthday present!"

First to arrive, Lou set about opening a box of Thai cigars. The concierge ran a small import business on the side and was excited to share his latest find.

"Thanks, Mister! We'll just have to make sure we don't set off any fire alarms. I don't *think* this is a non-smoking room but …"

"Well, some smoke in here might make you feel at home," he teased. "Man, you gals used to be at Kay's every night!"

"Like I was saying … we could've just gone to—"

Lynnie ducked as Kathryn threw the pillows back at her.

"Happy birthday, Joann!" George and Finn walked in next. Sam, Tory, Jed, and Sadie soon followed, then Beth, Kelly, and Stan.

"No other valets tonight?" George inquired, handing a beer to Joann.

"Robert's busy, Bill's out with friends, Bryce has a business dinner, and Matt's not around—he quit the hotel."

"Well, it's still looking like a nice turnout. Cheers!"

"Yay-party-yay-fun-yay! We don't need those boys! George, try these cigars!"

"Jeezus, Kelly. Settle down!"

"Never!" She pounced on Joann. "Come on, try one. You don't inhale."

Giggling, Joann took a puff.

"What a *risk* taker," teased Lynn.

"Jo, I've got a little something for you, too."

Kathryn held out a homemade book. She'd applied floral contact paper over cardboard for a cover, then glued verses by poets like Corinne Roosevelt Robinson and Grace Stricker Dawson to the inside. Between the cover panels, each of the five pages had a drawing featuring a letter from Joann's name:

J-Joy

O-utstanding

A-ngel

N-erd

N-ight owl

On the back of each letter page, smaller squares of paper were attached with birthday messages written by Sylvans. Caterers, cooks, food servers, chefs, cocktail servers, valets, concierges, sales managers, housekeepers, desk agents, event planners, and a room-service rascal had scribbled well-wishes and funny drawings. Bound with love, the whole thing was titled, "The Joann Book."

"Thank you *so* much, Kathryn." She turned the pages. "This is a *big* something!"

"Wait, there's one more."

Miss Emerson handed her another present.

Joann undid the wrapping paper to find *Frederick*, the children's book by Leo Lionni.

"Frederick is a storyteller. He uses words to help the other mice remember beautiful times," said Kathryn. "Someday … someday, you'll write it all down, Jo."

Robert had also once said that Joann should write books. But could she ever put words to any of *this*? To any of them? In college, Joann had finally mustered up the courage to try a creative writing course, but the instructor informed her that she "hadn't lived enough to be writing anything." Was she qualified now?

Joann hugged Kathryn and felt someone fly past.

"I think Lynnie just barfed," George announced.

"Don't worry, Joaaanna. I didn't get the throw pillows."

A week later, they were back at Kay's. Lynn and Joann flipped through jukebox selections while Kathryn and George snagged a table.

"How's she doing?" Lynn asked.

"I dunno. And I don't want to push, but then I don't want her to think I don't care."

"Kathryn *knows* you care. And really, what the hell *can* anyone say? Nothing's going to bring him back. Nothing will ever be right about what

The Sylvan Hotel

happened. And she's traumatized. Fuck, we all are. Just be her friend. When she wants to talk about it, she will."

"Thanks, Lynnie."

"Okay, pick some tunes."

"I want Patsy."

"Word."

They walked to their table, and the jukebox started *Walkin' After Midnight*.

"Patsy Cline is the best," declared Joann.

"Yeah, well, Natalie *Cole* can kiss my ass," grumbled Lynn.

"Um ... how did we get from Patsy Cline to Natalie Cole, and what did Natalie Cole ever do to you?"

"She's at the Sylvan, right now. And she's making the entire housekeeping staff sign an agreement not to talk to her." Lynn raised both middle fingers.

"What the hell," Joann muttered.

Poor Lynn couldn't ever catch a break. Maybe Ms. Cole was paranoid about privacy, but come on. That was sort of an asshole-move.

"Screw her *and* her Hawaiian Punch." Lynn took a long drag.

"Hawaiian Punch?" asked George. "Lynnie, what are you smoking?"

"I'm nooooot high. The woman wants red punch stocked in her room, 24/7. So put THAT in your pipe."

"Speaking of red, the new lobby carpeting looks like someone hurled Campbell's Soup all over the place!" Joann shook her head and hugged Lynnie in solidarity.

"The hotel's getting weird." Kathryn flipped her ponytail.

The hotel *was* getting weird. Carpeting was changing. Furniture was changing.

Faces were changing. Change was everywhere.

Joann sank into the red upholstery. Where was Kelly tonight? Might be time to throw on some boots and hit the Vogue.

But George wanted to switch it up.

"How 'bout we swing by Il Bistro?"

"Where's that?" Kathryn was not convinced.

"Under the Market, near the piggy-bank statue."

"Helloooo. Her name is *Rachel*. Have some respect." Lynnie threw back her drink. "But yeah, I'm up for it. Let's check out the bistro."

"It's not one of Joann's grunge dives," teased George. "Hey, and Murray Stenson's pouring tonight. He's an amazing bartender and a really great guy. Everyone loves him!"

"Okay, but let's call Kelly, too. She might wanna go!" Joann pulled out a quarter.

"Yay-yay-yay!"

Kelly was in.

Under Pike Place Market, Il Bistro dreamily smoldered in a pinkish-gold light. White textured walls, rounded arches, crisp linens, and dripping candles also set the scene—like a fairy-tale speakeasy!

Welcoming the Sylvans, Murray poured rum and cokes. Then the 'tender extraordinaire made a "hot angel" for Miss MacIntosh, and Kelly yelped, renaming it a "fallen angel."

Steamed Frangelico warm-and-fuzzies caroused in Joann's stomach. Headlights rattled along the cobblestones above, and rain was falling again. White-aproned servers kept watch, and Murray played host at the end of a marble bar. Kind of like *his* "front desk," mused Joann.

"Are you serious? No way!"

George, Lynn, and Kelly were debating something.

But Kathryn ... Kathryn looked as if she wasn't there.

Uncle John used to disappear like that, too. He'd be standing in a room full of people or seated at the dining table, then suddenly, he'd be gone—lost inside himself. Most of the time, he just "checked out" for a few moments. But, as Joann got older, the episodes got worse—like that afternoon she was sitting on the sofa next to him, and news about war shouted through the TV. Suddenly, her uncle's entire body was shaking. Crying out in terror, he sobbed, "His whole face is gone," and she had to shake him even harder to break the trance.

Kathryn wasn't shaking, but ... somehow she was sinking.

Kathryn. Come back.

Kathryn. Stay here.

Kathryn. I'm here. And, dammit, if there's a god, Todd's here, too.

Margaret, do you believe in God?

Tell me what to say to her. You always said the right thing to her. Help me.

The Sylvan Hotel

•

"Kathryn?"

"I … we should go soon!"

She struggled with her jacket and adjusted a heavy ponytail.

In the morning, Joann drove to her parents' house, parked, and headed straight into the Genesee meadows. She needed to run from something. She needed to run toward something. Circling the field, she breathed hard, and the trail breathed hard. *Crunch-crunch-crunch.* The pebbles rasped beneath her shoes. The laps were usually a challenge, but today she didn't want to stop. Miss MacIntosh was all lungs and worry, but the south-end world was all beauty and brightness. May skies. Sunlit grass. Breezy knolls teeming with tiny daisies in pops of pink and white.

She slowed, then cut over to the lake. Kneeling by a dock, Joann tightened a shoelace as Pearl Jam let loose. Turning down her Walkman, she gazed at the water. Oh, to be swaddled in the checkered life vest with the boat rocking her to sleep—and Jack rowing alongside the bridge, his hands steady at the green-handled oars. Her father could be volatile, but he'd stayed calmer out there. Even in the face of a storm.

She breathed in, thinking about the day a squall had kicked up choppy waters, whitecaps, and wind. The weather had raged, tossing them up and slamming them down. She'd been certain they would die, but her father just turned for shore and, quiet as a mouse, he'd just kept rowing. Back and forth. Back and forth. The water pushed. He pulled. And Joann had shivered with terror as the dark waves spilled over and into the aluminum boat.

Honk! Canada geese skittered past, then circled the shallows before paddling out to the depths. It was gorgeous all around her, but Joann was back in that storm; the boat rolling up and down; the shore close but far. She needed to leave the Sylvan. She couldn't leave the Sylvan. She needed to find a grown-up job. Maybe she wouldn't find a grown-up job. She couldn't stop caring about Robert. She wasn't supposed to care about Robert. She wondered about Bill. She wasn't supposed to wonder about Bill. Todd was gone. He wasn't supposed to be gone. She wanted to help Kathryn. She wasn't helping Kathryn.

Joann couldn't find the calm.

Tick-tock.

Work was just a few hours away.

"Good evening, Joann. It's been a while. How are you?"

"Hi, Conner. Welcome back!"

"Is it a crab-cake night, tonight? Ten-thirty work for you?"

"Sure, see you then!"

Whew! Everything seemed totally fine. He was all smiles and back to his professional self. And they were on for dinner! Just maybe … no walks to the car. Although, *maybe* he'd just had too much to drink that night—or *maybe* she really *had* imagined it. Whatever. She had another chance! So no more spinning of the wheels. She'd ask about junior writer opportunities—for real this time. Where did he suggest? Was there an opening in *his* office?

"Hey, Jo."

"Well, hey, Robert Bailey. What's new?"

He'd been absent for a few weeks, having opted to cover the day shifts.

"Work has sucked."

"Yeah, we've missed you."

"No more mornings, Jo."

Promise. Because work's not the same without you. Life's not the same without you.

"Well, that's good to hear!"

"Besides, someone's gotta keep an eye on you, Joann MacIntosh."

Are you trying to torture me?

She didn't care anymore. He was still there. In the world. With her. With all of them.

10:30 p.m.

Robert kept both eyes on Joann as she joined Mr. Mann in the lounge.

Tick-tock.

A plate of crab cakes was on deck, but uncertainty was starting to brew.

The Sylvan Hotel

♦

⇌ ♦ ⇋

11:20 p.m.

Captain Advertising walked Miss MacIntosh back to the lobby. Robert had left, and Ollie was busy in PBX.

"Joann, would you like to come up to my room? We could talk some more."

And there it was. Just another ad man … with a hook.

The waves crested high, and Joann clenched her fists, gripping the sides of the boat.

The wind was cold; the clouds vindictive. But she wasn't the one going overboard.

The Sylvan took a step back.

"No. I have to get going. Thank you for dinner."

"Any time, Joann. Good luck with … everything."

The crab cakes pinched at her stomach.

Goodbye to you, too, Captain Hook.

The elevator doors closed, and she turned on her heels.

There was Robert at the concierge stand. He *hadn't* left. He'd waited for her. Like he'd always waited for her.

"Robert, will you walk me to my car?"

"Yeah. I got you, Jo."

Waves rolled in her thoughts. *Hold tight, Joann.* The sea was rising. But he was the shore. He would always be the shore. And she would stand by him, once more.

TRIPPING

Mrs. Nirvana entered the lobby, clutching a small brown lunch bag. The Cobains' house was being remodeled, so Courtney Love and hubby had been staying at the Sylvan.

"Heroin," Alicia surmised in a whisper.

Joann gaped at her boss. To have that kind of success—and just shut yourself in a hotel room with a bag o' drugs? Go travel, she thought. Explore the world. Write more music. Make art. Plant a garden. Volunteer. Enjoy the freedom that you have. Why just sit around and do *that* all day?

Don't be judgy, Margaret.

Ms. Love trudged into the elevator. Well, maybe their own pains were too painful.

But how did they not die doing that stuff? And how could they so easily risk their lives?

They had money—all sorts of possibility. And other people … other people had been cheated.

Joann took another look at the elevator. Hmmm. Maybe the brown bag was just a meatloaf sandwich. Then she glanced at the valet booth where Andrew and Jed were organizing keys for the shift changeover. Yuck. Their tribe had sprung a leak, like a sneaky rip in an old fishing net. The wrong people were falling out; the wrong people were getting in.

She printed her lists, then pushed through the swinging door to the printer. Passing PBX, she waved to the new girl seated at the switchboard. At least Lily seemed nice. Engaged to the head chef, Lily had recently moved to the States from Germany. Then she'd taken on the Sylvan switchboard, armed with her English dictionary.

Joann thought of her grandmother's German book. How was Lily doing that? And she was so far from *home*. What would it be like to leave Seattle? Joann couldn't imagine being as far away as Europe. Her ex, Grady, had said that his brother Ian was thriving abroad. However, in a recent postcard, Ian had sworn to Joann that their city would always be the best.

The Sylvan Hotel

8:00 p.m.

A little kitchen loitering was in order. Joann had been spending more time across the lobby, which was a welcome break from the cycles of tension circling the desk. She was also getting to know Rhett, who'd started filling in for Finn. Rhett was "very gay," as he put it, but taking a dating break and in the market for a gal pal. So they'd meet up for lunch, drinks, or late-night meals—and they'd chat up a storm on slower shifts.

"MacIntosh," Stan yelled. The pastry chef pointed to the phone. "It's Brad! Check-ins!"

"See ya, hussy." Rhett whacked her with a towel, and she headed back to the desk.

Joann helped get the arrivals squared away, then Brad sat down for a break in PBX.

Swish. Rhett crossed the lobby, now joining Joann on her side of the "house."

"Well, look who's out front!"

"Yeah, yeah. So, what gives, sista? You spendin' the night? Just remember, I'm not spooning with you. I ain't nobody's teddy bear." His own version of an evil giggle followed.

Joann grinned. Rhett's "slumber parties" were the best. Originally from New Orleans, the Italian Southerner had so many stories to tell! She'd laugh late into the night with him, fascinated with his descriptions of the Big Easy—and his sassy-pants points of view. They just never seemed to run out of things to talk about. So Rhett was good with her staying over. There was just one condition: "No snuggling." But Joann didn't need a teddy bear; she needed a night owl!

"What about the Cloud Room? Wanna get drinks in the starry-starry-sky?" her buddy asked.

Located atop Seattle's Camlin Hotel, the Cloud Room was a lounge on high, serving up cocktails, piano tunes, and city views. Fifties decor and shades of teal put the place somewhere between down-on-your-luck and above-it-all—a perfect setting for *The Fabulous Baker Boys*, which had filmed there a few years prior. Stepping off the elevator, you almost expected a bejeweled auntie to glide by in black cigarette pants. And she'd be *carrying* a cigarette in one of those long holders. The whole thing looked like Lawrence Welk and a bar had a baby!

Rhett looked at his watch. "Or, I could eat: maybe hummus at Sit & Spin?"

Over in Belltown, Sit & Spin was a laundromat-café. The funky, art-filled hangout had a "people's-gallery" type of vibe. You could run a load, get inspired, grab a bite, see a band, play a boardgame—

"*Yo*. What's it gonna be?"

"Can't tonight, Rhett. I have to wash my hair. Haha! *Kidding*. Actually, I think I'm hanging out with the girls."

"Okay, then. You behave yourself out there." A deeper evil giggle followed.

Swish. Robert incoming.

"What's up, Bailey," Rhett challenged, his voice going full butch-baritone. Turning back to Joann, the room-service attendant couldn't resist.

"I'll see you, later, sweetheart. Pity you won't be sleeping over."

And with an even deeper evil giggle, he practically sashayed back to the kitchen.

Robert froze.

"Jo, you're staying *over* at his place?"

"Yeah, sometimes!"

"Do you sleep in his bed?"

"Well … sure. He's got a tiny studio, and I mean, he's gay."

The valet's face clouded over.

"Robert. Rhett is *gay*. He likes *boys*."

"And nothing happens? With Rhett?"

"*Robert*. He's *gay*."

Joann didn't know if she should laugh or get mad. And why did he care? Arrrrgh. *Here we go again.* Also, why was he worried about Rhett but didn't blink an eye about Bill? Um, and the only thing that would ever "happen" with Rhett was friendship.

The gay men she'd known had been some of her best allies. After all, they, too, knew what it was to be an outsider. She recalled the story her parents had shared about their honeymoon flight. A straight stewardess had refused to serve the newlyweds because they were a mixed-race couple. It was a gay steward who'd waited on them, hand and foot.

The Sylvan Hotel

•

Joann hadn't personally known any gay people 'til she was seventeen—at least, none she'd been aware of. Grady's brother Ian was gay, but that hadn't ever been acknowledged out loud. Then at seventeen, Ian invited her to move in, and she clued in.

Like Joann, Ian was the oldest of four in a Catholic family, and he'd fought his own share of battles growing up. So he'd offered her a sofa during one of her father's freak-outs. That day, Joann shacked up with a guardian angel on the verge of getting his wings.

Ian made eggs on toast for breakfast, while Classical KING FM floated through the radio.

He read the paper; she read her books, and petals blossomed in pots on the sill: pink, yellow, white, red. There were always flowers—and Joann's new roomie told her tales of fields that bloomed their boldest in faraway countries. But even in rainy Seattle, Ian could cultivate color almost all year round, forcing brightness from bulbs between winter and spring.

Garden gloves on, he'd use water, light, and stones, tending to hyacinth, paperwhite, and tulip bulbs sheltering under glass. It was a beauty-on-the-rocks revival, and it lifted one's soul amid the seemingly endless gray.

Ian had also kept spirits up ... by looking up. The friends would toast to their dreams on a co-op balcony, watching commercial airliners swiftly crossing Central District skies.

"British Airways. Northwest. Pan Am."

The travel agent who'd soon pilot those planes kept his own hopes soaring with regular play-by-plays.

"Look at the tail, doll. See the tail?" Ian *loved* flight.

In warmer months, they'd taken the show on the road, flying through the streets of Seattle on his Vespa. An itinerary of classic "pit stops" included Madison Park for lakeside naps or Cobb salads at Hank's—and Volunteer Park where you could peruse pretty plantings (and pretty boys). Polo shirts, madras shorts, and Ray-Bans on, the golden-tanned duo had been their own kind of "jet-set." Heads would turn wherever they went, and Joann would laugh, holding tightly to her friend.

Ian had them *all* in a tizzy, all the time. Old, young, guys, gals—but that's how it was with him. The men made eyes, the ladies swooned, and everyone whispered: *What's he doing with her?* But Joann knew. He was her wonder twin: a brother from another mother. He was family. Still, Ian had often flown solo and under the radar. Joann knew not to ask questions, although sometimes, he'd let her "stow away." After dark, they'd scooter under stars to a dive bar called the Nitelite. Nobody carded her, and they'd meet up with a man who she later learned was more than a "friend" to *her* friend. The nattily dressed Nordstrom model had been nice to her—but in a careful way, like he wasn't sure if she was really "okay" with things.

Putting the pieces together, Joann had discovered a new truth. As a teen, she'd been taught that homosexuality was something bad. But ... Ian was one of the best people she knew. Joann had been discarded; uprooted—and the "sinner" had saved the day.

It had been another big lesson. Homosexuality had been around since forever, and Ian was who he was. He was also a survivor. Just like her. Most importantly, he was a human being, a *decent* human being who'd handled a budding teen with his best kid gloves, tucking her in with grace and compassion.

"But, Jo—you sleep. In Rhett's bed. *With him.*" Robert was not letting this go.

"Yes. But he's *gay.*"

The valet was flustered. So now Joann was flustered.

You are tripping, Robert Bailey. And we are going on two years of this! How can you stand it?

"Joann," Brad announced from PBX, "Kath's on the phone. Come take a break."

Miss Emerson to the rescue.

"Hey, Kath! You wanna go to Kay's tonight? School's out, baby!"

"Sure! I'll come by the hotel at 10:30 and wait for you. How's work going?"

"Rhett asked me about sleeping over, and Robert freaked out."

"Rhett's gay."

"Yes. But—"

"So Robert Bailey thinks you have the power to change Rhett's mind? Hahaha ... well, I didn't see that one coming—"

"Kathryn, I'm serious! He was going on about 'does nothing happen'—"

"Jo, just stay in PBX. I don't know what his deal is, but oh-my-god, you two ..."

The Sylvan Hotel

◆

—◆—

Ten forty-five, and time to go back out there.

Robert counted bills, and Joann counted bills. She said that her car needed an oil change, and he said his line about "take care of your car, and it will take care of you." Then she mentioned needing to ask her mother for a haircut.

"But not too short?" the valet asked with that shy, melty voice.

He quickly looked down, and Joann almost fell down.

How much longer are we going to do this? How are we so close but so far at the same time? Robert Bailey. Will you please. Say something.

He opened his wallet.

"Jo, can I get one more twenty?"

Robert stared at the counter, and Joann tried not to stare at him.

"Hello, all." Kathryn pushed through the hotel doors. "Going to Kay's, Robert?"

"Hey, Kathryn. Uh, I can't tonight."

"Well, if you … *change your mind.*" Kathryn smiled at the valet.

He looked down again. "You girls okay to walk—"

"Yeah. We're going with Lynn, and George will join us in an hour or so."

"See you tomorrow, Jo?"

"See you tomorrow."

Swish. And off he went.

"Real subtle, Kath!"

"Well, it's time someone around here said something. *For god's sake.* You two need to get it over with, already!"

Ding.

"What's up, Front Desk?" Lynn exited the elevator.

"Hey, Lynnie! Same-old, same-old. Robert can't make up his mind, so Jo stands here in agony. And tonight, he was worried about her sleeping with Rhett!"

"But Rhett's the gayest … Oh. My. God. That is—"

"Yeah, yeah. 'Pure comedy!'" Joann stormed off to the locker room.

One block away, Kay was waiting for them. *Sigh.* How could you *not* want to be there? Joann liked grunge music, but she knew that she'd probably be trampled in a mosh pit. Her access to that scene was limited. Period.

Here at Kay's, somewhere between old Seattle and new Seattle, things weren't so extreme.

Miss MacIntosh stared into the mirrored walls. Where was Robert right now? She imagined herself sitting in the kitchen of a Shoreline apartment, asking all the questions. Favorite food? Favorite color? Favorite subject in school? Favorite place? Favorite season? Favorite books-movies-music-hobbies? What was his family like? What had he been like as a kid? What were his friends like, outside of work? What did he wish for? What were his dreams? Did he see himself staying in Seattle? Did he know what he wanted to do with his life? What did he want to be when he grew up? What made him scared? What made him sad? What made him happy?

And he'd be making sandwiches, bragging that his grilled cheese was the "best in the world."

Later ... a futon with soft, faded sheets and comfy old blankets. Vintage Pendletons? Crocheted afghans? Quilts from Grandma? He'd swear they were keepers. Giggling, she'd get up for a glass of water, and he'd beg her not to "leave." Jumping back in, she'd tease him about hogging the covers. He'd laugh, wrapping her up tightly while cursing the mattress—but she'd swear that it was still better than all those nights on a damp window ledge. But he'd say that those nights had been some of the best nights. And they'd be so happy. They'd be *together*. Then the rain would get louder, and they'd get sleepier. Or not.

Okaaay. Now *she* was tripping. Good god. Robert Bailey was going to be the end of her.

Joann thought about badass Matt and how he'd bailed from the hotel. Was it a relief? But had the "outsider" *missed* out, always doing his own thing? Was he lonely? Stronger? Or both?

She silently toasted the valet.

Stay gold, Matt Heulin. Wherever you are.

"There's my crew!"

George squeezed in next to Lynn and pretended to confiscate her cigarettes.

"Don't mess with my smokes, man."

"So Joann, you havin' an affair with Rhett, now?" Her friend snorted with laughter.

"Whatever, George."

"Give it up for Jo, guys. She gets around."

"Yeah, here's to me. What a floozy."

"Oh, Joaaanna. Don't be so hard on yourself. Ha, and you got *skills*. Rhett used to only like boys!" Lynn blew smoke at her.

"Nice, Lynnie. Real nice." Snatching Lynn's smokes, Joann threatened to crush them with her boot.

"Okay, okay. I'm sorry. I'll shut up. Please don't destroy my cigarettes."

"Lynnie, you are in big trouble." Kathryn warned with a giggle.

"What did Lynnie do?"

Marlboro boy incoming.

"Well, hellooooo, *Bill*." Kathryn giggled again and sat back.

The night was still young.

Lynn tried not to giggle and ended up coughing instead.

"Um, are you *sure* I shouldn't take these?" Joann held Lynn's cigarettes in the balance.

"What up, Joann?" Bill had questions.

"What do ya *want*, hon?" Kay needed answers.

"Thanks, but I'm not staying."

He was off to Goldie's on 45th, where beer, darts, and pinball awaited.

Whew. Joann didn't trust herself tonight. Too many routines were headed for replay.

After Kay's, nobody felt like going anywhere. Lynn dozed off in the back of Kathryn's car and, up front, Miss Emerson was suddenly drowning in tears.

"It's not fair."

Fuck. Where. Were. The. Words.

"I'm sorry, Kathryn. It *isn't* fair. And I'm so sorry he can't be here—at least, how he *used* to be here, and I'm sorry if I'm saying the wrong things—I'll keep trying."

But maybe sometimes there were no words.

Her friend's eyes went vacant again. Absent of light. Absent of life. It really was like part of her had burned out.

Like part of her had died with him.

Frannie James

◆

—≡ ♦ ≡—

Days later, the Cobains were leaving. Joann printed the folio form while Kurt leaned on the desk, watching quietly. His wife looked away, ready to be done with such tedium. Jeezus, and they obviously hadn't showered in days. Joann moved back slowly, trying to act as if she hadn't noticed.

Mostly, the pair reeked of disapproval—or pity. Little Miss Proper in her prissy navy uniform. Little Miss Sellout. Little cog in the machine. Little slave to the status quo. They signed the form and slunk away from the desk.

Had Joann missed her big chance? But ... chance at what? What could she have possibly said to them? *She* was sick of explaining "Honduran Mahogany" over and over, so imagine a band having to deal with "I'm such a fan," over and over. Plus, she wasn't a kiss-ass. And who knows? Maybe an attempt at conversation would've been met with annoyance or even contempt.

I'm not what you think! And Soundgarden's the best, but I like some of your music, too. And my friends buy your music. So you can buy your drugs—er, your meatloaf sandwiches. And hotel rooms where you can ... eat your meatloaf sandwiches. Yeah, I'm working for the "man" because I have to pay my bills. And I make a whopping $7.25 an hour in this prissy outfit.

But maybe they *were* just bored. Or highly out of it.

Alicia joined Joann out front.

"Are they gone?" she whispered.

"Yeah."

"Oh, my god, Joann. They totally trashed their room. I feel for Housekeeping."

But of course. Lynn loved Nirvana—her hometown band; the band that understood her struggle. And now she'd have to clean up their shit. Well, it wasn't the whole band, but still!

Alicia continued. "Styrofoam packing peanuts everywhere. Mattresses pulled off beds."

Some doll collection thrown around the room. Only thing they didn't touch? The towels."

"Yeah ... I could smell, er, tell." Joann crinkled her nose.

"Okay, I'll be around for a while if you need me or if Housekeeping wants to vent."

The Sylvan Hotel

◆

Swish. Robert pushed through the stair door.

List. Check. Newspaper. Check.

"Hey, Jo! You on 'til eleven?" Smiling at her, he straightened his collar.

Temperatures were rising in Seattle, and the valets had switched to their warm-weather uniforms: black knee-length shorts with white polo shirts.

Joann averted her gaze.

"Yep. Someone needs to keep an eye on you, Robert Bailey."

Chuckling, he walked around to the valet booth.

"Hey, Jo. Got some matchboxes for me?" Finn crossed the lobby.

"Not yet. In about an hour. What's new with you, Room Service?"

"Nothin' much. Oh, uh … who's the chick staying in 502?"

"Do I dare ask why, Finn?"

Three, two, one … *evil giggle.*

"Let's just say she answered the door without much on."

Joann rolled her eyes, and more evil giggles followed.

"Valet to Base. The McGee party is arriving."

Mr. and Mrs. McGee reached the desk, and Finn straightened up, moving to the side.

As always, he was an excellent conversationalist and offered his help to the visitors, should they require room service. Instantly charmed, they thanked him, and he turned for the kitchen—but stopped midway across the lobby to make faces at Joann.

Mr. and Mrs. McGee began to comment on the mahogany walls and turned, gesturing toward the lounge and lobby. Pivoting at warp speed, Finn escaped through the stair door.

"Housekeeping to Base."

"Base to Housekeeping. Lynn, call me!"

Beep!

"Good evening, Joanna."

"Lynn, oh my gosh—did you have to clean up the Cobain mess?"

"No, I got here after all that went down. Thank god."

"So lame. Glad you didn't have to deal with it."

"Fuckin' weirdos!" Lynn laughed. "Hey, we goin' to Kay's tonight?"

"Sure. But, um … I kinda want Robert to walk me to my car first. It's gonna be a busy night, so I won't get to see him as much, and he—"

"Uh, Joann? Now *that* is lame."

"Okay, I know. But can you just wait? Then I'll pick you up out front? Please???"

"Puuuuure comedy. See you later, Joanna."

10:00 p.m.

The lobby emptied, and a new hostess slinked over from the restaurant. Stopping at the concierge stand, she waited with her back to Miss MacIntosh. Robert rounded the corner, and Joann's stomach turned end over end as she watched Miss Slinky try to engage the valet in conversation. An intruder was checking out Mister Bailey. Big-time.

The hostess dialed up the charm.

Inhale.

Robert formally answered her questions.

Exhale.

Mission not accomplished!

Miss Slinky slinked back to the restaurant, and the boy Joann recognized hurried to the desk, tucking a pen behind his ear.

"One-ah-ah-ah. Two-ah-ah-ah."

Joann wanted to kiss the Count.

10:54 p.m.

Nightcap orders flowed in the lounge, and in the circle, a few last cars awaited their drivers. Joann clipped her receipts and counted out the cash. *One, two, three—*

"Hello."

Miss MacIntosh looked up, and the tall singer folded his arms, clearly waiting for her reaction.

"Well, hi. How are you?"

"My throat hurts. All that smoke on stage, and the fog machine …"

"Hmm. You should try some tea with lemon and honey. That might help."

He smiled. "Will *you* bring it up to me?"

"Let's see what I can do."

Joann picked up the phone.

"Hi, Finn. Will you please bring some tea, lemon, and honey to 308?"

The singer stepped back.

"Jo, that's the Candlebox dude, right? The tea order?"

Ding.

The elevator doors opened, and Mr. Candlebox waved goodnight.

11:00 p.m.

The Sylvan's night auditor walked frantically through the front doors.

"Sorry-sorry-sorry. I'm cutting it close."

"That's okay, Ollie. I'm cutting it close, too."

Joann wrote a shift note in the ledger and straightened the desk.

"Ready?" Robert was on his way.

Minutes later ... *Ca-clunk. Ca-clunk.* They were clocked out.

Holding the door, a valet shyly glanced at a desk agent. The pair started down a dark path, and lonely breezes blew alongside.

"Jo, I'm leaving in a couple weeks. I'm gonna load up the van and do a drive down the coast on my own. A summer road trip. I've wanted to do this for a while, and I ... well, I think it's time."

Joann's shoes clicked along the cement.

"How long will you be gone?" she finally heard herself say.

"If I come back to the hotel, it will be late August or early September."

If.

"Oh, wow. That sounds like a good adventure." Her voice caught in her throat.

No. Please. Not yet.

They should all be sticking together! After everything that had happened? He'd be out there ... by himself. And *if* he came back to the hotel? What did *that* mean?

"But, Robert, I hope you come back to the Sylvan."

Don't leave me.

"Thanks, Jo. I'll be checking up on you to make sure you're not making too many personal phone calls."

I can't do this. I can't act like it doesn't matter. Meeting you has changed my life. And I don't want to go back to how it was before. Please, Robert. Please don't—

"Very funny, Mister Bailey. So tell me where you plan to go …"

"Well, I wanna stop in Oregon, California …"

The rest was a blur.

Down the garage ramp, up Madison, and into the circle where a cigarette sparked like a tiny flare.

"Hey, Joann. One sec. Lemme put this out—"

"I don't care. Roll down a window."

"What's … are you okay?" Lynn climbed in.

Turn the corner. Straight to Kay's. Park.

Joann couldn't see through a thickening haze. It was all muddled; her focus gone.

Time … to pull over.

"Lynnie, uh, will you please grab a table? I need to call Kathryn."

—✦—

"Hello?"

"Kath—" It wasn't right to put this on her friend. Not with all that had happened. But … saying goodbye to *Robert???* Joann couldn't handle it. She didn't know how to let go. She didn't know how to give up. Two flannel shirts pushed past, and she tilted her head, hiding a flood of tears with her hair.

"Jo? What's going on? Should I come get you? You're at Kay's, right? I'm leaving now."

Joann hung up the phone but couldn't move. She was feeling everything and nothing, all at the same time.

Lynnie, help. Help me.

"Joann?"

Her friend pushed back through the foyer door.

"Hey, what's wrong?"

And the tears started up again.

"Dude, *talk* to me."

"Why did I have to meet him? I've never felt this way about *anyone*. And now … now he's going."

The Sylvan Hotel

•

"What do you mean he's—oooooooh, shit. He's leaving?"

"God, I am so stupid. I got too attached to someone who I had no business getting attached to, and now I have to say goodbye."

"Okay, let's … I got us a table. Or do you *wanna* stay here?"

"Yeah. Kath's on her way."

"Oh, thank Christ. I dunno what to do!"

"Sorry. I didn't want to freak you out."

"No, no—it's fine." The super friend took a super-long drag on her cigarette. "Fuck. The fucking drama around here."

Minutes later, Jim Morrison was breaking on through to the other side, and another super friend flew through the doors.

"What in the hell happened?"

"Bailey's out. He quit the Sylvan, and he told Joann tonight. I'm gettin' booze."

Lynn got up to confer with Kay, and Kathryn squeezed in with her friend.

"So … where—"

"Road trip. Driving down the coast. Doesn't know if he's coming back to the hotel."

"I'm sorry, Jo."

"No. I'm sorry, Kathryn. You've been through hell, and I shouldn't be leaning on you."

"We've all been through hell. Hey, and maybe Mister Valet needs to leave so he can come back to *one* of you, once and for all. Maybe this trip isn't just about destinations he wants to see. Maybe he needs to figure out … something."

"Yeah, maybe he'll 'figure out' that I've just been one big distraction—or that he thinks I'm bad, like some sort of 'temptation.'"

"Come on, now. Anyone can see you're more than that. Look, some space could be good. This thing with you guys is going on *two years*. And both of you are trying to get to whatever's next. There's a lot of 'in-between' stuff happening. So, time for a break. It's okay, Jo. I *got* you. Lynnie and I will both be here. We're not going anywhere."

Lynn returned to the table.

"You okay, Joann?"

"Yeah. Thanks, you guys. Sorry."

"Hey, we're your friends. No apologies needed. Shit! *Bailey pulled the trigger*. I can't believe he's leaving—and he's leaving Joann!"

"*Lynn.*"

Kathryn flipped her ponytail and said "Zip it," with a "zip-it" teacher face.

"What?!? I'm just surprised. I guess I thought it would never actually happen."

Lynn pushed her drink toward Joann in atonement.

But it's not like any of it could have lasted, thought Miss MacIntosh.

And now ... Robert Bailey is escaping the in-between. Without me.

An hour later, Kathryn took off, as she'd promised Scott that she wouldn't be gone long. Not ready to face the night alone, Joann took refuge at Lynn's place. At the apartment, she searched the darkness through windows decorated with purple and green Christmas lights. Potted plants, weepy candles, and sooty ashtrays lined the sills.

"Joann, you wanna hit?"

"No. I should *not* get high right now."

"Okay. I might fall asleep, but I'm queuing up some stuff for you."

Lynn pushed "play," then nodded off. Joann propped herself against the sofa, eyes heavy with everything. Maybe ... just ... for a minute ...

Over the river and through the woods.

She holds an orange book and says the funny words. But Grandma's tatting shuttle goes too fast. *Try again, Joann.* Wrap-loop-knot. The lace is very angry.

Now Mommy holds a golden book. She opens it and says the prayer:

Once upon a time.

Joann blinks. There's a piano book, plus a red book, plus a blue book, and a lot of problems. "Pay attention," the math teacher snarls. She tries to play the measures, but his numbers are yelling: *Six. Seven. Eight* ...Shhh, you'll scare the fish!

Inhale. Exhale. A nightlight can't breathe.

Up, up, up. Raise your arms, Joann. Fly, Joann.

Flashback! Cotton candy. Ice-cream uncle. Blue ribbons on Cinderella taxis. A purse is running ... then a father-boy is running, fast like the horses, still chomping at bits. Another boy runs, and his hands turn red. *Careful, child ... might not be so lucky next time.* She looks inside. It's all there, but ... enough for a prize? The goldfish stares back, then disappears behind a window.

Well done, Joann. That movie is starting again. In it, a teacher reads a tiny story. Then *ring-ring-ring*, and two tiny feet are running, running. *Ring-ring-ring*, and two tiny lungs are wheezing, wheezing.

Whee—here comes the bride! Two small cousins fling small petals, but now their baskets spill with sad. Near the deep end, pretty dresses wait for frosting and watch blossoms kissing blue. It's all so beautiful ... but Auntie says not to fall in.

Suddenly, water everywhere.

Daddy, the basement's flooding.

"Go, go, go!" the red whistle yells.

Breathe. Breathe. Breathe. The swimmer chases golden lures, silver hooks, shiny spinners, rosaries, rainbow trout, princesses, and peas.

She blinks once more. New classmates! A cute boy ... talking to *her*. "Are you rich? Your lunch ... always ... salmon sandwiches." Her face is red, red, red like a Sockeye fillet.

Whoosh. Mrs. Rollins reads *A Wrinkle in Time*, but there's a wind in the door.

Slam! At talent-show practice, the poles catch an ankle.

"You really *should* be in the Filipino dance."

I don't know how to—

Then both ankles ... wobbling on white boots and blades; a pair of fairy-tale hand-me-downs, creased with gray and tied up with memories. Pompadours. Poodle skirts. Fly me to the moon.

Joann skims across a cloudy pond.

Red light ... green light ... red light!

Freeze.

She stops in the middle, and cloudy gives way to clear. Underneath, miniature flowers float, suspended over rocks; another season's colors, now dull in the cold. A mermaid's down there, too, stuck like a statue asleep in icy layers—or an alabaster figurehead at the front of a sunken ship.

The skater twirls, and something's sparking. But downstairs, a doll cries—it's just too dark. Then someone lights a cigar. *Breathe, Joann.* A matchbox flies open, and inky feathers bleed light and fire, torching snow-covered pages.

Frannie James

♦

Ding! A blue Barracuda waits by the elevator. Joann climbs in, and a fish goes up. Winking, the godfather points to a window where the queen's candle still burns. Wind jeers at hot flame, but waxy tears hold fast in its wake—and five poets hoist ropes past roiling seas, shipwrecks, captains, stars, and souls. Wendy's out there, too. Her suitcase is sinking … but the lost boy flies by and blows kisses at her sails.

Whoosh! Joann is flying. Flying into the shadows like Peter Pan … flying, flying, flying—but these are tinsel stars. In a galley, mixers are mixing, and whisks are whisking, but at the helm, a dial is breaking; an arrow spinning, spinning. The Christmas lights go out, the sky goes muddy, and water catches stars. But meteors are fastening life vests, and two brown birds twinkle at the docks.

Help!

A father is running; a hard breather. Have you seen … my daughter.

He jumps in and down, then up, up, up.

She breathes through him.

Now he breathes through her.

Up, up, up. The fish has legs and many tales.

Up, up, up. Flashes catch fire.

Up, up, up. Past falling petals—and another lost boy who waves a melted wing.

Up, up, up. Past the thorns.

Up, up, up. Arms flailing; elbows rusting.

But greased lightning strikes through you, Xanadu—

And heavenly bodies are waiting to shine.

Pink scales. Green scales. Piano scales.

Big fish. Blue fish. Shy fish. Goldfish.

Pretty fish. Preppy fish. Punk-rock fish.

Swim, little fish. Breathe, doll fish.

Now back to gray.

Gasp! Opening her eyes, Joann slowed her breathing and tried to slow her heart. I don't like this, it punched. But not gonna crack, it hammered. I miss you, it thumped. But not gonna crack, it thrashed. I—

Condensation ran down the windows, water dripped in the kitchen, and the refrigerator softly hummed. In the living room, a diver bubbled at the bottom of a fish tank … and Lynnie's latest mixtape cycled through.

I DREAM, YOU DREAM, WE ALL DREAM

"Yay-yay-yay!"

Kelly snagged two phone numbers, then the girls made their way through a buzzy Wild Ginger. One of the Sylvan servers had recently picked up some extra shifts there, so the Western Avenue hot spot was becoming part of a new routine:

White wine. Satay. Steamed buns. Or on low-budget nights, the restaurant's signature sauce went well with small bowls of rice. It was a perfect pairing for whatever chardonnay you were swirling … while everything else was swirling. Wild Ginger was a Pan Asian fever dream with a menu that never disappointed—and huge sides of people-watching.

Joann had never been to such a "happening" restaurant, but she knew enough to leave the flannel at home. Loud dance music looped, and waitresses orbited in head-to-toe black, looking like they'd stepped off a catwalk. Dressed to the nines, nouveau northwesties were also circling.

The following evening, it was back to grunge land. Three Sylvans joined up and headed down to let off some steam at Belltown Billiards. Located under Queen City Grill, the pool hall was somewhere between high-stakes and lowkey—upscale and lowbrow. It was a slick but relaxed space with a wide bar that fronted all kinds of games. Out on the floor, dark woods surrounded a sea of green, and drum-shaped lights shined above crowds reaching for cues.

1:00 a.m.

Bill and his friend huddled in a booth, deep in conversation. Wandering around, Joann found Kelly scoring at the tables.

"Hey, Kell, I'm outta here soon. Will you be okay to—"

"Uh, tend to your *own* business, lady. 'Cause from what I can see, it looks like you're in for a long night, hahaha."

"What's up, Joann?"

One of Bill's hands was already under her cut-offs.

Cackling with delight, Kelly swiped his cigarette.

"What the fuck, Kell." Bill put both arms around his Sylvan grunge girl. "Let's go."

"Have fun, Fallen Angel!" Kelly shouted.

Joann drove her own car back to the Hill, where she found Bill waiting at the apartment. Sitting on the building steps, the valet watched his date walk toward him. As she got closer, he took the cigarette out of his mouth and blew a smoke ring. It looked almost effervescent in the darkness, like an elusive jellyfish: there one moment, gone the next. Then he fully exhaled.

"Dude. You and Lynn—" Joann batted at the Marlboro cloud.

The boy pulled the girl onto his lap and kissed her.

"Bill. Let's go inside. It's getting cold."

Smash. The heat was on—and the call-box phone receiver crashed to the floor.

Then they crashed to the floor.

What was with this guy? At the hotel, it was business-as-usual, but after a night out together, he acted as if it was the first time, every time. It must be the drugs. Who knew what he had taken at the pool hall. And what was going on with *her*? Why was she still *going* along with the weirdness? Ugh. This was not how it was with normal people. And he'd be back to the girlfriend, again, at some point.

Maybe Kelly was right. Joann should stop thinking so much and go with the flow: "Live in the moment." And it was time to give up the idea of control, because there was none—over anything, anymore. It was all mixed up. Sure, she liked the way he held her; the way he looked at her. But they weren't a match. And they were both trying to forget someone else.

Standing in the shower, Joann closed her eyes. The night began to replay under a cascade of hot water—but one of Bill's offhand comments also echoed through her mind.

I'm gonna marry a rich woman.

The water grew cold.

She toweled off, changed for work, then opened the fridge. Mayo. Bud Light.

The Sylvan Hotel

•

Yeesh. It was looking like lunch with Rhett. Joann picked up the phone.

"Hey! Have you eaten? How 'bout lunch at the Surrogate? Maybe Bauhaus? Poor Italian Café? Olympia Pizza? Or if you're feeling adventurous, Bryce told me about a good Hawaiian dive: The Kauai Family Restaurant!"

"Where the hell have *you* been?" He pretended to nag—then those giggles kicked in.

"Hanging out with ... you know ..."

"Which one? Heh. And I'm starting earlier today. But come by the kitchen when you get to the hotel, and we'll scrape somethin' together for you."

"Thanks, Rhett!"

"See you soon, Front-Desk girl ..."

Minutes later, the "Front-Desk girl" parked at a meter and pushed through Sylvan doors. Ross, another recent valet hire, stood guard at the entrance.

"Aren't you supposed to use the alley entrance?"

"It's fine; I'm in my uniform. It's not like I'm all grunged out."

And over to the kitchen to find Rhett.

"What's up, MacIntosh? You look tuckered. Why, Stan. I *do* declare: Joann got ravaged by one of those valets all night."

"Rhett! *Not* appropriate. Sorry, Stan."

"*Joann.* Well, as long as he was a gentleman about it."

"So ... was he?" Room Service was ruthless.

"What the *hell*, Rhett! *Yes. He was.*"

"My, my. And look at you blushing."

"Whatever. I gotta get to the desk."

"Okay then, sugar. Good luck out there with all those dirty little boys." He laughed as she pretended to kick him.

Crossing the lobby, Joann shuddered as Ross patrolled the area, his eyes both shifty and glacial. Yuck. Robert should be standing there. Not asshole Ross.

Robert.

No, Joann scolded herself. No more thinking about *any* valets. Mister Bailey was lost somewhere in road-tripping land, and the Sylvan Hotel was likely a distant memory.

If I come back.

Yeah. A month away, going on two. Not likely.

She started printing her lists and organized the desk while Brad attacked calls in PBX.

Swish. Bill pushed through the stair door. Smiling at her, he crossed the lobby.

She couldn't help but smile back.

A suspicious Ross now zeroed in on both of them, and a quiet Jed was looking especially sullen, having recently split with Sadie.

At 7:00 p.m., Joann lifted two chafing lids to see if any part of the staff dinner was identifiable. Nope. She turned toward the cafeteria door, but Jed was suddenly standing in her way.

"You need to stop using the front door."

"Jed, let's not get into it."

Who the hell did he think he was?

Okay. Breathe. She would try to be patient. He was still suffering from his break-up, and she knew how much he loved Sadie.

"Uh, we're gonna get into it. You need to follow the rules—"

Says the groper concierge who smokes weed on shift??? *What. The. Hell.*

Shaking her head, Joann moved forward, but he blocked her. Okay, this did not feel safe—and nobody else was around. Joann tried to force past, and Jed practically exploded with fury. Grabbing her by the shoulders, he shoved her so hard that she almost fell down.

Then the desk agent was capsizing on the inside—and a reflex pushed through her.

Bump. Set. Spike.

"FUCK you, Jed. Get the FUCK away from me."

The words came out of her mouth, loud and fierce, released from the depths of somewhere. Jed looked just as startled as she was, and Joann practically ran up the stairs and back to the front desk. She and the concierge did not speak for the rest of the night.

This place is going downhill fast, thought Joann. Time for *her* to pick up the pace on the cover-letter writing. Time to stop "hanging out in the joints."

The Sylvan Hotel

◆

When Brad returned from dinner, Joann asked him if she could switch to PBX.

The cafeteria incident had left her too shaken, and the damn desk was too close to the concierge stand. Why-oh-why couldn't Lou work more evenings? As fastidious as he could be, Lou didn't care about her walking through the front entrance, just like Mr. Alexander.

Yeah. Lou *never* bothered her. And he would never manhandle—er, jackass-handle her.

And what business was it of Jed's, anyway? No manager had ever made an issue of it, and walking through the front doors felt safer than the alley.

Beep-beep-beep. The switchboard was ablaze.

"Concierge, please. We want dinner reservations. Marco's Supper Club."

You and everyone else, thought Joann. Well, at least it would keep Jed busy. Both he and Lou seemed up to their elbows in finagling fine dining these days. Matt's in the Market.

Place Pigalle. Tulio. Chez Shea. Canlis. Ray's Boathouse. The Met. Maneki. Lampreia. Maximilien. The Pink Door. The Brooklyn. Seattle restaurants were getting hotter every day. The classics weren't slowing down, and new ones were popping up all around.

Grady had managed for Victor Rosellini at the Four-10, and she'd been to Daniel's Broiler once or twice—and maybe the Met—but that was the extent of her "fine-dining" knowledge. There *had* been that time she'd peeked into Dahlia Lounge. However, the place looked like a red-velvet jewel box, and she wasn't sure she belonged there.

Joann could hear Kathryn's voice in her head:

Why can't we just go to Kay's?

Well, it *was* good to try new things. It's just that …

She looked at the patch of worn carpeting.

Todd. Everything's changing so fast. It's getting weird.

◆

8:30 p.m.

Incoming call, valet booth.

"Hey, Joann."

"Hey, Bill!"

"Have a good one."

"You, too."

Since when did he call to say goodnight? Looking out the window, she watched him cut through the circle, his steps slowing. Pausing, he breathed in. The night air was cool but warm, and he unzipped a Cowichan sweater.

Beep. Eight more lines blinking. Three for the restaurant, two for the concierge, and three for the valets.

At nine o'clock, Joann pushed through to the front.

"Brad, you want to sit down for a while?"

"Just give me about fifteen more minutes out here, and I'll switch ya."

"Okay, sounds good."

Back to PBX.

Beep. Toll-free line. Aw, jeez. Nobody wanted to deal with reservations at this hour.

"The Sylvan Hotel. How may I direct—"

"Joann, how many personal phone calls have you been making this evening?"

Her stomach bunched into a familiar knot, and her heart began to pound.

"Robert! Oh my gosh! Where are you? I miss you so much!"

Okaaay. All *sorts* of words were tumbling out of her mouth tonight.

"I'm at a campground in Oregon. Lemme tell ya, Jo. The toilet paper in California sucked. Oregon has much better—"

"Oh, my god, *stop!* Tell me how you are!"

He told her it had been a peaceful trip—how it had been good to get away from it all. He described the fun of camping, and how he could rig an outdoor shower with water warmed by the sun. A boy on the road so wildly at home—but missing … home.

"How 'bout you, Jo? Still goin' to Kay's?"

"Yeah, remember? I'm 'not ready' for Beth's Cafe yet!"

A familiar chuckle followed.

"Joann, you are a pile of joy."

They both giggled, and she brought him up to speed on hotel life. Brad, soon figuring out who it was, instructed her to say hello for him as well.

Before she knew it, twenty minutes had passed, and the switchboard was picking up again.

"Well, I ... I should ... let you go," said Robert, his voice dropping.

"No! Not yet! Or ... um, okay, but *please* call again. So I know you're safe, and—"

"Now, Jo, I'll be fine. Are you getting someone to walk you to your—"

"Robert, please stay in touch, okay? I really miss you."

Oy. That was twice.

"Sweet dreams, Pile of Joy. Take care."

"You, too. Be safe."

Ready for a break, Brad pushed through the swinging door. Clicking a gold pen, he asked, "How's our boy? Is he doing okay?"

"Yeah."

"Do you think he'll come back?"

"I dunno. I didn't think I should pressure—er, ask him. He's probably still deciding."

Captain Front Desk took a seat, and Joann walked out of PBX, somewhere between miserable with longing and aching with happiness.

Marching over from the concierge stand, Ross halted directly in front of her.

"You look best when your hair is pulled back. Like when you wear a ponytail."

She tried not to flinch. More jackassery. *How* had he wormed his way onto the team?

Leave me alone.

"Yeah," he said, continuing to survey her face. "Makes all the difference in the world."

The creep walked off, content with his evaluation.

Why did she feel like she needed to shower again? God, he was gross.

Whatever. Joann wasn't going to let Ross ruin her evening. Robert had called her!

⇌ ♦ ⇋

Summer scorched on, and the toll-free line heated up as Mister Bailey checked in again and again. Joann found herself missing him even more, but she tried to be realistic. She doubted he'd return to the hotel grind after being away from it for so long. She wished she was out there with him, laughing camp-fireside in his arms; whispering secrets by the light of the moon; swimming and splashing in the sun. Was he missing *her*? Had he figured whatever out? Was he going to say something?

Maybe *she* should say something. But … what if it made things worse? Once you put those words out there, you couldn't take them back. He might be horrified and never speak to her again. It could kill their friendship, which she treasured more than anything. *No.* She wasn't willing to risk what she *did* have of him. So she had no voice in the situation.

Aaack. She was turning into the damn fish girl.

In college, Joann had taken a class on Hans Christian Andersen. She'd needed an extra credit and had been intrigued by the self-described "outsider" who'd authored *The Little Mermaid*, one of the saddest things she'd read as a child. Fish girl has a dream, then falls head-over-tail for a human boy. Fish girl gives up her voice for a chance with the boy. But the boy chooses someone else—a princess he thinks has saved him from a sinking ship. Turns out, it was fish girl. But fish girl can't say a thing. Worst of all, a clause in the chance-at-love contract leaves her with a horrible choice: If fish girl fails to gain the boy's heart, she'll have to kill him—or turn into seafoam and float in limbo. Unable to murder the boy, fish girl quietly accepts her watery fate. In the end, her mermaid heart is her salvation. She conquers depths, rises above, and hangs out with other "daughters of air," waiting for a soul.

Joann stared at the switchboard. *Yikes.* Not all fairy tales were unicorns and rainbows.

More like lost boys and shipwrecks.

At the end of August, Joann was counting her cash when Bill radioed.

"Valet to Base: I'll give you a ride to your car if you want."

"Thanks! I just need a couple minutes."

She filed her receipts, clocked off, and met him in front.

Bill circled the drive and continued onto Madison. At the top of the garage ramp, he turned up the radio and made a laughing sound as Dolores O'Riordan and the Cranberries defied the silence. A broken-sounding but

The Sylvan Hotel

strong-willed voice professed that someone was winning someone's heart but someone didn't want to get hurt.

Joann looked at the glove box, then she looked at Bill. But he wouldn't look at her.

He turned off the radio.

"Goodnight, Joann."

"Goodnight, Bill."

She got into her car, and sat there for a minute. What was *that* …? Did he—?

Oh, for god's sake. She was over-analyzing, and her imagination was over-tired. But … she didn't feel ready for sleep. Hmmm. Lynn was out somewhere, and Kathryn was with Scott.

Maybe … George! She pulled into the circle.

Ollie would let her park anywhere, especially this late at night.

Waving to the night auditor, Joann pointed to the bar as if to say, "Is this all right?"

Ollie, happy anytime she wasn't at the "notorious" Kay's, nodded vigorously.

"Hey, Jo." George set a Bud Light in front of her. "So … what's going on with those valets? You still, uh, seeing Bill?"

"Well, it's not like I'm 'seeing' him. We're just—"

"Okay, okay, I get it. I don't need *those* kinds of details. Are you being safe, Jo?

What *is* the dealio with you and that kid? Hasn't this been going on for a while now?"

"I dunno, George. I don't know anything, anymore. The last couple years have been a whirlwind—or a whirlpool. I walked into this place, and months later, my first real boyfriend dumped me. Then I got too attached to someone who isn't available. Then I somehow ended up involved with another someone, and yes, I'm being careful. Although … I seem to be failing at the 'fling' thing. It's … well, it's lasted longer than I anticipated. I mean, it *is* nice to 'be' with someone. As in, newsflash: Girls like sex, too. Uh, but I'm not someone who can just go out there and randomly 'hook up' with people. *Shit*, I couldn't if I wanted to.

"First of all, I need some kind of connection. Otherwise, there's no point. *Ideally*, I'd like to have a real partner. Do I see that happening anytime soon? These days ... not so sure. Outside of that, the options are limited. Because it's scary! There are just too many jerks—and freaks—out there.

"*Dude.* You're so lucky that you don't have to think about this stuff. Jeezus, it's not like 'connection' is an issue for boys when it comes to sex. Not to mention, you don't need to worry about psychos—or respect, for that matter. After all, it's not like *you* guys have been used, abused, and exploited for centuries."

"First of all, careful with the generalizations." George folded his arms. "Not all men are down with 'random'—er, stuff. And well, some women *are*. Not that I'm saying it's a good idea or that it's safe, but ... facts are facts. Thirdly, you don't owe anyone an explanation."

"Sorry. You're right. Generalizations retracted. Anyway, I'm stuck in this damn pattern with Bill, then Robert left, and—"

"And ... what?"

"And now he's calling."

George raised his eyebrows. "He's *calling*?"

"Yeah. He's been calling me on the toll-free number."

"What's up with that?"

"Well, now he's torturing me long-distance. Although, don't get me wrong. I'm always so relieved to hear his voice, and I always tell him to call again."

"Oh, boooy ... Toll-free torture!"

"Let's talk about something else. How's the dancing? Have you met anyone new?"

George excitedly described his Lindy Hop partner and how he was having feelings for her—how he could see them together. It was so amazing that this *straight* boy was able to talk openly about love, life, and everything in between. Was it because he was older? Or maybe he was just ... George. In which case, *big* gold star for the barman. Joann saw the hope on his face and crossed her fingers for him.

At 3:00 a.m., they walked out to the circle.

"Remember what I said about putting people on pedestals, okay, Jo? Keep in mind, people are just people. We all have our issues, baggage, and damage. None of us is perfect.

Got it?"

"Yes. Thanks, oh wise one. And thanks for letting me hang out."

"You're welcome in my bar anytime. Uh, but we're overdue for Kay's. Damn, for a while, you girls were down there almost every night! What happened?"

"Well, Kathryn's with Scott a lot, and Lynn's started dating, so ... things are changing,

I guess."

"Well, lemme know the next time you get a dive-bar hankering."

"Okay. Good luck with the dancing, and don't be afraid to ask your friend out. I bet she'd love to have dinner with you!"

An hour later, Joann was tossing and turning.

Then the phone was ringing. What the—what time was it?

"Joaaanna."

"Jeezus Christ, Lynnie. You scared me."

"I went on a date."

"That's awesome! So ... do you like her?"

"Yeah. But I missed you and Kathryn tonight."

"Well, let's go to Kay's tomorrow. It's been a while. We'll get the teacher out of the house, no matter what it takes. Besides, summer's almost over. We've gotta make the most of it before she's back on the school schedule!"

"Joann?"

"Yeah?"

"I'm so high right now." Then giggles were traveling through the phone lines again.

"Lynnie, put down the bong, and go to bed."

"Ten-four. Sweet dreams."

"You, too. Nighty night."

But Joann still couldn't sleep, so she reached for her Walkman. Then the Cranberries played on, and the beautiful Dolores sang on about a winner of hearts—about someone who was understanding; someone who was kind; someone who was a dream.

REDUX

Swish. Robert Bailey pushed through the stair door.

"Hey, Jo." He grinned.

"Hey, yourself." She grinned back.

At the desk, a check-in list was waiting with a copy of *The Seattle Times.*

Resting toned arms on the marble countertop, Robert pretended to review the headlines.

Joann couldn't believe it. He was right there in front of her. Tall and tan, young and lovely. Those kind but mischievous eyes—and that warm, wonderful heart that had always managed to rise above it all.

"You here 'til eleven?" Her friend looked at her shyly, even after two years.

"You know it. Welcome back, Mister. We sure missed you."

The valet struck his superhero pose, and Joann laughed.

Happiness *rocked.*

"Welcome back, Robert!" Brad pushed through the PBX door and shook his hand.

Alicia followed next and patted his shoulder, relieved. Getting Robert Bailey back? This was a win.

Finn and Stan crossed the lobby with some of the cocktail servers. It was handshakes and hugs all around.

George walked in next.

"Bailey! *What's up,* man?"

Joann's eyes traveled to the stair door. She wished Kathryn would walk through, her ponytail swinging, as she chatted with another valet following closely. But that time was gone. Things had changed and would continue to change.

The crew dispersed, and Miss MacIntosh wondered: Was there a way to keep moving forward but also hang on to what remained?

"Valet to Base."

"Go ahead, Valet."

"We've got the Michaels party checking in."

The Sylvan Hotel

◆

"Copy that. We're ready for 'em."

"Ten-forty, Base."

"What a gorgeous hotel, Miss. And the walls! What—"

"Thank you, and welcome! The walls are made of Honduran Mahogany."

Joann finished checking in the Michaels and sent them on their way with Jed.

Robert returned to the desk, still smiling.

Ding.

Lynn and Kiet walked off the elevator, and an annoyed Jed rolled on. They should be taking the stairs.

"Dude! Welcome back!" Lynn embraced the valet, and another happy housekeeper lightly punched him on the arm.

"Thanks! Have you guys been keeping an eye on Jo for me?"

"Don't you worry. We've *all* been keeping an eye on Joanna," Lynn replied, and Kiet watched quietly.

"So, uh … Lynn, did 401 get that iron?" Brad prompted.

Then Bill and Sam walked in from the valet booth.

"What up, Lynn. Hey, Kiet."

The junior valet searched their faces, and Lynn slowly turned toward the elevator, not wanting to miss whatever was happening.

"Hey, Bill. Yeah, and … Brad, we'll … um … yeah—the iron …"

The housekeepers were off, but no one moved from the concierge stand.

"Brad, can I cover phones—and maybe take a dinner break soon?" Joann asked.

"Sure, no problem."

She pushed through the PBX door, and Brad took the wheel.

"So, gentlemen, how are we tonight …"

Twenty minutes later, Joann hurried through the back office and into the hall. Holding her breath, she took the corner.

"Going to dinner?"

Bill rested *his* toned arms on the concierge stand, staring straight through her.

"Yeah," she answered, staring straight ahead.

"See you when you get back." His eyes didn't move.

Pushing through the stair door, Joann practically ran into George on the other side.

"Whoa, Joann. What's the hurry?"

"Just going to dinner … and …"

"Uh, huh. Looks like you've got your hands full, out there. Is Kath working?"

"No, it's Brad. And everything's *fine*."

"Yeeeah, okay. I think it's a Kay's night. Get the teacher on the horn, and radio Lynnie.

I'll see you guys around midnight."

He proceeded toward the bar, and Joann continued to the cafeteria where she found Kiet and Robert.

"Joann! Pull up a chair!" Robert happily tucked a pen behind his ear.

She picked up a plate but quickly put it back.

"Hmm. Maybe not as hungry as I thought. I'll just sit with you guys for a minute."

Robert talked basketball, but Joann's nerves were tightly skipping, like fishing lines jigging between the waves of a strong but invisible current. Her whole body had gone shy.

"Darn it—uh, I forgot to tell Brad something. I'll see you guys back up there!"

Miss MacIntosh climbed the stairs and returned to PBX, which was just as well, because the switchboard was starting to freak out. She routed all the calls, then dialed Kathryn.

"Hey, lady … orders from headquarters: George says Kay's at 11:00! See you then!"

Beep. Housekeeping was checking in.

"Yo! Kay's, tonight?"

"Yeah, Lynnie. Kathryn, too."

"Ten-four. Gotta go. Some jerk in 208 is bitching about a hair in his tub."

Joann hung up, then listened as Brad switched out a room for the latest check-in.

"But we wanted a view," whined Mrs. Whoever.

"Sorry about that, folks. This isn't a view hotel. Let's see what I can do for you."

Brad upgraded them to a slightly bigger room and dialed Finn, asking him to deliver wine.

Wow, thought Joann. The stuff people got away with.

Click.

The Sylvan Hotel

"Hi, Bill."

Be calm, Joann. Be calm.

"Hey. Wanna go to Belltown Billiards tonight?"

Oh, boooy. Had he broken up with the "girlfriend," again? Or was he doing the competition thing because Robert had returned? And how was it that their "situation" always followed *his* personal calendar? Plus, if she said yes, it would lead to an all-night roll in the hay followed by days or weeks of that be-careful-around-me vibe until he was "available" again or done freaking out. Hell, it was freaking *her* out. How were she and Bill still doing this, almost a year later? And, now that Robert was back, well … maybe there was a chance …

"Kathryn's stopping by tonight, so she and Lynnie wanna go to Kay's. Thanks, though."

"Have fun at Kay's."

He was staring at her again, but Joann couldn't meet his eyes—and PBX seemed smaller than ever.

Hell's bells.

Beep. Saved by the goddamn switchboard.

11:00 p.m.

Joann finished close-out procedures while Robert and Kathryn caught up.

"Well hello, Mister Valet! You wanna go to Kay's? George is going, too—"

"No, I gotta head out. But be safe down there, all right? And, remember, Jo. Don't do anything I wouldn't—"

"*Yes*, Robert." She waved, and he was all smiles again.

"So … how was the first shift back?" asked Kathryn.

"I feel like things are the same, but different. Uh, and Bill asked me to go to Belltown—"

"Oh my god. *Jo.* One of you is going to get hurt. How long can that go on—"

"I know, I know. And I'm not gonna lie. I do have fun with him, but we're never gonna be a match outside of this place. We're not 'going' anywhere.

Come on, all the drugs??? And sooo much drinking. Like I said—not a match. Besides, I … I want real. I want an actual relationship someday. And trust me, you don't have to worry about Bill. He only gets 'concerned' about things if he's on a break with the girlfriend—or um, apparently, when he thinks the convenience of whatever we're doing is being threatened in some way. It's not like he's actually stressing. The situation will run its course—if it hasn't already."

"You might mean more to Bill than you think. He just doesn't know how to communicate that. Plus, he's dealing with his own stuff. But he's still human, and he's not stupid. *Everyone* can see there's something between you and Robert. It's all getting quite … twisted. You need to resolve—"

"Yeah, this shit's getting *too* twisted."

Their favorite housekeeper appeared, smacking a cigarette pack against her hand.

"Hey!" Kathryn greeted Lynn with a hug. "Jo, hurry up and change. Lynnie and I will wait in the bar with George."

Swish. Jed incoming. Joann wondered if she should invite him to Kay's. He was probably lonely, and this awkwardness *had* to be smoothed out. They had to *work* together.

"Jed—" she began.

Then Bill pushed through the front doors.

"Let's go, dude."

"Yep, ready!" The concierge put away a rolodex and pulled on his coat.

"Have a good night, Joann." Bill waved at her.

"Bye! You, too."

Downstairs, Mister Bailey was almost through the door.

"Robert! Wait! Are you *sure* you can't hang out with us?"

"Well …"

"Pleaeeeze?"

"Okay," He looked down, shy again. "I guess … for a few minutes."

Joann ran to the cafeteria and picked up the phone.

"Bar, this is—"

"George! Robert said he'd go to Kay's! We'll meet you guys there!"

Locker open. Locker shut. Jeans. Flannel. Boots. Lipstick. Her heart was zinging all over the place.

Be calm, Joann. Be calm.

Pressing forward, the desk agent and the valet swapped work gossip and chatted about his trip. The dark alley was soon behind them, and Joann jumped around with excitement, hugging on her friend. She swore to the universe that she'd never complain again. He'd come *back*.

A few paces later, they stepped into a smoky Kay's. After waiting a second for their eyes to adjust, the pair found themselves in the middle of a very crowded bar. Lynnie and Kathryn waved from a fleet of tables that had been pushed together. Beth and Lee were also joining, plus Stan, Finn, and three of the hotel food servers. Kiet, too!

Kathryn elbowed Lynnie, Lynnie elbowed Kathryn, Kay grabbed her tray—

And Joann couldn't help but think that the "between" was actually quite beautiful. Everything they were aiming for; everything they were trying to get to; everything they were running toward—would it ever be as good as this? Obviously, the Sylvans would have to move on at some point, but …

"That's life," Frank Sinatra crooned.

Joann breathed in. She'd survived some painful goodbyes, but how bad was *this* one going to be? Maybe that *was* life, but could you really get used to the farewells? And how did people just "move on," especially when life was like this? How could you *not* get attached? And where did that time together … go? One second, you're huddled together in your favorite smoky bar, and the next, it's all just lost to the ether? Or shoved into a photo album and buried in a basement?

That's just too sad, Mister Sinatra.

Joann hugged Lynnie tightly. If only there *was* a way for the Sylvans to move forward but somehow stay together.

Tick-tock.

Laughter filled the ashy air. Standing in the middle of it all, Joann was drunk with happiness. Someone began to tell a dirty joke, and as she giggled, Mister Bailey crept up from behind and teasingly covered her ears. Continuing to giggle, she fended him off, and he surrendered—then wrapped an arm around the front of her. Leaning against him, she thought she'd burst with contentment. Then, in between the gold etchings of those mirror-tiled walls, she saw a life in full bloom—and so much of what she'd wanted. Hot cannelloni steamed on the table next to quarters and candles; a jukebox was an open book, and a girl was on an adventure in the best possible city with the best possible friends. A girl who was someone. Someone who mattered.

Turning around, she smiled at Robert again, and as his own smile lit up the room, she dared the stars to do better.

Otherwise, she'd be wishing on him forever.

Twenty minutes later, George walked in, and Robert left the table to meet him.

"Helllooo … Joaaaaaaannna. *Dude.* You're glowing like a little nighttime sun."

Kathryn elbowed Lynn again.

The boys returned, and Robert put his hand on Joann's shoulder.

"Jo, I gotta head out. George promised me he'd get you all to your cars."

"Okay, Robert. Thanks—and I'm sooo glad you're back!"

"See you tomorrow?"

"Same bat time. Same bat channel."

Waving to everyone, he exited the bar.

"Jeezus. It's kinda hot in here." George took a swig of beer.

Kathryn laughed—then Finn was yelling.

"Hey, Jo! What's with the chick in 301?"

"Do I want to know why you're asking me that question?"

Three, two, one … *evil giggle.*

She nudged Lynn.

"What about the guy with the hair in the tub? Did you get that sorted?"

Lynnie slowly raised both middle fingers, and Kathryn patted her arm.

"Jo, I think Lynnie's trying to say that she doesn't want to talk about Bathtub-Hair Man."

"Yeeeah. I'd rather talk about the prodigal Robert Bailey. Isn't it nice how he's returned to Joann—I mean … home?"

The desk agent made a face at the housekeeper, and the barman coughed into his beer.

Beth stopped stirring her drink.

"Joann, are you with Robert?"

"She wishes she was with Robert."

"Thanks, George. Thanks for that." Joann tried not to be mortified.

"Robert is—" she started, trying to play down George's comment. "Well, I just don't know if he likes me in that way."

Beth looked at her curiously. "Hasn't that guy walked you to your car for like two years? Oh, but weren't you out with Bill … ? I think I saw you at the Frontier Room."

George buried his face in his hands.

"*Joann*. What's going on at the front of the house?" Beth picked up her drink again.

"Nothing's going on, Beth. Bill's a friend, and Robert—"

The Girl from Ipanema began to play, and Lynnie choked on her ice. Kathryn elbowed her yet again, then finished the sentence:

"Robert … is back."

George smiled at Beth, Kathryn smiled at Lynn … and Joann sighed blissfully.

Across from them, the jukebox sighed, too, as it continued to sing the same old song.

GREEN LIGHT, GO

Late September neared, and autumn returned. A storm was creeping, but Joann shrugged off the melancholy skies, sipping her tea as the *Singles* soundtrack heralded in a new season.

"Get lost, clouds." She turned away from a window framing turbulent horizons.

The ominous view would not spoil her outlook. Summer was over, and hopefully, the Sylvans were in for a peaceful night.

Tick-tock—2:20 p.m.!

Off with the Walkman, out the door, and into fall! The sun was being lazy, but showstopping colors sliced through surrounding trees as if a wand had been waved, dressing them for send-off in their bittersweet best.

Bouncing by, a group of St. Joe's kids jumped in and out of falling leaves. Two mothers rolled into houses with strollers, their walks cut short with a sudden change of plans. Across the street, a mohawk passed a smoke to a briefcase, and two old-timers abruptly turned, their scarves losing a battle with the wind.

Joann steered the car up Madison to Broadway.

Red light.

Inhale. This intersection would never be easy.

Green light.

Exhale. Then onward, and—parking in front!

When she entered the circle, Joann spied Ross … circling. What in the hell was *he* doing there? Hopefully just a shift cross-over. She could have sworn the schedule said—

"Hey, Joann."

Lou held the door for her—but why the weird expression?

"Hi, Mister Concierge! Your day going okay?"

He nodded but quietly continued through.

The Sylvan Hotel

•

Mr. Alexander greeted her next. With a buttery welcome, he asked if she'd mind looking after Nicky. The child ran up, hugged her, scurried off, then reappeared ten minutes later.

"You gonna hang out with me, kid, or what?"

"No. Just wanted to say 'hi.' My dad decided that he *is* ready to leave. So hi, and 'bye!"

Jed incoming—and practically skipping his way over from the concierge stand.

Uh oh. Cheshire smile.

If he was unhappy, everyone else had to be unhappy.

"I'm so excited for Robert."

Mister Concierge cracked his knuckles.

"Yeah? What's up?"

"He's starting an espresso business ... East Coast ... Starbucks getting so popular here ... nothing like that yet in the town he picked ... closer to Tricia ... he can build a career ... gave notice."

Bump. Set. Spike.

He who laughs last. Or shoves last.

Joann was sliding across the court. She was out of time and out of the game.

"How about that *Bailey*?" Ross circled back and slapped the marble countertop. "Oh, but Joann, here, is probably bummed. She's gonna lose her special buddy."

Get away from me, you villainous asshole.

"Well, good for Robert," Joann smiled her perkiest front-desk smile. "I hope it works out."

The conversation continued, but it felt like something was getting muffled—or like something had fallen underneath. Then the desk phone started beeping, and Joann's arm was lifting the receiver.

"Front Desk, how may I help you?"

"Hi, um, I can't seem to turn down the heat."

She was walking into PBX and picking up a radio.

"Base to Engineering. Come in, Engineering."

She was putting the walkie-talkie back in its charger.

Piano. Violin. Flute.

Radios buzzing.

Frannie James

♦

Switchboard beeping.

Keyboards clacking.

What should I do ... Should I back off ...

I'm sorry ... trust me ... I get it ...

She was printing the check-in lists. Then she neatly placed *The Seattle Times* on top of one copy, straightened two newspaper stacks on the ledge, and closed the big window.

Four o'clock. *Swish.* The stair door.

Joann hurried into PBX.

"Brad, I have cramps. Can I trade you for the switchboard?"

Seven calls routed. Restaurant. Florist. Babs. Sales. The bar. Concierge. Reservations.

"Good afternoon, the Sylvan Hotel. How may I help you?"

"Hi. I'd like to plan a night for my girlfriend's birthday! I heard your hotel has a very romantic setting—and so much *history*—"

"Let me transfer you."

Joann spun the chair around and looked at the worn patch of carpeting.

What should I ... What should I do?

Static.

"Valet to Base."

She was turning the radios down.

And the switchboard was burning up.

Twelve more calls.

Minibar math.

Goodnight, Alicia. Goodnight, Leena. Goodnight, Tory.

Internal call. Room service.

"Hey, Jo. Amenities ready, yet?"

"No VIPs tonight. You're all clear."

"Cool! Thanks. So ... uh ... I heard that Rob—"

"Ooops, I've got all ten lines going. Catch you later, Finn."

Brad walked into PBX.

"Joann, do you want to take a dinner break?"

"No, I'm good—thank you!" she replied, keeping her eyes on the reservation computer.

"Okay."

He hesitated momentarily, then pushed back through to the front.

Joann now stared at the bulletin board. Not a red X in sight.

Green light, go.

Headlights in the driveway. Navy jackets. Gray slacks. Black shoes.

Branches scratched against the window, and it was raining again. Then a wind picked up, and Miss MacIntosh watched tiny gold leaves collide with PBX panes—then blow away.

7:00 p.m.

"Joann, can I sit down for a few?"

"Sure, Brad. I'll be right there."

Beep-beep-beep!

Be-calm-be-calm.

Out in front, the lobby was almost empty. Cocktail servers convened at the fireplace, and restaurant dishes clattered at the other end of the far hall. Nobody at the concierge stand or—

Incoming call.

"Hey, Joann. It's Jed. We're all in the garage. Just radio us if you need a valet."

George started across the lobby.

"Jo, what—"

Joann shook her head at him.

He nodded and retreated to the bar.

Incoming call. Housekeeping.

"Front Desk."

"Joann, George called me. Do you ... should I come up—"

"Nah, Lynn. It's cool. I'll see you later, okay?"

Swish. Robert, incoming.

She could hear herself talking.

Hi ... big decision ... when do you leave ... where are you ... what's the plan ...

Now he was talking.

Friends from high school ... business partners ... researched East Coast ... college town ... No espresso there yet ... U-Haul ... couple weeks ... big opportunity ... closer ... Tricia.

"Congratulations."

"Thanks."

"Welp, I'd better get my stuff done!" She quickly backed away and through the PBX door.

11:00 p.m.

Joann placed her receipts in the cash drop, stepped into the hall, and braved the lobby.

"Walk you to your car?"

"Oh, um … I'm gonna visit with George for a bit."

"See you tomorrow?"

"See you tomorrow."

The desk agent sat at the bar in her uniform.

"Just take off your name tag." George set a beer in front of her.

"Yep."

"Did you call Kath?"

"It's a school night. She needs her sleep. What she doesn't need is my drama."

"Well, I called Lynnie. She should be up any sec—hey, there she is!"

"Hey, Joanna. Do you want to get out of here? We can go to Kay's, or …"

"I—I don't want to go there. But I'm not tired, yet. Let's just go to your place."

At the apartment, Lynn dozed on floor cushions, and Joann sat near the sofa. Leaning against it, she breathed in cold cereal, weed, and cigarettes. Condensation ran down the windows, water dripped in the kitchen, and the refrigerator softly hummed. In the living room, a diver bubbled at the bottom of a fish tank.

The Sylvan Hotel

Tick-tock—four o'clock.

At 4:15 a.m., Miss MacIntosh left for her own apartment, steering the car through a late-night storm.

Green light, go.

Will you be here tomorrow ... walk you to your car ... how many check-ins ... if you got on a plane ... keeping an eye on you ... just checking on you ... personal phone calls ... lipstick on your glass ... thanks for the list ... be safe ... be good ... Happy Valentine's ... Happy Easter ... Merry Christmas ... Happy New Year ... you can do it, Jo ... wait for me, Jo ... let's get outta here, Jo ... I'll make it up to you, Jo ... I got you, Jo.

Tall and tan, young and lovely.

He is the shore. She is joy.

They have history.

Joann curled up, cocooning under the covers. What the hell was so great about espresso, anyway. Her eyes closed, and she saw herself in the boat with her father. He was rowing, and worms wriggled around in big, red coffee cans.

"The best part of waking up, is Folgers in your cup ..."

The ad jingle belted through Joann's clock radio. Time to get showered and dressed.

3:00 p.m.

Swish. An unsmiling Robert walked in.

An unsmiling Joann stared down at the computer keyboard. Down, down, down.

Lists. Matchboxes.

Babs. Alicia.

Ken Wolf. Khloe Wolf.

The florist is changing the orchids. Mr. Alexander needs his keys.

Check-ins. Reservations. Down, down, down.

Three o'clock. Six o'clock. Nine o'clock. Eleven o'clock.

Walk you to your—?

I'm okay, thank you.

But something was not okay.

Bud Light. Rum and cokes. Out of the bar. Into the car.

Lynn at a loss in the back seat. Kathryn trying to find anything that looks like tissue.

"I'm sorry, Jo. I'm so damn sorry. He looks totally torn up about this. He was staring at you all night. Believe it or not, I'm not sure *he's* sure about what he's doing. There's *something* between you guys, but, well … sometimes, timing is just timing. And they have *history*. There's nothing wrong with you. I promise—"

Joann could barely see. Her contact lenses were practically afloat. How was she so … connected to him? He walked into a room, and life was instantly better. But now—

"Jo, tell me how to help you." Kathryn was still desperately digging for tissue.

Breathe in. Breathe out.

Be calm, Joann. Be calm.

"Kathryn, Lynnie—please don't ever leave me. I don't know what I'd do without you. And I'm sorry I dragged us through two effing years of this. It's like something just sneaked up on me. Then, suddenly, I couldn't imagine life without him. Robert … he … well, goddammit, Robert Bailey just felt like *home*. But he's not. Or he can't be. Or he doesn't want to be. Or he was, and … now … now he's—"

"This completely blows." Lynn sat forward. "I can't hate him, though. I like Robert.

And you know I don't like people. Robert's a good guy. He's just confused. Yeah, he sees himself on some path or whatever. But the truth is, he also fits with you. And he can't fucking choose. So he's going with what he knows. And, yeah, they have history. But … maybe he's *hiding* behind history. Or maybe he's just doing what he thinks is right. Shit, maybe he's *hiding* behind his principles. Wait … is it *possible* to hide behind principles? Regardless, if someone is so 'right' for someone, then why is *another* someone even a … someone? Like, if Person A is 'it,' then why would there even *be* a Person B? Why would there even *be* any confusion? I give up. This is messed up."

The Sylvan Hotel

George knocked on the window.

"Dude. You scared me." Lynn rolled it down.

"Fucking *open the door, Lynnie*. It's raining."

"Oh yeah, sorry."

"Jo, you don't look too good. Kathryn, you don't look too good, either."

"Gee thanks. It's been a long night, George."

"Yeah. I figured I might find a steamed-up car parked in front of Kay's."

"Hey, Mister. Just what are you implying? I'll have you know that I've not taken advantage of anyone in this here vehicle." Lynn snickered, blowing a cloud of nicotine out the window.

"Didn't say ya had. But that does paint an interesting picture …"

Kathryn swatted George, then lambasted Lynn about "that goddamn smoke."

Joann breathed out. "I'm hungry. Can we go to the Coins?"

"Now you're talking. Hit it!" Lynn latched her seat belt.

Miss Emerson took the wheel, and Joann wiped the windows with her sleeve, trying to see beyond the thickening fog. Seasons were rolling by, and it was hard not to feel lost or behind—with so many words she might not ever find.

Green light, go.

DEAR JO

October 5, 1993. It was Robert Bailey's birthday—and his last day at the Sylvan Hotel.

Lists were printed, cars parked, phone calls answered, guests checked in, and receipts tallied. Cannelloni orders had been called into Kay's, along with a heads-up that a large party from the hotel would be there around eleven. Joann had made the rounds all week, encouraging as many people as possible to join them in giving their friend a proper goodbye.

At 10:40 p.m., food servers, cocktail servers, kitchen staff, desk agents, valets, a pastry chef, a bartender, a concierge, and a room-service rascal began their close-out tasks.

Robert counted up his dollar bills, and Joann traded him for twenties. Then she slipped one of his last valet tickets into her pocket and hit the stairs. Kathryn and Lynn met her by the cafeteria, and they headed for the hillside.

Inside the bar, Kay was pushing tables together at the center of the room. Tonight, the place belonged to the Sylvans. It was early in the week, and they would pretty much have it all to themselves.

Inhale.

Exhale.

Robert was through the door, still in uniform. He and Bryce were followed by Jed, Sadie, Kiet, Sam, Bill, Lou, and Finn. Stan and George soon appeared with Beth, Lee, and Sue, followed by Tory, Kelly, Brad, a few of the food servers, and some of the kitchen crew.

"Only Jo could pull this off." Robert looked astonished.

Lynn looked at her ice. Sighing, she counted out some quarters and queued up Frank Sinatra, Patsy Cline, *The Girl from Ipanema* … and a little Elvis.

Toasts were made.

A camera clicked.

Taps flowed.

The Sylvan Hotel

•

An hour later, the joint was jumpin', but a certain valet wasn't looking so festive. Finding his way back to Joann, Robert took a seat right next to her. Guessing this time was as good as any, she handed him an old shoe box tied with a ribbon.

"What's this?"

"Open it, and see."

Her friend undid the bow and pulled out a flannel shirt from their favorite store.

"No way!"

"It's a Chubby & Tubby special. You can wear a bit of home on the road!"

Robert held onto his gift for a few seconds, then put it back in its box.

Looking at Joann, he stirred a sea breeze.

"Jo, you *always* take care of me." Robert's voice was low and serious, his eyes searching.

"*No*, you always take care of *me*," she replied softly.

And in that smoky room, a boy and a girl began to see quite clearly.

Tick-tock.

The place was buzzing faster, but Joann was somewhere else. Somewhere with Robert in the space between themselves. Somewhere, together, between pain and peace; worry and wonder.

She crossed a leg, and he folded his own leg, tucking it back against hers. They were all tangled up.

Wait. *What?* Who flipped the script? What was happening?

Decisions had been made. Plans were in place. They'd had *two years*. And it was too late.

Robert shakily picked up his drink, and Joann desperately grabbed for her camera. She would try to take more photos. Literally ... focus. Her hand slipped, and a flash went off under the table. Great. Probably a freeze-frame of their legs. Well, at least there'd be proof when she thought she'd dreamed it all.

Aaack. Where was Lynn? Or Kathryn? Where was George? Everyone had broken into small groups, talking ... laughing—but she couldn't move. She didn't want to move.

Breathe, Joann.

Be calm, Joann.

Robert started talking to people in front of him and to his left. Joann talked to someone in front of her and to her right. The valet's leg had not budged.

Okay, maybe he was just being—

His eyes were on her again. Uh, no. He was looking at her *that* way. But … he was leaving! Moving to the opposite coast. To be closer to someone else. Everything was all wrong. It was—

"Bailey, come on, you gotta see the naked-lady painting one last time!"

Sam and Jed yanked Robert out of his chair, releasing Joann's leg as they careened into the hall.

Lynn appeared from somewhere with a beer.

"Drink."

One forty-five. Robert was answering questions about his new job, and Joann was trying to be a part of another conversation.

Two o'clock. Closing time. Kathryn had left earlier with most everyone else, but George, Lynn, Robert, and Bryce gathered in front on the sidewalk. Joann could also see another valet in her periphery.

"Who's driving Robert and Joann?" Bill asked soberly.

"They look fine to me. Come on, let's go."

George put an arm around the junior valet, and they disappeared.

Crossing the street, Joann, Robert, Lynn, and Bryce began the walk up Madison.

At the hotel garage, they started the climb to the roof. Lynn and Bryce fell back, talking.

Joann hadn't had much to drink, but the whole world was fading away—except for Robert.

Halfway up the ramp, his hand reached for hers and fingers intertwined.

This could not be real.

Robert Bailey is holding my hand.

The valet and the desk agent drew closer, anchored yet pushing forward, their steps weighted but unwavering. Bryce and Lynn grew quiet, but continued to follow.

Inhale.

Exhale.

At the top, shadowy concrete gave way to shiny patches of water brimming with reflection. A light rain began to fall, and two Sylvans paused as two Sylvans walked to the middle.

City lights. Seattle skies.

Navy jacket. Gray slacks. Black shoes.

The boy turned toward the girl, eyes awash with sadness, fear, and inevitability. The girl turned toward the boy, slowly raising her own eyes to meet his. There was no looking away. Robert braced his jaw, his beautiful face stricken with truth.

Tick-tock.

The girl threw both arms around the boy, and he pulled her to him.

"I don't want you to go. *Please*, Robert. Don't go," Joann tearfully whispered.

An ancient tide was crashing in.

The boy held the girl tightly, his heart pounding through both of them.

The girl clung to the boy, her soul screaming for both of them.

Then he was kissing her hair.

"Joann, you don't even know. *You don't even know.*"

Now the boy was crying, and the girl's knees were buckling. She did know. She had known for two years. She was in love with Robert Bailey. And he was in love with her.

The rain misted and glittered as the Sylvans stood between heaven and earth.

The boy was trembling, but his arms were strong and steady, wrapped around the girl.

Her soul was still screaming, but Joann couldn't make a sound. All she could do was hang on.

Don't let go. Something like this can't possibly happen again. This is everything that is good. This is everything that is right. This is real. This is truth. This is home. I love you with my whole heart, and I love life with you, Robert Bailey. I adore you, and I'll love you forever. I'll love us forever. Please—

And ... cut.

Bryce materialized from darkness, and Joann was no longer in Robert's arms.

The wind blew past, a course was set, and words were being said.

"Let's go. Lynn, we'll follow to make sure you girls get to Joann's okay."

Bryce got hold of his friend, and the boys vanished into a murky corridor.

"Holy. Shit. What the hell just happened?" Lynn whispered. "Oh, my god. That was *epic*. What the—Joann? Okay, don't freeze up on me. Come on, we gotta get in the car—"

They climbed into the Jetta and coasted downward.

Bryce's Cabriolet was waiting at the bottom.

Frannie James

◆

Joann turned onto Madison, and the boys followed. Lynn turned in her seat, but a heavier rain blinded any view of whatever was happening behind them.

"Holy-shit-holy-shit. Holy. *Shit.* Joann, did you see—okay, well you couldn't see. But I did. I fucking saw it all! Holy shit, *love is real*! I cannot *believe* you guys. Holy shit. Holy … shit. **Love. Is. Real.**"

Joann continued up Madison to 19th. Braking at the apartment building, she threw off her seat belt and ran to Bryce's car. Robert rolled down a window, and she tried to kiss his cheek.

He turned to face her but, wiping at tears, Joann pulled away too soon. Bryce hit the gas, and Robert called out to Lynn:

"Make sure … Jo's okay …"

―◆―

Lynn paced in front of the sofa, and Joann collapsed on the bed. Twenty minutes ago, she'd been in the arms of the boy she loved. How were they not together right now?

You don't even know. You don't even know.

"Joann! What the hell? Holy shit, dude! What are you gonna do?"

"Lynnie, let's just sleep for a while, okay?"

"Okay, Joann. *Holy shit.*" Lynn whispered.

"Goodnight, Lynnie."

"Goodnight, Jo. Holy …"

―◆―

Three o'clock, October 6, 1993. Miss MacIntosh walked into the hotel, and two morning-shift agents excitedly called to her.

"Joann, there are flowers here for you!"

She ducked into the bathroom and opened a small card.

"Dear Jo,
Thanks for everything. Especially the lists.
I'm thinking of you. I hope things are going
a lot better for you than they would have gone
for me at work if you would have left."

The Sylvan Hotel

Her knees were buckling all over again. *Thanks for everything?* It sounded so … final. And "at work?" It was like he was adding a footnote—a disclaimer. Like he was backpedaling.

No. Please, God. No.

Margaret, do you believe in god?

He would not just walk away. Not after everything. Not Robert Bailey. And they *hadn't* been drunk. He'd barely had two drinks; she'd had one beer. No. *No, no, no.* The goddamn bouquet was drunk!

Be calm, Joann. Be calm.

She just had to get through her shift. It-was-fine. It-was-fine. It-was-fine.

Back at reception, a quiet lobby was loud with loss. The desk agent could practically hear her wristwatch. *Tick-tock.* Hours; days; maybe months to go, and she was stuck on a ghost ship.

Joann tried not to look at the stair door. No land in sight, and a blackness rolled closer. Then torrential panic, battering down. She could still feel him, somewhere, somehow, missing with a part of herself, like a phantom limb—

Or a phantom half of a soul.

Swish. Bryce was reporting for duty.

"Hey, Joann. You okay?"

"Yeah. Um, is Robert—?" her heart skipped.

"Yeah, he's fine. Well, uh, hang in there. I'd … I'd better get outside."

Chop. Chop. *Bryce knew what worked.*

And Bryce was fresh out of advice.

Four days later, check-in lists were hot off the printer when a call rang through to the desk.

"Good afternoon, The Sylvan—"

"Jo?"

"Robert … hey."

"Hey. I, uh, was calling to tell Jed about the warehouse meet-up. We're testing gear …"

He still sounded close, but so far away.

"You should go … here's the … address …"

Write it down. Down, down, down.

Joann scribbled the information on a scrap of paper and transferred the call to Jed.

What should I do ... should I back off ...
You don't even know. You don't even know.

Two days later, the sun was shining unseasonably warm. Joann chose cream-colored shorts and a light gray turtleneck; finely threaded cable socks, and well-worn boots. Just enough preppy. Just enough grunge. Good girl. Rebel. Delicate. Strong. The fading light of summer. The foreshadows of autumn.

"Let's go, ladies!"

Kelly, Joann, and Lynn climbed into George's car. He turned the key, and it was off to the warehouse—and to see Robert, one last time. When they got there, the group watched their friend and his business partners demonstrate equipment and discuss their plans with a room full of well-wishers.

After an hour, Robert's associates started to walk people out, but the Sylvans held back. Then Miss MacIntosh stepped forward. Mister Bailey put his arms around her, and everything disappeared again.

Joann was being lifted up, up, up ...

And Robert held on, and on, and on.

Don't let go. I love you.

Joann was still on her tiptoes—

So George took the wheel.

"Okay, uh ... I think we'd better let Bailey get to it."

The girl stared at the boy. The boy stared at the girl.

"Bye, Robert."

"Bye, Jo."

Somehow, Joann made herself start walking. Halfway across the warehouse, she stopped, turned around, and looked at him. Steady, strong, good, sweet, kind, handsome Robert—now standing at the crossroads of everything ... and something.

He hadn't taken his eyes off her and raised an arm in a final goodbye.

The girls climbed into George's car. It had really happened. But was it really over?

"Yay-yay-yay! Oh, my god, Jo. Oh, my god!" Kelly fired up a smoke.

The Sylvan Hotel

♦

"Holy shit, Joann. What now?" Lynnie fervently smacked a cigarette pack.

"Jo, today *you* were the girlfriend," George proclaimed. "And love *is* real."

"Yay-yay-yay-love!" Kelly pulled a cassette from her purse. "Mixtape, George. Mixtape!"

She shoved in the cassette, and the Sylvans listened to Chaka Khan describe a love that would withstand fire, and how she'd take it all the way, right down to the wire, come what may.

WITH THE FREAKS AND GHOULS

Three and a half weeks. No word from Robert. Whatever had happened … was over.

Inhale. Exhale.

Caught in rip currents of grief, heartache, and shock, Joann was drowning. He was gone, she'd been left, and they were lost.

What *had* happened?

Two years of loving someone more than she'd ever loved anyone or anything. Two years of looking forward to seeing his face, every day. Two years of waiting for him to walk in. Two years of laughter; tears; longing. Two years that had led to an unforgettable moment.

Two years that had *been* an unforgettable moment.

And now? Joann's only hope was an undertow. A merciful force that could take her from above and tuck her somewhere below—far away from the eye of the storm. A force that would somehow suspend her underneath, until she could remember how to swim up top. Until she could figure out how to turn pain into a propeller … and push out past the middle.

Robert was no doubt dealing with his own stresses. New job; new life; new city—

But … three and a half weeks.

It seemed that distance had finally done the trick.

You don't even know.

I know you love me. *I know you do,* Joann silently declared. But maybe he thought he had love mixed up with something else. Or he did love her—but love wasn't enough.

She wasn't enough.

Swish. The stair door opened.

There was a new concierge in town. Tony had recently relocated from Boise, determined to find a more gay-friendly home. He'd recently worked at Portland's Heathman Hotel, then ended up in Seattle, finding the Sylvan.

Tony waved at Joann, then buttoned his jacket and adjusted a gold pin. Next stop: the bar for cocoa.

The Sylvan Hotel

◆

Swish. A not-so-junior valet walked through the front doors, just as the concierge returned.

"Hey, Joann."

"Hey, Bill." She straightened a stack of registration cards.

The concierge set a mug in front of the desk agent and sipped his own hot chocolate.

The valet hesitated, then—

"Uh, can I get some Marlboros?"

Joann handed him the cigarettes.

"So, I'll be outside if … anyone needs me."

He backed away from the desk and out to the valet booth.

"Okay. What is going *on* with the two of you—and drink your cocoa!"

Tony set his own cup firmly on the marble.

"It's a mess. I … um … the boy who used to work here—"

"The valet who moved east?"

Be calm, Joann.

"Yeah. He … I … Um, I guess it just wasn't meant to be. But it seemed … and then it didn't, and then one night, I just got tired of, uh … and then Bill … but we're not compatible. And … the other boy … but then Bill … and … well, I just … I thought it would naturally end, or … like I said. It's a big mess."

"Okay. Things are … sort of making sense? Because when I first got here, I was, like, 'What did I just *step* into?' Forgive me, honey, but you didn't look so good. And let's just say … well, I couldn't tell *what* the hell was going on. Uh, but the way *that* guy out *there* looks at you??? *Giiirrrl.*"

"Yeah, well, I'm done with all of it."

"Uh, huh. Ahem. So … where … what happened with the guy—"

"He's with the person he met before me. I have nothing against her—and she … she's everything. I just wish I hadn't been the one to help him figure that out. Anyway, it looks like I've been written off as a momentary lapse of reason."

"Well, it's his loss, sweetie. Come on, now. Chin up. You have a lot of friends who are still here and who love you."

Bill, incoming.

"Joann?"

"Yeah?"

"I've got tickets to the Smashing Pumpkins. You wanna go?"

"Ooo. That sounds *fun*." Tony scooped up the mugs. "I'm just gonna take these back …"

"So … how 'bout it, Joann?"

The boy looked like he was going to jump over the desk.

The giiirrrl kind of wanted him to.

"Okay. Sure."

Be calm, Bill. Be calm.

11:00 p.m.

Denim cut-offs, flannel shirt, tights, boots … and the Smashing Pumpkins!

Oz was a smaller venue, formerly the "Skoochies" roller rink Joann had loved as a kid. Now she was back, *still* going in circles. *Ha*, thought Miss MacIntosh. *So what.*

Bill wrapped her in his arms, and they moved close to the front. Then Joann gave herself over to the music: indelible tapestries that were anthems of something and everything. Rebellion. Sadness. Confusion. Desire. Joy—

Smash. The call-box phone receiver fell on the floor. Bill was inspired, too.

Sofa-bed out. Boots off. Nervous. Gentle. Angry.

Joann pushed Bill onto the mattress, and he pulled her to him.

How many more times can this happen? Remember this. Remember being wanted like this.

Four in the morning.

Were they crazy? But who decides? Who would right this night-owl song?

3:00 p.m.

Back to work.

Swish. Tony walked in and looked at Joann. He laughed, and they started their shift.

Over the next several weeks, the concierge and the desk agent became new partners in crime. Lynn was dating, Kathryn was teaching, George was Lindy-Hopping, Kelly was busy with beaus, and Rhett had moved back to Louisiana—so the two friends were on their own. They met for lunch, cooked dinner, and celebrated … because Tony had fallen in love with Seattle. He and Joann toasted to the Emerald City and danced the nights away at Neighbours, a popular gay bar on the Hill. Sometimes, Bill would meet them there—usually on Sundays when they'd toast to two-dollar pitchers. The beer-fueled disco party was always quite a scene, but he loved to cause an even bigger one, proudly making out with Joann and grabbing Tony's ass.

"Now just *stop* that, you little horn-dog!"

The concierge would roll his eyes, the desk agent would laugh for hours, and the valet would kiss her in the middle of the dance floor—until Tony yelled at both of them.

"Get a grip, you two. Freakin' breeders! You're scaring all the queens!"

But Joann was a dancing queen.

And life had become a blur. ABBA … The Village People … Bud Light …

Smash. The call-box phone receiver crashed to the floor.

Sofa-bed out.

Mouths.

Arms.

Legs.

Hands.

Joann didn't want to sleep—or think about anything, anymore.

And Bill was very willing to accommodate. Because honey, he was still free … and if she needed him, she just had to let him know.

Because he wasn't ready to let go.

It was 3:00 p.m. again.

Frannie James

◆

Lists. *The Wall Street Journal*. Minibar math. Marlboros.

Cocoa with Tony. Gossip with Tony. Stories with Tony. He had plenty of his own hotel tales, like the one about a midnight run from The Heathman to Safeway. Patti LaBelle wanted apple pie!

—◆—

4:00 p.m.

Tony left for a date, and Jed clocked in.

A couple hours later, Kelly cruised in, arm-in-arm with the guy she'd landed.

"Jo, is it slow tonight?" She giggled.

"Yeah, just dragging."

"I bet you are. Getting any sleep, mama? Yay-yay-yay!"

"I meant the *shift* was dragging."

"What up, Kelly?" A suspicious Bill walked around from the concierge stand.

She pounced on the valet, hugging him and laughing.

"Dude. Are you drunk?" He carefully peeled her off.

"Hahaha! I'm sooo drunk!"

Bill quickly retreated to the valet booth with Jed.

"Jo, can we get a key? Please-please-please?" she excitedly whispered.

"*Kelly*. I don't think … I can't just—"

"Oh, come *on*, Jo. No one cares. Seriously. NO. ONE. CARES."

Joann looked down. This would be breaking a big rule. And this was *not* respectable behavior.

No one cares.

Fuck rules.

Fuck respectable.

"Here. Take 606. Just … hurry up."

"Yay-yay-yay!"

Two hours later, Jed guided a small-framed gentleman to the desk.

"Joann, do we have any rooms available?"

An astonished Bill and Sam hovered a few paces behind. The visitor smiled shyly. Mister … Something … And he had such a way about him: Kind. Polite. Total class.

The Sylvan Hotel

◆

She checked him in and—

"*Joann!* Don't you know who that *was*????" Both valets proceeded to lose it.

"No. But he was very nice ... quiet, but—"

"Hahaha—she thought he was quiet."

"Okay, are you gonna let me in on the joke?"

"Joann. That was *Layne fucking Staley.*"

"Oh my gosh!"

Alice In Chains was in the house.

Holy grunge gods! How cool to have met such a humble and talented human. Joann wished she could have told Layne how his music had made her feel better. Then again, he probably heard that all the time. And with good reason. She'd never forget his voice that first night at the Vogue and how it had taken her to a different place—but also brought her back.

Joann filed the registration card. *Goodnight, sweet soul.*

And now it was time to clean up.

Beep.

"Front Desk—"

"Jo! Lunch tomorrow: Mama's Mexican Kitchen!"

"Hey. Um, I don't think I can make it. I ... I'm sorry. Well, and ... I gotta go. Bill's taking me to the Croc. Be safe out there, okay? See ya, Kelly."

◆

Eleven o'clock.

Empty lobby.

Flickering lounge.

Navy jacket. Gray slacks. Black shoes.

Leaning on the desk, the boy looked at the girl the way he'd always looked at her.

"Ready?" he asked.

"Almost."

◆

Two hours later, a chill was creeping at the boy's apartment. He held tighter to the girl, and the heat from his body quickly engulfed hers.

But the girl's mind began to race. Pulling away, she looked at the boy through darkness and saw herself already missing him.

His mouth was on hers again, greedy; searching; frenzied; as if to draw—or give—life.

Wrapping her arms back around him, the girl wished that, in the end, they could still be fr—

It doesn't work like that, her heart chided.

The girl hung onto the boy, but a tide of worries was rising fast. When would this end? How would this end? How badly would this end? Forged in desperation, "this"—whatever it was—had seemingly fueled even more desperation. The boy and the girl were never meant to be, and yet ...

Jealousy sparked in Joann. Jealousy of people who'd be able to know Bill long after she had—and when she no longer could. A Bill who was tenacious as always, but steadier, and a different kind of strong. She also saw the Bill in front of her. She saw that irreverent gleam in his eyes, daring you to wonder what he knew that you didn't. She saw curiosity, a thirst for adventure, and the doggedness he wielded like a superpower. Mostly, she saw someone who *did* belong—someone who was secretly smart, secretly loyal, and secretly decent.

Someone she cared about.

Tick-tock.

Joann closed her eyes. All she could see *now* was the end. But it was always going to end. *What* had she been thinking, allowing this to go on for so long? They both knew that they didn't belong together, so it should have been over that first night. Because you didn't want to get used to the wrong person—because it could lead you down a wrong road—which could lead to other wrong roads.

Joann felt a familiar panic washing over her.

What *were* they doing? But how could they really talk about anything if they weren't supposed to be anything? It had been so clear at the start: Too much risk, too many differences, too much damage, and all the wrong reasons between them. Still, there had been good moments between them, too.

And almost two years later, that *was* something.

It was nothing, hail spat at the window.

*It **is** nothing,* the wind screamed, cutting past.

But a fire was raging.

The Sylvan Hotel

♦

You're beautiful, the boy whispered.
And the girl cried out—
For something. For nothing. For everything.
For all of it. For all of them.

⋯ ♦ ⋯

A cold rain fell, and two Sylvans started to drift—
Click.
A cassette was spinning, spinning, spinning ... and a Russian Blue purred, circling the room.
"Bill. Allergies!"
Click.
A door opened.
Then the Cult began to play.
So the cat padded off, the heat was back on—and the world, the world turned around, as a boy and a girl found sanctuary.

CHRISTMAS CURSES

December 1993. Simon Le Bon handed Joann his key, then joined his bandmates in the lounge. She giggled. If only her high-school self could see her now. So many Academy lockers had been covered with photos of Duran Duran, and … flash forward to them standing right in front of her! A little more weathered, but definitely Duran Duran.

She watched them talking as they faced the fireplace, butts lined up in crushed velvet pants. The band had aged, but an elegance persisted—and a wildness.

And wild boys? Well, they never lose it.

Wild boys (and girls) always shine.

Turning around, Duran Duran made a move for the doors.

Quickly backing away from the musicians, a group of grownups tried not to come undone. Giggling again, Joann forced herself not to wave like a teenager.

Swish. Brad walked in with a stack of magazines, armed for what was shaping up to be a quiet night. The bar was jumping, but the arrivals list was looking fairly meager.

"Housekeeping to Base."

"Hi, Housekeeping. Call me at extension four if you want."

Beep.

"Yo."

"Hey, Lynnie!"

"*Dude.* We haven't gone out in—"

"I know, I miss you! But you're so popular with the ladies these days! I've just been hanging out with Tony—"

"Oh, I know who you've been hanging out with. And it ain't just Tony."

"Well, yeah, but …"

"Don't get hurt again, Joann. I couldn't take it."

"I'm *fine*, Lynnie. There have never been any false expectations. We're not 'ending up' together. And it's no secret that I'm a mess right now, and he's—well … he's a mess, too. The guy's hung up on an old girlfriend and probably back with the current girlfriend."

"Yeah, but, see? You're in-between again."

"Lynnie, it was never serious to begin with."

"Uh, yeeeah. And *when* did it begin? Have you looked at a calendar lately? You might not be a 'girlfriend,' but you're not a 'fling,' either."

"I mean, I *do* like him. There's something … he's just so … fearless. Probably too fearless for his own good, but yeah, he's fearless, even as he's figuring it all out. And it's like he wants to breathe that fearlessness right into you—like he wants you to hurry up and *catch* up, already. I also suspect that he's a pretty interesting guy. And I think he might be a good partner to someone, someday. But *we're* not happening. We just somehow found ourselves in a strange space, together, and … well, it sort of worked in that space."

"Okay, that is waaay too much for my tired brain to handle. Are we hangin' out tonight, or what?"

"Sure! Lemme call Kath. It's Saturday, so she might be up for it."

"But … I don't wanna go you-know-where. It's just not the same."

"Yeah," Joann replied. She couldn't blame Kay and Joe for retiring, but Lynn was right. "It's not … well, it's not what it was. Hey, but—I heard there's a trattoria that makes excellent tortellini in Pioneer Square. Maybe—?"

"Sure! Okay, see you at eleven—or earlier if I can get Kiet to cover."

Five minutes later, a concierge cracked his knuckles over the marble countertop.

Fuck. Cheshire smile.

"What's up, Jed?"

"Guess who's stopping in tonight?"

Oh, god.

"Who?"

"Robert and Tricia are in Seattle. They're planning to come by. Isn't that great?"

NO. It's a goddamn nightmare.

Jed waltzed back to the concierge stand, and Joann organized some forms.

Robert. Why are you doing this?

A pensive piano player wandered over from the lounge.

"Hey, Miss J."

"Hey, Santa Baby."

"So ... uh, some Charlie Brown?"

Margaret, how many times have you and Kathryn asked Frank to play—

"How about ... you choose tonight."

They stood there quietly for a minute, then Frank returned to the piano.

"Hey, Front Desk—how goes it up here?"

Beth incoming!

"Hey, lady. It's—well, I miss Kathryn and ... everyone."

"Yeah. You want anything from the bar?"

"No. Thanks, though."

"Sure."

"Hey, and can you let George know that Robert and Tricia will be stopping by? He'll want to say hello."

"They're stopping ... by?" Beth placed her tray on the marble.

"Yeah. Home for Christmas."

"You sure you don't want anything from the bar?"

"Nope. Gotta stay awake up here. You guys are slammed, but this is our slower season."

"Okay. I'll let George know about—"

"Thanks."

8:00 p.m.

Navy jackets stood up behind the big window, and conversation filled the valet booth.

It was time.

"Base to Housekeeping. Come in, Housekeeping."

"On my way."

Joann picked up the phone and dialed extension 107.

"Yo. What's up?"

"George, I—"

"Be right there."

Swish. His voice. Her voice.

The Sylvan Hotel

•

And … they were through the front door. Joann felt like she'd never get back to "normal," but Robert had moved on in the blink of an eye. It was like—

It was like he'd flipped a switch.

Joann pushed through to PBX.

"Hey, Brad. VIPs arriving."

Captain Front Desk joined her at the front, and Super George flew in from the bar. Cornering the couple at the entrance, he escorted them to reception, talking nonstop. Hugs. Handshakes. Happy Christmas. Robert and Tricia … dressed all wintry, wonderful, and—

Why, oh, why was Joann still stuck behind the damn desk?

Ding.

Lynn walked out of the elevator.

The special guests addressed Brad first. Joann waved politely, and Robert nodded formally at her and the housekeeper.

George kept talking, and Brad took a key out of a key box.

"Hey, guys. There aren't any tables available in the lounge, and it's so busy in the lobby. Why don't you take this key to 601. Just hang out there for a while, and we'll send everyone up for a visit. A lot of people will want to say hello. And, Lynn, be sure to radio Kiet. He'll want to see Robert for sure."

Was this a mercy killing? Was he trying to remove them from her line of sight? Or was he looking out for the upstanding duo? Did Brad think Joann had been an inconvenient distraction who'd almost steered Robert Bailey off the path of righteousness?

Tricia looked pleased. The Sylvans were so cute! She and Robert stepped onto the elevator. Then George went back to the bar, Joann stayed calm, and Brad retreated to PBX, leaving the girls at the front.

Lynn looked like she was going to cry.

"Oh, Joann. What the—that's just not—"

Make sure Jo's okay.

Incoming line. The bar.

"Jo, you okay?"

"Yeah, George. Thanks."

"No prob. Bye, baby."

Joann hung up the phone, and Lynn marched toward the elevator.

"Fuck this. I'm going up. I just cannot believe—I never thought he'd— What the … I've gotta see for myself. How—"

Ding.

"Lynn, be cool."

Captain Front Desk went up next with Sam, and Joann held down the fort.

Twenty minutes later, Brad returned.

Screw it, she thought, and headed for the elevator.

When she got to 601, Joann found Kiet, Lynn, and Sam sitting with their guests. She asked Tricia how school was going and made perfectly respectable small talk. Even then, two minutes was too much—and she couldn't look at Robert.

Joann stood to walk out, and Robert jumped up. Then everyone followed suit.

Christ.

Cramming into the elevator, the Sylvans were on their way down.

But Miss MacIntosh was going up in flames.

Kiet and Lynn stared at the floor. You could slice through their tension with a knife.

Sam grinned in oblivion, and Robert attempted to make a joke.

"Just remember, Joann. All guys want the same thing."

The desk agent wanted to scream.

*Really, Robert? Maybe now **isn't** the time to talk. And of all the things to … Just what are you trying to say? Are you trying to cheapen something? Minimize a memory? How did we even get to this point?*

Ding.

"Oh, thanks. I'll keep that in mind," she sassed, like just-another-day-in-hotel-land.

Tricia laughed.

Robert and Joann were such a pair.

Ding.

Ding.

Ding.

Ding.

Ding.

The Sylvan Hotel

◆

Joann quickly exited the elevator with Lynn at her heels. They stopped near the house phone and pretended to be talking, while Robert said his goodbyes at the concierge stand. Then a housekeeper and a desk agent watched as a valet prepared to exit the circle.

The piano played. The fountain trickled. The wind blew past.

Robert opened the car door for Tricia and defied any urge to look back. Seconds later, they were gone: off to grown-up parties, relatives, friends—and to destinations where caffeine most certainly didn't come from red cans.

Lynn stormed to the elevator and punched the button.

This is my girl. To hell with you if she's not good enough for you.

The desk agent walked down the hall and punched the combination lock.

Then through the office and out to the front.

"Brad, you can take a break in PBX."

She needed to breathe. She needed open space.

Be calm, Joann. Be calm.

"Joann."

Kiet appeared, then began to say his own goodbyes. He did not know the words, but neither did she. The houseman looked down at the marble. Then he walked to the opposite end of the desk, his hand sliding along the countertop. He turned, walked toward her again, stopped, and faced her.

"Robert—he—he—break your heart—into—million pieces."

Joann stared at him. He stared at her. Then she nodded.

Kiet glanced at the valet booth and at Joann. What had just happened? Where had it all gone? The way the boy and the girl smiled at each other. The way they looked after one another. The way a room instantly changed when both of them were in it. The laughter. The friendship.

The love.

Together, the boy and the girl had been magic. The boy and the girl had made this place magic. But something had vanished. And destiny ...

Destiny had come to collect its dues.

Joann gripped the desk. Then destiny had the wrong address.

No. She couldn't accept it. She would never accept it.

Swish. Kiet disappeared, and Joann called her teammate to the front again.

"Brad, I think I need a break, please."

In the bathroom, Joann leaned against tile, and piano notes piped through. Notes promising to be home for Christmas.

Notes promising that they could be counted on.

This was unbearable. There was no way that he didn't love her. It wasn't possible.

It hadn't been some stupid crush. For either of them. If there was anything she knew in her little life …

You don't even know. You don't even know.

"God, please make it stop," she sobbed.

Margaret, do you believe in God?

Push it down. Far, far down. No more hurting. Just push it … down.

Joann closed her eyes, but she could see herself as a kid again—locked in the bathroom and sitting next to the laundry chute as her father pounded on the door. In those years, Joann could fit into the chute and slide through to the basement. There would be a second of fear, then the realization that she'd done it and transported herself to a whole other level. She just had to believe she'd make it. She just had to push through. She just had to push down.

We will lock you up, Joann MacIntosh. We will put you away. Open this door. NOW.

She was burning up. And pushing down. Down, down, down. Past the fire, past the flames. Down, down, down. Then find the cold, and—

Go numb.

The desk agent adjusted her blazer, tucked everything in, and returned to the desk.

Swish. Ken and Khloe Wolf walked through the doors—but she was beneath them.

Midnight. Trattoria Mitchelli. Three plates of tortellini sat on a table, and three girls sat silently. Man, this night sucked. Joann wished she'd called in sick. She should've gone to watch the Christmas ships at Stan Sayres with her parents. If *only*.

She looked at Kathryn. Maybe this was a bad idea. They all knew that Pioneer Square was one of Todd's favorite places. Then again, maybe that's why they were there.

Lynn was over it.

The Sylvan Hotel

•

"Fuckin' tortellini. This should be cannelloni, and we should be up at Kay's. And Todd should be here. And Robert should be here. And Bill should be climbing under tables to put The Doors in for Joann. And where the fuck is George? Fuckin' holidays. And fuck no—I will not be attending the Sylvan Christmas party this year."

Kathryn and Joann laughed. You had to appreciate Lynn's honesty.

Joann raised a glass.

"The Christmas curse lives, y'all."

Kathryn and Lynn raised their glasses.

"Fuck Christmas," they said in unison.

"Maybe we should try and stop by Kay's. How bad could it be?" asked Joann.

"It's too depressing," Lynnie sighed.

"I haven't been in a while. I'm willing to try it." Kathryn pushed her fork around in the pasta.

She hadn't eaten much. Maybe it *was* time to leave.

Ghosts of Christmas past were everywhere tonight.

"What'll ya have?"

An unsmiling waitress looked at them sourly from under spiky lashes. On the other side of the room, a bartender with an unsavory mullet watched with an unsavory gaze. Over in an empty corner, freshly cut wires dangled from the wall, and a jukebox was missing in action.

"Okay, I'm done."

Now Kathryn was saying goodbye.

Lynnie guzzled her drink. "Oh-my-god. This is so *wrong*."

Yep. But maybe it was right that Kay's was all wrong. Maybe it should be vulgar.

Maybe it should be bad. Because so much of the good that had happened there ... was gone.

Two hours later, Joann sank onto Lynn's floor. Condensation ran down the windows, water dripped in the kitchen, and the refrigerator softly hummed. In the living room, a diver bubbled at the bottom of a fish tank.

What had happened to it all? Where was the life that she recognized? Gone. Gone far, far away. She would just have to learn to survive.

RUSTY CAGES

February 1994. Joann flipped through her mail. This had to be the year she would break into copywriting. Rent was going up, and minimum wage wasn't going to cut it much longer.

Phone.

Electric.

Visa.

Robert Bailey.

Another letter. The first one he'd sent had arrived with newspaper clippings about the espresso business. She'd written back, then his next letter included a stack of passes for an East Coast band that had come through his town. "Dave Matthews" was Seattle-bound and reportedly on the up-and-up—but Joann couldn't get anyone to go. Everyone was busy, and everyone was moving on from the space between.

Tracing her name in his writing, she wondered what the other was thinking. Then her soul was screaming again. *We just never say a thing.*

Joann turned the envelope around in her hands. She wanted to open it. She didn't want to open it. She had to open it.

> "Dear Pile of Joy,
> How are your lists doing? I'm lost without mine. Things are going good here. The sun has finally come out, so it's warming up. My other business partner got in a couple days ago, so we've been showing him the ropes. He'll lighten the load, and we'll have a chance to look into expansion. I'll keep in touch and call if I get rich to rub it in, or if anything else happens. I have to go now. I need to rest up. Tricia comes to town tomorrow.
> –Robert"

The Sylvan Hotel

And the tragedies between them grew deeper. Joann folded the piece of paper and placed it in a box at the bottom of her closet—along with an old valet ticket, one Minnie Mouse valentine, some candid photos ... and a card once sent between wildflowers.

March 1994. Joann clocked out, headed back up the stairs, and exited through the Sylvan lobby. She was on her own, but the car was parked close by. Leaving earlier and earlier for work, she'd gotten better at snagging good meter spaces so as to avoid the garage ramp or the alley. Or the roof.

Miss MacIntosh started the Jetta and headed for the Hill, because it was a straight-to-bed night. Tomorrow, she was waking up early to work on more job applications. The copywriter-to-be was in hot pursuit of a big break. Bryce had agreed to help her with a portfolio, and she was sending samples everywhere.

Sigh. Tricia got the boy ...

And Joann got a book.

Whatever. It was all about the future now. Her concepts were good, and she knew someone would bite eventually. She was determined—like a salmon trying to swim upstream.

Like a salmon swimming through the Locks.

When Joann was a youngster, her father would take them to see the Chittenden Locks in Ballard, a historic fishing and shipbuilding neighborhood. There hadn't been much else there except for old houses and Scandinavian grannies, but her father liked watching the workings of water-level control. The Locks linked Puget Sound with Lake Washington and Lake Union, so you could see boats pass between salt water and fresh water, the levels raised or lowered, depending on the destination. The Locks also helped salmon and steelhead to continue on their journeys. Joann would watch the fish heave themselves through water, trying to jump the ladders. The current had to push enough to attract them while not totally exhausting them. Still, it was a hard road to swim.

Like writing cover letters. There was just enough of a promise to keep going, but the process was draining and demoralizing. Sometimes, she felt that she'd become a fish with no ladder. The walls of her kitchen were papered with layers of rejection letters. Even so, Joann stuck with it. At some point, she would clear the hurdle.

Frannie James

◆

April 1994.

Job applications. Post office. Job applications. Post office. Job applications. And …

Parking right across from the hotel!

Dig for quarters. Feed meter. Then into the circle—

"Turn around and take your little ass down the hill."

Ross stepped out in front of her, his face red with hate.

"I'm in my uniform. Mr. Alexander doesn't mind, and no one's even around."

Why was she explaining anything to him?

The valet grabbed her by the arm.

"Hey! Get off me!"

"You're gonna go through the alley, like everyone else."

The Town Car sat silently, and the fountain had gone dry. The greenery was still, and the string lights were drab in the daylight.

"Ross, I said stop!"

Her voice was so small in the wind.

Joann tried wriggling away, but he was too big. And in an instant, she was seventeen again, being dragged on a hillside. Her heels were scraping along the cement, and she struggled to stay upright. *Ow!* He twisted her arm, and she almost fell for the second time. Should she shout? To who? So the valet hauled her all the way down.

Down.

Down.

Down.

When they reached rock bottom, he pushed her into the alley, and she stumbled again.

"See you up top, Joann." Smirking, he jogged off.

Wait for me … Be safe … Do not lay a hand on her. Ever.

Tears ran down Joann's face.

Robert. Come back to me.

Her arm hurt, her leg hurt, and the heels of her shoes were wrecked. Christ, what an asshole. But everyone knew that Ross was an asshole—and it was her heart that was hurting the most. Robert was good. And kind.

He'd taken care of her. Admired her. Respected her. Loved her. Until, suddenly, he didn't. So maybe that injury had been the worst of all.

Joann wiped her eyes and clocked in. Time to toughen up. Time ... to take the wheel. People had lived through much worse. Uncle John: Nazi survivor. Her Irish ancestors: Famine survivors. Grandma MacIntosh: Widowed-while-pregnant survivor. Joann also thought about her mother: a seven-year-old Bernadette, running through jungle; running from bombs; sailing to a land of red dirt and dreaming in fields of gold—then growing up, going to war, and living to tell the tale. Joann thought of her father, too. Poverty; near starvation; the fall from a horse: a shattered leg. "It's over," they'd said. Today, he owned a house and could walk for miles. They'd all been such warriors. Surely that kind of courage, perseverance, and strength existed somewhere in Joann's DNA.

Although ... people *did* need help now and then. She recalled the story about an activist who'd saved her tough-as-nails grandmother from a mugging. Back then, the Madrona neighborhood had some rough pockets that could have been dicey for anyone. Luckily, it had also been home to Seattle's Black Panther party. But what now? Superheroes were gone. They'd hung up their capes and their berets—and their navy jackets—for good. Joann had to learn how to save herself. She had to keep going. She had to figure this out. She had no other choice.

Taking a deep breath, she hit the stairs. Some new room-service guy passed her, avoiding hellos. Finn was only there part-time now, having discovered an opportunity in the beer biz. Stan wasn't around much, either, and Kiet had quit. As for everyone else? Alicia was having a baby, George was starting computer classes, and Lynn was gone a lot, picking up shifts at City Market. Meanwhile, Kelly was off to new adventures with new friends, and Kathryn was teaching full time. She'd also moved north, landing near Fremont. It was a funky, artsy-fartsy area where a big troll guarded a bridge. Maybe Mister Troll could keep ghosts away, too.

Joann pushed past the stair door. Across the lobby, Brad was waiting for her at the desk. At least some things hadn't changed. She glanced at the circle. But other things had gotten worse. Catching sight of Sam, she quickened her pace. Good god. Her valet problems were endless. That one had barely spoken to her in weeks, and she was sick of trying to do her job while walking on male-ego eggshells. Hopefully, he would get over it. Really, though, he needed to get over himself.

Frannie James

•

The newest nightmare had begun at a party, when she'd been out with the kitchen crew—and a Sylvan food server decided the coast was clear. Joann had never "officially" been with Robert, but apparently she'd been wearing an invisible cloak of bro-code protection while he'd been around. Then it *fully* disappeared when he disappeared, ripped away in the dark of night.

And she was bleeding out like easy prey.

As the Sylvan server started to hang on her, a fit of rage had pushed through Joann like hellfire. She'd wanted to scream—and die. But no one was the wiser. Hurting like the devil but sparkling like heaven, Joann MacIntosh had been a vision, smiling and laughing in aquamarine.

How charming. How exotic. How ... different.

What a pile of joy.

So the server had gone in for the kiss, and she'd gone into a tailspin.

*Sure, dude. At **your** service. Ready when you are.*

Out of her mind with grief and anger, Joann had been somewhere out of her body while the server smooched away. Then, reeling with disgust and despair, she'd finally pulled away.

But Miss MacIntosh went to the next party, because staying at home by herself was worse.

Enter Sam. Having split with Tory, the valet had happily cozied right up. Joann made polite conversation, but minutes later, he'd made his move. The anger bubbled right up again, but she'd managed to push his hand off her leg. What was this? Plug-and-play? Was the "word" out about Miss MacIntosh? Did Sam think she was the Sylvan *toy*? And of course, he'd been so offended when "the toy" appeared to be broken. Did he think he'd been deprived of his turn? Was she not worthy of *any* respect?

Joann pushed at the marble. Something had to give.

—=♦=—

WHOOSH. A sharp gust of air blew in.

"Jo, did you hear?" Sam opened the big window.

"Um ... what's up?" she replied, backing up carefully.

"Cobain. He's dead."

"No way. How? Where?"

The Sylvan Hotel

◆

"They found him at his house today. Suicide. At least from what they can tell."

The rest of the night felt especially foreboding—like something was getting farther off course, drifting toward oily, uncharted waters. In the circle, valets listened to Nirvana in a parked Town Car, their cigarettes flickering behind shadowy windows.

"Housekeeping to Base."

"Lynnie! I didn't think you were working tonight!"

Beep. Internal call.

"Dude! I can't believe he's—"

"I know. It's really sad. I remember when he and his wife stayed here. They seemed to have everything, but maybe not. Or maybe that was the problem. Jeezus. Everyone has a story. Everyone has problems. Everyone has pain. Maybe some people have too much pain."

"Fuckin' life."

"Word."

"Joann?"

"Yeah?"

"Shit's getting bad."

"Yeah."

"Later, my friend."

On Sunday night, the Sylvan crew watched vigil coverage from the small TV in the valet booth. Mourners crowded into Seattle Center, and candles blazed hard as if to signal the end of so *many* things.

*It's **all** going downhill*, Joann thought.

Seattle … was sliding.

But there were still moments. Weeks later, she held on tightly to Bill as Soundgarden ruled the stage. The crowd was crazy, but the Sylvans were safely behind the really rough stuff—and they gave it up for loud love.

Then the moment passed.

Frannie James

◆

Two months later, a Sylvan elder kept an eye on a very tired Joann as she circled the fountain.

The girl had been busy-busy-busy, writing cover letter after cover letter between hotel shifts. Meanwhile, other types of letters were dwindling—and certain "distractions" were on hold yet again.

Sighing, the wizened limo driver watched over the desk agent, concerned, but letting her work through whatever needed working through. Recently retired in the outside world, Edward was well-aware that sometimes people had to go in a few circles. He'd also seen how that girl had lit up around that boy—and how that boy had lit up around her.

Joann looked at the green-velvet drape.

What should I ... Should I back off ... I don't know what to do.

Maybe it was a bad idea. But she needed answers.

She needed him.

In the morning, Joann dialed the numbers.

"Jo! How *are* you? How many personal phone calls have you made today?"

They talked for an hour. And they talked again. And again. And again.

July 1994. Joann boarded an eastern-bound plane. It sat on the runway, delayed three hours before being cleared for departure. Stuck on the tarmac, she had plenty of time to second-guess herself.

Her friends had been worried, too.

When she'd brought up the possibility of a visit, Joann could tell Robert was unsure, but he hadn't flat-out said no. Although, maybe he'd agreed to it ... out of pity? Or maybe he—

Oh, *whatever*! Joann was sticking to the plan. She missed her friend so much it hurt. And she just couldn't shake her belief in him—and in them. Besides, this was what you were supposed to do, right? If you loved someone, you took the Hail Mary pass. *You rallied.*

You put it all on the line.

So, Joann booked her ticket. She even had a place to stay. Lily from Germany still worked mornings, and they'd become friends as their shifts often overlapped. And as it happened, Lily's in-laws lived in Robert's new town.

Miss MacIntosh was set for take-off.

The flight was touching down. Waking somewhere between hippy and preppy, a girl stepped into sandals, then retied her chambray shirt over a long, thinly striped sundress.

Be calm, Joann.

Inside a small airport, Robert was at the gate. He'd waited three hours.

She breathed in. All these months later, and he was real again. Not a voice on the phone; not a memory; not a letter; not a dream. With one plane ride, he'd reappeared. It sounded so simple, except that ... it wasn't. Trying not to run, she stopped just short of her friend.

"Robert, I'm so sorry for the delay—"

But the boy was hugging the girl. And the girl was home.

Robert picked up her duffle bag, and they were walking side by side, just like always. Afraid that he might disappear, Joann was already memorizing him. His hair was longer on top now, tied in a floppy ponytail. T-shirt. Long shorts. Small gold earring. He was more Robert than ever, but different, too.

Outside, the night air was cool but warm. In the shadows, two fireflies wildly blinked and bobbed like tiny wayward stars. Silent but bright, they lit up in tandem, sparking and circling like twins through borrowed time. To the right, a chorus of trees murmured.

Que sera, sera. Whatever will be, will be ...

Shifting the truck into gear, the boy eased them forward. The girl leaned back, relieved and happy. She strained to see the dark, unfamiliar roads ahead but breathed out, knowing her friend was right next to her.

When they arrived at Lily's in-laws', Robert let go of the baggage—then put his arms around Joann again. Standing in the entryway, her hosts patiently waited as he held on, and on, and on.

What was *going* on? Was Robert worried? This was a very nice neighborhood, and Lily's folks seemed like very pleasant people. Had he been this protective before? All of that seemed so far away now. Or ... was he scared that *she* would disappear?

Holy—! He was going to hug the life right out of her.

Tick-tock.

"It's okay, Robert. I'll be fine," she whispered.

No one had ever held her like that, and he still wasn't letting go.

The following evening, Robert Bailey and Joann MacIntosh strolled along Main Street. Finding a coffee house, they crowded in, taking their seats on the floor. Then a folk singer swept everyone up and away. Her voice was transcendent, the music honest.

The girl happily squeezed the boy's arm, and this time, *she* didn't want to let go.

Joann began memorizing him again: this person who could make her feel as if she was going to jump right out of her skin—*and* totally at peace. How was it possible to have such magnitudes of need and want for someone, yet the sense of having already belonged to that someone for ages?

What was this pull, this force … this gravitational alchemy? If it was possible for "feeling like home" to feel primal, that's how she'd have to describe it. It was unyielding. It was more than epic. And she'd never felt more alive.

MISSING PIECES

Robert was nearing the end of his shift.
Standing alongside the espresso cart, Joann watched him check off new lists and work through new routines. Mister Bailey was making his mark in a Sonics T-shirt and shorts; socks and sandals; briefcase at the ready. The boy-next-door-hippy-jock-entrepreneur. He was many things, like her.

※

The next afternoon, they were poolside, outside Robert's apartment. The friends sat safely away from one another, and Joann was warm in shorts and a tank top. But ... putting on a bathing suit would have felt kind of weird. He was still someone else's partner, and it seemed—

Robert stood, threw off his shirt, and dove in, slicing through the cool water. Joann nearly fell in. No navy jackets around here. She quickly closed her eyes.

※

Four days into the visit, a Sylvan walked along a hot, dusty road.

"Miss ... are you ... in trouble?"

After the tenth car stopped, she finally accepted a ride. Trucks with packs of white dudes hanging out the back had been a no-go, but an older black gentleman had convinced her to get in. His manner had been kind, and his concern had felt real, as he informed her that "nobody in their right mind walked around these parts in a heatwave."

"Why would you do that? Jo—you *hitchhiked*???"

Robert just about had a meltdown.

"It's not like I was trying to, and it's not like I ever did it before! But *every* car that passed me was stopping to check, because apparently *I'm* the one who looked crazy for walking! And the person I finally said 'yes' to was like a very polite grandpa!"

Needless to say, there wouldn't be any more treks into town.

That night, they landed on a movie. *Forrest Gump* was still playing, and neither one of them had seen it. Robert seemed curiously awkward, but Joann quickly pushed that thought from her mind. She was probably being paranoid. As they waited for the show to start, her date slumped in his seat, covering his face with his hat. The lights dimmed, and Robert sat back up.

An hour or so in, Joann wasn't feeling it. Tom Hanks and ... the Princess Bride?

He looked a little lost without his rom-com queen.

Suddenly, the film strip broke, and—lights on. Once again, Robert slumped in his seat.

Oh, no. *He didn't want to be seen with her.* Maybe someone in the theater knew Tricia, and he wasn't with Tricia. He was also a businessman, now. A businessman in a small town.

But they'd been on the town a couple nights ago, and what about that massive embrace?

An old feeling was returning—like Joann was falling down inside, and a piece of her was going missing. Maybe Bryce had called and put his friend back on track. Or a letter had arrived from New York. Or maybe all of it had just been too much; a reminder of something from even further back; something before the Sylvan. Something Robert wanted no reminders of. Or maybe he'd simply caught himself slipping, then recovered. The future was in motion, so he needed to be done with the past.

Joann pictured her friend weighing it all, starting on that cross-country drive. Had he struggled like she had? Had that pounding heart gotten too loud on some of those late-night stretches? Had it gotten too close to drowning out *any* map? She could only ... imagine:

*He leaned forward, pushing for cruise control between the centerlines. Were his feelings even real? Were **her** feelings real? Was **she** real? And who were "Joann and Robert" outside of the Sylvan? Were **they** real?*

Welcome to Montana ... Welcome to Minnesota ... Welcome to Indiana ... Welcome ... His foot was heavy on the getaway, his soul heavy with a memory. He could still feel her in his arms. He could still feel her hand in his. He could still see her at that desk, smiling every time he walked in. And he could still see them at that damn window together. Her laughing and him wondering if she felt what he felt. Him wondering what it would be like to push back that hair, to kiss that face. Him wondering what it would be like to—

Then the sadness. He'd just wanted to swoop her up—take her somewhere far away.

God, the way they'd held each other on that roof. And at the warehouse. It was like something—

No. Just stop. There wasn't supposed to be a "something." He was about to have everything. Fuck, he couldn't keep doing this. And now he'd probably confused someone else.

The signs blurred by, but his mind raced faster. Okay, he'd write her a letter, and that would be it. Or maybe two. Or three. But he'd have to be careful: not send the wrong message. Aw, jeez. It didn't seem right to say that anything about her was "wrong." And yet what kind of person would he be if he just started breaking all the rules? How strong were her feelings, anyway? How long had she even had them? And how well did they even know each other? What if … what if he wasn't the person she thought he was?

Bryce said they'd just gotten "caught up" on the roof; caught up in a moment … and …

Their emotions had gotten the best of them.

"Don't wreck your chance at a nice life—at having everything. You'll regret it, man."

But Bryce hadn't seen all the other nights. He hadn't seen all the happiness.

And how could anyone regret her? He adored her. He—

Fear rattled through the windshield, and he took a hard turn. Maybe the hotel "happiness" had just been a childish detour. A fairy tale. After all, the Sylvan wasn't real life. And his life was happy enough, wasn't it? Besides, what was he going to do? Just throw away a solid, established relationship? Risk it all for a … wildcard? There were just too many unknowns.

Too much uncertainty. Okay, but then why did it feel like a piece of himself was missing?

The thoughts about her picked up speed: How he looked forward to seeing her every day;

how when they were together, it felt like things were where they were supposed to be. How she could make him feel as if he was going to jump right out of his skin but at peace at the same time. How he wanted her—and how maybe she wanted him, too.

His heart was fluttering all over the place, then pounding too fast again.

Wanna feel the heat with somebody?

So maybe it was just a guy thing. And he was better than that. That was how people got into trouble; lost everything because of a little biology. Sparks were natural between humans, but they needed to be controlled—so that you didn't end up in flames. So temptation didn't—

No. That word was too gross. She wasn't evil. She was good. She was Jo. Clever, kind, lovely, stubborn, gentle, funny, secretly shy, wonderful, starry-eyed Jo.

*And ... he would never see her again. How could that **be**, he wondered ... and ... who would keep her safe? If anyone hurt her—but ... what if **he'd** hurt her? No: Bryce said she was fine.*

She-was-fine-she-was-fine-she-was-fine.

*Then the pain. Like a saw cutting into the deepest parts of him as the miles mercilessly ripped by—and she got farther away. But even now, he could still feel her. Like before, in the summer, the first time he tried leaving. But this wasn't summer. He was trying to start his **life**. Christ, this was what he'd worked for. And he was committed to someone else! Was he losing his mind? What was his problem? What was happening to him?*

*He looked over at his buddy, peacefully snoring as the highway rolled on. He thought of the smart, beautiful woman in New York with so many plans. She **was** the plan. Plans were in motion! There were expectations; responsibilities. He'd made promises. And he hated the idea of hurting anyone. So, at the end of the day, which road would do the least damage? But ... did **his** feelings even count in this? Then again, he wasn't even sure what they were. Which was making him unsure about who he was. Which was making him unsure about everything. Which would likely end in disaster. Which brought it all back to risk.*

Bottom line: Best to err on the safe side, for everyone.

But his eyes started to water, and panic took the wheel.

Joann. Her name burned inside him—

Then a voice was hammering through something.

Man up.

So he downshifted. Hit that brake hard. Because whatever this was had to stop.

And he'd made it stop. He'd left it all on the road; buried it deep out there, somewhere just past the middle, with no going back.

Then came Christmas. Probably wasn't the best idea, but admittedly, he'd been curious. And things had surely calmed down. Once through those doors, it did feel kind of jarring, but settled at the same time. Until months later, when

The Sylvan Hotel

•

she'd started calling. It was so good to hear her voice, although it always caused a bit of a rewind, messing up his fast-forward track—

Gasp! Joann sneaked a look at Robert out of the corner of her eye. What had she been thinking? This trip had been a bad idea. But ... what about the night she'd arrived? He'd barely let her go! Maybe ... maybe it had just been some kind of reflex. Like a muscle memory.

Like ...

A heart-muscle memory.

The screen now steadily flickered, but *Forest Gump* had become a blur—and her imagination was yelling louder than Dolby Surround:

*The night she got in really threw him for a loop. Once she was in his arms, he could barely bring himself to let go. What **was** this thing between them? He was getting confused all over again and feeling way too many things. Things that were supposed to have been buried.*

*Goddammit. He'd made a decision. Okay, he'd just keep reminding himself: Too many unknowns. Too big of a risk. Besides, who **was** Joann MacIntosh? Sometimes, she was too scared. Sometimes, she was too bold. Hell, she dared to jump on that plane. She dared to hitch-hike. She was also starting to look a little lost. **And** she was stuck at the Sylvan. Okay, that wasn't fair. He knew she'd find her way.*

*But ... where would the road take **her**? What would she do with her life? Who would she be with—*

No. *No. No. No. Push that stuff back where it belonged. Push it down, down, down.*

It was time to let go.

It was time ... to grow up.

Joann blinked, and the credits were rolling. Robert stood, then quickly moved toward the exit. He didn't rush *too* far ahead, but he didn't look back, either. For the first time, they weren't walking together. She tried to keep up, but in her brain, another "screenplay" was slowing her down:

Everything inside him was screaming. What were they doing on a movie date? An exit sign blinked green-light-go, and pushing through the door, he gulped for cooler air.

Joann froze. Yeah, she was taking liberties, speaking for him like that. But her imagination was also hurting—and on the run again.

She looked at the scar below her knuckle.

What should I do? Should I back off?

She had her answer. It was hard to accept, but her friend had his own story, and for whatever reason, it could no longer include her.

You don't even know. You don't even know.

She knew that he needed her to leave. She knew that he needed her to say goodbye.

So that's what she would do, because she loved him. But oh, how she also wanted to have it out, once and for all. To say what needed to be said. To laugh and cry about two years that had undoubtedly shaken, mystified, and changed both of them. She wanted to tell him to take a chance. She wanted to tell him they were worth it—but … at what cost? It would be unbearable to hear the person she loved try to explain it all away: to say she'd been a mistake. There'd already been too much damage, and she was free-falling deeper into numb. Joann had to be careful, or she might not find her way back.

No. She would let things be. That way, she could at least hold on to the good memories. She could protect them—leave them intact. Not mar them with regrets. The good memories were all she had left of him. She would not kill them.

The espresso entrepreneur dropped Joann at the airport with an easy-breezy goodbye. Then she waved and walked away, each step like a dagger cutting through something. Something that was over.

Joann breathed in. It was time for life to go on. It would *have* to go on. It's just that … she liked it better when her friend was in it. And she'd always be missing him. At least they'd had *some* time together, but it would never be enough.

Screw you, Universe. And thank you, Universe. In a big old world, the paths of Joann MacIntosh and Robert Bailey had somehow managed to momentarily collide—and she would have done it all over again, even knowing the outcome.

The flight was taking off.

"We are … headed to … relax … sit back …"

If you couldn't go home, where did you go?

The Sylvan Hotel

◆

Eight hours later, a plane started its descent toward Puget Sound and land masses thick with evergreens. Looking out a window, the girl lost herself in cold gray waters. Far below, waves were hitting bottom, breaking and crashing at the shore—then dissolving into seafoam chasing undertow and air.

At the hotel, word had gotten around about Joann's trip east. Bill never asked about it, but he didn't look at her anymore. So she whispered another goodbye into walls of Honduran Mahogany. It was for the best, though. Because in the end, they were courting *dead* ends. Each of them was in love with someone else. Each of them was desperate to be good enough. Each of them had sustained profound injuries, and too many wounds were still too fresh.

Time … to jump ship.

September 1994. It was 2:00 a.m. in a fireside lounge, just outside of downtown Seattle.

Sitting on a green-velvet sofa, Miss MacIntosh re-read the letters burning in her hands. Now she just had to be brave. Rising, she began to move past smoldering ashes and dark walls.

Click. Joann entered the back office. Shaking, she reviewed the offer letter again—then watched herself place a resignation letter on one of the desks.

Returning to the lobby, the girl glanced at a big window ledge one last time. Then she pushed through Sylvan doors. Outside, Joann looked up at faraway skies, then down at her scar.

Well, look who's checking out. Good for you, Margaret.
Why "Margaret?"
I dunno. I just thought it was a cute name.
I did it, Todd. Other things didn't work out, but—
Never say never.
*Ha. You **would** say that.*
Peace out, Margaret.
Peace out, my friend.

Frannie James

◆

The young woman patted a tired Town Car, then saw two quarters lying on the ground.

She picked up the coins and moved toward the middle of the circle. It was cold, but she didn't feel cold. Tossing the coins into the depths of an old fountain, she made a wish that they'd be happy, always. It was what she wanted. She knew they'd given her what they could. She knew they loved her. And she loved them. And nothing else mattered.

EPILOGUE

"*So, what was it all for?*" a brain sighed.

"The love!" a heart declared.

"*And the story,*" a soul whispered.

Then a woman sat back, glancing at the pages before her.

"Ooops! Sorry, hon!" A waitress bumped the table in passing.

Some ice sloshed and splashed about but quickly melted in the warm café.

The woman continued to look at the pages.

Yes, she nodded. It was what she wanted to say.

And now they'd always be together, sitting at a window … chatting by a switchboard … and holding onto each other through all that haze.

The woman shifted again, and turned toward a familiar horizon, her spirit soaring past old walls and watery panes.

"Looks like a storm's brewing," someone said at the counter.

But white-hot bolts were already striking, ripping through darkness—and re-stitching high roads to rightful stars.

City lights. Seattle skies.

The night was far from over, but—

I've got you, Joann, the woman promised.

Then the girl smiled and breathed out.

... Other pathways lead to Somewhere,
But the one I love so well
Had no end and no beginning—
Just the beauty of the dell,
Just the windflowers and the lilies
Yellow striped as adder's tongue,
Seem to satisfy my pathway
As it winds their sweets among.
There I go to meet the springtime,
When the meadow is aglow,
Marigolds amid the marshes,
And the stream is still and slow;
There I find my fair oasis,
And with carefree feet I tread
For the pathway leads to Nowhere,
And the blue is overhead.
All the ways that lead to Somewhere
Echo with the hurrying feet
Of the struggling and the striving
But the way I find so sweet
Bids me dream and bids me linger—
Joy and beauty are its goal;
On the path that leads to Nowhere
I have sometimes found my soul.

– "The Path That Leads to Nowhere,"
Corinne Roosevelt Robinson

ACKNOWLEDGEMENTS

Thank you, Sr. Mary Annette, for telling us to "read that sentence again; to really read it."

Thank you, Julia. Without your direction, this book would not exist.

Thank you, Maggie C. and Walt for your kindness and generosity.

Thank you, Bird Lady. Very grateful for your help and encouragement.

Thank you, Marcus, Maggie B., Nova, Marilee, and the Hinton team.

Thank you, Marti, Bridget, Jessie, and the Editing McKennas team.

Thank you, truest friends and guiding spirits. You know who you are.

Special thanks to J. and Freddy.

FRANNIE JAMES is a writer, Seattle native, and lifelong resident of the Pacific Northwest.

www.ingramcontent.com/pod-product-compliance
Lightning Source LLC
Jackson TN
JSHW022037290925
91818JS00005B/38